ALSO BY TATE JAMES

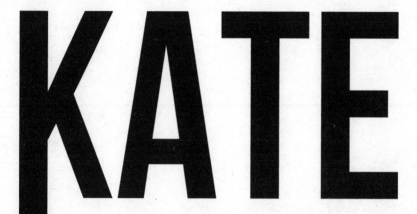

KATE

TATE JAMES

Bloom books

Published by Bloom Books, an imprint of Sourcebooks
P.O. Box 4410, Naperville, Illinois 60567-4410
(630) 961-3900
sourcebooks.com

Originally self-published in 2020 by Tate James.

Cataloging-in-Publication data is on file with the Library of Congress.

Printed and bound in Canada.
MBP 10 9 8 7 6 5 4 3 2 1

For my mum.
I miss you so damn much.

CHAPTER 1
STEELE

Seven and a half years ago.

A pout pulled at the pretty blond girl's lips as she scowled at us, and I grinned. It annoyed her that I kept smiling, so I did it more just because it was fun to see the fire in her unusual violet-blue eyes.

Her delicate, little hands clenched at her sides like she wanted to punch us both, this skinny little girl against two fifteen-year-old boys who'd been fighting since we were younger than her. It was funny, and it made me want to ruffle her hair or something.

"I don't *need* you to babysit me," the girl huffed. "I'm eleven years old. I can take care of myself."

My grin spread even wider. She had so much backbone; she reminded me of Arch.

He snorted a mocking laugh at my side, crossing his lanky arms across his chest. "Trust me, Princess Danvers, we have better things to do than babysit some spoiled little brat while her mom plays gang whore for a week."

"You take that back!" she shouted. "You don't know anything! You're just a—a stupid *boy*." The girl's face screwed up in fury, and she lashed out, shoving Archer in the chest with her little hands.

He stumbled back a step, not having expected her to actually push him. But he also had a quick temper, and I recognized the flash of anger in his face. He didn't care that this girl was four years younger than us with *no* clue what a vipers' nest she was standing in the middle of. He just saw someone challenging him, and Archer D'Ath never backed down from a challenge.

"Okay, come on," I said, angling myself to be slightly between the two of them. "Damien gave us an order," I reminded Arch with a hard glare. "And you have nowhere else to go right now," I said to the girl. Madison Kate. It was a pretty name, but it didn't suit her at all. Not that she wasn't pretty—she definitely was—but she had anger and stubbornness and bravado that contradicted that pretty, girly name.

"Let's just go hang out upstairs," I suggested, "before we get dragged into any more shit."

Archer gave me a grudging nod and turned to leave the seedy bar that we were way too young to be hanging out in. But no one was telling us what we could or couldn't do.

He didn't check if we were following, so I sighed and turned to the girl once more.

"Come on, Madison Kate," I coaxed. "We can just play Xbox and order pizzas. It'll be like a sleepover or some shit."

She frowned at me like I was stupid. "A sleepover with two gangster-wannabe boys? No thanks. That's not my idea of fun." Her thin arms folded over her chest, and I noticed the red marks on her wrist where Damien had grabbed her arm earlier. It was probably going to bruise, with skin as pale as hers.

I shrugged. "What else are you going to do? You heard your mom. She doesn't wanna see you for the rest of the week."

Her stubborn face faltered, and a flash of real pain showed through. Fuck. Poor kid. She didn't deserve that shit—none of us did.

I let out a sigh. "You'll be safe with us, Madison Kate," I

promised her, dropping the hard edge I usually used when I was in the Reaper clubhouse. "We won't let anything happen to you while you're here. Promise."

She scowled some more, then shot an uneasy look in the direction of the main bar, where her mom and Zane had disappeared to. Indecision was painted all over her pretty face, but eventually she sighed.

"What's your name anyway?" she asked as her shoulders drooped in defeat.

I smiled, knowing she'd made up her mind to trust us. "I'm Steele," I replied, holding out a hand to her, "but you can call me Max if you want. That's what my sister calls me."

She reached out and took my hand with her delicate, cold fingers. "Well, okay then, Max. You can call me MK."

I wrapped my hand around hers, pulling her after me as I made my way toward the stairs. "Nah," I said back, flashing her a grin. "You look more like a Cat to me."

Her blond brows dipped low, but she kept following me up the stairs. "You can't just change my name, Max. That's rude. And I hate cats; they're so mean."

I laughed because she was exactly like a cat, all pretty and soft but quick to hiss and scratch at anyone she didn't trust. *Just* like Archer...except, I guess, he didn't look even the slightest bit soft.

This assignment was either going to be a heap of fun or a god-damn nightmare.

Present...

Pain wracked my body, and I tried to draw a breath. Only a tiny amount of air made it into my lungs before blood choked me and my chest spasmed.

Fuck. I'd been shot.

I couldn't move enough to get up; I couldn't even turn my head if I wanted to. But I didn't. I never wanted to look away from those beautiful, violet-blue eyes that stared back at me. If she was the last thing I saw before I died…

My ears were ringing a high-pitched whine broken only by ragged, wet gasps as I tried to breathe. I was drowning in my own blood; there was no question about it. I guessed it was just a race to see which killed me first: the bullet wound or asphyxiation.

Movement jolted me back to the present before I even realized I'd started to drift away. Pain radiated through me again as someone scooped me up off the ground and ran.

I tried to scream, but no noise came out, just more blood spilling from my lips as I choked.

"Stay with me, you bastard." Archer's rough demand cut through the ringing in my ears, and I wanted to laugh. Of course he'd still be cursing me out as I died.

More jostling dominated my attention as he stuffed me into the back of the car, and the pain of it all made me black out.

Maybe that was it?

But soft, floral-scented hair brushed my face, dragging me back to consciousness as gentle lips kissed my cheek.

She was here. My girl was here. I couldn't leave her yet…not yet. She needed me; she needed *us*. I couldn't fucking die. Not now.

"Max, please don't go," she whispered, her voice choked with the tears that fell on my skin. "Please. I'm so sorry. I'm so, so sorry. This is all my fault. Please, Max, please…"

A low rumble of voices from the front of the car reached my ears, but I couldn't make out the words. No doubt Arch was driving like a damn bat out of hell to get me to a hospital. I wanted to shout at him to hurry the fuck up. My girl needed me, and I wasn't going out like this. To some cowardly fuck shooting from the shadows? Hell no. Max Steele wouldn't be wiped off the board that easily.

Except…I was pretty sure I was dying, no matter how fast my friend drove.

Blood choked me again, and my Hellcat turned my face so it could drain out. It gave me a fraction's respite. Enough that I could hear her next words clearly.

"You can't die yet," she whispered in my ear. "You can't. I've never even told you that I love you, but I do. I love you so fucking much, Max Steele. Please, *please* don't leave me."

Shit, beautiful girl…if only I had the choice.

Seven and a half years ago…

Zane's fist landed a hard blow across his little brother's face, and MK's hand gripped mine tighter. It was the only sign she showed of being afraid. Her face, with such delicate features, didn't betray anything as Zane beat the shit out of Archer in front of us.

"You're fucking pathetic, Little Brother," Zane snarled down at Archer. My friend was on the ground after that last punch, and blood spattered the wooden floors. "Is that the best you've got? Grandfather must be getting weak in his old age if that's as good as you've got for me." He delivered another heavy kick to Archer's ribs, and something snapped.

MK flinched this time, just the slightest bit, but I squeezed her hand in warning. I knew she wanted to say something to try to stop Zane from beating up Arch, but it wouldn't do any good. In fact, it'd only make it worse.

A few more kicks with his steel-capped boots and Zane decided he was done. He spat on the floor in front of his brother's body and sneered.

"You'll never go far in the Reapers, Little Brother. You're too weak." His disgusted gaze ran over me, then flickered over MK with somewhat more interest. It made my blood boil because she was a fucking *kid*. No bastard should be looking at her like she was a woman when she was barely even in a training bra.

I stepped forward, blocking her from Zane's line of sight and ready to stick my neck on the line. But he turned away before seeing the defiant glare in my eyes.

"I've got a hot date with my girl tonight," he told us with a lazy grin as he wiped his bloody knuckles on a rag. "Don't burn the fucking house down while I'm gone, yeah?"

He shot another sly smile in MK's direction, like he'd just remembered that *his girl* was *her mom*. Thankfully, he left before shit got any worse, and a few moments later we heard the roar of his motorcycle peeling out of the driveway.

The moment it was safe, MK dropped my hand and rushed over to where Archer remained lying on the ground.

For a second, I thought she was going to burst out crying. But then she slapped him across the face—hard, too, if his answering groan was any indication.

"What the heck is wrong with you?" she demanded, her little hands curled into fists as she glared down at him. "Why didn't you fight back? You could have killed him, and you know it!"

Archer just rolled onto his back, groaning as he laughed. "It's hilarious that you can't curse, Princess."

She whacked him in the chest, making him hiss with pain and cradle his ribs. Something was definitely broken there. A deep frown marked her brow, but she didn't apologize. It was cute as hell.

"You're so dumb, Arch," she mumbled, sitting back on her heels as I offered my hand to help him sit up. "Why did you pretend you couldn't fight?"

He flashed her a grin, and it tightened a knot in my stomach. Arch *liked* MK, despite treating her like an annoying tagalong. He saw something in her that spoke to his stained and damaged soul. I saw the darkness in her too, but I wanted to protect her from it. Arch wanted to draw it out and make her embrace it.

"Strategy, Little Princess," he replied with a grunt as he pushed himself up from the floor and limped over to the bathroom.

She wrinkled her adorable nose and turned to me for translation.

I just shrugged, offering her a hand to stand up too. "He means by not revealing our strengths to Zane—or to Damien—we're holding the power. If they don't know what we're capable of, they can't ever see us coming."

Her big, long-lashed eyes widened, and she followed Arch into the bathroom, where he'd started assessing his injuries. He'd pulled his shirt off. Bruises were already spreading across his midsection. Fucking Zane would pay for that one day. Just another mark against him when the time came.

"You guys are planning something?" MK demanded to know, folding her arms and raising her chin with stubborn determination. "Good. No offense, Arch, but people like your dad and Zane shouldn't have power. They just abuse it to make themselves feel better about their tiny dicks."

I choked on air, my cheeks heating in shock that she'd actually just said *that*. "Cat…what the fuck do you know about their dicks?"

Archer just snickered as he dabbed blood from his mouth. "You said *dick*. That's just one step away from *fuck*. I reckon we'll have corrupted you by the time you leave here."

Her cheeks turned pink, her gaze ducking to the floor. "Whenever that is," she mumbled.

"Hey," I said, reaching out for her again. I couldn't seem to stop touching her—in a totally platonic way. "It'll be soon. Did you say your dad comes back from Europe next week?" The *one-week* forced vacation her mom had brought her on was now coming up on three weeks…but selfishly Arch and I liked having her around.

She sighed, her shoulders rising and falling. "Yeah. I guess." Her gaze returned to Archer, and a deep frown creased her brow. "You're doing that wrong."

He raised an eyebrow at her in the mirror. The unsplit one,

7

that was. He was trying to apply butterfly stickers to the other one, but he hadn't cleaned even the worst of the blood away, which prevented them from adhering.

"You think you can do better, Princess?" He wasn't even subtle in taunting her, but she'd take the bait. She always did. I was starting to think she enjoyed the verbal sparring as much as he did.

Fucking hell. We needed to get her home to her cushy mansion before this life really did corrupt her irreparably.

She just huffed and slid out from under my arm to take the washcloth from the edge of the basin.

"Sit down," she snapped, shoving Arch to the side of the bathtub like he wasn't twice her weight. "Stupid boys," she muttered under her breath as she went to work cleaning up Archer's eyebrow.

He shot me a smug look while she was distracted with his wound, and I flipped him off behind her back. I didn't even know why we were being so competitive about her attention. She was a full four years younger than us, and neither of us was interested in her like *that*. But…there was just something there.

Like a past-life connection or some shit. I dunno. Karma.

_____

Present…

Every time I started to slide into the darkness, her voice pulled me out again. I clung to that sound like a lifeline, using it to drag myself back from the abyss when the pain became overwhelming.

Her hand gripped mine hard as my dying body was lifted from the back of the car and placed on a gurney.

My lids flickered as her hand tugged on mine like someone was trying to separate us; then they succeeded and her fingers fell away. I focused my eyes just in time to see her ball up her fist and punch a hospital security guard in the face.

I wanted to laugh. I really did. But my body wasn't under my control anymore.

The hospital staff raced my gurney through the doors, and my lids drooped. I *needed* her. Could I make it through without her voice, her touch pulling me back?

I had to. There was no other choice. I had to survive…because my Hellcat had finally said she loved me.

Love conquered all, right? Even a bullet to the chest.

CHAPTER 2
MADISON KATE

"I can't do this," I whispered, my hands balling into fists and bunching the heavy white skirts of the wedding dress I wore. "This is insane. I can't *marry* Archer." And certainly not in a dress that made me look like a fucking meringue. What the hell had I been thinking when I let him talk me into this *ludicrous* idea?

Bree snorted a laugh, dragging my attention back to my phone, which I'd propped up on the shelf to my left.

"Uh, newsflash, babe. You're already married to Archer." She was grinning, but her face on the video call was still a mess of yellow-brown bruises as she healed from our crash.

I rolled my eyes, releasing the dress fabric. The last thing I needed was to damage the designer gown and be forced to pay for the ugly thing.

"Not like *this*, Bree," I replied with a grimace. "This is the real deal. Everyone will know, and it'll be, you know, *legit*."

She gave me an indulgent smile. "No, the paperwork that was filed with the state registry eighteen months ago was what made it *legit*. This is just a party and a pretty dress." She paused, wrinkling her nose. "Or it will be a pretty dress if you can find a better one than that. Try the next one."

I reached behind me, tugging the dress clips loose so I could step out of the enormous gown and move it into my rapidly growing reject pile.

"No, not that one," Bree called out from where I'd placed my phone with a full view of the huge fitting room. I'd kicked the attendant out because she'd been driving me nuts with her questions about my *fiancé*, so Bree and I were doing it via video call instead. She was stuck in the hospital on bedrest for *months* yet and had more surgeries coming up to fix her wrist and leg. Not to mention her dodgy placenta placement.

I turned back to her with my hands on my hips. "Which one, then?"

"The lace one on the end. I wanna see that!" She grinned at me, her bruised face filling the whole screen.

Doing as she asked, I wiggled into a dress made almost entirely of lace, only to be met with the sound of Bree booing and giving me a thumbs-down from my phone.

Agreed.

"Okay, try the pretty one now," she ordered me with a huge smile.

I groaned. "Seriously? Bree, that looks like something a Disney princess would wear." But still, I pulled out the dress she wanted and hung it on the rack to change into.

"So what?" she challenged me. "If this isn't a *real* wedding, then why are you stressing so hard over what dress you wear? Just let me choose it, and you pay the lady with your husband's black Amex."

Damn. She had me there. And even I had to admit…the dress was freaking gorgeous.

"Yes!" Bree shrieked when I zipped it up, the sample size fitting me like it was fate or some shit. "Yes, oh my god, if you don't buy that dress, I'm going to discharge myself from this hospital, march down there, and kick your ass."

I laughed, hoping she was joking. "Bree," I groaned, "I don't even look like me in this."

"I know," she sighed. "You look like a fucking fairy princess. And it's a bit slutty too, with your rack. I'm totally in love. Buy it."

"Fine," I reluctantly agreed. Okay, not so reluctantly…the dress was beyond stunning and I couldn't wait to see what the guys' reactions would be to me wearing it.

Bree smiled in satisfaction. "Good. Now, I arranged a little something for you, seeing as I couldn't be there in person."

I frowned, crossing back to where I'd propped up my phone. "Bree, you didn't have to *do* anything. It's way more important that you and the baby are being looked after, and this isn't a *real* wedding. Right?"

Her smile was tinged with sadness. "Sure. Well…call it a late birthday present. Seeing as your stupid boys didn't include me in their *private* celebration the other day. Your surprise should be getting there right about now, so I'm gonna go. Call me later, okay? Happy birthday, bitch. I love your fucking face!"

She ended the call before I could question her any further on this *surprise*, so I just tossed my phone back in my handbag. I took another moment before taking the dress off, stepping up on the little platform to see the full effect of the gown in the mirrors all around the room.

Bree was right; I looked like a fairy princess. Archer was going to have a coronary. He probably expected me to show up in a black dress or something, to match his soul.

A soft tap on the fitting-room door made me sigh.

"I think I'm done," I called out to the bridal shop assistant, while still admiring the soft waves of the skirt in the mirror. "I'll take this lilac one."

"Holy shit," *not*-the-bridal-assistant commented. "Good choice."

My jaw dropped, and my gaze locked with a pair of silver-gray eyes in the mirror. "You!"

Steele grinned. "Me."

I whirled around in a storm of silk and tulle, launching myself at him before remembering he'd recently taken a bullet to the chest and *should* still be in the hospital.

"Fuck," I squeaked, jerking away just before I slammed into his body. "Fuck, sorry, shit."

He just laughed, grabbing my arms as I wobbled off balance. His strong grip pulled me in closer, and then he looped his arms around my waist.

"I'm not made of glass, Hellcat. You *can* touch me." His eyes flared with heat, and I knew he was thinking about more than just hugging me. Hell, I was too. But common sense won out, and I scowled.

"Max Steele, you weren't supposed to be discharged for another week. What the shit do you think you're doing here?" I tried to keep my tone stern, but I was too damn happy to see him. He knew it too, the sly fuck.

He tugged me closer still, and I draped my arms ever so gently around his neck. The need to kiss him was almost overwhelming, but I desperately didn't want to hurt him.

"Bree told me you were trying on wedding dresses, and I had to see for myself," he murmured, dipping his head to brush his lips across mine. "So I discharged myself early, and Dallas drove me over."

"Well, what do you think?" I stepped backward out of his arms and gave a twirl to show off Bree's choice. "Will it do?"

Reaching out to grab my waist again, Steele gave me a dark look. This time he didn't let me dodge away and kissed me until I was dizzy. Only then did he answer my question.

"You're easily the most beautiful woman I've ever laid eyes on, Hellcat. The dress is just garnish. But…do you want to explain to me *why* we're buying a wedding dress?" He leaned back and gave me a perplexed stare, and my cheeks heated.

Crap. Steele didn't know the plan.

"Let me get changed, and we can fill you in on everything back at the house?" I nervously bit my lip and mentally crossed my fingers that he'd be okay with this...*crazy*-ass plan.

A small frown creased his brow, but it eased off quickly when I leaned in to kiss him again.

"Trust me?" I whispered, searching his eyes from just an inch away.

He nodded, letting out a breath. "Always, Hellcat. With my whole heart and soul."

Smiling, I let go of his neck and stepped away to undress. "I'll be quick. Is Wade still out front? Maybe let him know to grab the car?"

Steele gave me a nod, then retreated out of the fitting room with a lingering look.

Wade was my heavily armed, highly skilled bodyguard for the day. After my stalker had damn near killed Steele, I'd agreed to never go out alone. Having Wade around—or one of the four other fully vetted security guards—meant that Kody and Archer didn't need to be glued to my ass twenty-four seven. Not that I'd have minded, seeing as we were on pretty good terms now, but sometimes we needed space. Like when I needed to go shopping for a wedding dress. Fuck me. I'd just chosen my *wedding dress*.

I quickly slipped out of the gown and tugged my jeans and sweater back on. Steele was waiting for me at the counter, fending off the doe-eyed shop assistant as she giggled and flipped her hair.

Placing the dress on the counter, I gave her a tight smile. "I'll take this, please."

She looked at me in shock, blinking a couple of times like she was trying to remember what her job was. "Oh, yes. Sorry. Gosh, I'm so sorry. I need to take your measurements and place an order with the designer and—"

"No need," I assured her, cutting off her panicked babble with a tight smile. "This size is perfect."

14

She blinked a few more times. Maybe her job wasn't usually so easy?

"Okay, well, great! I'll get this ordered—"

"Actually," I cut her off with a smile, "the wedding is in six weeks, so can I just take this one?" She'd already mentioned that custom orders could take up to eight months to arrive. I had neither the time nor the patience for that. If we didn't take the offensive soon, I wouldn't be *alive* in eight months.

The shop assistant hurried to package my gown up in a garment bag, then process it through the register, all while shooting coy glances at Steele. He just leaned on the counter like he had all the time in the world, but the tightness to his eyes betrayed the fact that he was in pain.

After the dress had been charged to Archer's credit card, the girl handed the garment bag across the counter to me, then handed Steele a folded piece of paper.

"My number," she told him with a suggestive smile. Under any normal circumstances, that'd be pretty appalling behavior in a *bridal* shop. But seeing as Archer had been with me when I arrived and had kissed me possessively before leaving me in Wade's care? Yeah, I could understand why she assumed Steele was single.

Steele just frowned at the paper, though, then handed it back to her. "Thank you, but I'm taken." Before I could say anything— even if I had something to say—he slipped his arm around my waist and kissed my hair. "Ready to go, beautiful?"

I bit my lip to hold back my laugh, because the shop assistant looked like her brain was mid-explosion. "You bet." I tipped my head back, pressing a kiss to his lips, then left the store with his arm still tight around my waist.

Once outside, I groaned and shook my head. "That was mean; it takes a lot of confidence to give a guy your number." A stab of guilt hit me, and I glanced back at the bridal shop.

"Except I'd already told her three times in the five minutes you were taking the dress off that I wasn't interested. She just didn't want to hear it." He gave me a small shrug, but I was distracted by the bead of sweat on his temple.

"Max Steele," I said in a stern voice, "you're overdoing it. Is Wade getting the car?" I glanced around, not seeing my bodyguard anywhere nearby.

Steele sighed and nodded. "Yeah. Here he is now." His eyes shifted past me to where our blacked-out SUV was coming around the corner.

The vehicle pulled up right beside us, and my bodyguard hopped out of the driver's seat to open the back door for us. Not that I was incapable of doing this myself, but it was one of those things that the security guys insisted on.

"Oh shit," I cursed, pausing halfway into the car. "Sorry, I left my jacket in the fitting room. Two seconds?" I gave Wade an apologetic smile, but he just nodded.

"I'll come with you," Steele murmured, taking the dress bag from my hand as I hurried back into the store. It was standard Steele protectiveness, but in his current condition I'd be the one saving *his* ass if someone attacked us in the bridal store.

I was glad he did follow me, though. We'd barely made it two steps back inside the shop when an explosion rocked the ground beneath our feet. Steele threw himself at me, knocking me to the ground and covering my body with his as glass from the shattered storefront windows rained down all around us.

The whole thing was over in seconds, but my ears rang as Steele cautiously eased off me.

Several car sirens went off in the street, and I already knew what I was going to find before crawling to my knees to look.

"Fuck," I breathed, staring wide-eyed at the flaming shell of our SUV. The charred, mutilated remains of my bodyguard lay several feet away from the wreckage, and my stomach knotted up with guilt and anxiety.

"We need to get out of here," Steele told me, then grimaced as he pushed to his feet.

He offered me a hand to help me up, but I batted it aside and yanked his T-shirt up to check on his still-healing wound. It was seeping blood, like I expected, and fear traveled through me. He shouldn't be back in the middle of this already. He'd just taken a bullet to the chest two and a half weeks ago thanks to my fucked-up life.

Steele pushed my hands away and smoothed his shirt back down. "Hellcat, I'm fine. But we need to go before someone realizes that you weren't in the car." He wrapped his hand around mine, stooped to grab my dress bag from where he'd dropped it, then led me quickly out of the shattered storefront.

We didn't hesitate even a second as we passed Wade's remains. Death was becoming all too familiar these days, and Steele was my priority. I couldn't risk his life again so soon. I just fucking couldn't. So we hurried away from the burning car without a backward glance.

One thing was for sure, my killers were still out there. Even if my stalker had been mysteriously quiet these past few weeks, he wasn't my only problem.

Not by a long shot.

CHAPTER 3

Kody and Archer were in the gym when we got back to the house and seemed just as shocked as I was to see Steele out of the hospital.

"Guys, give it a rest!" Steele exclaimed after they'd badgered him for a solid five minutes about the risks of early discharge. "My doctors cleared me, and I'm a grown-ass adult. I think I can make these choices myself." He glared at them both, then softened his gaze as he looked at me. "Besides, if I had to suffer through one more of those uncomfortable visits with nurses watching our every movement, I was going to lose my damn mind."

I bit my lip to hold back a smile, but I knew what he meant. We hadn't had a moment truly alone the whole time he was in the hospital. There was always a nurse hovering around or a doctor needing to check notes, probably because fucking *every*one in Shadow Grove seemed to be on the payroll of one gang or another. Undoubtedly, someone had seen the opportunity to listen for valuable information.

"Okay, if you're such a grown-ass adult," Kody challenged him, folding his arms over his bare chest, "explain why there's blood on your T-shirt. Huh? You couldn't even make it from the hospital to home without ripping stitches?"

Heading through to the kitchen, Steele rolled his eyes and flipped Kody off. "I got my stitches out a week ago, dickhead."

"Also, that wasn't his fault," I added, handing my dress bag to Steinwick, who'd appeared out of the dining room. The elderly butler took it silently, and I knew he'd see it safely stored in my closet.

"Why do I get the feeling you two have been causing trouble today?" Archer muttered, taking one of the beers that Steele pulled from the fridge. "And where's Wade? The security detail is supposed to check in when you get back."

Steele grimaced, then twisted the top off his own beer and took a long sip. "Wade's dead."

Kody and Archer both shifted their gazes to me, like I was somehow to blame for this mess. Okay, sure, I was in a way. But come *on*.

"Someone blew up the car," I told them with a wince.

Archer blew out a long sigh, scrubbing his hand over his face. "Someone blew up the armored vehicle I assigned to your bodyguard?"

I jerked a nod and accepted the bottle of pear cider that Steele handed me from the fridge. They'd appeared about a week ago, and I wasn't the only one drinking them.

"So the hit is definitely still active," Kody pondered aloud, leaning his elbows on the island countertop. "I think you were right on this plan, Arch."

Archer just grunted. "Of course I'm right."

"Yeah, about that," Steele said, leaning his hands on the counter across from Kody. "Anyone want to explain why my girl was trying on wedding dresses today?"

My face heated, and I gave Archer a pointed glare. I'd *told* him we needed to discuss the plan with Steele first, but he'd insisted the hospital wasn't a safe place to talk openly. He was probably right, but still…

19

Kody snorted a laugh and sipped his beer. He had no intention of helping out on that one.

Archer just smirked, that fucking prick. "You mean *my wife*?" he replied, smug as fuck. "Maybe we're just making things official in the public eye."

I glowered. "Don't be an asshole, D'Ath, or I'll replace you in the wedding announcement. If it's a fake wedding, then what does it matter *who* I marry, hmm?"

Kody grinned. "Oh, I like that idea. Pick me, babe. I'll look so fucking good in a tux."

Archer's response was to smack Kody in the chest, making him groan in pain. "No one's replacing me. We're legally married already, remember?"

Steele exhaled heavily. "Why did I want to come home so badly, again? It was so nice and quiet in the hospital."

"Bullshit," Kody replied with a snicker. "You had Bree forcing you to watch *Real Housewives* with her every day 'cause she was bored out of her damn mind."

Steele grimaced. "Yeah, good point. Okay, I'm just going to put two and two together here. We're going on the offensive to lure out anyone who might have taken the hit on Hellcat? This wedding is an ambush to eliminate three or four birds with one stone?"

My brows lifted. "Uh, yeah. Pretty much. Too obvious?"

He drummed his fingers on the counter a couple of times, thinking, then shrugged. "No. I think that sounds like a good idea. Fuck waiting around for them to keep taking shots at us; let's draw them onto our turf. I assume we're working on canceling the hit—even temporarily—so this is a hell of a lot better than sitting around and waiting for them to strike."

"Exactly," Archer agreed, but his gaze flickered at me too fast for me to calculate his mood. He took a long drink from his beer, then placed it down with a sigh. "I need to go deal with this Wade situation; Kody and Princess can fill you in on the details." He disappeared out of the kitchen again before anyone could respond, and Kody rolled his eyes.

"Fucking pussy," he commented with a laugh. "Totally just bolted before Steele could poke holes in his bullshit plan."

I wrinkled my nose. "You think it's a bad plan?"

Kody shrugged, his green eyes holding my gaze steadily. "Not really. But I do think he's got a pretty strong ulterior motive at play here."

My pulse raced, and my stomach knotted up. "Why didn't you say so the other day when we first discussed this idea?"

His smile was knowing. "I figured it was obvious, babe. I'm just pissed I didn't think of it first."

My cheeks heated, and panic swarmed my body. Kody was treading dangerously close to saying he wanted to marry me. For real. That was way too much, too soon, too fast. Yep, I was officially freaking right the fuck out, and yet I couldn't seem to smother the rush of oxytocin flooding through me at that idea.

"He's just joking, Hellcat," Steele reassured me, coming around the counter to loop his arms around my waist from behind. "Aren't you, Kody?"

Kody still held my gaze, and the way his brow twitched totally contradicted his words as he agreed. "Uh-huh, just joking."

Steele leaned his face down to kiss the spot on my neck where my pulse seemed to be trying to climb out of my skin. "Let's go sit down, and you guys can explain the rest of the plan. And for the love of all that's holy, can we *please* order pizzas? That hospital food has been slowly killing my soul."

I drew a deep breath, letting his change of subject ease the panic in my chest. "I'm always okay with pizza. You guys wanna try to teach me how to play that shooting game?"

Kody rolled his eyes skyward. "*That shooting game.* Ugh, you hurt my soul. Yes, babe, we will happily teach you to play *Call of Duty*. I won't even tattle to Archer if Steele wants to play too."

Steele huffed a laugh against my neck. "Thanks, bro, you're a star."

Kody shrugged, magnanimous. "You earned it." He circled around to the fridge to grab us all more drinks, then paused to clap Steele on his shoulder. "I'm glad you're not dead, dude."

He took the fresh drinks out of the kitchen, making his way to the den and leaving me alone with Steele once more. I turned around in his embrace, raising my arms to rest on his shoulders.

"I'm glad you're not dead too," I whispered. I'd never get tired of looking into his eyes. The brief moment when I'd thought his light had gone out was easily one of the worst I'd ever experienced, so I'd take every opportunity to remind myself that he was still here. Still alive.

His lips tugged into a smile. "I know. You've told me that every day since I woke up."

Rising up on my toes, I pressed my lips to his in a quick kiss. "Because it's true. But I'm also glad you're home."

His eyes flashed with lust, and he captured my lips in another kiss. "I have something I want to talk to you about. But it can wait until you and Kody fill me in on this plan for a wedding." He smacked me playfully on the ass. "Come on. Convince me this isn't just Archer's elaborate way to lay public claim to you."

I groaned but walked with him to the den, where Kody was on the phone with our usual pizza place.

"That's not…I'm sure that didn't even factor in," I grumbled, taking a seat on the sofa and tugging Steele down to sit beside me.

He snorted a laugh. "That *definitely* factored in. But I don't blame him." He hooked his arm around my shoulders, but I pulled back a couple of inches.

"Do you need to patch that up?" I reminded him, pointing to the dots of blood decorating the chest of his T-shirt. "Should you get a medic to look at it or something?"

Steele looked down and grimaced. "Nah, it'll be fine. I'll just put a silver dressing on it. I think there's some in the medical kit upstairs." He kissed me again, then stood. "Back in five."

Kody took the spot beside me the second Steele was out of the room, then hauled me into his lap without warning.

"Kody!" I exclaimed, but he cut any further protests short by grabbing my face and kissing me dizzy.

When he released my lips, he held me there, our foreheads pressed together. "I'm sorry I freaked you out before, babe," he murmured, his tongue swiping across his lower lip in a teasing way.

My heart thudded. "You didn't," I replied, then cringed when I heard the lie pass my lips. "Okay, maybe a little bit. Things are just moving at a really weird pace for us, aren't they? I mean, for all of us." I sat back in his lap slightly, my knees either side of his hips.

One of the many things I loved about Kodiak Jones was that he didn't dismiss my concerns as unimportant, even when he didn't agree. He genuinely listened to what I needed to say and considered my point of view before replying.

"Are they?" he asked after a moment, a small line creasing his brow. "I mean, yes, things are a bit unconventional with you and Arch being legally married. But it's been almost six months since you came back into our lives. Steele's been secretly harboring that crush on you since he was fifteen. Arch too, which he'd realize if he could pull his head out of his ass and see it for what it was."

I bit my lip, desperately holding all the big, scary emotions at bay. "And you?"

An easy smile curved his lips, and he gently brushed a lock of my pink hair away from my face. "Madison Kate, I fell in love the second you tried to kick me in the balls on Riot Night. Some people need years to *know*, but I only needed those few minutes in the dark."

My heart thumped faster, and my chest tightened. I wasn't used to...*any* of this. As a Danvers, I'd grown accustomed to the fact that we didn't share our feelings. Ever. So it was giving me sweats.

23

"I know this stresses you out, babe," Kody continued, letting me off the hook. "I won't keep going on. But I wanted you to know that if things were different, and if Arch hadn't already had the paperwork filed eighteen months ago"—he shrugged, his eyes glittering as his hands slid to my waist and clasped my body—"I'd have happily—"

"Taken one for the team?" Steele interrupted with a snort of laughter as he came back into the room with a clean T-shirt on. "I fucking bet you would have, asshole. Get out of my seat; Hellcat is all mine tonight."

Kody glared over my shoulder. "Screw you. Finders keepers." His fingers tightened on my waist, and I bit back a laugh.

"Kody, I don't remember *you* being shot with a hunting rifle two weeks ago," Steele pointed out. "Now fucking move. My doctor told me I need to relax, and I can't think of anything *more* relaxing than having my girl in my lap."

"*Our* girl," Kody growled back, but reluctantly released my waist and slid out from under me. "That excuse won't fly forever, bro."

Steele grinned, full of victory as he took his seat on the sofa once more. When he reached for me, I swatted his hands away.

"Think again, hot stuff. I'm not sitting *on* you this soon after life-saving surgery. I'll sit beside you, and that's the best you'll get." I gave him my very best no-nonsense glare, which was virtually impossible to maintain when he sent me back a pair of puppy-dog eyes. "Stop it," I scolded him. "You know I'm right."

Thankfully—because my resolve would have cracked in a second—he sighed and nodded. "Fine, I'll take it."

Satisfied with our negotiation, I got comfy snuggled under his arm and accepted my game controller from Kody. I was nowhere near as bad as I used to be, but my gaming skills still had a long way to go yet.

Steele shifted his grip on me, pulling me flush against his side

24

while his lips found my ear. "But I want you in my bed tonight," he added in a whisper.

A thrill of excitement shot through me, and I bit the inside of my cheek to hold back my feral grin. Tipping my head back, I gave him a narrow-eyed look of warning instead.

"To *sleep*?"

His answering smirk was all mischief. "We can discuss the finer details later. But sure, sleeping can happen…at some point."

I should have argued, but I didn't. I just cuddled him tighter because he was finally home and he was *alive*.

The second we were properly alone, I needed to tell him those three words that I'd only ever managed to say while he was dying or unconscious.

CHAPTER 4

After Steele fell asleep on the couch shortly after consuming a whole pizza, I decided we should call it a night. The sun had barely even gone down, but there was no harm in getting extra sleep—especially when Steele was still recovering from a gunshot to the chest.

Fuck me. He'd almost died. I still couldn't wrap my head around how lucky we were that he'd survived. That night we'd rushed him to the hospital, when there had been *so much blood*…

I shuddered, pushing the memory aside. He wasn't dead. That was all that mattered.

"Hey," I murmured, gently stroking a hand over his freshly buzzed hair. "Wake up, sleepyhead. You don't want to sleep here on the couch all night."

He mumbled a protest, his brow furrowing, but blinked his dark lashes a couple of times. When he focused on my face, he nodded, yawned, and let me help him up from the couch.

"You need me to carry his heavy ass, babe?" Kody asked, clearing up the pizza boxes and empty bottles.

I grinned but shook my head. "Nah, I got this."

Steele was only leaning a small amount of weight on me, and

there was nothing wrong with his legs. He was just drained, which was understandable considering the stressful events of the day.

"Just don't collapse on the stairs, okay?" I murmured to him with a grin. "I can't help you if you do something dumb like that."

He gave me a small smile back. "I'll do my best."

Once he was awake, though, he didn't need all that much help getting up to his bedroom. He sat down on the edge of his bed with a groan, and I stripped his T-shirt off to check the dressing he'd applied earlier.

Not that I knew what to check for—other than bleeding—but it made me feel better to do *something*.

"Do you have painkillers?" I asked, gently running my fingers over the edges of his dressing.

Steele let out an exhausted sigh. "Yeah. Over there on my dresser. I don't need them, though."

"Bullshit," I muttered, heading over to grab his pills. After checking the directions on the printed label, I shook two tablets out into my hand, then screwed the cap back on and returned to where Steele waited. "Here."

He rolled his eyes but took the pills from me anyway, swallowing them both dry like some kind of psychopath. Who dry-swallows pills? Gag.

"Lie down," I ordered him, fluffing his pillows up. "I'm going to get changed out of these jeans, then I'll come back, okay?"

"Or you could just wear my clothes," he suggested with a dark look as he lay back against the pillows and let me tug the blankets over him.

I grinned because that's what I'd intended to do all along. A quick hunt through his drawers and I found one of my favorite T-shirts, and then I slipped it over my head. I didn't bother stealing his sweats, just took my jeans off and climbed into the other side of the bed.

Steele reached out his arm, bringing me closer even as he

yawned heavily again. "Okay, talk to me. You guys haven't been telling me shit while I was in the hospital, so you need to get me up to speed."

I nodded, getting comfy on his pillows so we were face-to-face. "Right. So you're already caught up on the wedding plan now." Kody and I had explained it all over pizza.

"Yep, all up to speed and on board there. It's a good plan, even if Arch is getting the best part in it." He rolled his eyes, but his lazy smile told me he wasn't totally serious.

My cheeks still heated anyway, though. "Okay, so"—I quickly changed the subject—"we're working on the assumption that Scott was framed. At least a little bit. He knew that I was being stalked, but instead of being, you know, a decent human being and helping me stay sane, he used it to try to further his own agenda."

"Ugh, I knew I hated that guy," Steele muttered, wrinkling his nose.

I gave him a tight smile. "I know. Anyway, *some* of the stuff we found at Scott's place had his fingerprints on it but lots didn't, which suggests it was planted there. There was one pair of my panties, which proves he *did* touch my underwear drawer."

Steele nodded, understanding. "But not that he took the rest and left the creepy stalker note. Got it. Sounds like your stalker was also watching Scott and saw an opportunity there."

I sighed. "Yep. I mean, Scott was still a creep. He still tried to force himself on me that day; no one *made* him go off the rails like that. But...yeah, he definitely wasn't the one stalking me. I doubt he even knew who was."

Steele gave me a teasing smile as his fingers played with my hair. "Not to say I told you so, gorgeous, but what were you even thinking making friends with a random dude while you had a stalker on your ass?"

I cringed, rubbing my hands over my face. "I know, I know. Trust me, I've asked myself the same damn thing a hundred times.

My only excuse is that after everything went down…after I found out you'd all been lying to me…I was just a bit broken. I wanted so badly to have a normal life with normal friends that I blocked out the warning signs." I heaved a sigh, mentally kicking myself for being so stupid *again*. "At least Bree and Dallas are real friends. I shouldn't need anyone else, right?"

"I get it," he told me in a soft voice. "I understand where your head was at. Right now, though, you just need to be second-guessing everyone. Except Bree, because I can safely say that after two straight weeks of watching reality TV with her? She really just wants to make things up to you for Riot Night. She's a good egg."

I grinned at his approval of my friend. "Well, other than the Scott stuff, we don't know a whole lot more. Between visiting you and Bree in the hospital, it hasn't left us a lot of time to play Veronica Mars, you know?"

Steele groaned and wrinkled his nose. "Please don't compare yourself to Veronica. I really don't want to end up like Logan did."

I pouted, agreeing. "That was such bullshit. They were so in love too."

Steele's brows rose. "Speaking of…"

My heart beat double time. "Speaking of…what?"

He gave me a slow smile. "Hellcat, I've been wanting to get you alone since the moment I woke up in the hospital."

"But those nurses seemed to be everywhere all the time? Pretty sure the blond just had the serious hots for you," I grumbled, but he was right. I'd also been wanting to get him alone, and if I was totally honest, I could have made it happen if I wasn't being such a wuss.

Steele's grin spread wider. "I actually think she had the hots for *you*, gorgeous. I don't blame her either." He reached out a hand and stroked a gentle finger down the side of my face. "Hellcat, after I was shot—"

"I'm in love with you," I blurted out, cutting him off. Mainly because I had a pretty good feeling I knew what he was about to say.

His brows hitched, and his eyes lit with interest. "Sorry, what was that? I think I need to hear you repeat that."

I huffed at his sarcasm and squashed all my anxiety over voicing my feelings. He'd damn near died before I'd had the lady balls to tell him to his face, and I needed to rectify that. "You fucking heard me," I muttered. "I love you, Max Steele. I'm sorry it took me so long to make the words come out of my mouth, but when I thought you were dying, I just…" I trailed off with an awkward shrug.

He gave me a curious look. "I thought I heard you say something along those lines on the way to the hospital, but I wasn't sure if that was just panic talking. Was it?"

I frowned. "What? No. I'm not just saying this because you nearly died, Max. I'm saying it because I *mean* it. I've meant it for ages and just struggled to say it out loud because—"

"Because the last person you said it to died?" His words were quiet, but they struck a nerve as sure as a sharp blade. He was right. The last person I'd loved had died—brutally and just six feet away as I cowered in a closet and cried silently.

I jerked a nod, not trusting my voice.

Steele trailed the back of his fingertips over my cheek again, following the line of my neck down. "Hellcat, we know. We all know where your head is at, and we don't *need* you to push past these boundaries any faster than you feel comfortable doing. If it takes you ten years to feel at ease saying that you love me—or them—then so be it. Those words spoken out loud don't change what is in our hearts, right?"

My brow tightened, and that familiar feeling of panic swept through me, just like it had when I'd thought he was slipping away without ever hearing me reciprocate his feelings. "No. You don't get it. You nearly died, Max Steele. You nearly died because *my* stalker shot you, and I was still too hung up on my dead mommy to tell you I loved you. That's not okay; don't let me get away with that self-centered bullshit."

A small smile touched his lips, and his thumb brushed my lower lip. "Hellcat," he murmured, "they're just words. I *know* you love me."

I rolled my eyes. "Yeah, now you do 'cause I just said it." I drew a deep breath, my resolve firm. "I love you, Max Steele. Don't fucking die on me again, okay?"

His smile widened, and he hooked his fingers around the back of my head, pulling my face closer. "I probably can't promise *ever*, but I'll do my fucking best. Okay?" He sealed the deal with a tender kiss, one that made my toes curl and my heart race.

"Fine," I muttered when our lips parted ways. "I guess I'll take that."

I trailed my fingernails over his buzzed hair, then down his neck until finally resting my palm over his chest. Over his wicked scar from the bullet intended to take his life.

"At least we know something more about your stalker now," he commented, covering my hand with one of his own. His heart beat steadily under my fingers, and it was the most soothing rhythm in the entire world.

"What's that?" I asked, licking my lips and trying really damn hard not to let all my big emotions drown me. It wasn't often I let them all out of their cages because I was shitty at handling them. But I wanted to get better...for him. For all of them.

Steele arched a brow, a playful smile pulling at his lips. "He was wrong. He *does* miss, or I wouldn't still be here."

I never miss.

Motherfucker.

Regardless of his hubris, he was still going to pay *dearly* when we got our hands on his fucking crazy ass. I wanted revenge for every single crime. Luckily, I knew of the perfect soundproof torture room in the woods where we could make that happen... provided we could find him before his aim hit true. I had a sick feeling he wouldn't miss again.

"How many people know about the wedding?" Steele asked, changing the subject.

"Uh, not many right now. But pretty soon it'll be everywhere. Archer sent it in to the *Shadow Grove Gazette* for the engagements section." I cringed as I said that. Not because I had a problem with being fake engaged to Archer D'Ath, but because it was going to put us all under the public magnifying glass. I'd been pretty publicly involved with both Kody and Steele in recent months, and now I was announcing my "engagement" to Archer? Yeah, there would be questions. Lots of questions.

Steele gave a soft laugh. "No, I meant how many people know about the *real* plan? Does Sampson and his team know?"

I shook my head. "No, no one. Just us and Bree."

"Dallas?"

"Nope. Bree won't tell him either, not unless we want her to."

Steele nodded, thoughtful. "Good. I think it should stay that way."

"Well, except for whoever Archer is arranging our backup through? I sort of assumed that was going to be Sampson and his guys." I frowned, wondering what was on Steele's mind.

"No, not this time," he replied, seeming confident. "I need to talk to the boys, but I think they're of the same mindset as me on this. Someone on our security team is leaking info to your stalker. The less we tell them right now, the better."

My brows shot up, and my pulse raced. These guys were supposed to be fully vetted, one hundred percent trustworthy. Weren't they?

"Besides," Steele continued, "Arch won't trust anyone but the best on this job. He'll call in a favor with Hades and the Timberwolves."

Anxiety pricked at me. "What if they decide to double-cross us?"

"They won't. Hades quite literally owes Archer a life debt. Besides, it'd just be a shitty business decision." Steele reached out again, weaving his fingers through my hair and pulling me in close for another kiss.

When the seemingly innocent kiss took a heated turn, his

32

tongue stud coming out to play. I groaned and pulled away with gargantuan effort.

"Max Steele," I scolded teasingly, "you just got discharged from the hospital today."

"So?" he replied, challenging my resolve. "*Discharged* means they decided I was fine to resume daily life."

"You were shot in the freaking chest two weeks ago," I reminded him with a small scowl. But really, I was more trying to remind myself why it was a bad idea to let things go further.

He pulled me back to his lips for another kiss, this time holding me tighter as I squirmed. "Two and a half weeks," he corrected me, releasing my mouth only long enough to say those words, then kissing me again.

With a groan, I pried myself out of his grip and sat up. "Exactly! Two and a half weeks ago you nearly died, Max!"

He pouted, rolling onto his back to look up at me with the biggest fucking puppy-dog eyes. Bastard. "Does that mean you won't take those panties off and let me fuck you in just my Vanth T-shirt?"

I gave him a stern glare. "Absolutely not. It means you're just gonna have to lie back and let me do all the work." I shot him a wink, then pushed the covers back so I could straddle his waist.

"Well," he murmured, then swiped his tongue across his lower lip, flashing that metal stud at me and reminding me what he had waiting farther south of the border, "I'd hate to go against medical advice."

I smirked, leaning down to kiss him but not letting him get too carried away. My mouth had other places it needed to be.

I shifted backward, sliding down his body until my breasts rested on his thighs and my fingertips curled under the waistband of his light gray sweats. We both knew he didn't have anything underneath, so it was just that one layer of cloth doing a terrible job of hiding how hard he was.

"Hellcat…" Steele groaned as I tugged his sweats out of the

way and wrapped my hand around his rigid, pierced shaft. "You're seriously going to torture me like this?"

Humming an agreement, I circled his tip with my tongue, then looked up to meet his hooded gaze. "Don't give me that face, Max Steele." My fist stroked down his length, and I watched as his lashes fluttered in response. "You love the torture."

He made a pained noise as I took him in my mouth, but when his hands gripped my head, it wasn't to pull me away. Quite the opposite.

"Fuck," he breathed as I relaxed my throat, taking him deeper, as his tight grip was begging me to do. "Fuck, I do. Holy shit…" The rest of his sentence faded into groans as I let him pull at my hair and still did what I wanted anyway. He wasn't in control this time. I was.

Using my tongue, I explored every one of his new piercings and tested his limits, tugging them gently with my teeth. It wasn't until Steele's hands were firmly fisted in my hair and his hips bucking up to meet my lips that I decided I wanted to torture him a little more.

"What—" he started as I pulled away with a teasing lick down his ladder. "Hellcat, what are—" His words cut off again with a sharp inhale as I wiggled out of my panties and straddled him.

"Shush," I teased, lining him up with my aching core and sinking down onto him ever so carefully. "Just lie back and take it, remember?" My snarky comment was ruined by the whimper that escaped my throat as his hips bucked up and fully seated his dick inside me.

His grin was wicked, but I braced my hands on his abs to remind him that I was running this fucking show. Okay, fine. I might have been on top, but there was no way I was in charge. As I started to move, riding him with my knees planted on either side of his hips, he just smirked evilly.

He reached out, his hands finding my ass cheeks and grabbing on tight as his pelvis rocked up, taking my control away and increasing the pace until my breathing was ragged and my cunt was pulsing with the start of an orgasm already.

"Steele," I moaned in weak protest as his eight shaft piercings tortured me as surely as I'd just tortured him.

His only response was to sit up in a half ab curl and seize my lips in a bruising kiss that somehow ended with me flat on my back with Steele on top.

"What the—" My startled protest was cut short by his bruising kiss once more.

His hips surged, his cock filling me over and over, drawing my orgasm closer with every damn thrust.

"Shh," he chuckled, kissing down the line of my neck and sucking the skin over my thundering pulse. "Just lie back and take it, Hellcat."

I groaned long and low as he fucked me senseless, my well-intentioned protest about his health dissolving into a scream as I came. He followed me just a few thrusts later, grunting with each strike, then letting his breath rush out as he finished.

"You're in so much trouble," I mumbled, my head still swimming and my breathing quick. He was semi-collapsed on top of me, his lips still kissing and nibbling at my neck and his cock still buried inside my pussy.

He chuckled and rolled to the side with a pained groan. "Worth it, though." He turned his head, facing me. "I love you, Hellcat."

I groaned, covering my face with my hands to hide the rush of fucking *feelings* that he'd just caused. But then I gave myself a stern mental word about making smart choices and swiped my palms up to my tangled hair.

"I love you, Max Steele," I whispered back, meeting his eyes and fucking owning that statement. Because I did.

I was in love with Steele...*and* with his two best friends.

When the fuck did my life get so complicated?

CHAPTER 5

Before falling asleep, I set my alarm for the exact amount of time until Steele could take another dose of his painkillers. Even though he would probably rather stick a fork in his eye than admit he was in pain, I could tell.

I needn't have bothered, though. With the restless way he slept and the overwhelming anxiety tripping through me—fear for what was to come—I wasn't getting any serious rest. So I wasn't startled when the bedroom door opened slowly and Archer padded in on silent feet.

He crouched down beside the bed and lay a finger to his lips while I curled up slightly.

My glare flattened. "No shit, smart ass," I whispered. Like I was going to start yapping at the top of my lungs and wake Steele up? What did he fucking take me for?

Archer just rolled his eyes and indicated for me to follow as he slipped back out of the room. I took my time, mostly just checking that Steele was still asleep, then hunting for my panties. They were nowhere to be found, though, so I gave up and just tugged Steele's T-shirt back on.

Slipping out of his bedroom, I closed the door softly behind me, then turned to Archer, who waited with his back against the wall opposite and his huge arms folded over his chest.

"What's up, Sunshine?"

He didn't respond immediately, just headed down the hall and opened his own bedroom door in silent invitation.

I gave him a narrow-eyed stare as I took the bait, stepping into his bedroom and waiting as he closed the door behind us. His bedside lamps were on and the bed perfectly made, like he hadn't been to sleep yet, which was probably true, considering how early Steele and I had come upstairs.

"Did you seriously just yank me out of Steele's bed to come and sleep with you?" I asked, folding my arms over my chest with a mocking smile. "Come on, Sunshine. You're not actually that jealous of your besties, are you?"

He glared back at me, closing the space between us, then backing me up until my calves hit the edge of his bed and I sat down heavily.

"Princess," he murmured with a wicked smile touching his full lips, "if that were my intention, I'd have your legs already wrapped around my face and you damn well know it." He leaned down, crowding me until I was flat on my back with him hovering just inches away. "And you damn well know that I *am* jealous of those fucks. But not to the point where I'm going to beat on my chest and make you choose monogamy with one of us."

I smirked up at him, fighting the urge to hitch my legs up and wrap them around his waist. "Why? Scared you'll lose?" Yeah, yeah, I couldn't help myself.

Something dark flashed across his face, then he gave a low chuckle. "That's cute, Princess. Real cute." One of his hands moved to my leg, his palm dragging up the side of my thigh, pushing Steele's T-shirt up. When he encountered my *lack* of underwear, he paused. "Fuck," he muttered.

"Problem?" I asked, my hands finding a mind of their own and slipping beneath his T-shirt to stroke hot, hard abs.

A small growl of frustration left his throat, and he moved away abruptly. "Yes. No, not…" He shook his head, scrubbing a hand through his hair. "I didn't actually steal you away in the middle of the night to make you scream my name and remember that I goddamn *own* your ass." I shivered because the way he said it wasn't antagonistic. He wasn't pointing out the fact that he'd bought me from my father and married me behind my back.

Nope, he meant that in a purely sexual, primal kind of way. And in that category? Yeah, I'd let him claim it. When we were alone anyway. I had yet to see how well he might play with others… Hopefully I'd find out soon, though. It was the sort of scenario that frequently popped into my head while I was showering alone.

"So the fact that I know you're naked under that shirt is somewhat distracting," he admitted, his eyes scorching a path up my bare legs as I hitched one up on the side of the bed. His brows twitched as I did so, and I leaned up on my elbows to grin at him. Luckily, I'd taken a minute to clean up in the bathroom after Steele had fallen asleep, so I wasn't still dripping with his best friend's cum.

"Sorry, did you not want to be distracted?" I shifted my legs farther apart. "My bad."

Archer glared, but he made no moves to try to hide the hard length in his pants. "You're plain, fucking evil, Kate. I just got back from sorting out the whole car-bomb situation."

Now *that* had my attention. I dropped the slutty bullshit and sat up straight. "And?"

"And it was a completely different type of bomb than was used on Steele's car. Other than the fact that they were both our vehicles, there would be no links." He leaned his butt on the dresser, like he didn't trust himself to sit on the bed with me. Fair call.

I pursed my lips, thinking. "So, one was my stalker, obviously." Because he'd left one of his signature notes beside Steele's exploded Challenger. "And the other was an assassination attempt?"

38

Archer nodded. "That's my guess."

"All right, so what now?"

"Nothing," he replied with a shrug, his eyes locked on my face. "It changes nothing in our plan. Actually, that was the other thing I wanted to talk to you about."

I cocked my head to the side. "You got cold feet and don't wanna marry me in front of hundreds of guests? I'm hurt but not surprised. I guess Kody or Steele can take your place, but you'd have to grant me that divorce first."

He just scoffed a laugh. "As if you still even want those papers, Princess. No, but I did get a call from Demi Timber while I was dealing with the cops about the exploded car."

Something in his tone hinted that Demi hadn't called about my divorce application. She'd spoken to me about it a few days after Steele was shot, and I'd given her the instruction to let it lie for now. We had bigger fish to fry, and Archer wasn't exactly the *worst* surprise husband in the world.

"And?" I prompted when he just stared at my legs with a heated gaze for way too long. Or not long enough, depending on how this conversation was going to play out.

His gaze snapped back up to my face. "She said she was trying to call you, but it went to voicemail. I guess you and Steele were busy *talking*."

I gave him an unapologetic smirk. "Yeah, sure. If talking involves his hard dick inside of me."

Archer glared, and I just grinned wider. There was something crazy addictive about pushing his buttons until he snapped and lost control.

"Okay, okay." I chuckled, rolling my eyes. "What did Demi want? Or she wouldn't tell you?" Because attorney-client privilege and all that.

His brow twitched, and I guessed I was right. "She wants to meet tomorrow night. Says she has some information for you." His jaw tightened, and I got the distinct impression he wasn't pleased that Demi had refused to tell him directly.

Hah. Too bad, sucker. Big-dick energy only gets you so far in life. Sometimes you actually have to be a nice person or, you know, accept the fact that you don't get to know everyone else's secrets.

"Cool. At her office?" I kept it casual as fuck, like I hadn't noticed his burning curiosity. He was worse than me sometimes.

His eyes narrowed. "No, she asked to meet at 7th Circle. Apparently this is the sort of conversation she feels better having on neutral ground."

"7th Circle?" I asked, trying to think if I knew where this was.

"Yeah, that warehouse-conversion club we did the photo shoot in? Official opening isn't for another couple of weeks, but that's where she wants to meet up anyway." Archer gave a one-shouldered shrug, like he didn't particularly care *where* Demi wanted to meet. There was no way I was going alone, even if it was on so-called neutral territory.

I wrinkled my nose. "Why *is* it called neutral territory?" I pondered aloud, leaning back on my hands. "It's not, not really, if Hades and the Timberwolves own all those venues."

A small smile hitched his lips, and he pushed off the dresser, stalking toward me. "No such thing as totally neutral ground, Princess. Someone has to be in charge of enforcing the rules after all." He stopped just in front of me, then nudged my legs open once more. "It just so happens that Hades's crew are scary enough bastards to get the job done, and everyone knows it."

"So why let anyone onto their turf at all? Why create these pseudo-neutral zones?" My breath caught as he pushed my legs wider still, sinking to his knees in the gap between. Apparently now that he'd delivered the important information, he had other things on his mind.

"Why not? Hades has legal businesses, like the bars and clubs, that need patronage. Partying patrons often like to indulge in

40

something harder than alcohol, so there're business arrangements in place. One of the perks of those business relationships is that the Reapers and Wraiths are welcome in Timberwolf clubs without fear of gang violence breaking out. It's just all about dollars." His hands clasped my knees, then slid up my thighs and disappeared under my borrowed T-shirt to clasp my hips. "But do you really want a lesson about the politics of Shadow Grove gangs right now? Or do you want to lie back and let me tongue fuck you until you scream?"

I gave him a sassy eye roll even as my fingers threaded into his hair and pulled him closer to my throbbing pussy. "Some might say, Sunshine, if I'm not screaming every time, you're probably doing something wrong."

He gave me an indignant glare, then chose to retaliate in actions rather than words. The first touch of his mouth on my cunt made me gasp and fall backward onto his bed. Then I froze.

"What now?" he growled, sensing me tense up.

"You replaced this whole bed, right?" I asked, raising my head enough to give him a worried look. While Steele had been in the hospital fighting for his life, it hadn't felt right to be sleeping in the guys' beds, so I'd mostly kept to my room. "I mean, since Jase…"

Archer recoiled, looking horrified. "Are you serious? Yes. God, yes. Steinwick had it removed that same night. This one is brand-new and custom made. It even has a few fun features that I can show you if you stay in here tonight…" His gaze turned wicked again, and excitement flooded through me. Fun features? Color me intrigued.

His mouth returned to my cunt, and I fell back against the mattress again, safe in the knowledge that Jase's DNA wasn't still lurking nearby. Archer lacked the bonus of a tongue piercing, but he more than made up for it in raw talent and enthusiasm. Nothing he did was gentle, and eating me out was no exception to that rule.

Not that I was complaining. I fucking loved how rough he was

41

with me. Despite how often he called me *Princess*, I was anything but his delicate flower. He knew my limits, and he damn well pushed them. Every. Fucking. Time.

"Oh, shit," I gasped when his thick fingers plunged into my pussy and his thumb teased at my ass. His mouth was sealed over my clit, sucking and flicking it like he was determined to make me lose my freaking mind. Ah, heck, who was I fooling? I'd already lost my goddamn mind.

My panting moans escalated as his fingers fucked me and his mouth worked me over. I held his short hair in a punishing grip, my hips bucking up off the bed as my orgasm took over.

"That's more like it," Archer murmured as my screams died off. He kissed my inner thigh, nipping my soft flesh with his teeth and making me quiver.

I groaned because I wasn't totally capable of words and watched with hungry eyes as he stood up and stripped his shirt off one-handed. Fuck, that was hot. Where did guys even learn that skill?

"So?" he prompted, unbuckling his belt. "Are you staying the night?"

A dazed smile played across my lips, and an emotion way too soft and fuzzy to just be *lust* filled me. Fucking hell, how did we get from hate to...*this* so damn fast?

"It's cute that you're even asking," I told him, licking my dry lips. Orgasms always seemed to dry my mouth out, like all the moisture got sucked south. "But..."

Archer's brows shot up, and he paused with his pants halfway open. "But?" He sounded so shocked it almost made me laugh. It was such a fine line between confidence and arrogance.

"*But*," I repeated, biting my lip, "it's Steele's first night out of the hospital."

Archer just stared at me for a moment like he wasn't totally sure if I was serious or not. Then he sighed. "Bastard," he muttered. "Next time I'll have to get shot instead."

My eyes narrowed. "Don't you fucking dare."

He just shrugged, then stripped his jeans off the rest of the way. Then his boxer briefs. "Well, shit. Now what do I do with all of this?" he asked, fisting his hard cock in a way, *way* too sexy way.

It was on the tip of my tongue to offer up a quickie...but this was Archer, not Kody, and our whole dynamic worked off our never-ending desire to piss each other off. So I just grinned and stood up, tugging Steele's T-shirt back over my bare ass.

"I figure you've got this...*handled*, big guy." I rose up on my tiptoes, pressing a quick kiss to his lips. "But make sure you think of me."

With a quick, sultry wink, I ducked back out of his bedroom and hurried back into Steele's before I cracked up laughing. But honestly, the dumbstruck look on his face as I'd left his room had been pure gold.

My heart still thundering, I checked the time and grabbed Steele's painkillers from the dresser, placing them on the nightstand instead so he could take them easily when my alarm went off. Then I slipped back under the covers, trying my best not to disturb his sleep.

I should have known better, though. He stirred immediately, rolling over, snaking a tight arm around my waist, and pulling me into his warm embrace.

"Hellcat," he mumbled, his voice thick with sleep as he buried his face in my hair. "You smell like Archer."

I tensed up, a wave of panic sweeping through me. It was one thing for them all to be knowingly sharing me; it was kind of another for me to bed-hop within the same night. Wasn't it?

"He had something to tell me," I replied, then bit my lip at the half-truth. Steele was no idiot, though, and he knew Archer all too well. He just chuckled against my hair, his grip on my stomach shifting lower until he found my still-slick cunt.

He let out a small groan as his fingers danced over my heat, and his own hard length nudged at my back. "I fucking bet he did," he muttered, sliding one of those long, talented fingers into me.

I whimpered under his touch, feeling a swirl of guilt and excitement and…fuck knows what else. It seemed so *wrong* to come straight from Archer tongue-fucking me to Steele—he withdrew his fingers then hitched my leg up, sinking his cock into me with a low groan—actually fucking me.

Fuck it. Wrong never felt so good.

CHAPTER 6

In the morning I left Steele to sleep and hurried back to my own room to shower and change. It wasn't until after I'd dried off and found fresh clothes that I checked my messages.

Sure enough, there was a missed call from Demi from the night before, along with a message that she'd try calling Archer. It was the next message—from Archer D'Ath—that made me blush, though.

The time stamp said it'd been sent about fifteen minutes after I'd left Archer's bedroom. Probably right around the time Steele was coming all over my tits.

There was no text in the message, just a video link.

Biting my lip with anticipation, I clicked on the play button because good god, I'd give Alice a run for her money chasing that white rabbit. Archer's hard cock filled my screen, his fist wrapped around it as he took care of business, and I grinned. Shaking my head, I saved the video into a folder to watch later. Minus pants.

Of fucking course, he had to have the last word on that one. Too bad he didn't know I was busy with Steele when the message came through.

"Babe!" Kody called out from down the hallway. "You up here?"

Tucking my phone into my pocket—along with my butterfly

knife—I exited my bedroom and found Kody coming down the hall toward me. "Sure am, what's up?"

He grimaced. "Is Steele awake? The gate guards just called. There was a package delivered overnight."

Sick anxiety rolled through me, and I swallowed heavily. "Um, no, not yet." I shook my head, my brain already rolling with ideas of what could be in today's package. "No, he's still asleep. We should leave him to rest anyway."

Kody gave me a smirk. "Yeah, you guys *rested* real hard last night." He winked, heading for Steele's bedroom door. "Besides, he'll wanna see this one." He turned to shoot me a worried look as he pushed Steele's door open. "It's addressed to him."

Shock held me immobile as Kody barged into Steele's room and yanked his blankets off in one harsh tug. "Wake up, you half-dead bastard," he ordered in a loving manner. "MK's stalker sent you a present."

Steele groaned in protest as he rolled onto his back, making no attempt to cover his half-hard morning dick. "What the *fuck*, Kody?" he mumbled. "Fuck off."

"Jesus Christ, man," Kody hissed, standing at the foot of the bed with his nose wrinkled in horror. "Put that away! Just looking at all that metal hurts my own dick. Fucking hell, you seriously did want to punish yourself."

A smug smile crossed Steele's lips, and he cracked his eyes open to look up at Kody. His hand drifted down to his cock as if to highlight the piercings. "Don't be jealous, bro. Hellcat *loves* them."

"Okay!" I snapped, parking my hands on my hips where I stood in the doorway. "That's enough of that."

Steele shot his gaze to me, clearly seeing me there for the first time as his sleep haze faded. "Oops, sorry, gorgeous. He started it."

I rolled my eyes, marched across to his pills on the dresser, and measured two out into my hand while Kody threw clothes at his friend.

"Here." I handed the pain meds to Steele as he sat up with a small groan. "Don't even try to tell me you don't need them." I arched a brow at him, silently reminding him of the less-than-gentle exercise from the night before.

He smirked back but took the pills. "Thanks, gorgeous. I could get used to this Florence Nightingale routine, you know?"

Kody groaned. "Stop it, dickhead. Now I'm picturing MK in a slutty nurse costume when we have a stalker package to open downstairs." He looped his arm around my waist, then dipped and flipped me over his shoulder.

I let out a surprised shriek and smacked his ass, but Kody just laughed.

"Babe, come on, let's leave the Tin Man to get dressed in private. Otherwise we will never get this package open, and it already kinda smells bad." He spun around, gave Steele a mocking salute, then carried me out of the room.

He didn't put me down when we reached the stairs, just bounced down them like he was carrying a load of laundry, not a whole grown person.

"Kody," I huffed, "I can walk."

He smacked my ass, conveniently located beside his head. "I'm aware." When we reached the kitchen, he finally put me down on the countertop beside my espresso machine, and I gave him an unamused glare.

"Happy now?" I asked, sarcastic as fuck.

He clasped my face between his hands, bringing my lips to his for a kiss that completely took my breath away and turned me to putty under his touch.

"Now I am," he replied, his voice husky and dark as he released me. His hands trailed down my arms; then he looped his arms around my waist. "Good morning, babe."

I grinned. I couldn't fucking help myself; everything Kody did made me grin. He was *impossible* to stay mad at, even when he'd just caveman-carried me out of Steele's room.

"Did Archer tell you we have a date with Demi Timber tonight?" I asked, snaking my own arms around his neck because, damn, I just loved being near him.

Kody nodded, then dipped his face to kiss my neck. "He did. I'm guessing this isn't about your divorce if he knows about it."

A small sigh escaped my chest. "No, I don't imagine so, although she didn't give any details. But I told her not to bother with that...for now."

Kody stiffened with tension, his lips pausing against my neck. "You're staying married to him?" He pulled away a short distance, a frown creasing his brow and his eyes searching mine.

"No," I was quick to reply. "Not... I don't know. No, I'm not. I'm too young to even think about marriage, right? No, I just meant that we have way bigger problems to deal with. The whole divorce thing can be put on hold until after people stop trying to kill us all. Besides, it wouldn't really do much for the fake wedding if anyone found out I was already applying for a divorce."

Crap on a cracker, even *I* thought I was protesting too hard on that subject, but it was like verbal diarrhea.

He still looked uneasy, but he made a visible effort to clear the frown from his brow as he shrugged. "Yeah, good point. Anyway, I told Dave to keep the package outside this time. He's got it in the security office with Arch right now."

I cringed. I didn't even remotely want to see what had been delivered, yet I knew we needed to.

"All right, let's go check it out," I said, hearing Steele coming down the stairs to join us.

Kody reached around my espresso machine and produced my huge travel mug, already full of coffee just the way I liked it. I beamed and took the mug with a happy hum.

Taking a sip, I groaned. Kody's barista skills had definitely improved. "Aww, you *do* like me," I teased, then licked the edge of my mug as I met his eyes.

48

He just smirked back. "Babe, I *love* you." Kody playfully slapped my thigh. "Let's go."

He stepped back to give me some space to slide down off the counter just in time for Steele to scuff into the kitchen with a sleepy scowl on his face.

"Where's the creepy gift?" he asked, glaring at Kody, then spotting my coffee in my hands. "Hellcat…" He held his hand out, his eyes pleading.

"Shit no," I replied with a laugh, holding my coffee closer to my chest. "Get your own."

Steele started to pout—damn it, he was going to win me over with that—but Kody saved the damn day by producing an extra travel mug.

"Here, cyborg," he said, handing Steele the coffee. "Don't say I never do anything nice."

Steele took the coffee, sipped it, then glared. "Cyborg's are part machine, not just metal. Keep thinking, bro."

Heading out of the kitchen with my coffee safely in hand, I rolled my eyes at the two of them. At the front door I stuffed my feet into a pair of Ugg boots, then headed outside. The new security office—new, since we never used to *need* security like this—was around the corner of the house in what used to be a storeroom.

The door was open, but before I got there, our cook—*Anna*, not Karen like I'd thought her name was for way too damn long—came rushing out with her hands pressed to her mouth.

"Oh, I'm so sorry," she exclaimed when we almost collided. Tears streaked her face, and her hands were shaking as she reached out to steady me. "I'm so sorry; I wasn't looking."

I shook my head, dismissing her apology. "It's fine, Anna. What's going on? Why are you upset?" Worry and anger rippled through me. If one of the guards had been harassing her—

"It's so silly," she told me with a self-deprecating laugh. "I don't even know why I'm so upset. I didn't even know the poor thing. It's just…" She trailed off, shaking her head. "I think I must be getting soft in my old age."

Confused as hell, I made no move to stop her when she reached out to hug me. It was just a quick squeeze but still left me a bit shell-shocked. Aside from the guys and Bree, I couldn't remember anyone *hugging* me since my mom died.

"I need to get back to work," she told me with a soft smile, then extended it to Kody and Steele behind me. "I'm cooking a proper roast for your dinner tonight, and if I find pizza boxes in the morning, someone will feel my wrath, understood?" She seemed to already be pulling herself together, sniffing away the last of her tears. "You four need to eat some good food. Especially you, Max Steele."

Kody and I shared a grin. Steele was usually the first to suggest pizzas. Now he was catching Anna's ire for all the beautiful meals we'd never ended up eating.

"Yes, ma'am," he mumbled, sounding sufficiently scolded.

Anna nodded, propping her hands on her hips. "Good. I've gone ahead and changed my hours to be sure you're all eating better. Not only is it important for your health, it seems to me that you just keep tempting fate with all these takeout dinners. Don't you realize how easily someone could poison your food? Good lord, for some smart people, you're very stupid sometimes."

She walked away without waiting for our response, and I couldn't escape the rush of embarrassment that swept over me. Goddamn it, she was right. No pizza or Chinese was good enough to risk my guys being poisoned.

"Shit," Kody cursed, "she has a point on that one."

"Dammit," Steele muttered. "I *like* pizza."

I scrubbed a hand over my face and glared at them both. "Guys, how many freaking times have we basically opened the damn door for someone to poison us? I'm feeling next-level stupid right now. But more to the point, why was Anna crying just now?"

"She found the package," Archer said from behind me. I spun

around and found him leaning on the doorframe with his arms folded and a grim look on his face. "It was in the driveway when she got back from the grocery store this morning."

"Well shit," Steele muttered, "don't keep us in suspense. What's he sent this time?"

Archer just stepped back, indicating we enter the little security office.

Inside, Sampson—our head of security—and Dave the gate guard were standing around one of the desks, looking somewhat repulsed. The gift box sat there seeming innocent enough—or it would have if we hadn't already received countless similar packages. There was a stomach-churning odor in the small office, and I immediately blocked my nose.

Whatever was in the box, it wasn't flowers and chocolates.

"Addressed to me this time?" Steele murmured, coming closer to the box to read the label scrawled across the top. "I take it you've already looked inside?"

Dave grimaced. "I wish we hadn't."

Sampson huffed an annoyed sound. "Be glad you weren't here to deal with the human heart before Christmas, then. You can head back to the gate now."

The gate guard didn't protest as he hurried out of the office, leaving us alone with Sampson and the box.

"Weak-stomached fuck," Sampson grumbled. "Gonna have to fix that if he wants to keep working here."

Steele just raised a brow, then reached out to flip the lid off the box and reveal its contents. I was still breathing through my mouth, but I could tell by the way Steele blanched the smell had gotten worse.

"Sick fuck," he muttered, peering into the box with a scowl. "Is there a note?"

"Underneath," Archer replied. "We didn't want to disturb things until you'd seen it as is."

I took a step forward, needing to see what my stalker had decided to send to Steele directly. If it was a Ken doll, I might die laughing.

"Oh, come *on*," I groaned, seeing what was causing the smell. Inside the gift box was a very dead cat. A gray one, wearing a name tag and collar. This was someone's *pet*. Fucking hell.

Sampson held out a pair of latex gloves to Steele, who placed his coffee down, then pulled them onto his hands. Gingerly, he reached into the box and moved the dead cat until we could read the name tag. Max.

Somehow, my stalker had managed to find someone's pet cat called Max with fur in a soft shade of gray all too similar to Steele's eyes. Or his name.

Carefully, Steele extracted the note from under the cat and laid it on the desk; then he pulled a bullet casing from the box to lay beside the note.

Welcome home, Max Steele. You must be almost out of lives by now.
Then, on the bullet casing: *LUCKY CAT.*

"Well, someone's pissed that he's a lousy shot," Kody murmured.

Archer and Steele were all but vibrating with anger, though, and I got the distinct impression I was missing something important.

"You guys know something more," I accused. "Spill it."

The two of them exchanged a long look; then Steele snapped his latex gloves off with a heavy sigh and an angry headshake.

"Cat," Archer replied, his voice a furious rumble, "is what Steele used to call you."

I frowned, confused. "What? No, I've always been Hellcat to him."

Archer gave a grim laugh, shaking his head. "Not now. Back when we first met, when you were eleven. He changed it to Hellcat when he started thinking about your nails dragging down his back during sex."

"Shut up," Steele snapped, glaring. "Sex had nothing to do with it."

Kody snorted a laugh. "Sure it didn't."

I held my hands up, my brain whirling. "Wait. Hold up. You're saying my stalker *knew* what you called me almost eight years ago when we hung out for three weeks?"

Steele just shrugged. "It could be a coincidence."

"Nothing about this sick fuck is a coincidence," Sampson commented, folding his thick arms over his chest and scowling down at the dead cat. "He was stalking your mom back then, Madison Kate. He would have known, and this is a deliberate message to Steele."

"So what is that message?" Kody looked to Steele and Archer. It was pointless to ask me; I remembered *nothing* of meeting them prior to Riot Night.

Archer looked to Steele, who just gave a shrug.

"No idea," he muttered. "Sampson, can you document this and dispose of it?"

Our head of security assured us he would, then Steele exited the office without making eye contact with me. When he was gone, no one else made any move to follow him.

I frowned in the direction Steele had disappeared. "Why do I get the feeling he just lied to us?"

Archer let out a heavy sigh. "Because he did." My brows shot up, and he scrubbed a hand over his short beard. "Let me talk to him."

Before leaving the security office, he pressed a quick kiss against my hair, his arm tight around my waist.

"Stay with Kody. I don't trust anyone." His words were whispered in my ear, and my eyes widened. I gave him a small nod of understanding, though, and he left the office to track down Steele.

Sampson muttered something about getting a trash bag and left as well. Kody blew out a breath, slinging an arm over my shoulders.

"Just you and me this morning, huh, babe?"

I winced and looked at the stalker gift. "And a dead cat."

A dead, steel-gray cat named Max.

CHAPTER 7

Steele evaded me for most of the day, and when I ran into Archer, he just told me not to worry about it. Like that wasn't going to make me worry *more* about it. Fucking boys just didn't get it sometimes.

Which is why I finally snapped as we were about to leave for our meeting with Demi at 7th Circle.

Archer, Kody, and I were already waiting in the Range Rover when Steele came out in a pair of distressed black jeans and a dark gray T-shirt, basically looking like he'd stepped off the pages of *Bad Boy Weekly*.

If that wasn't already a magazine, it needed to be.

"I'm taking my bike," Steele called out to Archer, bypassing the Range Rover to head toward where his motorcycle was parked.

Annoyance sparked, and I climbed out of the car. "Wait up; I'll come with you," I called out after him.

He paused, then spun around to eye my outfit critically. We were meeting Demi in a nightclub, so I'd dressed for the occasion in a sequined, silver minidress and strappy, black high heels. My hair was up in a high bun and my makeup was heavier than usual. Because why the hell not? I looked great, and with people trying to kill me every second day, I deserved the boost to my own confidence.

Also, having the guys watch me like predators every moment I moved was a hell of an ego stroke.

"You're gonna ride on the back of my bike in that, Hellcat?" Steele's lips curved in a challenging smile, and I propped my hands on my hips.

Batting my lashes, I threw him an arrogant smirk. "What, like it's hard?"

Steele just snorted a laugh and indicated for Archer to go without us. Security would be following both them and us regardless, so we weren't concerned about splitting up for a short drive. As for my lack of protective clothing? Fuck it. A little part of me enjoyed the danger.

We stared at each other until the Range Rover pulled out of the driveway, then Steele folded his arms over his chest.

"I'm not avoiding you, Hellcat. It just makes sense to have a secondary vehicle in case something goes wrong." Bullshit. The tight set to his shoulders told me a whole different story.

Holding up a finger, I started pointing out some facts. "One, you lied to me this morning about the cat thing. Two, you've most definitely been avoiding me all damn day. Three, you shouldn't even be driving right now, let alone riding a motorcycle. Are you suicidal? And four, you swore you wouldn't lie to me anymore, Max. What the hell?"

He deflated, his shoulder slumping and his eyes on the ground. "I'm sorry, Hellcat. I shouldn't have lied to you."

I waited for more of an explanation, but none came. *What the fuck?*

"Give me the keys," I demanded, holding my hand out to him. "I'll drive."

Steele's gaze snapped back up to mine, and he scoffed a laugh. "Not a chance, Hellcat. Come on, I promise I'll spill all my secrets when we get home."

He took a few more steps toward his motorcycle, but I needed to push him harder.

"Why not now? This obviously has something to do with me, so just tell me now, Max." I folded my arms and ignored the scratch of my sequined dress.

He let out a heavy sigh, holding out a helmet for me to take. "Because, Hellcat. It also has to do with Rachel, and I'd really, *really* appreciate the distraction of your naked body when I need to drag up painful memories of my dead twin. Okay?"

"Oh." That was the best response I could muster up because I hadn't expected *that* response from him. *Crap, now I feel like a total bitch.*

Steele gave me a weak smile and helped me fasten my helmet. "So can you just wrap those gorgeous thighs around me for a few minutes and let me park this topic for a few hours? I promise it's not detrimental to your safety; it's all ancient history."

I jerked a nod, then climbed onto the back of his bike after he was seated. No verbal response was really needed, so I just did as he asked. I pressed my whole body to his, my arms tight around his torso without hurting his chest.

The drive to the warehouse district where 7th Circle was located went by surprisingly fast, but when Steele pulled in to park and helped me off, my teeth were chattering.

"Told you that dress wasn't suited for my bike," he scolded as he wrapped me in his warm embrace and rubbed my frozen arms. "It's sexy as sin, though."

I shot him a grin. "No pain, no gain, Max Steele."

He grimaced and rubbed a hand over his chest. "You can say that again. Come on; the guys are probably inside already."

With our fingers linked together, Steele walked straight past the burly security guard at the front door with nothing more than a small nod. Inside the old warehouse, the whole place had been fully transformed since the last time I'd seen it. Where it had still been a work in progress during our photo shoot, it was now fully finished and totally polished.

"I thought Archer said this place wasn't open yet," I said over the music as we wove our way through the crowd.

"It's not," he replied. "This is a trial-run night. Everyone is here on invitation only to put the staff through their paces and ensure they're ready for an official opening."

"Makes sense," I commented, then spotted Archer and Kody at the bar. I pointed them out to Steele, and we made our way over there to find drinks already waiting for us.

"That was quick," Kody teased, handing me a fruity cocktail identical to his own. "All that metal giving you dysfunction, bro?"

Steele scoffed. "You fucking wish. Demi not here yet?"

"She's in the mezzanine bar. We wanted to wait for you two before heading up there." Archer indicated the area toward the far end of the warehouse where a bar overlooked the main hall. The two featured runways, each ending in a spinning pole that extended all the way past the mezzanine level—dangerous as hell if one of the dancers fell from that height. Also a seriously cool design feature.

Archer laid a gentle, yet possessive, hand on the small of my back as we made our way up the staircase that took us up to the next bar. A security guard waited at the top, but he simply stepped aside to let us pass.

Inside, the entire bar was all but empty, just one bartender and my lawyer, who sat at one of the tables near the balcony.

"MK, good to see you," Demi greeted me, standing up from her seat. "Come and sit." She was dressed in a sharp, white pantsuit with the edges of a royal-blue lace bra peeking out of her blazer. Her Louboutin shoes were a matching royal blue, and she looked exceptional.

I sat down on the sofa she indicated, opposite her, but when Demi held up a finger to Archer, none of the guys sat. Archer huffed an irritated sound.

"MK, I have information for you about your mother. I'm happy to tell you in confidence if that's what you'd prefer." Her

57

gaze was locked on me, and I filed that little power dynamic away for future reference.

With a smile, I shook my head. "No, it's fine. They can stay. Archer and I have…started working out our differences."

She grinned back at me, making a small signal that the boys could join our table. "I thought as much but wanted to give you the choice."

Archer, the petulant fucker that he was, decided to reinforce my statement. He slid onto the couch, then pulled me into his lap and looped his arm around my waist. Like he fucking owned me.

Bastard.

"Sunshine," I said with sugary sweetness, "are you lost? There're plenty of other seats." And by plenty, I meant there was enough space between us and Steele for us both to sit. Kody dragged over an armchair.

Archer just dropped a kiss on my shoulder. "Hush, Kate. Demi has something important to tell us."

My cheeks flamed at his unnecessary display of big-dick energy, but Demi just smiled.

"Working through your differences looks entertaining," my lawyer commented with a cheeky grin. "But let's get down to the important things, shall we? I located your mother's family."

Shock froze me. "You did?"

She jerked a nod. "I did. After Archer provided me the paper trail he'd originally covered up, it was enough of a thread for me to follow through to the source."

"That was quick," Archer commented, his fingers flexing against my dress. "My people have been working on that for over a year and still coming up blank."

Demi was pure smug satisfaction. "You need better guys."

"So it seems," Archer murmured. His grip around my waist relaxed slightly, and he brushed a soft kiss across my shoulder, almost like an unconscious gesture.

Demi reached into her designer handbag and pulled out a folder of paperwork. She placed it on the small table between us and flipped it open. On the top page was a photograph of a beautiful, older woman, maybe somewhere in her seventies. There was something shockingly familiar about her face.

"Meet Katerina Orlova of Moscow, Russia. Your maternal grandmother." Demi watched me closely as she tapped a long, nude-painted fingernail on the photo.

My mouth went dry as I studied the image. "I know her," I whispered as fuzzy edges of long-forgotten memories tried to resurface in my mind. But the harder I tried to grab on to them, the further away they seemed. All I could grasp was that I *knew* this woman and that I'd loved her…once.

"Katerina, I believe, is why your mom added Kate to your first name. She died a little over ten years ago," Demi continued, "which seemed to be the catalyst for your whole matriarchal line being buried by your mother."

My gaze snapped up to meet Demi's curious gaze. "My mom hid it? I thought…I just assumed my dad had something to do with it."

Demi shrugged. "Your dad is a piece of shit, no question there. But this was done by Deborah herself. I can only imagine it was an attempt to keep you safe from whoever killed her mother."

I swallowed heavily. "And whoever ended up killing her."

"Probably," Demi agreed.

None of my guys spoke, but I could feel their strength and support like a tangible thing. I was glad not to be learning these truths alone.

Shifting in Archer's lap, I reached out to flip the page. The next sheet of paper showed a photograph of an unfamiliar man. He was younger than the image of Katerina, but the photo also looked a whole lot older.

"Abel Wittenberg of Pretoria, South Africa. Your grandfather.

Died when your mom was fourteen and left full control of his company to his loving wife, Katerina." Demi paused, sitting back and linking her hands together in her lap. "The rest of the information is all there, but I'll give you my summary on what I think happened. Take it with a grain of salt because maybe I'm adding two and two, then coming up with twelve. But…" She gave an elegant shrug.

I nodded. "But in your *professional* opinion, what do you think happened?"

Her smile was sharp. She knew I didn't mean her profession as a divorce lawyer. "When your grandfather died, he left *everything* to his wife. From what I can deduce, they were very much in love, despite their marriage originally being a business arrangement. She was heartbroken, understandably, and apparently lost interest in running Abel's company. Instead, she assigned it to a trusted CEO and then left South Africa with her teenage children. She came to America and set up a new life."

"Children?" Steele commented, voicing the same question echoing through my head.

Demi nodded, then reached out to show us the next photograph in her folder. It was of a handsome boy, maybe only sixteen or seventeen years old. His blond hair and blue eyes were vaguely familiar, but I'd never seen him before. Or I was pretty sure I hadn't.

"Declan Wittenberg," Demi told us, "your mom's twin brother. He was killed during a home invasion several years after they arrived in America. I've included the case notes, but it's still an unsolved crime."

I ran my fingers through my hair, thinking. "Okay. So, what then?"

"Then, nothing much…until the man your grandmother assigned as her CEO died of a heart attack. A week later, Katerina was flying back to Pretoria to attend the funeral, and her plane crashed somewhere over the Middle East." Demi pursed her lips, looking grim. I'd put money down that my grandmother's crash hadn't been deemed an accident.

"Someone wanted her dead," Kody muttered, like he was just thinking out loud. "Someone who stood to gain from her death."

"But my mom would have been the only heir, right?" I asked, puzzled. "She'd be the only one to gain."

Demi nodded. "Which probably explains why two days later Deborah employed a very highly skilled gentleman to start erasing her paper trail. She went into hiding for her own safety, and for yours."

Archer's fingers flexed on my stomach, making me guess he'd thought of something. I turned slightly to meet his pensive gaze.

"Of everything, it was *your* records that had been most thoroughly wiped. I bet Deb was hiding the fact that she had a daughter at all"—Archer's brow was tight as he thought it through—"eliminating you as a target for the killers who would eventually be coming for her."

Annoyance rippled through me. "So what? She just went into hiding here in Shadow Grove, got some guy to do a half-assed job covering her tracks, then crossed her fingers and hoped for the best?"

"What would you have done?" Demi asked, genuinely curious. "In her position as a woman in a loveless marriage with an eight-year-old daughter to care for…what would you have done differently?"

I gaped at her in disbelief. "Seriously? *Anything* else. She just stuck her head in the sand and hoped whoever had just murdered her mother would give up and move on? No way. I'd hunt that fucker down and make damn sure he wasn't threatening the people I loved any longer. I sure as hell wouldn't be content to live in fear."

My heart was pounding and my palms sweating, but Demi just gave me a long, considering look. "Yes, I can believe you would do that. You're a strong woman, MK. Was Deborah? I never met her; I couldn't say."

Her question made me hesitate. What did I really know about

my mom? She'd died when I was only eleven, and more and more I was realizing huge chunks of my childhood memories were missing. Had she been a strong woman? Something told me that Katerina had been, but Deb?

"No," I admitted with a long exhale. "No, I guess she wasn't."

Every little girl wanted their mom to be perfect, and I used to think mine was. But with the clarity of hindsight, I had to admit she'd been deeply flawed. She'd been selfish and impulsive, quick to anger, then quick to forget. But she'd loved fiercely, and I knew she'd loved me. Sometimes, that was enough.

Sometimes, it wasn't.

She probably could have left Shadow Grove when she suspected someone had found her. She could have done any number of things to keep herself—and me—safe from this fucked-up life of death and violence. But she'd stayed…because of Zane. Of that, I was sure.

"Okay, so then I guess the only question here," I said, gritting my teeth against a spike of bitterness toward my dead mother, "is who inherits if I'm dead? Archer?"

His muscles tensed, his arm around me going rock-hard. "Kate, if you're asking whether I killed your mom—"

"I'm not," I cut him off. "I'm just pointing out the fact that people are *still* trying to kill me now, eighteen months after we were legally married. Although, you said you wouldn't get access to my trust until I was twenty-one, didn't you?"

Archer nodded, his rough cheek brushing my shoulder. "That's right. If you die before you take control of your trust, it goes to the next blood heir."

I frowned. "Right. So there is something more complex going on." Then another thought crossed my mind. "Demi, what line of business was my family in? What was Abel's company? I'm assuming that's what is up for grabs here."

Demi's brows rose. "You don't know that much?" Her gaze

shifted to Archer behind me. "You paid Samuel Danvers fifty-two-million dollars to purchase his daughter and her trust fund. How was that even put on the table without seeing the financials?"

I turned my face to catch him glare daggers at Demi. "It wasn't about the money, Demi. You, of all people, know that."

Well, color me curious. Demi gave a tight smile in return and dipped her head. "Fair point." She cleared her throat and turned her attention back to me as Archer's arms tightened around my waist. Like he was reminding me that he wouldn't let go…

"Wittenberg has a number of smaller businesses under the parent company, but the jewel in the crown, so to speak, is Brilliance." Demi paused, letting that information sink in.

I blinked at her several times. "Brilliance," I repeated, dumbstruck. "Wittenberg owns Brilliance."

Demi cocked her head to the side, seeming amused by my shock. "No, sweetheart. *You* own Brilliance, as *you're* the heir to Wittenberg."

I spluttered a laugh, sure I must have somehow slipped into a delusion. "What the fuck is even happening right now?" I whispered, running a hand over my face and shaking my head.

Kody blew out a long breath. "That…was not what I expected."

"Fuck me," Steele muttered.

"Well. Suddenly all the assassination attempts make a shitload more sense," I murmured.

Because if Demi was telling the truth, then I was the heiress to South Africa's—and the entire world's—largest and most profitable diamond mine.

Holy. Fuck.

CHAPTER 8

Demi had unraveled a whole shitstorm for me—about my mom, my grandmother...about an uncle I'd never even known existed, and most of all, about my *real* inheritance. It was a lot.

Archer insisted I ride back with him in the Range Rover—apparently my silver-sequined dress made me too easy of a target on the back of Steele's bike—but none of us really spoke much.

It wasn't an uncomfortable silence, though, and I filed that away as one of the many things I loved about our unconventional four-way relationship. No one felt the need to fill silence with aimless chatter. Everyone was just on the same page that we needed to process internally first.

Demi hadn't had much else to tell us, except that the current CEO—Karl Kruger—didn't seem to have any familial connections. Despite saying that, though, she intended to keep her guys digging in case there was a link that had been buried.

After we parked, we all made our way into the house. Steele was in front, making a speedy exit, which reminded me we had a conversation to finish.

"Max Steele, don't even think about it," I snapped and he halted midstep on the stairs. "You and I have cats to discuss."

His shoulders slumped, but he shot me a good-humored grin. "Fine. My room or yours?"

"Yours," I replied. "I'll be up in a couple of minutes. I need a word with Archer first."

Kody snickered and jogged up a couple of stairs. "Everyone's in trouble tonight. Feel free to come sleep with me when you're done spanking these two, babe." He shot me a wink, then carried on up to his room.

Steele followed him, and the sound of their banter faded away as they reached the second floor.

Archer waited patiently with his thumbs hooked into the pockets of his jeans. "Something on your mind, Princess?"

I leveled a deadpan glare at him. "Understatement of the decade, Sunshine."

One corner of his mouth slanted up in a half smile. "Come on; I stashed some of those gross pear ciders you like in the back of the fridge so Kody wouldn't find them."

He led the way through to the kitchen, then handed me one of my favorite drinks. Then he opened one for himself too.

"Uh-huh, so *Kody* doesn't find them?" I teased with a nod to the open bottle in his hand. "Sure thing, liar." I completely ignored the barstools and boosted my ass up onto the island. I just really liked sitting on the counter. It put me at a good height against all three boys.

Archer smirked and took a sip, then licked his lips when he was done. It shouldn't have been as sexual as it was, but nonetheless...

"Stop it," I growled before taking a sip of my own cider.

"So, what did you need to talk to me about?" He stepped closer and trailed his fingertips up my bare thigh. My tiny dress didn't cover a whole lot when I was sitting down. Or standing, for that matter. "Or was that a convenient excuse to get me alone and make up for last night?"

I grinned, sipping from my bottle but held his heated gaze.

"Nah," I replied, before I placed my bottle on the counter beside me. "You looked like you had a great time all on your own."

His smile spread wider and more wicked. "So you *did* get my video. You never answered."

"I was busy." I licked my lips. His gaze dipped to my mouth, his body gravitating closer, but I placed a hand against his chest, stopping him. "I actually wanted to discuss something Demi brought up."

He let out a sigh, moving away slightly and running a hand over his facial hair. "Yeah, I figured you would." He took a long sip, then placed the bottle down on the counter. He laid his palms on my bare thighs, and I shivered at the cold from his cider bottle. "Ask away, Princess. I don't have anything left to hide from you."

I bit my lip, suddenly nervous. "Well, that's comforting," I muttered, somewhat sarcastically. "That certainly implies there's a bucketload that I don't know, but I just haven't asked the right questions."

His grin returned, and his fingers flexed against my skin. "I love that you read between my lines so easily. But you don't need to know all my dark and dirty past right now, do you?"

I arched a brow. "Don't I?"

"Nope," he confirmed. "Because we have the rest of our lives to learn those things, and none of it would change how you feel about me right now."

My heart sped faster. *The rest of our lives?*

"Oh yeah?" I couldn't help pushing him. "And how do I feel about you now, Archer D'Ath?"

His hands gripped my thighs, parting them and pulling me to the edge of the counter. My legs hugged his hips, and he dipped his face to feather a teasing kiss over my lips. "I think you know, Kate. You're just too stubborn to say it out loud."

I love you.

"Or maybe you're wrong," I countered, full of bullshit. "Maybe this is just a bit of fun and the second I have my shit handled, I'll take off into the sunset with my diamond fortune and never give you a second thought."

Archer let out a low, dangerous chuckle. His hand left my thigh and wrapped around my throat as his lips brushed my earlobe.

"You run, and I'll chase you, Princess." With his tight grip on my throat, he brought my lips to his for a kiss hot enough to set my panties on fucking fire. His teeth grabbed at my lower lip, biting me hard enough to draw a little blood and make me pant like a bitch in heat.

Archer laughed again, releasing my throat before he skated his fingers down to my wet-ass pussy. "But something tells me you'd get off on that, huh?"

"Fuck you," I replied, but it came out sounding a whole damn lot like a plea, not an insult. It didn't help that my cunt was already aching and my nipples were tight. Damn him for being right.

Archer just grinned and stroked me through my panties. "So, what did you want to discuss? I'm guessing it has to do with the financial transaction with your father."

My breath shuddered, and I tried to find my train of thought. Easier said than done with Archer teasing me like he was. "Yeah. You paid fifty-two million dollars for me?"

His expression didn't change. "I did."

"Is that the going rate when a debt-crippled businessman sells his underage daughter?" The whole concept made me sick, but Samuel Danvers would get his the next time our paths crossed.

Archer shook his head slightly. "Not even close." His jaw tensed, and he stopped teasing me through my panties. Instead, his hands rested lightly on my thighs. "There is no *going rate*. Every sale is unique and will attract a unique set of bidders. But if you're asking the average purchase price? Anywhere from one to twenty million isn't uncommon. Much less in the mainstream human-trafficking rings, but the market your father intended to place you in caters to a specific clientele."

I swallowed hard. It was a lot to wrap my head around. "What do you mean by that?"

Archer shrugged. "Heiresses, celebrities, models—basically anyone of a certain status in society. People who would be noticed if they just up and disappeared. People who are easily controlled, despite their public profile."

I shook my head, hardly believing what I was hearing. Archer wasn't being an asshole about it; he was just that desensitized. That jaded toward such a vile underbelly of the one percent.

"So why pay so much?" I asked him, my voice rough with emotions that I desperately shoved aside. So many what-if scenarios crowded my brain whenever I thought about the fact that my father had *sold* me…but they did me no good. What-ifs held no weight in my present because none of them had come to be. Archer had been the one who'd purchased me. Archer had been the one to save me.

He dragged his thumb over his lower lip and took a moment before he responded. "It was personal."

My brows rose. "Oh? How so? Fifty-two million dollars is a hell of a lot of money, Arch."

A small smile touched his lips. "You hardly ever shorten my name like that. I think you're going soft on me, baby girl."

I rolled my eyes. "Shut up and answer the question, asshole." He cocked a brow at me, and I stifled a frustrated growl, knowing damn well what he was about to say. "Just answer the question," I amended.

His eyes searched mine for a moment; then he ran a hand over his hair and let out a pained sound. "All right, but before I answer, I need to tell you something. Okay?"

Nervousness fluttered in my stomach. That didn't sound good.

"Okay," I replied, intrigued as hell, even though I was dreading what he might say.

His fingers ruffled his inky hair again; then his hands dropped back to my thighs and his gaze held mine. "I love you, Kate. I've been in love with you for a really long time, but I just needed you to smack my own stubborn bullshit out of the way before I could see the truth of it."

There was nothing but sincerity and—fuck—*love* in his gaze, which only made my heart race faster.

"Now I'm really worried," I whispered back, not brave enough to blink for fear of losing this moment between us. "Answer the question, Archer. Why did you pay fifty-two million dollars to buy me?"

His eyes tightened a fraction in a wince. "Because I knew it would piss you off."

What the—

"If it's any consolation, I also wanted to save you. I couldn't *stand* the thought of one of those other revolting, depraved fucks on the exchange buying you, *owning* you, doing whatever the fuck their sick fetishes demanded. But yeah, my first thought was how furious you'd be when you found out, and I liked that." He didn't look pleased by his own confession, but he did look honest.

That was something, I supposed.

"Why?" I asked, for lack of any other coherent thoughts. "Why did you want to piss me off? What did I do that hurt you so much?"

Despite my irritation at his motives, I couldn't deny how he'd inserted himself into the very fiber of my being. He was tattooed on my damn soul, and he owned a third of my heart. At this stage, there wasn't much I wouldn't forgive him for.

I was so totally screwed.

"That's the thing," he replied, looking somewhat ashamed. "You didn't *do* anything. Or nothing to warrant the grudge I held for so fucking long." He snagged his cider bottle again and drained the rest of it.

"Are you deliberately killing me with suspense here?" I muttered, scowling. "Or is that just a bonus?"

He coughed a short laugh, placing his empty bottle back on the

69

counter. "Just searching for my balls, Princess. I thought maybe I'd left them in the bottom of that cider bottle."

Despite the conversation, I snickered. "Just spit it out, Arch. We've already established the fact that we...you know...*don't hate* each other. Tell me what the hell happened in the past so we can move on."

A smirk touched his lips. "Yeah, all right. We *don't hate* each other." He gave me a sarcastic eye roll. Fucker. "Back when we met, when you came to the Reapers HQ with Deb...I know Steele told you a little bit but not everything."

I nodded. "Yeah, but he gave me the impression you weren't a big fan of preteen me?"

He gave a soft laugh. "Uh, yeah, pretty much the opposite of that. I was *too* much of a fan—but so was he, so he can't judge. Anyway, some shit went down on the last night you stayed with us. Reapers shit that should have stayed Reapers shit, but you were sneaking around and saw something that frightened you. Steele and I tried to calm you down, but the second my back was turned, you called the cops." His lips tilted in a nostalgic smile, but I was shocked.

"That seems like a pretty stupid thing to do," I commented with a small laugh. "What the fuck was I thinking?"

Archer stroked his fingertip down the side of my face, then tilted my chin up to meet his eyes. "You were thinking you'd just seen a guy get shot, and you were scared. It was dumb of us to think that you were okay when you hadn't grown up around that kind of violence."

"So what happened next?" None of this was jogging my memory, but I didn't question the truth of his story. One day, I'd work harder on recovering those missing memories.

He winced. "Cops came, of course, but the SGPD know better than to stick their noses where they're not welcome on Reaper turf. After they were gone, Damien was out for blood. He was in a murderous rage, wanting to know who'd tattled to the PD."

For the first time since he'd started talking, a flicker of recognition hit me. I sucked in a sharp breath. "You took the blame for me," I whispered, horrified at my own past self.

Archer nodded. "He would have killed you without a second thought," he said softly. "We knew it. Steele tried to come forward first, but I tripped him and took the blame myself."

I swallowed heavily. "What did he do to you?" My voice was hoarse, thick with guilt and regret.

"Nothing he hadn't done plenty of times before," he replied with a shrug. "I was probably the only one he would have let off still breathing, though. That's why it had to be me, not Steele."

"He beat the shit out of you, didn't he?" I murmured, jagged slices of memories flashing across my mind. It was all so broken, just a jumbled mess of fear and anxiety and pain.

Archer gave me a humorless smile, sliding his hand into the hair at the back of my head like he needed to constantly touch me. I was the same with all three of them, so I *got* it. "Yeah, that's putting it mildly. Anyway, afterward his guys dragged me home and dropped me on the front porch. You, Steele, and Rachel had to carry me inside and call the Reapers' medic."

I gasped. "I knew Rachel?"

"You only met her that night," he replied. "She wasn't in the Reapers; she just came around to spend time with Steele during school breaks."

"Oh." I bit my lip and tasted a trace of blood from where Archer had kissed me so roughly only a short while ago. "So we called the Reapers' medic for you?"

Archer nodded. "He'd been told by Damien to only provide enough care that I wouldn't die and nothing more. Part of my punishment. That meant no painkillers. It was a *rough* night that first night, but you stayed with me the whole time. You sat on the floor beside the couch and stroked my hair and talked to me to provide a distraction when the pain was too much to sleep."

71

"Is that…" I almost didn't want to ask. "Is that what made you hate me? Because my stupidity caused you to be beaten so badly?"

His smile was soft and his lips, when he brought them to mine, filled with apology. He kissed me tenderly, then gave a small sigh when it ended.

"No, baby girl. I fell in love with you then, even though I was too young and dumb to know that's what was making my heart hurt so bad when you were gone. We all knew you were going home the next day. Your dad was getting back from his trip, and Deb needed to play her part as the faithful wife once more. I was all bitter and twisted up that we'd never see you again, but you swore to me over and over you'd come back, that you wouldn't forget your first *real friends*. That's what we were to you. Friends."

I gave a small laugh. "Yeah, well, I didn't know any better."

"I know. It was adorable. But then the next day your mom dragged you home, and that was it." He tried to smile, but I could see the shadows of hurt in his eyes.

Shaking my head, I frowned. "Wait, what? We never saw each other again?" Until Riot Night, of course.

Archer wrinkled his nose. "I came to Deb's funeral—Steele and I both did—seeing as Zane was in lockup and couldn't attend. We stayed near the back, not wanting Samuel to see us, but then when everyone was leaving, you headed straight toward us. I thought you'd seen us and wanted to… I dunno. You walked straight past like we were total strangers."

My heart sank. "I'm so sorry; I never—"

"I know that now. We figured you had some trauma-based memory loss but just never realized *how much* until Halloween when you blew up about Zane." His fingers massaged the back of my head, and his body was warm between my knees. He was comforting me when it should have been *me* apologizing.

"Arch, if I'd known…"

He shook his head. "You didn't. Not then or at the party

when you were sixteen and I punched out some punk rich kid who was bragging about fucking you to his buddies." I gasped, and he smirked. "You were pretty wasted; it was no surprise you didn't recognize me then. But it wasn't until Riot Night that I fully comprehended the fact that you had *no clue* who we were. Then I was just bitter and pissed off, so when I saw the email about your contract of sale an hour after we left you on the side of the road…" He shrugged.

"Wow." That was the best response I could muster up. "I kind of get where you were coming from. I mean…nothing really justifies *buying* a human being, but you did save me from a potentially nightmarish fate so, yeah. I guess I'm glad you were pissed enough to pay that much money."

He scoffed. "Yeah, that's true. If I hadn't spent so many years obsessing over that feisty little girl who'd held my hand and told me I had *worth*, then maybe I wouldn't have looked twice at your contract."

"Wait," I said, another worrying thought occurring to me. "Why *did* you see my contract? How do you even join that mailing list?"

Archer's fingers trailed through my hair; then he rested his hands on my waist once more. "It's not a mailing list, Princess. It's…well yeah, I guess it's like that in a way. I have access because of Phillip. He worked a lot of anti-trafficking cases, and when I inherited everything, I also inherited his passcodes. I don't use them often because I don't have any interest in becoming a civil servant or even a vigilante. But I'd used it once before, and *something* sent me to access it a couple of days before Riot Night. I couldn't even say what it was, but I logged in and forgot to log out. That's how I saw your name pop up."

My stomach churned, and I fidgeted with one of the buttons on his shirt. "You used it once before?"

He jerked a nod. "As a favor to a friend. There was a girl,

Seph. She was barely thirteen when her father listed her contract, a punishment for someone else's infractions."

"Oh fuck," I murmured, and pressed a hand to my lips, disgusted. "Your friend...am I right in thinking it was a favor for Hades?"

"It was." He met my gaze steadily, not giving anything away.

He didn't need to, though. "You saved a thirteen-year-old girl from sex slavery? Yeah, I can see now why Steele said Hades would take our side if push came to shove." Then another piece clicked together in my brain. "Seph. Cute. What's it short for?"

Archer grinned. "Persephone. It's not her birth name, but it's the name she uses, much like Hades. It works for them."

"Can I meet them one day?" Because I was all kinds of curious to put faces to names. Not that they were integral to my story, not at all. But I got the feeling real friends were few and far between in Archer D'Ath's world. I'd like to meet one of the few he had outside of our house.

He nodded, smiling. "Of course. They'll probably be at our wedding after all."

I spluttered a laugh, then groaned. "Fuck, I almost forgot all about that."

"Rude," he murmured, his gaze turning playful. "This could be the happiest day of your life, you know."

I shivered, dread rolling over me. "I hope so," I whispered. "Because that will mean it ends with the reception hall painted red with the blood of our enemies."

Archer gave a small groan. "Fuck, baby girl. Keep talking dirty to me and I'll have to give Kody a run for his money on this countertop." His hands drifted to my ass and squeezed.

My hips rolled under his touch before I could even catch myself, but then I shook my head. "Tempting. Very fucking tempting, *Husband*. But I need go and deal with Steele's secrets now." I frowned. "Does it have anything to do with that night? When I met Rachel and you almost died at Damien's hands?"

He just shrugged. "Let him tell you. Talking about Rachel is really hard, but it's helping him heal. *You're* helping him heal, Kate."

"You're weirding me out with all these compliments, Arch," I muttered, awkward and uncomfortable under his praise.

A wicked smile crossed his lips. "I'll make up for it later if you come to my room." He stroked my wrists. "These would look so pretty cuffed to my headboard while I fuck your ass."

My pulse raced, this time from excitement. "Well, that's more like it. But you'll have to take a raincheck on that idea." I pushed him away with my hands flat on his hard chest. "Steele already said I needed to be naked before he spilled his secrets."

I hopped down off the island and left Archer grumbling to himself about why *he* hadn't thought of that rule first.

Truth be told, I was a bit disappointed he hadn't. Then again, like he'd said, we had our *whole lives…*

However long that turned out to be.

CHAPTER 9

By the time I crept into Steele's room, he was already fast asleep. Fair enough too. My "couple of minutes" with Archer had gone much longer than intended, and Steele *was* still recovering, no matter what he pretended.

I hesitated a moment beside his bed, then decided I'd had enough confessions and secrets for one day. Besides, he needed his sleep. So instead of waking him up, I fetched a glass of water from the bathroom and set it on his bedside table with some pain pills.

Silently, I slipped back out of his room and closed the door behind myself. It had been crazy tempting to slide under his blankets and curl up in his warmth, but I knew that wouldn't result in a restful sleep for *either* of us. So I headed back to my own bedroom instead.

I went to sleep alone, but I woke up to the warm glow of a building orgasm as a skillful set of lips caressed my bare pussy and a talented tongue found my pulsing clit.

A low moan rolled through me, and I arched my back, threading my fingers into his hair and silently pleading for more. He chuckled against my clit, making me shudder, then slid two fingers into my cunt.

"Fuck," I hissed as he brought me to the edge, my brain still fuzzed with sleep and my eyes still closed. But I didn't need to see to know who was waking me up in the most delicious way. "Kody..."

My thighs tightened around his head as he pushed me off the cliff, and I groaned through a soul-deep, toe-curling climax.

"Good morning, babe," he murmured when my body stopped trembling and my legs released his face.

I let out a low laugh as he nuzzled my inner thigh, then clambered up the bed to lie beside me. "*Good* morning is right," I whispered, my voice husky as I licked my lips. "What time is it?"

Propping his head up on his hand and lying on his side to face me, Kody gave me a satisfied smile. "Time to get up. You promised me an hour of training before my bookings today, remember?"

I groaned, dragging a pillow over my face like I could pretend to still be asleep. Maybe I was still asleep? It could be a dream, right? A shitty dream, if he was serious about dragging me from my post-orgasm bliss to work out in the gym.

"Come on, babe," Kody said with a laugh and pulled the pillow off my face. "If you work out hard, I'll spare a couple of minutes at the end to reward you." His smirk was all mischief, and my stomach fluttered in response. Damn him for being so gorgeous.

"Fine," I replied with a scowl.

He leaned over and kissed me, leaving the taste of my own pleasure on my lips like a promise for what was to come. "Five minutes. I'll meet you in the gym."

I mumbled something that probably passed for an affirmative, and he climbed out of my bed.

"Don't go back to sleep, MK," he warned me from my doorway. "Five minutes, or you'll be paying for it."

He left my room with a smirk, and I mumbled curses under my breath. I knew all too well he didn't mean that I'd be paying in a fun way. More like he'd kick up my training a notch until I ended the session a boneless heap of exhaustion.

In retaliation, I dressed in just a pair of booty shorts and a crop top. If Kody was going to make me suffer through an early morning workout—because he and Archer had been taking my training seriously since Steele was shot—then I'd damn well make *him* suffer as well.

After all, I'd already come once, while he was sporting one hell of a hard-on when he left my room.

Snickering to myself, I jogged down to the gym and strutted in while weaving my hair into twin braids. It was the only way to keep it out of my face during a workout.

"Oh, really?" Kody scoffed from the far side of the gym where he was selecting a playlist from his phone. "That's how you wanna play it, babe?"

I grinned. "You're damn right it is."

Finishing my braids, I tied them off with rubber bands from around my wrist, then proceeded to start warming up. Lots of bending and stretching was involved.

Kody just shook his head and grinned. "You're cruel, you know that? And here I was thinking you'd be in a good mood after a wake-up like that."

I bent over in front of him, touching my toes and waggling my butt way more than was strictly necessary. "I'm in a fantastic mood, Kodiak." I peered at him from between my knees. "Can't you tell?"

He groaned and ran a hand through his hair. "All right, let's do this, then."

I had to hand it to him—when he set his mind into trainer mode, he didn't let *anything* distract him. I knew because I'd tried everything short of turning up naked. It was totally worth it, though. An hour of training with him in the gym was like foreplay on steroids.

By the time he announced we were done, I was sweaty and panting. Only part of that was due to how hard he'd made me work out. After my bruises from the car crash began fading, Kody and

78

Archer had sat down and worked out a training plan for me, and I had to admit, they knew what they were doing.

In just ten days—since they started training me—I already felt more confident in my strength, endurance, and ability to fight back if anyone attacked. I still had a *long* way to go before any of them would feel confident that I could defend myself without them around. Hell, I doubted that day would ever come, regardless of how highly skilled in mixed martial arts I became, but it was nice that I no longer felt like a weak little girl.

"Here," Kody said, tossing me a water bottle. I caught it and took a long drink, trying to calm my breathing. My face was hot, and little strands of hair stuck to the back of my neck. Gross. I needed a shower.

I sat down on the mat, stretching out my leg muscles while Kody went to collect his phone from the sound system. When he came back over to me, though, there was a small frown marring his brow.

"What is it?" I asked with dread. He was looking down at something on his phone and handed it over as he sat opposite me on the mat.

"No turning back now," he commented as I scanned the article. It was the online version of the *Shadow Grove Gazette*, and the article was one that Archer and I had answered pages and pages of questions for a week ago. It was our official engagement announcement, splashed all over the tabloid newspaper for all of Shadow Grove—and most of California, probably—to see and read about. There was even a sickly sweet photo of the two of us that the reporter had taken.

"This feels so weird," I muttered, handing his phone back with a sigh. "We're announcing a fake engagement a solid year and a half *after* being actually married, all to lure my wannabe assassins into a trap where we can turn the tables and wipe the slate clean."

Kody didn't reply, just slipped his phone into his pocket and stretched his own hamstrings out.

"What?" I demanded after a moment of tense silence.

His gaze shot back up to mine, and he sighed. "Sorry, I'm…" He trailed off with a guilty smile. "I'm jealous as fuck. I know it's not a real wedding, but it feels like this plan is robbing us of that whole experience."

Surprise flickered through me. "Um, you think about that? About us getting married for real?"

Kody met my gaze unflinchingly, and the answer was undeniable without him ever saying a word.

Shit.

"When you know, you know, babe," he told me with a lopsided smile. Without waiting on me to say something back, he pushed up off the mat and held out a hand to me. "Come on; we've got twenty minutes before I need to go. Let's hit the steam room."

Now that was a plan I could get on board with. Twenty minutes with Kody in the steam room? Hell yes, that was a worthy reward for the torture he'd just put me through.

The steam room was attached to the indoor pool, and I eyed the water with longing as we passed by. Maybe I'd take a swim after the steam room; I wanted to make the most of the twenty minutes before Kody had to leave for his client.

We didn't bother grabbing towels, instead stripping out of our workout clothes right there outside the steam room and entering totally naked. Why not, right?

Except we weren't alone.

"Jesus fucking Christ," Kody exclaimed when someone moved in the fog.

A familiar laugh echoed back. "It's just me," Steele replied. "But you two should *probably* have checked first. What if Steinwick were in here?"

"Ew," I groaned. "Thanks for the visual." I made my way over to where he lay on the highest bench, a towel draped loosely over his waist and his skin still slick with chlorinated water. Steele had been swimming.

"Good morning, gorgeous," he greeted me, arms linked behind his head as he eyed me with open appreciation. "What happened to you last night?"

I wrinkled my nose, taking a seat on a bench lower than him but turned sideways so we could talk. Kody sat behind me, then settled his magic hands on my aching muscles.

"My chat with Archer turned into a whole thing," I admitted. "You were so peaceful when I came up, I didn't want to disturb you."

"Hellcat, you can *always* disturb me." He gave me a sleepy sort of smile, his gaze skating down to my tits and lingering there. His chest was bare, the red line of his healing scar exposed. It was such a strange thing that an injury as life-threatening as a bullet to the chest could be reduced to just a line of scarring.

I reached out and traced my fingernail gently beside it, reminding myself for the thousandth time that he was still here. My stalker hadn't succeeded in taking him away from me. From us.

Kody's hands on my shoulders slid lower, his thumbs finding a tight spot near my spine, and I moaned on reflex.

"Fuck," Steele breathed. "Do that again."

Kody let out a soft chuckle. "This?" he repeated the movement, kneading the tight knot in my back and dragging an even longer moan out of me. Holy crap. I had my own personal masseuse and had never even known it.

"Shit yeah," Steele murmured back. His eyes were locked on mine now, his gaze heated. "How is it that you can get me so god-damn hard with just one sound?"

"Probably because it's the same sound she makes when your dick enters her for the first time," Kody offered, his hands drifting around to cup my breasts. My nipples were already tight, and just

81

the lightest brush of his thumbs sent a shudder of arousal rushing through me.

Steele watched with hunger, and I licked my lips.

"How hard does it make you, Max?" I dragged my fingers down his torso, dancing them across each of his defined abs until I reached his towel. His tented towel.

A sly smile curved his lips, and I caught a flash of his tongue stud between his teeth. Fuck, I loved his piercings. "Careful, Hellcat. You're playing with fire. I dreamed about your body all damn night."

"Didn't we all?" Kody agreed. One of his hands left my breast and dipped lower, sliding between my legs and finding my slick folds. I'd been wet from the moment he woke me up with his face between my thighs; I was practically gushing now. "Go on, Steele. Show her what she's doing to you."

With small nudges, Kody shifted my position until I was on my knees facing Steele as he lay on the higher bench. Steele sat up slowly and swung his legs around until his knees bracketed my body and his towel-draped waist was in front of my face.

Kody's hand was still between my legs, his fingers sliding up and down my wet cunt but only teasing, never giving me what I wanted. Fuck. *Fuck.* They were feeling evil this morning, I could already tell.

"I dunno," Steele murmured as he tugged his towel free and wrapped his hand around his hard length. "Maybe I wanna hear you beg for it, Hellcat."

Kody's fingers slipped inside me, and I let out a sound of protest.

"Max…" I groaned and glared up at him. He knew full fucking well how badly I wanted his cock in my mouth.

He just grinned back at me, though. "Ask nicely, gorgeous."

Kody snickered, his lips trailing over my back. The steam had us all slick with condensation and sweat, which only seemed to enhance his touch. He tweaked my nipple with the hand still on my breast, and I gasped.

"Max…" I started again, then stopped to arch into Kody's touch more. The two of them were messing with me, but I was one hundred percent on board for that ride.

"Yes?" Steele prompted, stroking his hand down his metal-studded shaft, teasing me.

I gritted my teeth, despite the fact that I was quietly getting off on his game. Sometimes a girl just needed to be pushed, and Steele was definitely in the mood for that.

Dragging my tongue across my lips, I held his gaze as Kody's fingers pushed back into me. "Max, *please*?"

A smirk touched his lips, but I saw his breathing hitch. "Please what?"

Fuck it. He wanted to play that game? I was all in. "*Please* will you fuck my mouth while Kody takes my pussy? I want you to pull my hair and make my eyes water. Choke me on your dick and come down my throat." I batted my lashes and smiled sweetly. "Please?"

Steele's jaw dropped, his eyes wide.

Kody started laughing, then bit the side of my neck playfully. "Well shit, bro. When she asks *that* nicely…" His lips brushed my skin as he spoke, but my eyes were still locked on Steele's.

A wide grin spread across his face, and he shook his head. "It'd be rude to say no when you're so damn specific." He brought his free hand to my head and wound one of my braids around his fist to drag my face closer to his cock. "Open wide, gorgeous."

I did as he said. Kody shifted his own position behind me, his hands moving to my hips as he angled my body the way he wanted. Steele used his grip on my hair to hold me still as he rubbed the head of his cock on my tongue, giving me a moment of warning and letting me taste his salty precum.

"You asked for it, Hellcat." He smirked, then filled my mouth with his dick. At the same time, Kody impaled me on his huge cock, not bothering to work his way in like he often did.

Fair enough too. Nothing about my request had implied I

wanted soft and gentle loving. I wanted rough, dirty fucking. And that's exactly what they were delivering.

For a second, I couldn't breathe. But it didn't take long for me to relax and take Steele deeper. Not that I had much choice. He was taking me at my word, fucking my mouth while Kody pounded my pussy from behind. The metal of Steele's piercings clicked against my teeth, but I just took that as a cue to push myself harder. To take him deeper.

Grunted curses slipped from both boys' lips, but I was incapable of sound. Caught between two of the three hottest specimens gracing this planet, I was just hanging on for the ride. My hands were braced on Steele's thighs, my knees on the edge of the bench, and my orgasm threatened an early appearance.

"Fucking shit," Steele growled, both hands now on my head as his hips bucked and his cock choked me, exactly like I'd asked him to do. "Holy fuck, Hellcat."

"Agreed," Kody grunted. He was huge, and he wasn't holding back. My pussy ached, throbbing around his thick shaft, and all I could think of was how all the stalking and murder attempts were *worth it*. I could deal with *anything* when I had sex like this in my life.

Steele's hands left my head as he leaned back, bracing himself on the bench as his hips bucked up to meet my lips. Kody was a true friend, though. He grabbed my head from behind, shoving my face down onto Steele's dick while he ravaged my cunt with hard, fast, punishing thrusts.

"Holy shit," Steele laughed, his breath coming in harsh pants. "Fuck me, I'm gonna lose it."

"Hold up," Kody replied, releasing my head. "Let me make our girl shatter." His fingers dragged down my spine, slick with moisture from the steam and sweat, then dipped into my ass. Fuck. *All* the way into my ass.

A strangled scream escaped around my mouthful, and Steele groaned.

"Bro…"

Kody chuckled. "Two seconds. Promise." He withdrew his finger, then plunged two back in.

My whole body tightened like a damn bowstring, and Kody's hips started moving again. He fucked me hard and fast with his thick cock and with two fingers in my ass while Steele matched his pace in my mouth. Seconds later, I exploded.

I came so damn hard I was seeing stars and my entire body went fuzzy with pins and needles. Steele joined me, his hot seed pumping down my throat as he slammed into my mouth.

There was a sharp slap of skin on skin; then Kody grunted his own climax on the tail end of my orgasm. My cunt was still tight, pulsing around his dick as he filled me up.

Steele eased out of my mouth, his gentle touch stroking my face as he leaned down to kiss me. His tongue explored every damn inch of my worn-out mouth, totally unconcerned by the taste of his own arousal as he kissed me stupid.

"I fucking love you, Hellcat," he muttered when he let me go.

I swiped my tongue over my swollen lips, giving him a knowing grin as Kody collapsed on the bench beside me.

"That…is exactly how all training sessions should end," he commented, and I snickered. My legs were like jelly, so I needed to move slowly to sit down. Then I winced. Yeah, I'd be feeling that one for the rest of the day.

"Did you fucks high-five while I was coming?" I asked, giving Kody a suspicious glare.

He just grinned. Fucker. "Hey, babe, you know if Arch had been here, I wouldn't have needed to use my fingers." His brows waggled suggestively, and my goddamn pussy fluttered in agreement.

I just rolled my eyes, though. "Aren't you late for your client, Kodiak Jones?"

His smile slipped. "Fuck. Uh, whatever, this was totally worth it." He grabbed my face with one hand, bringing my lips to his for a possessive, dominating kiss that left me panting all over again. "Think about it, though. I bet it'd be fun."

With that, he took off out of the steam room and left Steele and me alone.

Tipping my head back to rest on the higher bench, I looked up at him with total adoration. "I love you too, Max."

His grin spread wide. "I know."

CHAPTER 10

"Miss?" Steinwick called out as I was finishing off my coffee at the kitchen island. I'd been on my phone, chatting with Bree and randomly browsing wedding Pinterest boards. Don't ask me why; I had no idea.

"Yes?" I looked up from my phone to see him coming closer with the house phone in his hand.

Steinwick gave me a brittle smile. "A call for you, miss." He held the phone out for me to take but didn't release it immediately. "It's your father."

Oh.

My stomach churned, and Steinwick gave me a sympathetic look as he let me take the phone from his hand. "Perhaps you're indisposed, miss?" His voice was pitched low enough that it was unlikely my father had heard, but still...I shook my head.

"No, it's fine. After all, there's not much he can do to hurt me now." I said that, but I didn't wholly believe it. Was there something he could still do? Why was he still hanging around playing the role of *father* when he'd already sold me? He already had his money.

I waited until Steinwick left the kitchen, then drew a deep breath and brought the phone to my ear.

"Hello, Father."

"Madison Kate," he replied, his voice clipped with anger. "Where's D'Ath? I asked to speak with him."

I rolled my eyes. Of course he had. Steinwick was clearly not a fan of my father and had decided to bring the phone to me instead.

"He's busy," I told him, keeping my tone just as curt as his was. "What do you need? I'm sure I can help."

My father scoffed a laugh. "I seriously doubt it, Madison Kate." His tone practically dripped with scorn, and I was utterly dumbfounded that I hadn't noticed it sooner. Why had I needed the guys to shove my face in it for me to realize that my father didn't love me? He'd never loved me.

Why had I been so totally blind to that fact until now?

"Just tell your *fiancé* that I'll call back some other time." My father must have seen our engagement announcement. He clearly had no idea I was already aware of the marriage contract.

I stifled an irritated sigh. "Sure thing, *Dad*." But also, I hope you choke on a chicken bone and fucking die, you pathetic excuse for a human.

"Great," Samuel Danvers snapped back. "I'll see you at the wedding, then."

I spluttered. "Wh-what?"

"You don't think I'd miss my only child's wedding, do you?" The sneer in his tone spoke volumes. Yeah, fuckface, I know perfectly well that you were in full attendance at your *child's* wedding. What a shame *she* wasn't there. "Cherry and I will be back at the end of the month."

On that ominous threat, the call ended, and I had to resist the urge to throw the fucking phone through the window. It wasn't the phone's fault that my father was a slug on the cabbage of life.

"Hey," Archer said, coming into the kitchen all sweaty and delicious, straight from the gym. Kody was still out on client sessions, so Archer was working out alone. He had another big-ticket fight booked for the week after our wedding, and he was taking training pretty seriously.

I didn't reply, just stripped him naked with my eyes. Shit's sake, I was turning into a sex addict.

"You okay?" he asked, putting his phone and earbuds down on the counter and circling around the island to me. "You seem...I dunno. Tense and angry."

It was on the tip of my tongue to snap back at him with an insult. That had been our pattern for so long that it came naturally to us. But Archer wasn't being a prick with that statement. In fact, he looked genuinely concerned.

Dammit. All these mushy feelings were really messing with that angsty, hate-sex thing we did so well.

I let out a long sigh, scrubbing my hands over my face. "I'm fine," I finally admitted. "My father just called, wanting to speak to you."

Archer's brows rose. "He did?"

"Steinwick brought the phone to me instead. Sly old fox. Anyway, my dad said he would call back another time and wanted to wish us congratulations on our engagement and gushed about how happy he was that his little girl had found love." I kept my tone flat as fuck; there was no way Archer could hear anything *but* sarcasm there. Yet for some reason, he was grinning. "What?"

"You said *love*."

I scowled. "I was joking."

He just smiled wider. "Sure you were."

I rolled my eyes and considered stabbing him with a fork. "Whatever. He said he'll be back for the wedding—with Cherry. Actually, explain that to me."

"Explain what?" he asked, pulling out the stool beside me and sitting down close enough that our thighs touched.

I waved a hand in the air, gesturing to my prior statement. "Cherry, your *mom*. How are you okay with her dating my dad

89

when you *know* what a piece of shit he is? He's keeping her all drugged up and shit too."

Archer just shrugged, his expression never shifting. "So?"

I frowned. "So? She's your mother."

"And Samuel is your father. Is that going to stop you from putting a bullet between his eyes the second he steps foot into our wedding in five and a half weeks?" Archer gave me a knowing look, before he snagged my last piece of toast.

I frowned, considering that perspective. "Well, no. But he tried to fucking sell me on a human black market. He deserves to die."

"Didn't *try*, baby girl. He *did* sell you. It's just fate that your Prince Charming swooped in and saved the day." He shot me a teasing wink.

I glared. "Prince Charming? More like Harvey Dent. But you want to tell me your mom did something equally bad? What was it?"

He finished his mouthful, then sighed heavily. "Cherry isn't as bad as your father, Kate. But she's no fucking *mother*. She never did anything inherently evil; she just didn't care. She doesn't hold the capacity for love. Having a baby with Damien was just an attempt to climb the ladder of the gang's hierarchy. When she realized Damien didn't give a fuck about her or his kid, she lost interest in me. I wasn't raised by her, and thank god for that."

My heart ached for baby Archer, and I placed my hand on his leg, squeezing to show I was listening.

"She's a gold-digging whore, Princess. She's exactly what someone like Samuel Danvers deserves, and in the meantime, it suits my interests to have eyes on him at all times." He gave me a small shrug, crunching down the last of my toast, then dusting his fingers off over my plate.

"She's spying on him for you?" I'd never even considered that possibility.

He jerked a nod. "In exchange for a monthly stipend, yep.

When they return to Shadow Grove, which was bound to happen at some point, your father will die and Cherry will move on to the next rich, horny idiot who takes her fancy."

What a sad pair we were. Then again, I'd never met Steele's parents, but they didn't exactly sound like exemplary loving parents. And Kody had never even mentioned his outside of his deceased grandma.

"Why keep my dad alive this long?" I propped my elbow on the counter and leaned my head on my hand. "Why not just kill him and reclaim your money?"

"Because it's just money, Kate. I can make more money, but I can only give you one chance at vengeance. Don't you want to cut your pound of flesh from his body with your own blade?" He was so casual, like we were discussing whether to serve chicken or beef at the reception dinner, not considering murder. It was hot as hell.

I bit my lip and groaned. "That's actually one of the most romantic things you've ever said to me," I muttered, heat rising into my cheeks. It was one thing to tell a person you loved them; it was another to play a long game and keep an adversary alive at significant financial loss just to let the woman you love seek closure in the form of patricide.

Be still my heart.

Archer shot me a grin. "Anyway, I should get back into the gym. Kody left me strict instructions this morning about what to work on." He leaned forward and kissed me, then hopped off his stool.

I frowned. "So why'd you come in here if you're supposed to be training still?"

He quirked a lopsided smile as he walked backward out of the kitchen. "'Cause I missed you."

My jaw hit the floor, but he was already gone. Hot and cold motherfucker was constantly throwing me for a loop.

I picked up my phone, unlocked it, and found some new

messages from Bree. Instead of answering them, I hit the video chat button. It only rang a couple of times before she answered, because she was stuck in a hospital bed and constantly had her phone in hand.

"Hey, girl," she greeted me when the call connected. "Oh, you have your freshly fucked face on. Did you just have a quickie?"

I gaped. "What? No! Jesus, Bree, I just messaged you like ten minutes ago."

She shrugged. "I did say *quickie*. What's up?"

"I was thinking about stopping by the hospital today. Are you up for a visitor?" I was hopeful but wouldn't be surprised if she said no. She'd been going through a lot with the aftermath of the crash and coming to terms with her totally unexpected pregnancy.

Her smile beamed, though. "Yes, hell yes! Come and save me from my downward slide into insanity at the hands of *Gilmore Girls*."

I laughed. "What season are you up to now?"

"Five," she replied with a pained groan. "Girl, you don't understand. Logan is so…ugh, so freaking hot. Rory needs to ride that pony."

Thank fuck she was team Logan. "I'll check which of my shadows is free and head over soon."

"Awesome, I'll kick Dallas out when you get here." She blew me kisses, then ended the call. It made me smile to think of Dallas sitting there in the hospital with her while she binged chick-flick TV.

My phone went back into my jeans pocket beside my butterfly knife as I wandered upstairs to find Steele. I already knew Kody wasn't home, and Archer was in the gym. If Steele was out or sleeping, I could ask one of the security guards to go with me, but I'd rather hang with one of my guys.

As I reached the second floor, the soft sound of piano music drifted out of Steele's bedroom, and I paused a moment to listen. He played with so much soul, I could hardly understand how he'd gone so long without it.

"Hey," I said softly, pushing his door open when the tune ended. "That was beautiful. What's it called?"

Steele looked over at me from his seat in front of his instrument and quirked a grin. "It doesn't have a name. What's up?" He was shirtless, his jeans not even buttoned up and no underwear in sight. Fuck, he was gorgeous.

"I want to go see Bree at the hospital. Would you come with me?" I leaned on the doorframe, keeping a safe distance between us. That early morning ménage à trois had only set my mood for the day, and I was panting for more. But I guess I couldn't deal with stalkers and assassins with my legs in the air twenty-four seven, so I was practicing some self-control. It sucked.

Steele nodded. "You bet. Let me just find a shirt." He stood up, showing off that drool-worthy V at his waist and confirming the fact that he was commando under his jeans. My pussy clenched, and I bit the inside of my cheek.

Down, girl. You've had plenty of vitamin D to last the day.

"I'll…wait downstairs," I said reluctantly, letting my eyes run all over his toned, tattoo-covered body as he bent to grab a T-shirt from his floor.

He smirked when he stood up and caught me looking. "You sure? I doubt Bree would mind if you were a bit late."

I let out a pained groan and retreated into the hallway. "Meet you downstairs!" I called back before I could change my mind, then raced back down to the foyer to pull my boots on.

Steele followed me just moments later, thankfully wearing more clothing, and led the way to a ruby-red Mustang that I'd never seen him drive before.

"Is this new?" I asked, sliding into the passenger seat and buckling my seat belt.

Steele buckled himself in, then turned over the engine with a rumble. "Not new, but I haven't driven her in a while. We decided to start changing it up with cars, though. Create less predictable targets."

I nodded my understanding. "Keep them away until we're ready to go on the offensive. Good thinking."

He shot me a smile, and we glided down the driveway to our front gate, waving at the guard as he let us out.

"I'm actually glad to get a few minutes alone with you," Steele told me as we drove out of the mansion district. "Not that this morning with Kody didn't blow my fucking mind"—he shot me a wicked grin, and my pulse raced in response—"but I need to explain that shit about the dead cat."

Oh yeah. That.

"If it's dragging up painful memories—"

"It is," he said, "but I still need to tell you. You don't remember anything about that time, so it's unfair of me to withhold information."

I disagreed; I didn't *need* to know everything. But he seemed determined to tell me. "Okay. So, why the dead cat? Why *Lucky Cat* on the bullet? I assumed he was just implying you had nine lives, but you guys seemed to read more into it."

Steele jerked a sharp nod, his hands flexing on the steering wheel. "Arch mentioned I used to call you *Cat* back then, and he said that he told you about your last night with us."

I cringed, ashamed of eleven-year-old me for running to the cops and getting Archer halfway killed. "Yeah, he explained."

Steele pulled in a deep breath and released it in a long sigh. "So, Rachel always had a crush on Arch. He never paid her any attention; she wasn't one of us, you know? She went to Rainy Prep and only hung out with us when she was feeling guilty."

Surprise rippled through me. "Rachel was at Rainy Prep? I never knew that." They were the sister school to Shadow Prep, where I'd gone to high school. Surely our paths would have crossed somewhere.

"She was four years above you," Steele reminded me. "Anyway, she developed this *huge* crush on Arch around the time we were thirteen, and it just got worse the more he ignored her. When she came around that night, she saw how he was with you, or how we both were, really." He shrugged.

I wrinkled my nose. "Was that a bit weird? I was just a kid."

Steele barked a laugh. "Okay, hindsight and extensive self-reflection have afforded me this level of insight. What we were feeling back then was love like a…I dunno, kindred-spirit connection thing. It wasn't a sexual, creepy predator thing." He shot me a grin. "That came later."

"Okay, so Rachel was jealous?"

Steele grimaced. "Understatement. When she worked out that it was you who'd called the cops on Damien, she blew up, wanted to run straight into the Reapers HQ and tell them it was you, not Arch."

"So why didn't she?" Because shit, I would have deserved it.

He sighed heavily. "I threatened her—made her scared enough that she'd keep her mouth shut. We had a huge blowup on the lawn outside Damien's house, where we'd been staying with you. When it clicked with Rachel that Arch had deliberately taken that beating to save you, she was…" He trailed off, lost in the memory for a moment.

I didn't want to intrude on his thoughts, but I also didn't want to leave him alone with them. So I just reached out and placed my hand over his where it rested on the gear shift.

He glanced down, then turned his hand over to link our fingers and rested our combined hands in his lap.

"Anyway, she knew I called you Cat. I'd basically stopped calling you anything else by that stage. I finally laid it out to her that we would protect you no matter *what* the price, and she shut down. I could tell she was hurt that I'd basically chosen some *random kid* over my own twin, but I couldn't take the words back. The last thing she said before leaving that night was that you must be one *lucky Cat.*"

Lucky Cat.

Fucking hell. It'd all been in capital letters on the bullet, so I'd thought my stalker meant Steele was lucky to be alive…but he didn't. He was reminding Steele that he'd been lurking in the shadows much, *much* longer than we were fully appreciating.

I couldn't believe we'd really thought we'd beaten him in Scott's death.

With every delivery, every message, my stalker was proving his point. He was smarter than us. Far too smart to be caught so easily.

But sooner or later, he'd slip up. We just needed to push him a bit harder.

CHAPTER 11

Steele and I stopped by a fancy baby store on our way to the hospital, and I let him choose a gift for Bree's baby. She would be twelve weeks in just one more day, so I was taking a gamble that it was all going to work out okay.

When we got to her room—a private one with a gorgeous view over the park below—Dallas was just leaving.

"Hey, Katie," he greeted me with a tired smile. "You're looking good, girl." He wrapped me in one of his signature bear hugs, lifting my feet off the ground. Thankfully, he set me back down again before Steele threatened to shoot him, but damn, Steele was probably close.

"Steele." Dallas nodded to my... Fuck. My *boyfriend*? That seemed weird, even inside my own head. Maybe I needed to edit that to *one of* my boyfriends. Like that made it any less strange.

"Moore," Steele replied, oblivious to my train of thought as he looped a possessive arm around my waist. "How's business?"

Dallas quirked an amused grin. "Same old. You?"

Steele just glared. Talk about awkward.

"Well, if we're done with the dick-measuring competition," I muttered, sliding out of Steele's grip, "I'm going to go see Bree."

He let me go, but the way his eyes followed me said he wanted to yank me back under his arm. Not that I blamed him when just two days ago someone had very nearly killed us in a car bomb. It'd made us all a bit paranoid while out in public.

I left the two of them in the corridor and slipped into Bree's room with the baby gift under my arm. Once the door was firmly closed behind me, I grinned at my bestie.

"Hey, girl," I said, holding up the enormous plush rabbit with a satin ribbon around its neck. "Brought you a friend to watch trash TV with."

Bree raised one brow at me. "Excuse me? It is *not* trash. But the bunny is gorgeous. Gimme." She held her hand out for it, so I delivered it into her grip. "Oh my gosh," she groaned, then hugged the stupid thing and rubbed her face against its fur. "It's so soft. Thanks, MK."

I shrugged and took a seat in the guest chair beside her bed. "Steele chose it, actually."

She gave me a sly grin. "Oh yeah? Max Steele escorted you today, hmm? And how is your little reverse harem going? Tell me everything; leave out *nothing*. Have you had a four-way yet? Oh man, you'd totally be walking funny after that, right?"

I groaned and covered my face with my hands as a rush of embarrassment flooded my cheeks. Why was everyone so interested in four-ways today?

"Remind me why I'm friends with you again?" I asked, scowling at her playfully.

She just beamed, petting the rabbit. "'Cause I'm awesome and you love me," she replied without even hesitating a second. "But also, spill. Tell me all the juicy details because lord knows it's going to be a long-ass time before I get any D in my V. You know how often the nurses just *pop in* here? Too often, babe. Too damn often."

I snickered, picturing her and Dallas trying to get frisky while her arm and leg were still in casts and she was confined to her hospital bed. "You just need to get creative, girl. I have faith in you. Maybe Dallas can help you wash your hair or something." I jerked my head to the private bathroom attached to her room.

Her brows rose, and she gave a considering nod. "I hadn't thought of that. Good work, you sex-positive queen. Now, back to this gang bang of yours."

"Bree!" I shrieked, knowing full fucking well Steele could walk into the room at any minute—if he couldn't already hear us through the paper-thin door. Fucking hell. "Can we change the subject? Please? Tell me more about how you're on team Logan. He just shits all over Dean, right?"

She shot me a look that clearly said I was insane to ever think otherwise. "Or we can discuss Mrs. Jones forever."

I blinked at her in confusion. "Come again?"

Bree rolled her eyes. "Of course, you have no idea what I'm even talking about. Here." She pulled out her phone and scrolled until she found what she wanted, then handed it to me.

It was an Instagram profile with the username MrsJones4eva and a photo reel full of pictures of Kody. Most seemed to come from his own profile, some were reposts from companies he'd modeled for, and some were just objects or locations that the profile owner associated with him.

"Um, Kody has a stalker?" I asked, grinning. But as amusing as it was, my stomach churned with fear for him. We badly didn't need another stalker in our lives.

Bree shrugged one shoulder. "Nah, she doesn't seem like a stalker so much as just a really big fan. Superfan. Anyway, she is *not* a fan of *you*." She reached for her phone, then brought up a browser page. She typed in a web address, then handed it back to me. "Case in point."

My eyes widened as I scrolled through the blog, skimming over all the nasty things this girl was saying about me. None of it came anywhere remotely close to the threats my stalker delivered on the regular, but…this was different. This was straight-up mean-girl behavior.

"What the hell?" I muttered, clicking a link that took me to an open forum where MrsJones4eva was encouraging random internet trolls to tear me down in every way imaginable. From my pink hair (totally trashy, okay?) to my boobs, which were so clearly implants. They attacked the way I dressed, the classes I took, the shops I visited. There were even photocopies of my report cards from high school. If something about me could be insulted in some way, it'd been done.

"When's the last time you even checked your socials, girl?" Bree asked me with a wrinkled nose. "I knew you'd ghosted them a bit, so I hadn't checked in forever. But this chick tags you *all the time* and is *never* nice."

I shook my head. "Not for months. Why would I need to borrow internet drama when I have enough in my real life?"

"Good point. Anyway, I don't think this is something to *actually* worry about. Not like…well, you know." She gestured to the fact that she was in the hospital, and I rubbed at the headache building behind my eyes.

"Yeah. Not like how people are trying to kill me and everyone around me. Still, it's probably something I need to get the guys to look into. My stalker seems to have a bit of a protective thing going on, remember?" I ruffled my fingers through my hair, then cringed as I remembered some of the bitchy comments about my choice of hair color. Women could be *so* cruel.

Bree nodded. "Right, but Drew was trying to have you date-raped. That sort of deserved *something*. Maybe not, you know, what happened. But still, fuck that bitch. Who even thinks of something like that?"

"Messed-up people, girl. Anyway, thanks for showing me this. I'm sure Kody will have something to say about it." I heaved a sigh, slumping back in the chair and tossing Bree's phone onto the bed.

"Girl, I'm so fucking tired. Seeing a whole we-hate-Madison-Kate forum barely even scratched the surface there."

She gave me a sympathetic smile, still petting her giant bunny with her good hand. "I'm not surprised. But it'll all be over soon, right? That's the plan, isn't it?"

I shrugged. "That's the plan. Whether it'll actually work remains to be seen. Change the subject, though. We ran into Dallas outside your room; he looks like he hasn't been sleeping much."

Bree's smile faded to a sad pout. "Yeah, that's actually something I've been wanting to talk to *you* about. Or maybe your harem." My brows shot up in surprise, unsure how we could help with Dallas's exhaustion. Bree bit her lip, like she was reluctant to say what she needed to say.

"Well, now I'm curious," I told her with a laugh. "How can we help?"

She let out a long sigh. "Dallas needs to get out of the Wraiths."

"Oh."

She cringed. "Yeah."

I sat forward, leaning my elbows on my knees. "Hun, the Wraiths are a life gang. Once blooded in..."

"I know," she replied, sounding both annoyed and pleading. "I know this. Dallas has told me a million times. But there has to be *some* way. I just...they're demanding so much of his time, and I'm scared something is going to happen. I can't—" Tears welled in her eyes and her voice broke. "MK, I can't have this baby alone. I can't let her grow up without a daddy. That's not what I want for my life."

Oh *fuck*. That'd turned real heavy, real fast. I couldn't even imagine what she was going through... It was one thing to fear for yourself or for your lover. But fear for what the future holds for an unborn baby? I couldn't possibly comprehend that.

"Bree, it's not that easy," I said as gently as I could. "I'm sure Dallas has already tried—"

She cut me off. "He has—but got nowhere, obviously. If

101

anything, they've been using him more than before, like a punishment for even suggesting he leave the gang." Tears rolled down her face, but she didn't fall to pieces. "I'm just *so* scared he's going to get killed, MK. I love Dallas so much it fucking hurts, and I don't know what I'd do if something happened…"

I reached out and squeezed her fingers where they poked out of the cast on her wrist. "For one thing, you're a tough chick, Bree. You'd make it work, and you'll be an exceptional mom. But I know where you're coming from. If Dallas could get out…" I trailed off with a shrug. "I just don't know how."

"But…your guys got out of the Reapers, right?" she pointed out, hopeful. "So it has to be possible."

I cringed. I hadn't told her about their past with the Reapers or what they'd done to get out. I sure as fuck wasn't going to suggest Dallas attempt something similar.

"I'll talk to Archer, babe. See what he can suggest, okay?" It was the best I could offer. Fuck knew I had no ideas how to handle that situation alone, and I didn't know Ferryman well enough to know how to bribe him. This was a job for Archer…if he could be convinced to help Dallas, that was.

Suddenly I was regretting having told him that Dallas took my virginity.

"Thank you," Bree replied, wiping her tears away with her hand, then taking the tissue that I offered her from the box beside her bed. "Okay, sorry. I didn't mean to go all emotional; I know that weirds you out."

I snorted a laugh. "I'm not *that* bad."

Bree rolled her eyes, dabbing at her nose. "Okay sure. Whatever you need to tell yourself."

The door clicked open, and Steele slipped inside, his eyes instantly locking with mine as he entered the room.

"Hi, Steele," Bree greeted him with a small laugh. "Nice to see you again too."

"Hey, Bree," he replied, coming over and kissing my hair before turning his attention to my friend. "You look like you've been crying. Did you get to a sad part in *Gilmore Girls*?"

I snickered. The two of them had been hanging out way too much while Steele was still in the hospital.

Bree pouted. "No, but thanks for implying something sad is coming up. Jerk. I fucking hate spoilers."

Steele grinned, then turned his gaze back to me. "I actually came to let you know that Bree's parents are on their way. I spotted them talking to her doctor down the hall. I figured you girls might want a heads-up in case you were loudly comparing notes on dick sizes and creative positions." His eyes sparkled with mischief, and I couldn't wipe the fucking smile from my face.

Ugh. I was so in love it was disgusting.

"As *if* girls talk about smut like that," Bree blatantly lied, "but you should probably go, MK. Carol is really not a fan of yours at the moment and will *probably* cause a scene if she sees you."

I groaned but pushed out of the chair. I'd had run-ins with Bree's parents before and was definitely not in the mood for another one.

"I love you, girl, but your mom is a total bitch." I leaned down and kissed Bree on the cheek. "Take care of yourself. I'll chat with Arch and see what he can suggest about Dallas, okay?"

"You rock my world, MK," she replied with a warm smile. "Call me later and tell me more wedding details. I'm living vicariously through you."

I just shook my head, then left the hospital room with Steele's hand already wrapped around mine. We hurried down the corridor, dodging behind some orderlies when I spotted Carol and Greg Graves still talking to a doctor.

Just as we stepped into the elevator, though, Carol saw me.

Her face twisted with fury as she locked eyes with me, and a rush of adrenaline flooded through me. More and more, my fight-or-flight reflex was pushing me to fight.

Carol said something, but she was too far away for me to hear her. She started storming toward us, though, and I knew it wasn't a compliment.

Just as she came within a few feet, the elevator doors slid closed and cut off whatever scathing insults were about to fall from her filler-puffed lips.

I let out a long sigh of relief, and Steele tucked me under his arm in a hug. "She looked like a lovely person," he murmured, sarcastic as all fuck. "I see where Bree gets her...uh...spark from."

I snorted a laugh, then shook my head. "Carol hasn't liked me for a while, but it's Greg who *really* hates me. In this situation, though? I don't blame them. If not for me, their daughter wouldn't be in the hospital right now. She has *every* right to curse me out."

Steele's arm tightened around me. "You didn't crash that car into her, Hellcat."

I said nothing. My guilt over Bree's injuries wasn't going to move for any amount of logical thinking. Regardless of who crashed that car, they wouldn't have done it if I hadn't been inside.

My phone buzzed in my pocket, and I pulled it out to find a message from Bree.

Bree Graves: Steele is so in love with you it's insane. You're adorable as hell.

"She's not wrong," he murmured, having read the message as well.

I just smiled, tipping my face back to kiss him before the elevator reached the ground floor. Words couldn't even describe how thankful I was to have him. To have all three of them. I wasn't in it alone, and that was a pretty special feeling.

It was a feeling I'd *do* anything, *kill* anyone to protect.

CHAPTER 12

Now that my "engagement" to Archer had gone public, we were all fending off calls from every faction of the wedding industry, as well as from journalists wanting the inside scoop on Madison Kate Danvers marrying a rising UFC star and billionaire businessman.

That part made me laugh. Calling Archer a businessman seemed so wrong, even if that's what he was.

"You guys need a new manager," I commented, flopping down onto the sofa beside Kody as he battled Archer in some monster-versus-alien fighting game.

Kody shot me a grin. "More like *you* need one, babe."

"Uh-huh, maybe I'll see if Mrs. Jones wants the job? She seems to have enough time on her hands." I gave him a pointed look, and he groaned, tossing the Xbox controller aside as Archer won their fight.

"Where are we on her?" Kody asked Archer. When Steele and I had arrived home the day before—and Anna forced us all to sit down to eat the creamy garlic chicken she'd cooked—I'd filled them all in on MrsJones4eva, and Archer had added it to his guys' research list.

"Nothing, yet," he replied, tossing his own controller onto the coffee table. "But I also didn't prioritize her, so it might be a few days before they even look into her."

"Fair call," I commented. "She doesn't seem dangerous on the scale from annoying online troll to psychotic serial killer."

"Hell of a scale, babe," Kody replied with a grimace, "but I'm inclined to agree."

Steele came into the den, wiping his grease-covered hands off on a rag. "Are we talking about Kody's fangirl?"

Kody scowled and threw a cushion at Steele, who caught it easily.

"Hey, don't get grease on the sofa," I scolded. "Steinwick will murder you if he finds out."

Steele dropped the cushion like it was made of magma. "Good point. I better go wash up." He started to leave the room, then shot me a suggestive look. "Unless you want to lend a hand?"

My cheeks heated, and I fought back a smile. Damn him.

"She's busy," Kody declared, dragging me into his lap and locking his arms around me like a straitjacket. "Fuck off and wash your balls yourself."

Steele just cracked up, the sound of his laughter echoing as he left the den and headed upstairs.

"Of course *he's* laughing," Archer muttered, mostly under his breath. "Don't think I didn't notice his smug fucking grin after his early morning swim yesterday." He narrowed his eyes at me, but they were glittering with interest. He wasn't actually mad, but he was plotting.

I shivered in anticipation.

"Mmm, yeah, that was definitely the most fun I've had in a steam room," Kody commented, innocent as all fuck as he loosened his grip and reached for the Xbox controller again. Archer's eyes widened for a flash, and I groaned. I suspected he hadn't known Kody had been party to that, uh, *party*.

His cool blue eyes locked with mine, and I sucked in a sharp breath.

Uh-oh.

"Hell no." He unfolded from the armchair in one smooth motion, plucking me out of Kody's lap before either of us had time to react. When Archer sat back down, I was straddling his lap with my wrists locked behind me in one of his huge hands.

I let out a small sound of protest—okay, maybe not *protest* but surprise—but it faded into a sigh as Archer's lips found mine.

"Stay or go, Kody," Archer growled, barely letting my mouth go long enough to speak.

Kody made a thoughtful hum, then a small laugh. "I think I'll stay. Fair's fair, right? How *did* you like watching us on the kitchen counter that night?"

I groaned as Archer's freshly trimmed stubble scraped over my throat and his teeth nipped at my skin.

"Guys, we can't just…" I trailed off as Archer's grip on my wrists tightened and his hips rolled under me. He was hard already. So damn hard.

Wait, what was I saying?

"We can't just fuck twenty-four seven," I protested.

"Are you sure?" Kody asked, his voice full of amusement. I shot him a narrow-eyed glare and found a look of dark hunger painted all over his face.

Fuck. These guys…

Archer's free hand slipped under my shirt, gliding up my rib cage to cup my breast. As much as I thought we probably shouldn't fuck right there in the den in the middle of the day, I was having a seriously hard time thinking of reasons why.

Until the doorbell rang.

"Who the fuck is that?" Archer sounded legitimately murderous.

Kody groaned, standing up and rearranging his dick. "I'll get it, I guess."

He made his way out of the den, and Archer wasted no time. His mouth found mine, his tongue plunging in and making sparks fly. I'd never known I could get so turned on by just a kiss, yet here I was, damp panties from just a little make-out session.

I moaned into his kiss, my hips rolling to crush his hard length against me, but raised voices cut through the lust.

Archer's hand released my wrists, and we both scrambled out of the armchair. Whoever was at the door wasn't fucking welcome.

"...don't let me speak to Miss Danvers immediately," a man was shouting, "then you'll be arrested on obstruction of justice!"

Kody's response was just to laugh. Of course it was.

"Whoa, what's going on?" I demanded as I hurried into the foyer with Archer right on my heels. Kody stood there beside the open door, looking bored as shit, but the uniformed policeman on our tiles was considerably less so.

In fact, he looked ready to blow his top any second. His face was red and his eyes narrow with fury, but worse yet was the way his hand hovered over his gun.

"Can we help you, Officer?" I asked the man, who just glared at me with pure disgust.

"You," he spat. "You're the little slut my brother was fucking. Where is he? If your criminal lovers have hurt him again, I swear—"

"You're going to want to take a damn breath, Shane," I said in a cold voice. This had to be Scott's brother. Now that I had made the connection, I could see the resemblance to Scott in his face. "Can I get you a drink? If you have questions, we can discuss it like civilized adults. If you're just trying to commit suicide, then please go ahead and keep insulting me."

My heart pounded and my palms were sweaty, but I'd be damned if I showed that fear to this fucker. I already knew he was on the Wraiths' payroll, and now he'd charged in here calling me a slut? Things weren't going well for Shane so far.

Officer Shane's face twisted up in a sneer. "I'm not dealing with a civilized adult, so that would be hard. Just tell me where to find my brother, bitch. If he's hurt—"

"Do you have a warrant to be here harassing me, Shane?" I asked in a dry voice. I was all bravado, but the strong, silent support of Kody and Archer gave me that confidence. I doubted I'd be so ballsy if Shane had caught me alone. Then again, maybe I would have done worse. Maybe I'd have ended up shooting him in the head, just like I'd done to his brother.

Fuck. I was already a murderer twice over. I needed to not make that a habit.

By the way Shane's glare sharpened, I knew full well he *didn't* have a warrant.

"Okay," I continued when he didn't reply, "in that case, I'd like you to leave."

Shane's gaze flickered over Kody and Archer, then back to me. He knew he was out of his depth—I could tell by the sheen of perspiration on his brow and the nervous way he licked his lips.

"Look, I just want to find Scott," he tried again, his tone marginally less aggressive. "I know he was hanging around with you, and you're bad fucking news. So just…just tell me where he is. I'll leave you alone."

Kody scoffed a laugh, giving me a look that clearly said, *Can you believe this idiot?*

Shit, maybe I was handling it all wrong. We knew where his brother was after all. We knew he was dead and had disposed of the body so thoroughly there was nothing left for Shane to find. Nothing left for him to mourn over.

Shane took a step toward me, his fists clenched and murder written across his features. Instantly I found myself remembering a similar scenario with Scott, just a few weeks ago. There was no doubt in my mind Scott had meant to harm me that day. Just like Shane wanted to now. The only things holding him back were Kody's and Archer's threatening presence.

"Get out of our house, Officer Shane," I snapped, folding my arms. "Don't come back again without a warrant."

Archer let out a dark chuckle from beside me, his arm looping around my waist. "And good luck getting one of those. Do give my best to your captain, Shane."

The officer looked like he wanted to pull his gun and start shooting, but a moment later his better judgment kicked in. He turned on his heel and stormed out, not looking back once as he slid into his patrol car.

Kody kicked the door shut and turned to me with an expression of admiration. "Babe, you handled that really well."

Archer's hand on my waist squeezed. "He's right. You did good. It's not easy, the first time you face questions from a family member."

"That happens a lot?" I asked with a weak laugh. In Shane's absence, my skin was chasing with shivers and my head swirled.

Neither of the boys responded immediately; then Archer let out a small growl. "Not if you don't leave anyone alive to ask questions."

A deep shudder rolled through me. "You guys are fucking scary, you know that?"

Kody came closer and kissed my hair as his hand trailed down my arm. "Yeah, we are. And we'd do anything to keep you safe, babe."

I leaned into Archer's hold as I let the two of them wrap me in their big-dick energy for a moment. It would be so easy to sit in my ivory tower and let them clean up my mess...but then I'd never be able to live with myself. I needed just as much blood on my hands because we were *equals*.

"I think I might go take a shower or something," I said with a sigh. "Officer Shane gave me all kinds of creeps, and I need to wash all of that away."

The boys let me go, but I'd only made it a couple of steps up the stairs before Archer spoke again.

"Actually, I forgot to tell you. We have an appointment this afternoon. Can you be ready to go in an hour?"

I paused with my hand on the stair rail, giving him a pointed look. "We have an appointment in an hour, and you were going to tell me this…when?"

A devilish grin crossed his face. "Probably *after* you'd come all over my cock while Kody watched."

I rolled my eyes and flipped him off, but Kody's laughter was infectious. By the time I'd made it up to my room, I wasn't even mad, just cursing Officer Shane for interrupting *that* scenario.

Still. There was plenty of time for do-overs.

It wasn't until I was halfway through my shower that I realized I had no idea what our appointment was even for. Apparently I'd reached the blind-trust phase of my relationship with Archer, because it hadn't even occurred to me to ask.

CHAPTER 13

Archer stuck his head back into my bedroom after my shower and told me to wear something "pretty," which immediately made me suspicious. I was tempted to throw on a pair of ripped jeans and one of Steele's band T-shirts just to piss him off, but I was curious enough to play along.

Which was how I found myself wearing a body-contoured dress in pastel purple and a pair of nude heels as I shook hands with our *wedding planner*. Yep, legit wedding planner who gushed all over how pretty I was, how handsome Archer was, and what a gorgeous couple we made.

Then she asked to see the ring.

It was on the tip of my tongue to ask, "What ring?" but then it hit me. Archer and I were fake engaged, and I wasn't wearing a ring.

Major plot hole in that plan.

"It's being resized," Archer smoothly lied. "My Princess has such delicate fingers, it just kept falling off. Didn't it, sweetheart?" He damn near purred the endearment, and I bit my cheek to stop from elbowing him in the ribs.

"Uh-huh," I replied instead. "Sure did."

Alyssa, our wedding planner, was gazing at us with hearts in her eyes like she was feeding off all the love in the air. An emotional vampire.

"Princess," she whispered with a happy sigh and wide smile. "That's adorable. I can see the two of you are like a match made in heaven, and I swear I don't say that to all my clients." She laughed at her own joke, and I forced a chuckle in response.

"Something like that," Archer murmured, leaning down to kiss my cheek; then he brushed his lips over my ear to whisper, "or Hell."

I smiled and let Alyssa think I was just smiling at her compliments.

"Okay, let's get started, shall we?" She clapped her hands and indicated for us to follow her over to a table. "I have all my samples ready to run through, and the cakes will be ready for tasting by the time we're done."

She bustled over to a table set up with stacks of color swatches and papers. We were in a bakery café in the Shadow Grove business district, but the place was totally empty, which was odd, given that it was lunchtime and the streets were busy.

"Now," Alyssa continued, sitting down opposite us, "you were so clear with your instructions over the phone, Archer, I thought it'd be best for us to lock in *every* imaginable detail today and save you from having to do more meetings with me. After all, we're very tight on time, aren't we?" Her smile was still pasted in place, but her gaze flicked over my midsection ever so quickly.

Great. Either she'd just assumed it was a shotgun wedding because I was pregnant or Archer had *told* her that. We'd have words about that later.

"I appreciate that, Alyssa," Archer replied, ignoring the glare I was drilling into the side of his head. He shifted his chair closer to mine and slipped his hand onto my leg, his fingers curling around my thigh just below the hem of my dress. "As I mentioned, my fiancé is still such a public figure, we really prefer to keep a low profile."

Oh. Sure. *I* was the public figure. That was rich, coming from Mr. UFC-fighting, male-model billionaire. Did he practice these lies in the mirror to have them come out so smoothly?

"Of *course*," Alyssa gushed. "And that new campaign for Copper Wolf you're both featured in must be bringing so much extra attention already, even without the wedding."

Ah yes, the billboards, magazines, freaking *buses* painted with Archer and me in fuck-all clothing looking like we were about to devour each other whole. I mean…we *were*. But it was taking a bit of getting used to, seeing my face everywhere.

I licked my lips, then gave another tight smile. "Uh-huh."

Yeah, this was going to be a painful meeting if we were going to be lying through our teeth the whole time. Then again, that was probably the only way we could plan a fake wedding. Archer knew that people would be watching us—he knew that my killers would be watching. We couldn't give them any reason to suspect the wedding would be an ambush, so we had to go through all the motions.

To my surprise, though, Archer had no concerns about giving his opinion to Alyssa as she ran through everything from the color scheme to floral arrangements to silverware and linens.

"Now, these are my choices for a photographer," Alyssa said sometime later, presenting us with three portfolios.

I hadn't actually *needed* to speak for ages, only offering my agreement when Archer gave me that look that said I'd been silent too long. But otherwise, I was pretty pleased with the choices he made. I'd never been the type of girl who thought about her wedding. I had zero clue what flowers I wanted in my bouquet or whether the dishes with gold trim matched the centerpieces.

Archer, apparently, did have a clue.

"Oh, I thought we would use Nicky," I commented, and

Archer gave me a curious look. "Or is that not a thing? I know she's not technically a wedding photographer—"

"No, I think that's a great idea," he cut me off, giving me a smile that was a thousand times more genuine than the ones he'd been giving Alyssa. "Nicky would be honored, I'm sure."

"Oh," Alyssa said, blinking a couple of times. "Okay, sure. Just send me through her details, and I can coordinate. Will you do an engagement shoot too?"

Archer's fingers had been stroking gentle circles on my inner thigh for the better part of an hour, so I blamed partial brain failure for the fact that I agreed.

He gave me a surprised look, and I shrugged. "What? Maybe your, uh, *best men* will join us." I flickered my brows up, and a slow smile curled Archer's lips.

"Oh, that's a great idea," Alyssa chimed in, oblivious to the sexual tension crackling between my husband and me. "The whole bridal party! Actually, I see, Archer, you listed two friends as your groomsmen, but, Madison Kate, I don't have anyone on your side?" She clicked a pen on, poising it over her notebook like she was waiting on me to tell her some names.

But Bree was the only person I'd have ever asked. And she was confined to the hospital for the foreseeable future, so I legitimately had no one to be a bridesmaid.

"We will get back to you on that, Alyssa." Archer covered for my moment of speechlessness. "Kate's best friend was recently involved in a car accident, so it's just—"

"Oh no! I'm so sorry," she exclaimed, pressing a hand to her chest. "Oh, my apologies, yes of course, just let me know when you know." She gave us a tight smile, and I released the breath I hadn't known I was holding.

Why the hell should it be expected that a woman needed *multiple* best friends in order to get married? Seemed like a pretty stupid rule to me.

Alyssa checked her watch. "I think we should be ready to choose cakes now, unless you have any other questions for me here?" She patted a hand on her stack of samples and gave us another bright smile. Her cheeks must have hurt with all that smiling. It wasn't natural.

Archer cocked a brow, looking at me questioningly, but I shook my head. "Nope," I said with a smile of my own. "No, you've been very thorough." I took a sip from my water, which the one and only staff member working in the closed café had brought over some time ago.

"Great!" She scooted her chair back and checked a message on her phone. "The cakes are in the kitchen. Shall we?" She gestured for us to follow her through to the huge commercial kitchen. Evidently, either Alyssa or Archer had arranged for the whole place to be empty because only one cook was back there, washing his hands.

"Maurice, this is our happy couple," Alyssa introduced us to the man, "Archer and Madison Kate."

He gave us a polite nod, drying his hands off, then came over to the stainless steel bench where six different mini-cakes were presented.

"Congratulations," he said, then proceeded to run through the flavors of each of the cakes he'd prepared. When he was done, he gave us a nod and exited the kitchen.

Alyssa handed us each a fork and indicated that we taste the cakes, but...there was just something a bit uncomfortable about eating while she was standing there watching us with that fucking smile.

"Um," I started to say, then glanced up at Archer. He just quirked a brow at me and dug his fork into the first cake. He brought it to his mouth, then held my gaze as he *slowly* licked the frosting.

Fuck's sake. He was trying to kill me.

"Alyssa, sorry, do you mind if we have a couple of moments alone?" I turned back to our planner with a pasted-on smile of my own.

She hesitated a second, blinking at me. Then she checked her watch, like she was late for something. "Of course, sure. I'll just pop outside, shall I?"

"Actually, you can go," Archer replied for me. "I'll email you later which one we decide on."

Her brows rose. "But I told the staff to go, for your privacy. I need to lock up when we're done." She showed us a key from her planner and gave an apologetic smile. "And I'm actually running late for a walkthrough of a reception venue…"

Ah, that was her hesitation. She wanted us to hurry the hell up.

"No troubles." Archer reached out and plucked the key from her hand. "We can handle locking up. You may go." There was a thread of command in his tone that told Alyssa this matter wasn't open to negotiation. "I'll see that the key is returned to Maurice tonight."

Alyssa's cheeks pinked, and she nervously bit her lip. Fair reaction, considering we were asking her to break the trust of the café owner. But no one refused Archer D'Ath when he really wanted something. Not for long, anyway.

"Thank you, Alyssa," Archer added, giving her that final verbal push. The subtle dismissal. "I'll be in contact later via email."

She jerked a nod, her smile brittle, but gathered up her things and hurried out of the kitchen. I stared after her for a moment, then turned to Archer with a frown.

"Was it just me, or did she seem cagey about something?" I couldn't help reading too much into our wedding planner's behavior.

Archer gave me a half smile. "You're adorable when you're paranoid, Princess."

I scowled. "Fuck you, Sunshine."

"Only if you ask *really* nicely," he countered, quick as a whip. "After all, we do have the place to ourselves now." He held up the key, and a rush of warmth filled my belly.

"Okay, sure, but what if this is a trap?" I pushed, ignoring his offer of sex that I was about one heated glance away from taking. "What if she was all squirrely because someone is coming to kill us? Hmm?"

His grin turned wicked, and his hands landed either side of me, his body pressing me into the countertop. "Well then, we probably need to fuck quickly so we don't get taken by surprise." His voice was a dark, husky whisper in my ear, and his statement punctuated by a gentle nip of my earlobe.

I groaned, pushing him back an inch. "I'm serious," I protested. "We can't get complacent, right?"

He kissed my lips, a gentle peck that was equally loving and mocking. Fucking bastard. "Princess, I love the fact that you're thinking more like a predator every day, but please trust me on this one. Alyssa works for Hades; she wouldn't *dare* betray us. She has a family to think of."

My jaw dropped slightly. "Oh shit. Okay, then."

Archer brushed his lips across my cheekbone, then found my lips again. He kissed me longer this time, and I almost melted under his touch. Almost.

"Wait." I pushed him away harder this time. "Wait. When Alyssa mentioned how soon our wedding was, she gave me *that* look."

"What look?" he asked, his expression neutral.

I scowled. "The look that said she thought I was pregnant. Did you tell her I was? Because I'm gonna be *real* fucking clear on this one, Archer D'Ath: kids are *not* on the cards."

His brows shot up, and he took a deliberate step back. Apparently he didn't like that statement. Well, too fucking bad.

"I never *told* her that, Princess. She assumed and I didn't correct her because it lends credibility to our story." His tone was cold, and I was pretty sure he had more to say on the subject. Damn, there goes that orgasm.

I folded my arms, glaring and gearing up for a fight, but he wasn't done.

"But now that we're just laying it all out there," he continued, cutting me off before I got any words out, "kids may not be on the table *right now* because you've got an IUD. But—"

"Whoa!" I held my hands up like I could physically wipe the *insane* from the damn air. "Whoa. Just fucking *whoa*. Stop right there. This has *nothing* to do with my birth control—which, I might add, is the only thing allowing you to fuck me bare and not mess around looking for condoms. Kids are off the damn table because, for one thing, people are trying to fucking *murder* me on a weekly, if not daily, basis. I'm being stalked. My father sold me. I only just found out that I own a goddamn diamond mine. Oh, how about this one? I'm too fucking young, Archer!" I emphasized my point with a solid shove to his chest because sometimes I felt like my words lacked the necessary impact.

Also, yeah, sure, I enjoyed seeing that flare of anger that it sparked in Archer's eyes. It was addictive as all hell.

"None of those things hold any weight in this argument, Kate," he snapped back. "Not for long. The killers, the stalker? They're temporary. The shit with your dad? You'll get your closure when he returns to Shadow Grove. The diamond mine? Fuck it. Give it away for all I care. We don't need it."

My jaw just about hit the floor. I couldn't actually believe what I was hearing from him.

"Archer," I snarled, "I'm nineteen. I'm not even *having* this conversation right now."

He gave a shrug that made me want to deck him. "You turn twenty soon-ish."

"I *just* turned nineteen!" I shrieked. "What the actual fuck is happening right now? Jesus *Christ*, Archer, we're not having kids. Period."

His jaw clenched, and the vein over his temple throbbed. Oh good, I'd flipped his alpha-male asshole switch on.

"Kate—" he argued, but I wasn't entertaining any more crazy.

"No!" I shouted, slamming my hand down on the counter beside me. "No. Archer, this isn't even just about you and me. Did you forget that Steele and Kody are in this too? They're not fucking going anywhere."

His face shifted, and I realized too late that I'd given him a flicker of hope. "So you're saying this is a question of majority rules?"

I blinked, dumbfounded at his shift in tack. "What? No! Arch—" I broke off with a frustrated snarl. Then I did the only thing I could think of to end the totally ludicrous argument we were engaged in.

I picked up one of the mini wedding cakes and smashed it straight in his sexy, stubborn face.

CHAPTER 14

Sometimes in life, we've all made choices that might have seemed really stupid, really reckless in hindsight. Sometimes, those choices worked out impeccably well, and the result was better than we could have ever anticipated.

Sometimes...it didn't.

This thought flashed across my mind as Archer stared back at me from a strawberry-champagne-sponge and cream-cheese-frosting covered mess.

The serving plate slipped from my fingers and shattered on the floor, but neither one of us paid it any mind. Archer reached up in goddamn slow motion to wipe the creamy frosting from his eyes, all so he could death glare at me even harder.

"Oops," I whispered.

He swiped another handful of cake from his face and threw it on the ground. "Oops?" he repeated in disbelief.

Yeah, maybe that hadn't been the *most* mature way to end an argument. But hey, that just proved my point, right? There was no way in hell I was mother material.

Fuck it, the damage was done now; may as well just double down on it. "Oh, don't be dramatic, Sunshine," I drawled, propping my hands on my hips. "It's just cake; it won't kill you."

He moved lightning fast. One second he was standing two feet away, dripping frosting—damn, that cake had a lot of frosting—and the next he had my hair wrapped around his fist and a plate of cake in his hand.

"No!" I shrieked. "Come on, Arch, I'm sorry, okay? That was childish. I shouldn't have smooshed cake on your face."

His brows rose. Or I think they did. He was still pretty coated in cake, so it was hard to get a real reading on his expression.

"Oh, you're sorry, huh?" His tone was *so* hard to read without those subtle facial cues I often relied on. Like the way a small dimple appeared when he was fighting a smile or the way his temple throbbed when he was feeling murderous.

"Yes!" I squeaked, my eyes on the cake in his hand. I really didn't want to wear that one. It was my least favorite of all the flavors Maurice had prepared. "Yes, I'm sorry. Forgive me?"

His grip tightened on my hair, pulling it hard enough to tilt my face up to his. It was *such* a turn-on, even with the threat of cake.

"If you're so sorry," he taunted me, "then prove it. Kiss me, baby girl. Show me how sorry you are."

I groaned, eyeing how much cake was still smeared over his face. *Why* had I picked up such a moist cake? There was so damn much frosting. "Arch…"

"Kate…" He was mocking me playfully, and apparently that was my kryptonite.

Fuck it, he'd wiped a decent amount of the cake off. I crashed my lips against his, licking frosting from his skin and letting the sugary cream roll over my taste buds. I didn't bother trying to get away with a quick peck; there was no way he'd allow that. Instead, I kissed him hard, plundering his mouth and ignoring the sticky mess transferring to my face. It was nothing a washcloth couldn't wipe off, and kissing playful Archer was worth it.

He hummed against my mouth, his teeth pulling at my lower lip before releasing me.

"Are we even now?" I asked, grinning way too wide. Why did I get off on pushing his buttons so hard? Definitely a question for my future therapist.

"Hmm." He gave me a considering look, tugging on my hair again to create a small distance between us. I should have seen it coming. I really should have. But the fucker held me locked on his gaze, so I never even flinched when the cake in his hand smacked into the side of my face.

I gasped, taking in a mouthful of sickly sweet caramel icing. Then just for good measure, he smooshed it in harder before tossing the plate back on the counter.

"*Now* we're even," he told me, smug as fuck.

Outrage boiled under my skin—even though I'd totally started it—and I tried to shove him away from me. He wasn't budging, though. Instead he just started laughing.

"Oh come on, Kate, what better way to sample the wedding cakes, huh?" His grip on my hair held me helpless as he leaned in and licked a long line up the side of my face. "Mmm, not my favorite. Shall we try another?"

"No!" I shrieked, seeing him go for another plate. This time I reacted faster and dodged out of the way before the red velvet cake could find my face to join the caramel swirl. Unfortunately, he still had a fistful of my hair, so I couldn't avoid it completely.

I groaned in disbelief as the cake splattered all over my chest, half of it on my dress and half of it in my cleavage. Mother*fucker*.

"Archer!" I protested as his grip loosened on my hair, and I pushed him away properly. "How the hell am I going to get that off? It's all over my dress!"

His wicked grin was broad as he swiped a finger through the mess on my tits, then brought it to his lips. He licked it off way too damn sexually, humming his approval. "Easy," he replied, licking his lips. "Like this."

Reaching behind me, he tugged my zipper down in one swift

motion, then pushed the dress from my shoulders. The cake-splattered fabric pooled at my feet, and he palmed my breasts through my lace bra.

"I think I like this one." He dipped his face down and licked some of the red velvet cake from the curve of my breast. I groaned, despite my better judgment, arching my back into his touch.

"You're fucking dead, Archer D'Ath," I told him, but my threat lacked any real weight. Probably didn't help that my hands were already at his waist as I tugged his shirt free of his pants. I mean, fair was fair; if I lost my dress, he deserved to lose his shirt…and pants.

My fingers made quick work of his shirt buttons. I pushed the fabric off his broad shoulders as he kissed my chest, my neck, my mouth. Suddenly I didn't care about the cake all over us. All I could focus on was getting his pants off so I could—

Archer stepped back, trying to kick his pants and shoes off at the same time, but stepped in the blob of cake and frosting he'd wiped off his face. Next thing I knew, he was flat on his back and groaning.

"Oh, shit." I laughed. "Are you okay?"

He just groaned in response, and I knelt down beside him, still laughing. His pants and boxer briefs were tangled around his ankles, but his dick was still hard, so he couldn't have hurt himself that badly. Big baby.

"Princess?" he asked with a totally fake pained groan as I sat back on my heels to scoop the worst of the cake from my face and chest. "I'm pretty sure I broke my back." There was a sly smile on his lips, though, so I rolled my eyes.

"Oh yeah? What a shame. Guess you won't be fucking me over this table after all." I rose up on my knees and wiggled my panties down, then tossed them aside. "Maybe I'll sit over here *just* out of reach and scratch that itch myself."

His eyes widened like he was *daring* me. He should really know better by now. I reached behind myself, unhooked my bra, and tossed that in the same direction as my panties, then proceeded to swirl pale pink frosting over my erect nipples.

Archer just watched me, his eyes blazing, and I brought my finger to my mouth to suck the icing off.

"Mmm," I moaned in a hugely exaggerated way, "delicious."

"Fuck," Archer whispered. He kicked his pants off the rest of the way, then pounced on me. My back slammed into the hard floor, but his hand under the back of my head prevented me from getting a concussion.

"Oh my gosh," I gasped, sarcastic as hell, "it's a miracle! You're cured!"

He snickered. His hips rolled and ground his hard cock against my core. "Amazing what your smart mouth can do to a guy." His hips rocked again, and his tip pushed into me, teasing and making me whimper.

"My smart mouth?" I arched my back and desperately tried to top him from the bottom. It was a futile attempt, though. Archer was *never* letting me get away with that, a fact he proved by shifting his hands to my hips and pinning me to the floor.

"Yeah." He kissed me in slow strokes that made me all the more wound up with needing him. "This mouth."

"Archer," I groaned, squirming as he teased me with his dick only barely inside me. "This smart mouth is going to fucking bite you in a second if you don't fill me the hell up."

He let out a sharp laugh but did what I wanted. The air rushed from my lungs as he slammed into me, giving me the whole damn thing in one thrust.

"Like that?" he teased.

I was incapable of words, so I just nodded frantically, my fingernails clawing into his back.

Archer dipped his head back down. His tongue swiped more sticky cake from my neck, and then he caught my earlobe between his lips.

"I love you, Kate," he whispered, his voice rough with sincerity as his hips started to move between my legs.

I groaned as I bucked up against him while he started fucking me slowly, giving me what he'd been taunting me with all damn day. His teeth scraped over my neck, his lips kissing, sucking, worshipping my cake-covered skin…yet I knew he was waiting for me to say something in response. He was holding back.

"I…" I started, but then his fingers found my nipple and I moaned.

"Yes, Princess?" he purred, rolling my flesh between his fingers and making me thrash. "You *what*?"

I hissed a breath. "I…"

His hips rocked as he fully seated himself within me. Then paused there. "Yes?"

I groaned, then licked some cake from his cheek. "I…guess…I don't hate you."

Archer barked a sharp laugh and shook his head. "Fuck it, I'll take it."

This time when his mouth met mine, there was nothing teasing about it. He was all business as he claimed my lips. His hips pumped harder, faster, and I wound my legs around his body to pull him tighter into me.

Incomprehensible curses and moans fell from my lips as Archer kissed my neck, and my nails raked down his back. I marked him just as surely as he was marking me, and the cavewoman in me went wild for that. It was almost disappointing that those marks faded so easily when Archer and I were so permanently inked into each other's hearts and souls.

By the time I shattered into an orgasm, he'd fucked me halfway across the kitchen floor and my ass was freezing from being pounded into the polished concrete. Not that I was complaining. Despite the mess from the cakes, Archer was rocking my goddamn world.

He came just a few moments later, pushed over the edge by the way I shuddered and thrashed under him in the throes of my climax.

He pulled out, rolling to the side to rest beside me on the cold floor, then propped his head up on his hand to peer down at me. Bits of cake and icing still clung to his hair and stubble, but it did nothing to detract from his sex appeal. Fuck me, I was one lucky bitch.

"You're perfect," he whispered, his eyes soft as he trailed his fingers over my sticky cheek. "Every time I look at you, I can't totally believe that you're mine."

I quirked a brow at him as his fingers skated across my bare breasts. "Because you tried so damn hard to push me away?"

"And I almost succeeded," he murmured, his expression turning sad. "It would have been the biggest fuckup of my entire life."

My whole body was like a wet noodle, but I mustered enough strength to reach up and pull his face to mine, kissing him with all the unspoken feelings burning in my chest. I loved him. I knew it, and he knew it. But I just wasn't ready to force the words past my lips. Things between us were still too fresh, too raw.

I was terrified that the next time he pushed me away, it'd break me.

He didn't pressure me for more words, just slid his fingers down to my throbbing, hypersensitive pussy, where I was slick with his own seed. I groaned as he stroked me, his fingers becoming soaked with the result of our combined climaxes.

"Fuck, that's hot," he muttered, his lids heavy as he stared down at his fingers sliding in and out of me. I was still aching, but I parted my legs wider, letting him play. His thumb found my clit and I cried out, but that just got him hard all over again. That shit wasn't normal, but I wasn't going to question it. Maybe the alien theory was right.

"Arch," I moaned, reaching for his rapidly hardening dick.

My hand wrapped around him, pumping down his shaft while I watched his breath hitch. Seeing his reactions almost got me off as easily as his fingers in my pussy could.

"Turn over." He took his hand away and sat up. I scrambled to do as he ordered, my own heart thudding with excitement as he amended that command. "On your knees, Princess."

He positioned himself behind me, the tip of his cock nudging against my swollen cunt as I tried to rock back onto him. He let out a low chuckle, then reached forward and gathered my hair all up in one hand. His other hand gripped my hip hard enough to leave fingerprint marks, and it just made me pant.

"Just so we're real crystal-clear, baby girl," he murmured as he pushed his way back into my body, making me shudder with waves of arousal, "we're not done with that argument."

Shock rippled through me, but he didn't give me a chance to retort. His hand in my hair pulled tight, forcing me to arch my neck. His hips slammed into me, his huge cock filling me up over and over. His pace didn't falter once until I was screaming my way through another orgasm. Only then did he slow, waiting me out.

When he withdrew without coming, I made a sound of protest.

Archer just chuckled a dark and lust-filled sound as he got to his feet, and I sat back on my heels. No encouragement was needed for me to part my lips and take him in my mouth.

"Fucking hell," Archer groaned as I swallowed him deeper and sucked him hard. His hands came to the back of my head, his fingers tangling in my cake-covered hair, pushing and pulling at me as he set his pace.

When he came a few moments later, I swallowed eagerly, then licked him all over before sitting back with a satisfied grin.

Archer started laughing. He sank to his knees in front of me and kissed me like his life depended on it. "Totally goddamn perfect," he murmured between kisses, "for me."

CHAPTER 15

As fun as it had been to throw cake in Archer's face and then fuck all over the bakery kitchen, the cleanup was significantly less enjoyable. Washing cake from my face, hair, and breasts was easy enough in the restroom, but trying to get it off my dress? Impossible.

"Dammit, Archer," I snapped as I exited the bathroom in my stained dress with my hair scraped back into a ponytail. "I can't go out in public like this!"

He threw a smirk, swiping his tattooed hand through his wet hair. "Why not? You look good enough to eat."

My glare turned venomous. "Ha-fucking-ha, wise guy. Look at this! I look like I've just taken a load of cum all over my tits." Because no shit, that's what cake frosting looked like when it dried onto fabric.

Archer snagged me by the back of my neck and pulled me into his huge frame. "Not yet, but that could be arranged."

Typical. With an irritated growl—and more than a little arousal—I shoved him off me and stormed back through to the kitchen to find my shoes and panties. I'd managed to find my bra and dress before washing up, but the rest of my outfit had been elusive.

"Don't worry, Princess," Archer told me as he followed me into the kitchen. "You can wear my coat. No one will find out that you're into sploshing."

I paused, my arm halfway under the oven, where I'd just spotted one of my shoes. "Into *what*?" I frowned up at him in confusion.

"Sploshing," he repeated, giving me a mischievous smirk. "You know, the sexual act of covering your naked lover in food?"

I wrinkled my nose at him, then retrieved my shoe before standing up to address *that* pearl of wisdom.

"For one thing, Sunshine, I'm curious as to how you even know this term. For another, *you started it*!" I found my other shoe on the complete opposite side of the kitchen—however that had happened—and slipped my feet back into them.

Archer scoffed a laugh. "Pretty sure I remember *you* throwing the first cake, Princess. Don't go blaming your fetishes on me; I'm just here to get you off in whatever way you want." His wink was next-level condescending, and I needed to suppress the desire to kick him in the dick. Mainly because I liked his dick fully functional.

"Whatever." I looked around for my underwear but came up blank. "Can you please help me find my panties? I really don't think Maurice needs to find my lace thong in the middle of his workday tomorrow."

"This one?" Archer replied, pulling a familiar scrap of lace from his pocket and dangling it.

"Yes!" I reached for my panties, but he snatched them out of my reach with a smile. Fuck's sake. "Seriously?" I demanded as he pocketed my thong once more. "Oh my god, you're as bad as Steele."

Archer's only response was to drape his coat over my shoulders and link his fingers through mine, "Come on, Kate. Let's get home so we can wash this cake off properly."

I grumbled shit under my breath about possessive deviants who stole their woman's panties, but I quietly loved it. I loved all the stupid, caveman bullshit they pulled on me. Call me damaged, whatever, I had no intention of changing anytime soon, so it all just *worked*.

He was right that no one would notice the state of my dress; between his coat and the fact that we hadn't parked far away, I doubted anyone looked twice. Not that it would have mattered, really.

When we got home, there wasn't even any discussion. Archer followed me straight into my bathroom, stripped me naked, then showed me exactly how dirty we could get while getting clean.

Anna called us all down for dinner—this new thing she was enforcing—and my legs were like jelly as I made my way to the table. When I sat down, I winced at the raw ache between my legs. Archer had taken me at my word in the shower when I begged him to give it to me harder.

"Babe, you okay?" Kody asked as I gingerly pulled my chair into the table. "You look like you're hurting. Did something happen?"

My cheeks heated, and I started to formulate a bullshit answer. But Kody's green eyes were sparking with amusement and a teasing smile played across his lips. Oh yeah, his bedroom was across the hall from mine. He more than likely had heard me screaming as Archer fucked me against the wall of my shower.

Whoops.

Thankfully, Anna came back into the dining room at that moment, carrying a steaming dish of aromatic Thai curry. She placed it down in the middle of the table beside the bowl of fluffy coconut rice she'd already brought out, then planted her hands on her hips.

"Now, this has plenty of good vegetables in it and tastes a thousand times better than the crap you've been ordering from Sawadeka." She gave a nod, like she was agreeing with herself. "You'll see. None of that takeout mess is needed in this house." She bustled back out of the dining room without waiting for any of the boys' smart remarks, and I grinned.

Since telling us that we were risking our lives by ordering in, Anna had made it her mission to re-create all our favorite takeout meals with her own gourmet spin. I had to agree; her versions really were delicious.

"How was the wedding planning today?" Steele asked as he dished himself up a bowl of food, then filled mine too. "Did you have fun?" His grin was teasing, like he knew how painful it had been for me. Well…until it wasn't.

"All part of the plan," Archer replied. He was sitting beside Kody, opposite me, so there was no avoiding the heated look he gave me. "I particularly enjoyed sampling the cakes."

Yep. I was blushing. Fucker. One of these days, I'd be comfortable enough to discuss my sexploits openly between all three of them. That day was not today apparently.

Clearing my throat, I took a sip of my wine and searched for a change of subject.

"Do we need to worry about Officer Shane?" I latched on to the first thing—okay, the first nonsexual thing—to pop into my head. "He seemed pretty torn up about Scott's disappearance; I don't think he'll let the matter drop easily."

"Officer Shane won't be a problem, babe," Kody told me with a small smirk, licking his fork.

My brows rose. "Oh? What does that mean?"

"Kate, did you tell the boys that your father and my mother are coming home?" Archer not-so-subtly changed the subject. I let him, only because I trusted them. That, and I had a fair idea that Officer Shane was probably going to learn a harsh lesson about who *not* to threaten in Shadow Grove.

"They are?" Steele sat back in his chair beside me and dropped a hand to my knee. "For the wedding, I presume?"

"Yep." I cringed. "God forbid Samuel Danvers ever give society something to gossip about. Like they haven't already noticed he's just dropped his company to go on a world cruise with his girlfriend."

"But we're going to kill him, right?" Kody pointed out, like we were discussing what to have for dessert.

All the horrible things my father had done floated through my mind. All the hurtful comments when I was a child, the total lack of affection, the way he'd tried to have me committed on several occasions, the fact that he'd *sold* me to escape his bad debts. He hadn't cared if I'd wound up in a whorehouse or dead. Why the fuck did he deserve anything better from me?

"Yeah," I replied, my resolve hardening. "Yeah, we are."

Steele squeezed my thigh and gave me a lopsided smile. "Want to do more target practice with me tomorrow? It's always good to work on marksmanship in our world, beautiful."

I looked around at the three of them, a rush of fizzy affection filling me up inside. They had my back one hundred percent, but they weren't going to stick me in a glass box. Killing my father was personal, and none of them would rob me of that moment just because I wasn't as skilled as they were. Instead, they'd just do their best to train me.

That, right there. That was true companionship and respect.

"You guys are kind of amazing, you know that?" I murmured, taking a mouthful of my food to cover the emotion that was threatening to spill out of me at any second.

Steele squeezed my knee again, silently telling me he thought the same. Archer just shrugged, like that was a known fact.

Kody snorted a laugh. "Well, I mean, I know *I* am," he said with a grin. "But my shoulders are getting a bit sore carrying these two deadweights."

Archer cuffed him around the head, and Kody just laughed harder.

It was nice, though. Having dinner with the three of them every night was making the whole relationship bond sink in deeper. We were a team, a family. I loved it.

"Anyone up for the new Keanu Reeves movie?" Steele asked

as we packed away the empty dishes at the end of the meal. "It's supposed to be on par with *John Wick*."

Archer scoffed. "Bullshit."

Steele just shrugged. "Don't know until we watch it, do we?"

"Sounds good to me," I offered. "But only if there's ice cream involved."

"To eat? Or to rub all over your body?" Archer whispered in my ear as we headed into the den.

I smacked him in the abs with the back of my hand, which probably hurt me more than him, and declined to respond. Prick.

In retaliation, I curled up in Kody's lap on the armchair so Archer couldn't get handsy on the couch. He knew it too, giving me a narrow-eyed glare as he sat down. I smirked back and flipped him off.

Who said romance was dead?

Steele returned from the kitchen with four bowls of ice cream and handed them out before flicking on the movie he'd mentioned. I snuggled into Kody's warmth, eating my ice cream slowly as the movie began.

He finished his quickly, then spent more time watching me lick my spoon than watching the movie. It was distracting and amusing all at the same time. It didn't help that we had the lights off, so it was all too easy for his hands to shift from my waist to my breast.

"Stop it," I whispered at him, fighting a smile.

"Stop what?" He kissed the exposed skin of my neck.

"Stop staring at me while I eat." I gave him a pointed look. "It's weird."

Kody's grin just spread wide. "Stop licking that spoon like how I want you to lick my dick, and I'll stop watching."

"Both of you stop it," Archer snapped. "I feel fucking creepy watching Keanu Reeves while my dick is hard."

"Agreed," Steele added.

Kody just grinned and playfully kissed my neck right over one of the dark marks Archer had left littered across my skin, which made me shudder.

"Quit it," Archer growled when I squirmed in Kody's lap.

I exchanged an amused look with Kody, but we were both smart enough to know when Archer was no longer kidding around. My lady bits were already hurting enough; I definitely didn't need to be spanked on top of that.

Or did I...

Archer caught my eye in the glow from the TV, and I shifted in Kody's lap. Nope, no, I really didn't. Maybe tomorrow, but definitely not tonight.

We watched the movie in silence for a while, but Kody couldn't seem to sit still if his life depended on it. He didn't even seem to notice what he was doing as his fingers traced patterns over my skin or his lips brushed gentle kisses over my neck. It was almost like he was just letting his subconscious take the reins for a bit.

The fact that his subconscious just wanted to touch me constantly? Total bonus in my book.

"Babe," he whispered in my ear somewhere around the climax of the movie, where the hero was shooting people left, right, and center while acting totally impervious to bullets himself.

"Hmm?" I turned slightly to give him my attention and found myself just an inch from his face.

His lips twitched in a playful smile. "Can I sleep in your bed tonight?"

I groaned and bit my lip. "Just sleep? I'm sore as hell."

Kody's eyes were wicked, and he pecked a kiss on my lips. "You love the pain." Damn him, he was so right. I smothered a laugh by tucking my face into his neck. "I'll be gentle."

"Bullshit," I whispered with a snicker. He didn't deny it, but his hand found the gap between my T-shirt and sweats, and he stroked the skin there.

"So, can I?"

"You know you can," I murmured back, tipping my head back to meet his eyes. "You don't need permission."

His eyes brightened. "I'll remember that."

"Pretty sure we need a fucking schedule or something," Steele grumbled from the sofa, clearly having overheard us. "This first-in, first-served bullshit is making me all paranoid and desperate."

"What's new there, bro?" Archer teased, and Steele retaliated by whacking him in the face with a pillow.

Kody took the opportunity of their distraction to kiss me properly. His mouth moved against mine, and his tongue traced the seam of my lips, demanding entry.

A small moan escaped my throat as his tongue explored my mouth and his hands kneaded the flesh of my waist. If I wasn't careful, our movie night was going to have a whole different rating.

Thunder crashed outside, and I startled, breaking away from Kody's kiss. It hadn't even been raining earlier, but with a thunder crack that loud, it was bound to start soon.

My pulse raced, my love of storms burning through me as I looked to the windows. Sure enough, a second later the clouds opened up and the steady, white-noise sound of rain filled the house. One of the most calming sounds in the world.

"You guys wanna watch another movie?" Steele asked as the credits rolled on the one we'd been watching.

"Nah," I said, settling back into Kody's embrace with a happy sigh. "Let's just chill and listen to the storm."

"You and Archer are cut from the same damn cloth, babe," Kody told me with a laugh. "I've never met anyone who loves rain as much as he does."

Archer and I shared a grin through the darkness. How strangely appropriate for us, then.

The credits finished rolling, and the TV went dark. Now, the only light in the room came from flashes of lightning flickering across the sky outside the windows. It was romantic as hell.

"I'm going to grab drinks," Archer announced. "If we're all hanging out in the dark, we can at least get a bit drunk."

That...sounded equally fantastic and dangerous. We'd call it a team-bonding moment.

I tipped my face back to the windows and watched the beautiful flashes of light across the dark clouds. Then the next flash of lightning lit up something I wasn't even remotely expecting.

With a startled gasp, I sat bolt upright, staring at the place I'd just seen a silhouette of a man. Or that's what I thought I'd seen.

"What is it?" Steele asked, instantly going on alert. "What did you see?"

"Someone's out there," I told him, my voice hushed with fear. "Someone was standing outside the window."

I stared at the spot where I'd seen the figure, but no more lightning came for way too long. When another flash lit up the yard, the figure was gone.

Had I just imagined it? Maybe the stress was finally cracking me.

"Let's check it out," Kody said, shifting me off his lap to stand. "Arch! We need a perimeter sweep!"

Archer came bolting back into the room but didn't ask any questions. None of them turned the lights on, which I filed away under things they were scary smart about. Turning the lights on inside would only cripple our night vision and illuminate us to anyone peeping from outside. The den had privacy glass like the rest of the house, but even privacy glass could be seen through when someone was close enough.

The boys operated with efficiency. Archer and Kody grabbed guns from hiding places around the den and split up to check outside. Steele stayed behind, pulling two more handguns from under the TV unit and passing one to me.

"It might be nothing," I told him in a quiet voice. "I might have imagined it."

"I doubt it," he replied with a grimace. "Just stick with me. I'm calling the security team to sweep the boundary and check for any breaches."

We moved through to the kitchen, where there were considerably fewer windows, and Steele called Sampson. Flashes of light outside the window made me flinch, but it only took me a second to realize they were flashlights. Probably Archer and Kody.

"Don't worry, Hellcat," Steele murmured, wrapping his arm around me and placing his gun down on the counter. "We've got you. We won't let these sick fucks hurt you again, okay?"

I snorted a bitter laugh. "Me? I'm worried about *you* guys. My stalker doesn't want to kill me, not yet. But he definitely wants you three out of the picture."

"And he's doing a shitty job of it," Steele replied, his tone firm. "He's underestimated us, gorgeous. All of us. We will catch him sooner or later, and then he'll pay for every *single* thought he's ever had about you."

The cold violence running through Steele's voice made me shiver, but it also warmed my heart. This man would watch the world burn for me. They all would.

"No one out there," Kody called out. He stomped into the kitchen a moment later, soaking wet as he placed his flashlight and gun down on the counter. His T-shirt was plastered to his muscles and his bare feet covered in mud.

"I found footprints," Archer announced, joining us from a different doorway. He, too, was soaked through and looking all kinds of pissed off. "Here." He handed his phone over to us. On it was a picture he'd taken of boot prints in mud. "Took a photo before the rain washed it away. That was right outside the window where Kate thought she saw someone."

"Smart thinking." Steele zoomed in on the picture. "Men's size eleven, it's printed in the center of the tread."

"The team is sweeping the grounds now," Kody informed us.

"I saw Sampson out there. This rain will wash evidence away crazy fast, though."

Archer swept a hand through his wet hair, sending droplets flying. "Now that he's been spotted, no doubt he's taken off. We need to sort out the security situation sooner rather than later."

"Agreed," Steele said.

My stomach twisted all up in knots. "We really think someone on security is involved? I thought they were supposed to be iron-clad."

"It's the only logical explanation," Kody replied, looking grim. "No one is totally trustworthy. No one outside this room, anyway."

"I hope it's not," Archer murmured. "Sampson is an old family friend and went through Phillip's program."

Steele grunted a noise. "So did Hank."

He had a point.

"James is on his way," Kody told us as he read a message on his phone.

I frowned in confusion. "James the groundskeeper? Do we think it could be him?"

Kody shook his head. "No, James is helping us look into the backgrounds of all our security guys. They were all thoroughly vetted prior to being hired—they're all either ex-military or ex-police—but sometimes records get buried or altered. We suspect one of them slipped through the cracks. Whoever *he* is, that might be how the stalker is gaining access where he shouldn't."

"Trouble is," Steele added, his arm still tight around me, "there's been no consistency with which guards are on for each incident. It seems improbable that more than one of them is involved too."

I shook my head, still not following. "But James is a groundskeeper. How is he—"

My question cut off when the loud wail of our alarm system screamed through the house. I clapped my hands to my ears, giving Archer a panicked look. He jerked a nod, gave Kody and Steele a hand signal, then took off with his gun in hand. Kody went the other way, popping open a panel near the pantry to reveal an alarm control screen. The number four key was flashing red, and Kody quickly keyed our passcode in to stop the noise.

"Zone four!" he called out in a loud voice, presumably to Archer, who'd gone to investigate.

Kody raced after him while barking commands into his phone to Sampson. Steele and I followed somewhat slower. Steele's hand on my wrist told me what he didn't need to say.

Stay behind me, Hellcat.

He'd get no arguments from me. Three of the four of us were qualified to deal with situations like home invasions and violent assaults, and I wasn't one of them. Yet.

Steele and I had only just reached the top of the stairs when Archer called out, "Zone four, clear!" His voice was a harsh bark, like he was barely holding his grip on his temper.

Kody called out to confirm he'd cleared the other upstairs zones—presumably our bedrooms, as there wasn't much else in this wing of the house—and Steele headed for my bedroom.

Oh fuck.

"Seriously?" I hissed. "Zone four is my room?"

He didn't need to answer me. When we walked into the room, I saw for myself that it was definitely the source of the alarm. My window had been totally smashed, and the desk chair was missing. No prizes for guessing where I'd find that.

"Oh come on," I groaned at the box sitting in the middle of my bed.

"It gets better," Kody announced from the doorway. His face was grim, and he jerked his head at us to follow him.

Sure enough, his room across the hall had been visited by my friendly neighborhood stalker as well. His bed had been slashed up, and a massive hunting knife left stabbed into his pillow.

Same thing in Archer's room. And in Steele's, except here he'd also taken the extra time to tear up the stack of handwritten sheet music and scatter it all around like confetti.

Kody's phone beeped and he answered the call on speakerphone with a scowl. "Tell me good news, Sampson."

"None to give, boss. Just found how your guy got through. Kyle's dead. So is Craig. You better come down here." Sampson sounded grim, and my stomach knotted up even more. Two guards were dead? That was a step up from killing a couple of low-tier gangsters. These guys were supposed to be highly trained ex-military.

"We'll be there in five," Archer replied. "Some gifts were left up here too. I want to bag the evidence in case he slipped up and left a print."

Sampson swore, and I heard a crack like he'd punched a wall. "Right. Take your time; these two aren't going anywhere. Just keep eyes on your girl at all times. I'm calling for reinforcements."

"What type?" Steele asked, his scowl deep as he stared down at Kody's phone.

"The expensive type," Sampson replied. "You boys can afford it, though."

"Good," Archer replied. "Secure your scene and we will be there soon."

The call ended, and I looked around at the guys, feeling adrift in an ocean of *what-the-fuck*.

"Reinforcements?" I asked in a small voice. I didn't think I could handle bringing in *more* people to grow suspicious of. But we couldn't go it totally alone. Not if we wanted to survive.

Archer gave me a nod, then kissed my forehead. "Steele, get these knives bagged. Kody and Kate, go see what's in that box. I need to make some calls."

He was gone before I could ask more questions—not that I could fully form complete sentences anyway. Kody placed his hand gently on the small of my back and led me back into my bedroom, where rain was soaking the carpet through the broken window and the curtains blew like crazy.

"Want me to open it?" he suggested, and I jerked a nod.

He flipped the lid off, and I breathed a quick sigh of relief that there were no bloody body parts or animals inside. There was a Barbie, but this time her hair wasn't pink like mine. It was blond and cut into a messy bob, and she wore a ripped dress. Her little doll face had smeared makeup, like she'd been crying, and her lipstick almost looked like blood.

A torn photograph confirmed that the doll was meant to be my mom. In the picture, she was so young, but the style of her hair and clothing matched the doll to a T. Someone had their arm around her, but the picture had been ripped in half, cutting whoever it was off.

"Fucking hell," Kody breathed, pulling out a scrap of lace from the box. It was a bra. Or it used to be. One of the straps was snapped and one of the lace cups torn. There was a dark smear across part of the band that looked a whole lot like old, dried blood.

The note in the bottom gave us the full picture, though.

What's a wedding without something old?

I gagged. It was my mom's. He'd gifted us my mom's bra, torn and bloodied like it'd been involved in an assault.

CHAPTER 16

Two guards were dead, another was missing. Archer came back to the house around an hour later and filled us in on the details. Kyle had been on the front gate; he'd been shot between the eyes. Craig had been walking the eastern side of the grounds—the side that my bedroom window faced—and his throat had been cut with a shard of broken glass.

The missing guard, Trevor, was now our top suspect. He was supposed to be patrolling the western line of the property but was nowhere to be found. He also wore a size eleven shoe.

"Sampson's guys are on their way," Archer told us, sitting down at the table with a heavy sigh. There was a streak of blood on his cheek, but his hands had been scrubbed clean. "They'll be here by morning."

I wrapped my hands around the warm mug of cocoa that Kody had made me. "Who are these guys? And why do we think they're any more trustworthy than the guys we have now? Or *had*." Seeing as two were dead and one was missing in action.

"Mercenaries," Archer replied, "to put it simply. They're an organization of some of the world's most highly skilled, deadly operatives for hire. They're not easy to get ahold of, very fussy about what clients they accept, have a waiting list a mile long, and most of all…" Archer trailed off with a shrug.

"Expensive as fuck," Kody finished with a grim smile. "But coin is king with these guys—and girls. Their loyalty is to whoever pays the contract, simple as that."

"So, what if someone pays them more than us? Do they sell us out?" Maybe that was a dumb question, but I'd never hired mercenaries before.

Archer shook his head. "No, once they accept a contract, they won't take anything conflicting, no matter what the price. It's part of their business structure, and it's what gains them their reputation. Selling a client out would be the end of any future business if word got out."

"Makes sense, I guess," I murmured, then took a sip of my cocoa. Kody made it so damn good, with whipped cream and little marshmallows and everything. "They'll be here by morning?"

"Yep, but they could only spare us a week or so." Archer confirmed. "Steele is making arrangements to convert the master suite into accommodations, as they'll be here around the clock."

I wrinkled my nose. The master suite was my dad and Cherry's room. I'd never even stepped foot in there and had no desire to change that now.

"Why *did* you let my dad live here?" I asked, the thought suddenly occurring to me. "Why pretend he owned this place?"

Archer just shrugged. "I did a lot of dumb shit in those months after buying your contract, Princess. I couldn't explain my thought process now."

Kody snorted a laugh. "Pretty sure you were deep in the pits of self-hatred and wanted to pretend like nothing had changed so MK wouldn't find out what you'd done."

I quirked a brow at him, fighting a smile. "Okay sure, I could buy that. But then why move in here yourselves?"

Archer's lips curved into a grin. "Because I'm clearly a masochist

144

and needed to torture myself daily by having you so damn close yet untouchable."

I shook my head, smiling back. "Idiot."

Steele came back into the room then, his phone in his hand. "All done," he told Archer. "I'll oversee the work in the morning."

Archer jerked a nod of acknowledgment. "Thanks."

"So, now what? I'm not sleeping in my bedroom tonight, and I get the feeling that leaving to go to a hotel falls into the purview of slasher-film dumb shit." I looked around at the three of them, but they all gave me confused faces back. "You know, like in the movie when the ditzy blond chick gets her house broken into and her bedroom trashed so she leaves the property only to get stabbed six billion times because she walked into a trap? No? Okay cool, you guys need to watch more slasher films."

"Or you need to watch less," Steele commented with a lop-sided grin.

"We have a safe room," Archer told me. "It's not luxurious by any means, but it *is* safe. You can sleep there tonight, and by tomorrow we will have all the damage repaired and our friends will have arrived."

I frowned. "Me sleep there? What about you guys?"

"I'm taking all that evidence to a friend in the SGPD," Archer told me, running a hand over his stubble. "I want the knives tested for prints and the blood on that bra tested for DNA. More than likely we'll find it's Deb's, but on the off chance that it's not…" He shrugged.

"Fair call," I murmured. "It'd be stupid not to check, just in case."

"Come on," Kody said, pushing his chair back from the table. "I'll show you the safe room. You look like you're about to fall asleep in your drink."

I wanted to argue, but he was right. I couldn't stop yawning, and I was super curious to see this safe room. Of course they had

145

a safe room. Archer D'Ath thought of legitimately everything, it seemed.

Kody led the way through the house to the garage, past the collection of Ferraris, and clicked open a hidden panel on the far wall. It revealed a set of stairs leading down into darkness, and I arched a brow at him.

"Creepy, much?"

He grinned. "Why not? Adds to the drama, right?" He flipped on a light and made his way down the stairs to a narrow corridor that seemed to run along under the house. As we walked down it, I noticed another staircase leading down.

"Where does that come from?" I asked.

"You know the linen closet between my room and Archer's?" Kody replied, glancing at me over his shoulder. "There's a false panel in the back of that."

"Huh," I said, "cool. Wait, how come this is the first I'm hearing about it? If it's a safe room, I feel like you probably could have shown me sooner."

Kody shot me a grin. "We probably should have, yes. But we were pretty confident it would never actually be *needed*. It was an addition Arch put in while the house was being built post–Riot Night, then we never really gave it a second thought. The three of us are capable enough to handle any intruders, but—"

I sighed. "But I'm not."

He stopped, spinning around to face me, his hand going to my waist. "*Not* what I was going to say. Back then, when you got back from Cambodia, none of us had any idea the lengths we'd go to, to keep you safe, babe. We couldn't have anticipated how this all would escalate, but now that it has, I'm pretty fucking glad for this."

After he nudged me to follow him once more, we continued to the end of the hall, which held a single door. Kody opened a hatch beside it and indicated I come closer.

"Press your hand here, babe." He pointed to the smooth surface.

I reached out hesitantly, pressing my palm to the screen like he told me. The surface lit up with a blue light, and then almost immediately the door slid open soundlessly.

"Sweet," Kody said as we entered the room. "Apparently Archer *has* thought about this recently. Last time I was down here, it was just an empty room."

"Um, do I want to ask how he got my prints to give me biometric access?" I squinted at Kody, and he just grinned back.

"Babe, come on," he teased, "don't underestimate the sneakiness."

I rolled my eyes, then looked around the room. It was far from empty, like Kody had said. In fact, it was fully set up like a little studio apartment complete with a king-sized bed, sofa, and TV. There was even a little kitchenette to the side, but a quick check of the fridge showed it was empty of food.

"This doesn't look so cramped," I commented, looking around. "Archer's such a fucking diva."

Kody snickered as he searched the closet and came out with an armful of fresh linens for the bed. "Here, let's get some sheets down so you can sleep."

"Unlikely," I grumbled but helped him make the bed nonetheless.

When we were done, Kody pulled the blankets back and pointed for me to get in. "You need sleep, babe. This isn't just about the fact that it's almost two in the morning. You're dealing with a crapload of mental stress, and the only way you're gonna get through is if you sleep when you can."

"Easier said than done," I argued, folding my arms over my chest. "He was *inside* the house tonight, Kody. While we were home."

He pulled me into his warm embrace and ran a hand over my hair. "I know, babe." His tone was soft and understanding. "But trust me on this one. When that door closes? No one is getting in."

I huffed. "Yeah, sure. Unless my stalker kills Archer or Steele, then cuts one of their hands off and uses it on the sensor."

Kody pulled back so he could give me a *look*. The kind of look that questioned his own sanity for being so attracted to me. "Babe, that's messed up. But no, even then it won't work. Once someone is inside, the door can only be opened *from* the inside. We'd have to let them in."

"Oh," I murmured, glancing at the door in question. It was still open for now, but that was actually quite comforting to know.

"Exactly," Kody said with a laugh. "Now get into bed and *sleep*, babe."

I started climbing into the surprisingly comfortable bed, then frowned at him. "You're staying, right?"

He hesitated only a second, then jerked a nod. "Of course." He headed over to the door and hit the button to close it, locking us in securely, then flipped off the lights. A faint glow came from a strip of LEDs around the base of the walls, breaking up what would have otherwise been total blackness.

Kody returned to the bed, stripped off his jeans and T-shirt, then slid under the covers with me. His arms closed around me, holding me tight to his chest, and his fingers trailed through my hair.

"Sleep, babe. I've got you."

Despite my total conviction that there was no possible way to sleep after the break-in, the next thing I knew, I was waking up to the soft murmur of voices.

"Shh," I mumbled, not bothering to open my eyes. I recognized those voices. "Sleeping."

Their conversation paused; then one of them chuckled. A moment later the bed shifted, and Steele wrapped me up in his arms, taking the place Kody must have abandoned to let them in.

"Go back to sleep, Hellcat," Steele murmured with a kiss to my hair. "We don't have anywhere to be today."

Kody gave a soft scoff and Archer murmured something too soft for me to hear, but Steele didn't leave. In fact, he just hugged me even tighter still, like he couldn't bear to let me go.

The feeling was mutual.

Another hand stroked over my hair, and Archer leaned down to kiss my cheek. "Sweet dreams, Princess."

He and Kody left the safe room, and Steele stayed behind with me, humming a vaguely familiar tune softly under his breath.

CHAPTER 17

Steele and I slept most of the day, curled up in the darkness of the underground safe room, and only resurfaced when my stomach growled loudly enough to echo.

Upstairs we found Archer and Kody sitting at the kitchen table with a handsome, black-clad man who appeared to be only a couple of years older than them. Anna was fussing around the kitchen preparing dinner and muttering under her breath about all the extra mouths to feed. It was cute because she also clearly loved having people to cook for.

"Zed," Steele greeted the guy. "I didn't know you were on this job."

"Steele, good to see you," the stranger replied as he stood up and held his hand out to shake. "This your girl?"

"Also known as Madison Kate," I muttered, eyeballing the guy with suspicion. Logic told me he was one of these mercenaries, but I didn't like being talked about like I wasn't standing right freaking there.

"Yeah," Steele replied with an edge of amusement and looped his arm around my waist, "Hellcat, this is Zed. He's...not an enemy." But not necessarily a friend, I assumed.

Zed gave me a look up and down, and his brow quirked. "Cute."

Steele's grip on my waist tightened a fraction and Archer's head snapped up to glare at Zed's back. Kody just folded his arms and shook his head, like he could hardly believe the balls on this guy.

Zed shifted his attention back to Steele, oblivious to or unconcerned with their protective reactions. "And I'm not on this job. Not really, anyway. Conflict of interest now that Hades is buying up real estate here in Shadow Grove."

Steele nodded like that made perfect sense to him, but I was lost. I was also starving. Slipping out of Steele's grip, I made my way over to Anna in the kitchen and left the boys talking about whatever the fuck they talked about.

"What are we having tonight?" I asked our cook, leaning my elbows on the counter and watching her finely chop garlic.

"Pizzas," she replied, giving me a stern look. "Proper wood-fired ones, not that cardboard shit Steele keeps ordering to the house."

I snickered. Anna didn't swear often, but somehow Steele's choice of pizza shops brought it out of her.

"Well, it already smells delicious," I told her with a smile. I'd always grown up with my father's staff floating around in the shadows, never really *existing* as real people. But now that Anna was around more, I was finding her company all kinds of enjoyable.

She scowled, but it was playful. "Of course it does," she muttered. "It's made with love, not preservatives."

I grinned, then turned to look over at the guys. Zed was leaving, so I did the polite thing and gave him a tight smile.

"Nice meeting you, Madison Kate," he said with a small, sarcastic smile. "Congratulations on your upcoming nuptials."

"I'll walk you out, Zed," Archer offered, then left the kitchen area with his friend. Or his *not enemy*.

Folding my arms over my chest, I headed over to where Kody still sat at the table. Steele took the seat Archer had just vacated.

"So, who wants to explain Zed?" I arched a brow at the two of them. "He's not one of the mercenaries? Or he is? I'm confused."

Kody tugged on my hand, pulling me into his lap, and kissed my temple. "Good morning, babe."

"Zed is a member of the organization, yes," Steele answered, "but he's not working on this contract. He was here to discuss the guest list for your wedding." His pointed look implied more than his words.

"He's Hades's second," Kody murmured in my ear, soft enough that no one could remotely overhear—not even Anna—because we trusted *no one*. "He'll be coordinating our security for the wedding day."

I nodded my understanding. But also, curiosity rippled through me with this new information. I knew that we were leaning heavily on the Timberwolves for this plan to succeed, and Archer had told me that the whole thing would be held on one of Hades's properties, but I had yet to actually *meet* anyone from their gang. Aside from Demi, that was.

When the boys had said their new management was serious about keeping the gang out of the media, out of public eye, they hadn't been wrong. It was actually impressive. Not to mention scary.

"He's the Timberwolves second in charge?" I murmured thoughtfully. "He doesn't seem much older than you three."

"He's not." Steele shrugged but didn't elaborate. I supposed it wasn't good form to gossip about other organized crime syndicates.

Archer came back into the kitchen and yawned heavily. "Princess, come with me; I'll introduce you to our new guards."

I climbed out of Kody's lap and took Archer's outstretched hand, letting him lead me out of the kitchen. He kept my hand in his as we headed up the stairs, but instead of turning left to the wing housing the master suite—where our mercenaries would be staying—he went right.

"Uh, are they in your room?" I asked with a laugh when he pushed his own door open and pulled me inside.

Kicking the door shut behind us, he shot me a smirk. "No, but *you* are now." A tug on my hand pulled me closer, and a moment later I found my back against the door as Archer's mouth explored mine in a hungry kiss that made my heart race and my skin tingle.

"Sneaky," I murmured when he released my lips some moments later, his eyes heated as he met my gaze. "If you wanted to get me alone, you could have just asked."

He cocked a brow. "Are you kidding? Steele threatened to stab me in the leg when I tried to get him out of bed with you a few hours ago. Possessive bastard. I've been going out of my mind needing to hold you all damn day."

It shouldn't make me so amused to hear that. If this whole relationship was going to work, the guys needed to find some sort of balance. Or at least drop some of the jealousy. Yet I couldn't deny the warm glow I felt whenever one of them threatened violence to stay around me a little longer. It was hot as hell.

Still, I tried to hide my grin as I peered up at Archer. "Well, you have me alone now," I told him. "What do you want to do with me?"

He groaned, his body crushing against mine harder. "So, *so* many things, Kate, you have no idea." His lips came down on mine again with a crash, and I let him devour me.

Just when I thought things were getting good, he stopped and cupped a hand at the base of my skull. "I do need to introduce you to our guys, though. They're going to be living here for at least a week to sort out our security and run extensive checks on Sampson's team. Also to try to weed out Trevor, wherever the hell he ended up."

I pouted. "So...you didn't drag me up here to fuck me?"

A grin crept across his lips, and he kissed me again, but quickly and not letting me push it further. "I wish," he murmured, his voice pained. "But your safety comes first. Let's go."

Linking our hands back together, Archer led me out of his room and headed for the master suite wing. I pouted the whole way, and when he glanced over at me, he barked a laugh.

"Stop it, Princess," he scolded me gently. "I thought you needed a break after yesterday, anyway."

I grinned, remembering how sore I'd been before going to sleep. I was fine now, though, so...

We reached the double doors to the master suite, and Archer pushed them open without knocking. Rude, yes, but then it was his house, I supposed.

"D'Ath," one of the room's occupants greeted him, not even glancing up from the laptop he was working on. He sat on one of the single beds, his back against the wall and his computer in his lap. "This her?"

"Madison Kate," Archer corrected, his tone sharp. "Yes, it is. Kate, this is Leon." He indicated to the guy on the laptop, who looked up at me with a quick, curious glance. He was maybe in his late twenties, his head shaved and tattoos covering his arms all the way to his fingertips. A set of square-framed reading glasses perched on his nose, totally at odds with his whole gangster image.

"Hi," I said, giving him a small wave. Leon jerked a nod, his gaze already back on his computer and his fingers flying over the keys.

"Good to meet you, Madison Kate," he said, sounding distracted. "You've got a hell of a mess on your hands, huh?"

I bit my lip. I had no idea how to respond to that. "Um, yep. That's one way to put it."

The corner of his mouth tugged into a smile, but he didn't look up again. Whatever he was working on, it must have been important.

"This is Danny," Archer said as someone came out of the en suite bathroom. My brows shot up, and I ran my gaze over Danny, which I was going to guess was short for *Danielle*.

"Hey." The girl came over to us with her hand extended. "You must be Madison Kate. Nice to meet you."

Her hair was tightly braided and a fascinating shade of silver, and she seemed to be roughly the same age as Leon—younger than I expected any of these super-badass mercenaries to be, but also with more vagina than I'd imagined. What did that say about me that I'd assumed our hired helpers would all be men?

"You too," I murmured. Her grip was impressively firm as I shook her offered hand.

She grinned. "You didn't expect a chick, huh?"

I frowned, searching for the right words. "Um…no? Not that I have a problem with it at all. I'm just at least ninety percent sure everyone has been talking about you like you're all guys."

Danny shrugged. "It happens. I can count the number of women in the organization on one hand, so most jobs *are* a sausage fest."

Leon snorted a laugh from his bed and shot Danny a look. "Thanks for the visual, Dan."

She smirked back at him. "You're welcome."

"Danny and Leon are working on our security team," Archer told me, his hand on my lower back like he had an unconscious need to touch me. "They're working out whether the missing guard is actually our guy or if he's been killed too."

"Also looking into this blogger chick that has a hard-on for Kody," Leon added, still with his eyes on his computer. "She seems…interesting." A smile tugged at his lips as he said that, and Danny rolled her eyes.

"He means she's hot. He hacked her server and found a whole album of masturbation porn she makes while pretending to be with your boy." She wrinkled her nose. "Classy girl."

Leon shrugged, unapologetic. "I like them a bit fucked in the head. Makes them filthy as hell."

Danny gave me a pointed look. "He also means she has huge tits, and he's very much a boob man."

I bit back a laugh, and Archer gave a sigh.

"Is she a threat, though?" Archer asked, his fingers tracing circles over my lower back. "That's all we really care about."

Leon shook his head. "Nah, I doubt it. She probably needs some hardcore therapy for her obsession with Kody, but otherwise she appears harmless."

"But," Danny added with a glare at Leon, "we will still be paying her a visit to shut down her blog site."

That information shifted a bit of weight off my shoulders, and I gave Danny a grateful smile. "Thanks for that."

The silver-blond woman smiled back. "It's what you're paying us to do."

Archer checked his watch. "Sampson should have the rest of his team here in about half an hour, and Anna is cooking dinner for you both. She won't accept no as an answer, so haul ass down to the dining room around seven, all right?"

"Yes, sir," Leon shot back, giving a small salute.

"Nice meeting you, Madison Kate," Danny said. "I'm sure we can get your security breach plugged up in no time."

Archer and I left the room, leaving them to carry on with their work, and headed back downstairs.

"They seem nice," I commented.

He gave me a quick grin. "Nice. I don't think they'd get described as *nice* very often. Those two have more blood on their hands than Kody, Steele, and me combined."

I winced. "Seriously?" Because that was a *lot* of blood. Danny had seemed like a normal woman, albeit a feisty, well-toned one. Leon came off as a regular, ink-enthusiast computer nerd.

Archer gave me a smile, then caught my chin with his fingers. "They're the best for a reason, Princess. If anyone can sort out our security breach, it's those two. And who knows, maybe they'll catch us a stalker while they're here."

"That'd be nice," I agreed, then closed the distance between us to kiss him. "Thank you for this."

A frown of confusion creased his brow. "For what?"

I shrugged. "This. Hiring these mercenaries to overhaul our security. For building a safe room in the basement and furnishing it *just in case*. For, I dunno, taking this all so seriously. My stalker has been sending shit to me for fuck knows how long and my dad didn't give two shits, but you do. Even when you hated me, you still kept me safe. So thank you."

Archer's eyes searched mine for an extended moment; then he shook his head slowly. "Baby girl, I thought we already cleared this up," he whispered, his thumb brushing over my lower lip. "I never hated you. Even if you hadn't forgiven me for what I did, I'd still do everything imaginable to keep you safe. I won't stop until these threats are eliminated for good, Kate. On that you have my promise."

When he kissed me, there was no doubt in my mind that he meant every damn word. The problem was, he was only human. No one could promise forever. Not even Archer D'Ath.

CHAPTER 18

Just as Archer had predicted, Nicky was over the moon excited to be our official wedding photographer. A couple of days after the break-in, we found ourselves back at her warehouse studio in Rainybanks for our "engagement photos," as that was what was expected of us.

Unlike at the last two photo shoots, though, I didn't mind being involved in this one. For one thing, I didn't need to fight that magnetic attraction with Archer anymore. For another, I'd insisted that Kody and Steele be a part of the photo shoot. We'd used the excuse that they were Archer's best men, but quietly, I just wanted some photos with my guys.

After a whole morning of posed shots with Archer and me together, Nicky moved on to taking some frames of the boys together, then of just me, then of the four of us. She'd worked with all three of the guys enough that it wasn't an uncomfortable experience. In fact, it was entirely *too* comfortable. So much so, that I didn't even notice how cozy I was being with Steele and Kody, all while supposedly taking engagement photos with Archer.

Nothing slipped past Nicky, though. She was all too obser-vant and all too good at fading into the background. So when she showed me some of her favorite frames at the end of the day, my jaw almost hit the floor.

"Don't worry," Nicky murmured when I said nothing for the longest time. "No one else will see these. But I couldn't *not* capture those moments." She reached over and clicked the button to skim through her highlights, pausing on a couple that painted a very clear picture.

Except it wasn't a picture of two people madly in love and preparing for their wedding. It was a picture of one girl madly in love with three different men and them with her. Fucking hell, they were perfect…for our eyes only.

"Here are the ones your wedding coordinator wants." Smiling, Nicky clicked into another folder showing all the cookie-cutter "couple" poses she'd had Archer and me do at the beginning of the day. "I prefer the other ones, though," she whispered, giving me a knowing wink.

"They're stunning," I admitted, still mentally berating myself for letting all of that show. If my assassins caught wind that this wedding wasn't exactly what it was meant to be, then the whole plan could be for nothing.

They guys were changing out of their suits across the room, joking around with a relaxed ease that I hadn't seen in…I don't know if I'd ever seen them like that. Maybe we needed to do more stuff together as a group. Maybe that was the key to making our relationship work.

"Will you send these to me?" I asked Nicky quietly. "Then delete them? Arch—"

"Say no more," she murmured. "They're all yours. But maybe when your life is less crazy, you might consider coming back again? With all three of your boys? I'm just dying to get you all in a bed together." She grinned, and I almost choked on air.

My cheeks heated, and I shook my head but couldn't hide my smile.

"You and me both," I muttered under my breath as I left her to take my white satin evening gown off and remove about an inch of makeup.

"Everything okay?" Kody asked when I passed them on the way to the dressing room. My cheeks were still warm from Nicky's comment, and my brain was turning in loops picturing the three of them all covered in oil like the first shoot they'd brought me along for. Except in my mental image, I was in the middle of it all and no one wore underpants.

Groan.

"Yup," I replied with a too-bright smile. "Just getting changed; then we can go." He gave me a suspicious look but didn't push the issue any further.

I changed quickly, throwing on my jeans and tank top, then returned the designer evening gown to the clothing rack outside the changing room.

We said goodbye to Nicky and headed back out to the parking lot, only to find two familiar gangsters waiting beside our car.

"Zane," Archer snapped, his whole posture stiffening with anger. "What the fuck are you doing here?"

The leader of the Reapers pushed off the side of our car, where he'd been leaning, and came toward us with an exaggerated swagger.

"Little Brother," he sneered, "fancy seeing you here."

"Cut the bullshit, Zane. What do you want?" Archer folded his arms over his chest and stepped slightly in front of me. I wasn't even totally sure he knew he was doing it.

Cass remained where he was, standing beside their motorcycles with his hands tucked in his pockets, looking like he wanted to be anywhere but here. He gave me a small nod, though, his eyes sharp like he was checking I was okay.

I should have checked in with the big grump more regularly. The last time I'd sent him a message had been just after Steele woke up from his surgery and the doctors told us he was going to be okay.

"We're not here to see you, Archer," Zane replied, craning his neck to look at me around his brother. "Madison Kate, I wondered if I might have a word?"

Kody snorted a laugh. "If it's anything like the last *word* you had with her, I'd rather you didn't."

Zane's brow lifted, and he gave Kody a predatory smile. "You mean when I informed her of her marriage into the family? I'd have thought you'd thank me for that. Saved you three the trouble of all those lies you were spinning to keep her in the dark. Besides...are there more skeletons that need to be exhumed?"

I stifled a sigh. This shit was going to end up in bloodshed if I didn't intervene.

Stepping around Archer's human shield of stubbornness, I parked my hands on my hips and leveled Zane with a hard look. "What can I do for you, Zane?"

Of course, I knew he was pissed to have lost his bargaining chip in the form of my security, but Archer hadn't done anything in retaliation...yet. Maybe Zane just didn't like the paranoia of waiting for his brother to strike out against him.

"A word in *private*, Madison Kate," Zane clarified, narrowing his eyes at all three of my guys. "If you don't mind."

"Actually," I replied, "I do. I'm not keeping any more secrets from Archer, Kody, and Steele, so I'm sure whatever you want to say, you can just say. It'll save me the trouble of repeating it the second you leave."

Zane's snakelike grin turned sour, and his glare darkened. Either he had nothing of any real consequence to tell me, or he wasn't eager enough to say it in front of everyone. Either way, his mood had shifted pretty firmly.

"So, that's it then? All just happy fucking family now? I saw the *engagement* announcement." He clapped sarcastically.

"Congratulations, Little Brother. Except, is it still an engagement when you're already married?"

Archer gave a tired sigh, like he'd run out of patience for his brother's bullshit. I didn't blame him.

"Zane, seriously? Don't tell me you're upset you weren't invited to the wedding." Archer's tone was dry and mocking, deliberately poking at Zane's temper.

The older D'Ath brother curled his lip in disgust. "I find it ironic, Archer, how quick you were to purchase yourself a child bride. After all the high-and-mighty opinions you held toward our great-grandfather for his extracurricular activities, here you are, following in his footsteps."

From the corner of my eye, I caught the way Archer stiffened. This wasn't going to end well.

"I'm *nothing* like that pervert," Archer hissed, stepping forward to jab Zane in the chest. "He was a sick, twisted, deranged bastard drunk on power and money."

Zane gave a casual shrug, smug in the fact that he'd pushed Archer's buttons. "Sounds a lot like you, Brother. All that money and power has gone to your head. You *bought* your wife just the same as he *bought* Ana."

Smack.

Dammit, Archer was *fast* when he was pissed off. One minute Zane was standing there slinging shit, and the next he was on the ground, knocked clean out.

"Fuck's sake," I muttered under my breath, then looked up at Cass. He hadn't moved even an inch from his position by the bikes, but now he just looked annoyed. "Cass..."

He huffed a heavy sigh and slouched his way over to us. "He deserved that," the big guy rumbled, looking down at his gang leader with disappointment. "You okay, kid?" His question was directed at me and only me. The guys might as well have not even existed for all the attention he paid them.

I jerked a nod. "I'm good," I replied. "You?"

Cass's lips twitched in what was probably meant to be a smile. "I'll deal with Zane. You four better get going before he wakes up, yeah?"

Archer said nothing but clapped Cass on the shoulder in a way that seemed to say, *thanks for that, I really appreciate you*. Or… something.

My guys started toward our car, but I lingered behind a moment. I had no interest in talking to Zane in private, but I trusted Cass. He'd kept me safe when he hadn't needed to by sending me back to Archer.

"What did he really come here for?" I asked the big, tattooed gangster.

He shrugged. "Fuck if I know. He wouldn't tell me. He found something out that had him excited, though."

I sighed, folding my arms. "All right, no worries. I'm sure if it's important, he'll try again."

Cass jerked a nod, then ran a hand over his short beard. "You really okay, kid? Those boys treating you right?"

My brows flickered up. "Uh, if you're asking about my relationships—"

"I'm not," he said, cutting me off with a huff of Cass laughter. "I just mean if they're still pulling their bullshit with you, you know what to do. Call me and I'll clean up the bodies."

I laughed properly this time. "Aw, Grumpy, you do care. Don't worry, though. I'd just chuck them to the pigs, and no one would ever find the evidence." I gave him a feral grin, and his eyes widened slightly.

"Well shit," he muttered, "that's more like it. Get out of here. Text me and let me know you're home safe."

"Can do," I replied, heading across the parking lot to where the guys waited with our car. Then a thought crossed my mind, and I spun back around to look at Cass. "Hey, how's your girl?"

The glare he shot me was pure violence, and I just grinned wider. Still unavailable was my guess. When my own drama was all wrapped up, I was going to have to work out who this mystery woman was. She had to be someone pretty cool to have Mr. Grumpy all tied up in knots.

"All good?" Steele asked as I slid into the backseat beside him. I jerked a nod. "Yep, Cass is cool."

Archer huffed a short laugh as he pulled out of the parking lot, leaving Cass standing over Zane's unconscious form. "Yeah, he's not bad."

"Hell of a lot better than Zane," Kody added. "We should sort that out one of these days."

I wrinkled my nose. "Sort what out?"

Steele shot me a grin. "Zane. He's outlived his usefulness and is starting to become an annoyance."

"You're going to kill him?" I don't know why I was startled by that idea. Maybe because he was Archer's brother? Or because he'd once loved my mom? I didn't know.

Archer was the one to answer me. "Not today," he said, his tone thoughtful. "But one of these days, he'll push me too damn far. The only reason he's alive now is because I'm grateful to him."

I blinked at him in the rearview mirror. "For what?"

He gave a small shrug. "He told you what I was hiding, and I'm glad he did."

His gaze held mine far longer than was safe, then slowly shifted back to the road ahead of us. I said nothing back because he was right. Zane had done us all a favor, whether he'd meant to or not.

CHAPTER 19

The next week was uneventful. Too uneventful. By the time the following weekend rolled around, I was jumping at every shadow, flinching at every beep of a phone or knock at the door. Put simply? I was a fucking mess.

Which was why it was such a relief when Leon came strolling into the den with his laptop tucked under his arm. For a mercenary, he was awfully attached to that thing. Then again, what the fuck did I know? I'd never met mercenaries before him and Danny.

"Madison Kate." He greeted me with a short nod. "Your men around somewhere?"

I arched a brow at him, the spoonful of ice cream halfway to my lips. "Why? You have something wrong with talking to me directly?"

There was really no reason to take that attitude with Leon, except that I was all kinds of twitchy and snapping at anyone who so much as looked at me. My stalker had been *silent* ever since the night of the break in. No packages, no notes, no creepy phone calls. It was like he'd just gotten bored and disappeared.

Leon didn't take the bait, though. "Actually, I don't want to repeat myself. Danny and I have another job to get to tomorrow, so I need to debrief on everything we've sorted out here."

I sat up in a rush, placing my ice cream on the table. "Shit, sorry, I totally lost track of the days. I'll grab them and be back here in five."

Leon just waved a hand like he didn't care, and I scurried out of the room. Kody and Archer were in the gym training—my session wasn't for another two hours, which was why I'd been pregaming on ice cream—and Steele was swimming laps in the pool.

By the time we'd all made it back to the den, Danny had joined Leon, and she had a thick folder of papers in her hands.

"All right," Leon said, checking his watch as we all sat down. "We have five minutes before the next guard passes by this window." He pointed to the one opposite where he sat. "So we'll keep this short and sweet."

"Suits us," Archer said. "What have you found?"

"Okay, first of all, you have three members of your security team with fabricated backgrounds," Danny said, handing her folder of papers over to Archer. "Which, as you know, isn't uncommon in our line of work. But we'd suggest removing them as a precaution."

"Done," Archer agreed. "What else?"

"Trevor, your missing guard?" Leon said, opening his laptop and tapping a few keys. "Not missing any longer." He turned the screen around to show us an image of a dead man with a bullet wound between his eyes and at least one to the chest. It was hard to tell with the amount of blood soaking his shirt.

"Murdered?" I gasped.

Danny shrugged. "Not quite. I located him and went for a chat. He didn't want to chat." I raised my brows at her, and she gave me an impassive stare back. "No one shoots at me and lives."

I almost wanted to laugh, but she was dead serious.

"So he could have been our leak?" Archer asked, tapping at his chin thoughtfully.

"It seems that way," Leon agreed. "There were several items at his crash pad that suggested it, like a collection of women's underwear and some image stills taken from the security feeds around the property."

"Wait, are we saying that Trevor was the stalker himself?" I blurted out, frowning in confusion.

Leon gave me a curious look. "You don't think he was?"

I shook my head. "It's too easy. My stalker is way too smart to be caught with evidence like that."

Danny nodded. "That was our thought too. We suspect Trevor was just his inside man and the evidence was either planted or given as a payment of sorts. In our digging, we found Trevor has a history of swiping ladies' underwear from laundromats."

"Gross," I whispered, horrified.

"Right?" Danny wrinkled her cute nose in disgust. "Anyway, if Trevor was the inside guy, then at the very least your stalker will have a hard time getting access to the property. He definitely won't be able to override the camera feeds to hide his package deliveries either; Leon's taken care of that."

Leon jerked a nod. "Your digital print is now tighter than a nun's nasty. Only people with access are you four and Sampson."

Kody snickered at that metaphor, and Danny rolled her eyes.

"Another thing," she said. "We paid a little visit to your obsessive blogger girl a couple of days ago. She's harmless and damn near peed her pants over the whole thing. *However*, she didn't take her blog down as requested, so we're going to pop over there now before we leave for Serbia and have another chat with her."

"Also, we dug up who put the hit out on you," Leon announced like a fucking afterthought. My jaw fell open when he didn't immediately continue. He shot me a grin like he knew he was dragging out the suspense.

Danny clearly wasn't in the mood for games, though. She sighed and shook her head at him. "After Archer gave us the information he and Demi Timber had gathered, it wasn't too hard to chase the right threads," she told me directly. "Archer said he thought you had an uncle or cousin who stood to gain in the event of your death, and he was on the right track there. You already knew that Katerina and Abel had twins, Deb and Declan. What was very well concealed was that Abel's considerably younger sister, Josephine, had a daughter, Serena."

"She's the one trying to kill me?" I asked, dumbfounded.

"Unlikely," Leon grunted. "Josephine and her husband, Gunther Zukman, died when Serena was three. She was raised by her paternal grandparents in a strict Catholic household with no contact with the Wittenberg family whatsoever."

Archer scrubbed his hand over his stubbled cheek. "So Serena was the one who would have inherited prior to Kate's marriage to me?"

Leon nodded. "Yep, technically."

"Technically?" I repeated, sensing more to the story.

Danny nodded to the folder of papers. "Page forty-seven of the report. Serena Zukman took a nasty fall down a flight of stairs around ten years ago. Left her paralyzed and brain damaged. She was declared mentally unfit, and power of attorney passed to her husband."

My brows shot up. "Ten years ago? So...just before Katerina and my mother were both killed? As well as the trusted CEO Katerina assigned to run Wittenberg? That's not a coincidence."

Leon yawned, then nodded. "Our thoughts exactly. Serena's husband is on page fifty-three."

Archer flipped the report open to that page, which showed a photo of a totally ordinary-looking man somewhere in his forties with a receding hairline and glasses.

"Karl Beymen. Married Serena Zukman three years before her so-called accident. Also goes under the fabricated name Karl Kruger." Leon paused then, his sharp gaze on me.

I frowned. "Should that name mean something to me?"

"It should," he replied. "He's the current CEO of Wittenberg."

"It doesn't add up," I muttered after Danny and Leon had left. They were paying another quick visit to MrsJones4eva before catching their flight.

"I agree," Steele said, leaning forward with his elbows on his knees. "Based on the assumption that estates pass to the next living blood relative in the event of a death without a will, then Samuel would be next in line to inherit. He'd be MK's closest blood relative."

"Unless he's not," Kody offered.

The silence that fell after that suggestion was thick enough to suffocate, and I shifted nervously in my seat. Was my dad not biologically my dad? That might explain his total lack of human emotion toward me and his willingness to sell me off.

"Bear with me," Kody continued. "We know that Deb did a lot of cover-up to hide MK from her family, right? What if Kruger *never* knew Deb had a daughter, then came here and killed her, or hired someone to do it, when he found out she was pregnant—"

"With Zane's baby," Archer murmured, his expression thoughtful.

Kody nodded. "Then his wife inherits the company because there are *supposedly* no other heirs. Deb had specifically edited her will to cut Samuel out in the event of her death, but instead of naming MK, she had put *blood relative*."

"So what changed?" I pressed. "What caused him to find me six years later and put a price on my head?"

"Your father," Steele offered. "Your father was up to his neck in debts and might have been looking into how to access your trust fund. It was set up by Deb and Katerina, though, and he had no clue what he was poking around at. Maybe *somehow* he found out that he wasn't your biological father, and that's why he sold you off."

"Cutting his losses," I muttered, bitterness coating my words.

"And alerting Kruger to your existence at the same time," Archer added with a sigh.

"It's just a theory," Kody added, "and not likely to be something we can ever work out for sure, but…" He trailed off with a shrug.

I nodded. "You're right. It's a theory, but it's a pretty good one. It makes sense. Except if Samuel isn't my father…who is? And why don't we just make my marriage to Archer public knowledge. Our prenup safeguards my assets from passing to anyone but him, right?"

Kody shrugged. "So Kruger's guys kill Arch first, then you. Boom, boom, done."

Archer's phone rang, cutting through the heavy tension of our hypothesizing, and he frowned when he looked at the screen.

"What's happened?" he asked when he answered the call on speaker.

"You might want to get over here and check this out," Leon replied. Danny was cursing something wicked in the background, and I shot a worried look at Archer. "I'll send the address and a couple of pics. Dan and I have to get going, but chat to management if you want us to loop back when we get a couple of days off."

Archer grimaced. "Will do. Thanks, Leon."

"Thank *you*," he replied with a laugh. "It's nice to be hired for brains over brawn sometimes."

Danny muttered something to him in the background, and he cracked up laughing, then ended the call.

A second later, Archer's phone beeped with several incoming messages, and he clicked them open, then groaned and shook his head before handing the phone to Steele.

"Someone else paid Mrs Jones a visit before Danny and Leon got there," he informed us, "and left a pretty clear message to claim credit."

"Fuck," Steele breathed, then passed the phone across to Kody and me. We were sitting together on the couch and could both look at the images.

Then I immediately wished I hadn't.

The Kody-obsessed blogger had been brutally murdered, her body duct-taped to her desk chair and mutilated in what looked to be a horrendously painful way. But worst of all was the little brunette Barbie doll sitting on the computer keyboard with crosses drawn over her eyes and the little plastic hands hacked up.

"Why'd he do this?" I whispered, bile rolling in my belly. "Danny said this chick was harmless. Why'd he kill her?"

Archer took his phone back from Kody's hand and gave us a grim look. "I guess we're about to find out."

I swallowed heavily and nodded, rising out of my seat. He was right, of course. We needed to get there in person and investigate any other clues or messages my psychotic stalker had left behind, and we needed to do it *before* someone reported the murder to the cops. The last thing we needed to be dealing with was some bullshit power trips if Charon's or Zane's pocket cops showed up.

None of us spoke as we headed for the car. We'd been expecting *something* soon. It simply wasn't in my stalker's pattern to go dark so long without something explosive as a result.

The only shred of hope I pulled from this latest message? He hadn't delivered it to the house. So maybe with Trevor gone, his access had been cut off.

Hopefully, we might be a fraction safer inside our own home once more.

Nothing could have prepared me for the *smell* that hit as soon as we entered the studio apartment of MrsJones4eva.

"Oh, wow," I murmured. Using my hand to block my nose, I tried to breathe shallowly. "This isn't so fresh."

"Couple of days old would be my guess." Steele handed me a pair of latex gloves, then pulled some onto his own hands. I guessed we would leave this crime scene for someone else to clean up when we were done.

"Didn't Danny say she and Leon visited a couple of days ago?"

I asked, my voice strangled as I tried not to gag on the smell of decaying corpse. Not to mention the *blood*. It was everywhere. I almost didn't want to go any farther into the room for fear of what I might step on.

Kody nodded. "And they said she kept posting on her blog *after* that."

"My guess?" Steele offered from where he stood beside the woman's corpse. "Your stalker followed Danny and Leon here the first time they visited, then killed the blogger after they left."

"The blog posts after she died?" I pointed out.

Steele reached over and carefully tabbed down the open browser window. "Most likely posted by our guy. Take a look. These aren't her usual Kody-obsessed junk; these are specific messages to MK."

"Stop," I gasped, pointing to an image on the feed. "That's my mom. That's the photo from the gift box with the bra."

The four of us all peered at the computer screen, ignoring the decomposing corpse beside us.

"Is that…" I squinted at the photo or, specifically, at the man with his arm around my mom. "Is that groundskeeper James with my mom?"

CHAPTER 20

Patricia Sparrow. That was MrsJones4eva's real name. Patricia Sparrow had been a twenty-two-year-old girl who'd seemingly formed an obsession with Kody after meeting him at a party when they were seventeen. He, of course, had no recollection of ever meeting her, but she'd kept extensive journal entries detailing the brief encounter that had sparked her obsession.

Patricia had also been hosting a much more sinister discussion thread on the dark web under the username MadisonSLUTneeds2die, which showed she had a much crueler streak than her Kody fan page suggested.

It was likely because of that page that my stalker had killed her, considering all her fingers looked like they'd gone through a meat tenderizer and her own hateful comments from the discussion threads had been cut into her skin with sharp, familiar handwriting.

"He's protecting me," I murmured as we arrived home from the crime scene. I needed to take a shower and to scrub my skin with a pot scourer, but even then I doubted I'd get the stench of old blood and decaying human from my nose.

Kody took my hand, linking our fingers together. "In his fucked-up serial killer way? Yeah, it seems like that."

I sighed, scrubbing my hands over my face. "At least that's one person who doesn't want me dead."

"That's looking at the glass half-full," Kody agreed with a crooked smile.

Archer grunted a sound of disagreement. "Yet."

I blinked at him in confusion, my brain too fuzzy to connect the dots. "Huh?"

He shrugged. "One person who doesn't want you dead *yet*, but whatever he *does* want to do to you would probably make you wish you were dead. Given how many people he's killed in rather brutal ways, we know he's capable of some fucked-up shit."

I blinked a couple more times, then shook my head. "And on that depressing note, I need a shower. Night." I untangled my hand from Kody's and hurried up the stairs to my bedroom. It'd been refurbished since the night of the break-in, with smash-proof privacy glass installed.

My shower was quick but scalding hot, and I scrubbed every damn inch of myself with antiseptic wash. God only knew what crazy diseases a person could pick up from decaying human bodies.

When I emerged from my bathroom wearing only panties and a T-shirt, I found a freshly showered Archer climbing into my bed like he owned the damn thing. Which, I guessed, he did.

I didn't comment because it'd become a habit for one of them to sleep with me every night since the break-in, like they all had an agreement that there was no way I'd actually *sleep* if I were left alone in my bed. They were right too.

Yawning, I crawled into his arms and curled up with my cheek against his hard chest. He stretched out and flicked the lights off, then stroked his fingers through my hair.

For a while I just lay there, listening to the steady beat of Archer's heart and picturing all the horrible things that had been done to that poor girl. A deep shudder ran through me, and my stomach churned. The *pain* she must have experienced prior to death was unfathomable.

"Sleep, Kate," Archer whispered, kissing my hair. "I promise, you're safe tonight. I won't leave."

I huffed but didn't argue his phrasing. Because he was right. *Tonight* I was safe. But what about tomorrow? Or the next day? Or the next week? Sooner or later, my luck was going to run out.

With that depressing thought, I slipped into a restless sleep filled with nightmares of cut-up bloggers and shadowy figures at my window. Yet every time I startled myself awake, Archer was there to soothe me back to sleep. Eventually, though, my mind must have given in to exhaustion because the next thing I knew, I was waking up *well* past my usual time.

I was all tangled up with my brooding bad boy, but he wasn't asleep. His breathing was steady, but his fingers traced a pattern down my spine that lit up all my nerve endings and made me groan.

"Good morning, Princess," he murmured in a low rumble.

Words were too hard, so I just yawned and snuggled into him tighter. Fuck dealing with stalkers and serial killers and assassins. I just wanted to stay in bed with my guys and ignore the world. Was that so much to ask?

I let out a sigh. Of course it was. Because none of those external forces would disappear simply because I wasn't in the mood to deal with them.

"What time is it?" I mumbled, not bothering to open my eyes more than a crack. It was daylight, that was for sure, and I never usually slept past dawn.

Archer let out a long breath of his own, tightening his arms around me like he also wanted to stay exactly as we were forever. "Ten-ish."

Surprise rippled through me. "Did you skip training?"

Archer usually met Kody in the gym around five a.m., and lately—if it'd been one of them sharing my bed—I'd come along to spectate. I was, and always would be, a *huge* fan of The Archer in the octagon.

"Yep," he replied. "You had a rough night, and I didn't want to sneak out."

I tilted my head back so I could look at him, a bemused smile crossing my lips. "That was awfully sweet of you, *Husband*."

His lips twitched in a sleepy smile back. "There's nothing on this earth I wouldn't do for you, *Wife*. Skipping a training session with Kody is the least of it all." His palm cupped my face, his thumb tracing over my lower lip, and his gaze heated.

I drew a quick breath, desire flooding through me as his eyes locked with mine and his open, raw emotions shone through. Never in a million years could I have guessed he'd been hiding all of that behind his asshole mask. Never would I have anticipated the depth of his love for me. This was no casual flirtation or fleeting college romance. He was all in…and so was I.

"Arch…" I started, then trailed off as my voice dried up in my throat. He was all in *now*, but I'd seen how fast his mood could shift. I believed he loved me with every inch of his stained soul, but I also believed he would push me away if it meant keeping me safe.

He didn't press me to say what I was thinking, though. He just brushed a soft kiss over my lips. One that I leaned into and deepened because, although I still couldn't say the words out loud, I knew I could *show* him how I felt.

"Kate…" he murmured with a groan as my hands ran down his sides and hooked into the waistband of his boxers. "You're testing my resolve something wicked."

"What resolve?" I kissed his chest and tugged on his boxers teasingly.

He let out a frustrated growl but slid his fingers into my hair and brought my lips back to his for another deep kiss.

"My resolve not to fuck you senseless *every* time I get my hands on you," he confessed with a hint of wickedness in his gaze. "But you make it so damn—"

"Hard?" I suggested. My hand slipped inside his shorts and grasped his thick erection. "What's wrong with fucking me every chance you get? I'm not complaining."

His lips pulled up in a smirk, and his hips rolled as I stroked his cock. "Maybe not, but…" His protest dissolved into a groan as my thumb circled his tip, playing with the slick bead of precum.

"But *what?*" I teased, kissing his chest once more.

As he drew a deep breath, his hands found my shoulders, and he flipped me onto my back. His thick thigh crushed against my core, pushing my legs apart. Like I really needed any encouragement.

"You're fucking trouble, Princess," he told me, as if this was new information.

I just grinned and rocked my hips against him. "You love it."

He muttered curses and kissed my neck, biting me gently on the spot that made me shiver and moan. "I love *you,*" he corrected me in a gruff voice as he hooked a hand under my thigh and spread my legs wider still.

My T-shirt was all tangled up, barely covering my breasts, and my panties may as well have been made of tissue paper as his hard length ground against my core. *Wet* tissue paper at that.

A knock on my door came just a moment before it opened and Steele wandered in. His brows only hitched slightly when he found Archer on top of me, and I caught the flash of desire in his eyes as he realized what he'd walked in on.

"Bro," Archer snapped. "What the fuck?"

Steele just grinned. "What? Don't tell me you get stage fright, big guy. I have it on good authority Hellcat doesn't mind an audience." He shot me a wink as he dragged his thumb across his lower lip.

I tried to swallow my moan, but it sneaked out nonetheless as my pussy pulsed with that suggestion. Kody's suggestion of a four-way kept rattling around in my brain, but Archer had yet to even partake in a *three*-way.

"Fuck you, dickhead," Archer shot back at his friend. "Watch if you want; maybe you'll learn something."

Oh, hell yes.

When Archer captured my lips in another toe-curling kiss, I held Steele's gaze and watched as he ran his tongue over his lower lip, showing off that piercing. Then he gave a pained frown.

"As badly as I want to call your bluff, Arch," he said with a resigned sigh, "I actually came with news."

I groaned, and not in a good way. Archer let out a curse and rolled to lie beside me, where the thin blanket did nothing to hide his hard-on.

"Dead, mutilated people news?" I cringed. "Or exploding cars news?"

Steele quirked a grin. "Hell of a scale, Hellcat. But…somewhere in the middle of those." He shifted his gaze to Archer. "My parents were just on the phone."

Archer cursed again with more passion. "What the fuck did they want?"

The biting edge to his tone told me exactly how Archer felt about Steele's parents. The fact that Steele had likened them to a car bomb said it all.

"Rachel's memorial is next weekend," Steele said in a tight voice, his expression pinched. "They want me home for it."

Archer scoffed. "I fucking bet they do. Did you tell them to screw themselves?"

Steele gave a minuscule cringe, and my heart ached for him. Whatever had happened between him and his parents, he was still hurting over it.

"It's not that easy, bro," Steele told Archer with a sigh as he hooked his thumbs through the belt loops of his jeans.

Archer groaned and swept a hand over his face. "I know."

I scrambled to sit up and give Steele my full attention. "When do you have to leave?"

His shoulders drooped as he sighed. "Today. Now. They've planned all these stupid *events* in Rachel's name that she would have *hated*. But they're demanding I attend all of them. Play the part of their dutiful son and shit."

Archer threw the covers back and grabbed his jeans off the floor. "All right, give me ten, and I'll sort us out a jet."

Steele shook his head. "Nah, dude, you're not coming with me." He gave a short laugh. "I appreciate the offer, don't get me wrong. But this shit is going to be painful enough without you punching out my dad in front of the press."

Archer huffed. "That happened *once*, and he deserved it."

My gaze bounced between the two of them. I was dying for that story, but now wasn't the time to ask.

"Well, he always deserves it," Steele agreed. "But I'll be fine. I'll just spend the entire weekend drunk off my ass and get in a fight with any rich prick who talks down to me. It'll be therapeutic."

Archer grimaced. He buttoned his jeans up, then scrubbed his hand through his hair again. "I think we should go with you. If Kevin tries to—"

"He won't," Steele snapped, cutting off whatever Archer was about to say. "He won't try *shit* or I'll kill him, and he damn well knows it. Just leave it alone, Arch; I'll be back first thing Monday." He cast a warning glare at his friend, then softened his gaze to run over me. Then he turned on his heel and stalked out of the room without another word.

Alarmed, I turned my wide eyes toward Archer. "Is he…?"

Archer just shook his head. "He's far from okay. Can you talk to him? It's not safe to split up right now. Maybe he'll listen if it comes from you."

I was already nodding before he'd even finished his sentence. "Yes, of course." I scrambled out of bed and pulled on a pair of jeans.

Archer caught my arm before I left the room, pulled me back to him, and kissed me hard. "Thank you, Kate."

I shook my head. "Nothing to thank." Because I would move heaven and earth for Max Steele if it meant never again seeing that pained look on his face when Archer mentioned *Kevin*.

Rising up on my toes, I kissed Archer again, quickly, then hurried my ass into Steele's bedroom. He stood at the end of his bed, tossing clothes into a bag like he didn't much care what he was packing, with a deep frown marring his beautiful face.

"Hey," I said as I entered his room. I perched my backside on the bed beside his bag. "Wanna talk?"

He flashed me a quick, humorless smile. "Not really. Archer send you in here?"

I shook my head. "Archer D'Ath doesn't send me fucking any-where, thank you very much. I came in here because I'm *worried*. Can we please talk a moment?"

He hesitated, a folded T-shirt still in his hand hovering over the open bag; then his eyes met mine and his shoulders slumped.

"There's nothing to talk about, Hellcat," he murmured, his gaze sliding away from mine and making me scowl.

"What did we say about lies and secrets, Max?" I kept my tone hard, and his nose wrinkled.

Tossing his packing aside, he collapsed onto the bed beside me. "Yeah, good point, beautiful." He buried his face in his folded arms for a moment.

I lay down beside him, propping my head up on my hand. "So talk to me. What don't I know? Why is Archer so worried about you going alone? I get the impression it's about more than just your safety from my stalker, which, I might add, is a very valid concern right now."

Steele shifted his face on his arms, turning to look at me. "Because my parents are disgusting human beings who never should have had children in the first place."

I bit my lip, sadness for Steele's childhood washing over me. "I gathered that much. Kevin is your dad?"

Steele grimaced. "Yeah."

He didn't elaborate on why that was a cringe subject, and I didn't push him to. He'd tell me when he was ready. But I did need to understand a little bit more about Rachel's memorial to know why he was so out of sorts.

"Aside from my stalker, is there any other reason to fear for your safety if you go alone?" I asked him carefully. I was concerned for him but didn't want to come across pushy and prying.

He shook his head. "Not unless you count the damage I'll do to my liver while I'm there."

I frowned. "You're not even supposed to be drinking yet. You're still healing."

Apparently that was funny, because he snickered and gave me a look like I was being cute. Fucker. I'd show him cute with my foot up his ass in a second.

"Hellcat," he murmured, snaking an arm around my waist, "I'll be fine. I promise."

I scowled but let him pull me closer. "Don't make promises you can't keep, Max Steele." I kissed him softly on the lips and tucked my body closer to his as he rolled onto his side. "What about just taking me? I'd like to meet your parents, even if they are pieces of shit."

A slow smile crept over his lips. "You wanna meet my parents, Hellcat?"

"Well, yeah. At some stage you probably need to introduce your parents to your girlfriend, right?"

Steele's smile spread wider. "My girlfriend, huh? I like that. But no. To be totally honest, Hellcat, I never want you to meet them. You bring out the best in me, and they deserve nothing but the worst." He heaved a tired sigh. "I'll get this memorial for Rachel out of the way—because she was my twin sister and I loved her

181

with my *whole* heart—but then I'll go out of my way to cut ties with my parents."

I bit my lip, wanting to argue but also knowing I couldn't. Not when I didn't have the whole story. Instead, I needed to trust him and just be the support he needed when he got home again.

"Okay," I murmured. "But you need to take one of the security guys with you." His brow creased, and I knew he was going to argue.

"Not up for debate, Max," I told him in a hard voice. "Take a bodyguard, wear some body armor, do whatever the fuck you need to do, but get back to me in one piece. Understood?"

His frown faded into a smile. "Yes, ma'am."

I squinted at him, suspicious. "Good. If I hear that you got shot or blown up or strangled or—"

"Hellcat," Steele said, cutting me off with a grin, "I'll come home to you, safe and sound. You have my word." I scowled and he smoothed his thumb over my forehead creases. "I'll be back in four days," he whispered, "and I'll be thinking about you every goddamn second."

Smiling, I pushed his shoulder until he rolled onto his back so I could straddle his waist. "Well, can you spare five minutes before you need to go? I want to make double sure you have something to remember while you're away."

Steele's grin spread wide, his hands going to the hem of my T-shirt. "Five minutes? Beautiful girl, don't sell me short."

And then we fucked like rabbits.

CHAPTER 21

Nervous as hell, I drummed my fingers on the tabletop and tried really damn hard not to chew a hole in my lip as we waited for James to arrive. Kody was sitting back in his chair, the folder of information compiled by Danny and Leon in his hands as he read.

"There's not really anything suspicious in here," he murmured, then closed it when he was done. "Nothing we didn't already know anyway."

"Then why was he in a photo with my mom?" I argued with a frown. "That's not mentioned in there. How come?"

Archer cocked his head to the side. "Danny and Leon are thorough, but they're not the all-seeing eye. If there was no record of James and Deb's connection, then there would have been nothing to find."

I huffed, folding my arms. "Fair point."

"I guess we'll just have to ask." Kody pushed back from his chair and stood up as the groundskeeper in question entered the dining room. "James, thanks for coming in."

James quirked a brow at Archer and me, then gave Kody a short nod. "No worries." He took a seat at the table opposite us. "Is this about Sampson's team? I thought the mercs took care of that."

Archer shook his head. "Actually, James, this is about Deb."

James didn't react. Not a single flicker of emotion passed over his face, not even surprise or confusion.

Kody pulled a printout of the photo from his folder and slid it across the table to James. "Wanna explain that to us?"

James looked down at the image, then sighed heavily. He didn't respond immediately, taking his time staring at the photo. "This photo..." he said in a husky voice. "Where'd you get it?"

My temper flared. "What does that fucking matter?"

His eyes met mine, and they were awash with guilt. "It *matters*, MK, because this photo was mine. It was in my wallet for..." He trailed off, shaking his head as his gaze returned to the image. "I don't even know how long. But I was mugged one night outside a bar, my wallet stolen. I'd never made a copy of it."

My brows shot up, and I gave my guys an uncertain look. Was James telling the truth? Because that would be awfully convenient...

"James," Kody said in a slightly softer tone, "explain that to us. We've trusted you with a lot, but right now all signs are pointing at you for being Deb and MK's stalker."

James's eyes widened. "Seriously? I'm going to take a leap here and assume this photo was gifted by the stalker. Right? Well, why would I out myself if that was me? Doesn't make sense, and you know it. That's why I'm sitting here right now and not being tossed off the back of a boat with rocks in my pockets."

He was right. If we really thought he was my stalker, he'd be dead. Except he'd be digesting somewhere in a pig's belly, not getting tossed overboard.

"James," Archer growled, "start talking. Maybe you're not *the* stalker, but you're sure as fuck not telling us the whole story."

The groundskeeper blew out a long breath, then ruffled his fingers through his brown hair. He was a good-looking guy, no question. I could see why my mom had been into him twenty-odd years ago.

"Yeah, I knew Deb," he admitted, but carefully avoided eye contact with me. "We were briefly involved while I was home on leave after my first tour. I met her at Murphy's when I went to see some buddies play."

"Scruffy Murphy's?" Kody asked. "The live music venue over on the south side of town?"

James jerked a nod. "Yep, that's the one. Anyway, Deb was there with some girlfriends for, she told me, her friend's bachelorette night." He grimaced.

"You hooked up," Archer commented, his tone flat and pointed.

"Yeah," James admitted with a sigh. "That night. Then we ended up seeing each other almost every day for the next two weeks."

"So what happened next?" I asked, my voice cracking as I processed this. James didn't strike me as an unbalanced nutcase. He sure as fuck wasn't coming off as a deranged serial killer with an unhealthy obsession with me.

Instead, he just seemed to be a guy reminiscing on a lost love… and that made me sad.

James met my eyes briefly, then looked back down at the photo. "Then…nothing. I was deployed, and by the time I made it back, Deb was married to Samuel. She seemed to have the perfect life here in Shadow Grove, with her filthy-rich husband and adorable little girl." He flashed me a short, bitter smile. "Turns out, that night was *Deb's* bachelorette party. She married your father the day after my leave ended."

Oh shit.

The conversation we'd had about Samuel *not* being my real father flickered through my brain, and I shot a startled look at Archer.

He was on the same wavelength, though. He placed his hand on my knee under the table and gave me a reassuring squeeze.

"Why come and work here, James?" Archer asked, instead of the question burning on my tongue.

The groundskeeper shrugged. "Honestly? Fate or something. If you remember, I took the job as *your* groundskeeper, Arch. Not Samuel's. When he turned up and started his charade as lord of the manor, I just stayed under the radar. Samuel and I never had any bad blood; hell, we'd never even met. But I couldn't bear to face the man who'd held on to Deb for so long."

"Sounds like my mom had some serious issues with remaining faithful," I muttered under my breath. Sure, it wasn't fair considering I was currently in love with three guys, but god*damn*. First Zane, now James?

James just cocked a brow at me. "Can you blame her? Samuel Danvers is a right piece of shit, girl. I don't think Deb loved him for even a second."

Good point.

Kody tapped his fingers on James's folder. "If we look into your stationing over the months when Deb was stalked and murdered, will we find an alibi?"

James gave a half smile. "As if you haven't already done that. I'm still breathing, aren't I?"

Kody smirked back. "That you are."

James turned his attention back to me. "I'm sorry I wasn't more upfront about knowing your mom, MK. But she died some time ago, so I simply didn't think it relevant. I can't shed any light on what's happening to you, but I *am* doing my best to help your boys any way I can."

I pursed my lips, weighing his sincerity. Kody and Archer had filled me in on James before we called this meeting. I knew that he'd spent the better part of the last twenty years in the marines, in some highly classified division. He'd been upfront with the boys when he took the job as groundskeeper, and they'd hired him because they liked the idea of having an extra layer of security in plain sight.

"Okay," I said with a sigh.

James nodded, then frowned. "Except now I'm wondering why your stalker has drawn your attention to my relationship with Deb. It was so brief, barely a couple of weeks. Deb would have—no offense—undoubtedly had other affairs over the years, ones that lasted much longer than mine. So why point the finger at *me*?"

"Maybe just because you're here, right under our noses? If you hadn't been so forthcoming with your military records and locations of deployment, then maybe that would have caused us to be suspicious of you." Kody seemed to be mostly thinking out loud. "Or he thought we would shoot first and ask questions never."

James hummed a thoughtful sound. "It'd strip one more layer of your defenses away, even if you just fired me and didn't kill me."

"He laid low while Danny and Leon were here too," Archer commented. "Like he knew we only had them for a short time period and that he was no match for their skill."

"Who were the other guards the mercs flagged as suspicious?" James asked.

Kody flipped a few pages to check. "Grant Silas and Niell Grosmon. Both had doctored their employment history in some way. Sampson released them from employment yesterday and is already interviewing replacements per Leon's list of possible candidates."

"So one of those two could have still been feeding info to my stalker," I murmured, frowning.

James shrugged. "Or they're totally innocent and had something embarrassing to cover up. Did all the other guards check out?"

Kody grunted. "What few were left, yeah. Nothing hinky about any of them. Sampson, Gill, and Dave all trained with Phillip when he ran the camp, then went on to law enforcement or private security. Ryan and Adamson both came from the marines, same as you. All aspects of their files are squeaky clean."

James let out a sigh and scrubbed his hand over his face. "So much for a nice, quiet retirement pruning roses," he muttered with a short laugh. "I knew I should have taken the job for Mrs. Greenborough instead of this mess."

Archer huffed a laugh. "Except we pay you double and let you use the mountain shooting range on your days off."

James grinned. "Good point."

"Just one more question before you go," Archer said, his fingers tightening on my knee. "Did you ever suspect that maybe Samuel wasn't MK's biological father?"

That question was delivered with the impact of a Mack truck, and James looked like he was about to fall off his chair.

"Wh-what?"

"Did it ever cross your mind that you might be MK's biological father?" Kody elaborated, his hands linked on the table in front of him and his gaze intense. "It must have, when you worked out her birthday and counted backward..."

James winced, then shook his head. "No. I mean, yes the thought crossed my mind. Of course it did. But aside from the fact that I was meticulous about using protection—"

I cringed, thinking about my mom having sex with James. Come on, no one wanted to picture their mom getting fucked.

"—I ran a DNA test."

Wait, what?

Shrugging one shoulder, James gave me a sheepish look. "You were born almost exactly nine months after your parents got married. Yeah, it occurred to me that you might be mine. It's part of the reason I stuck around when Samuel showed up with his new girlfriend."

"So..." My voice was rough and dry, forcing me to clear my throat. "So, you did a paternity test?"

James nodded. "Just using hair from your brush. Results were negative; you're not my kid." He offered a small smile. "Although I admit I was a bit disappointed. I see a hell of a lot more of me in you than I do Samuel."

Archer was frowning hard, his fingers still gripping my knee. "What lab processed the test?"

James's brows shot up. "You think the results could have been tampered with?"

Archer shrugged. "Anything is possible with Samuel Danvers. Especially if he thought he was still going to bleed more money out of this arrangement I made with him. Would you be willing to take another test?"

"Uh, of course. I don't know that it'll change anything, but yes, for sure." James nodded, then stood from his chair when Kody did. He started to leave the room, then hesitated in the doorway. He turned back to look at me. "For what it's worth, Madison Kate, I'll still do everything I can to help. Regardless of the result. You're a good kid, and you deserve better than this mess."

He left with Kody then, and I turned to Archer with a long exhale.

"So, do we believe him?" I asked in a weak voice. I wanted to believe him...but life had conditioned me that everyone was a suspect these days.

Archer cupped the back of my head, bringing my face to his to kiss me gently. "Right now, Kate? I don't trust anyone."

I gave a bitter laugh as I thought how he'd just read my mind. "But we don't think he's the stalker?"

Archer shook his head. "I don't. Do you?"

I shrugged. "I have no fucking clue. I hope not. Though...it kind of seems likely he might be my real dad, and that would be all kinds of fucked up, right? My stalker has a clearly sexual interest in me, which would be so, *so* gross if he turned out to be my biological dad."

Archer wrinkled his nose. "Not many lines that haven't been crossed so far, Princess. Incest probably falls way lower than torturing and mutilating a blogger for being a bitch online."

I groaned, then shuddered. He had a good point. But James just didn't give off those kind of crazy-killer vibes. But...did anyone?

"Hey, speaking of DNA testing," I said, a thought occurring to me, "what were the results of the blood on my mom's bra?"

Archer wrinkled his nose and shook his head. "Dead end. It was hers, like we suspected."

I deflated a fraction more. Not that I'd thought he would hide it from me if there'd been anything more eye-opening about the results, but part of me had been holding a little hope.

Dead end. Fucking hell, those seemed to be everywhere lately.

CHAPTER 22

The cold rush of blankets being yanked off me wrenched me from my pleasant dream, and I groaned a protest. I fumbled around with my eyes still shut as I tried to find the blanket again, but the bastard had taken it out of my reach.

"Kody!" I whined. "Why do you hate me?"

His chuckle made me want to hurt him. Except that would mean waking up properly, and I *really* wanted to go back to sleep. We'd been so damn cozy; why'd he have to go and ruin it?

"Babe," he murmured, tucking his face into my neck as I huddled in a ball against the harsh, cold air of morning, "you and Arch both owe me for yesterday's missed session."

His lips worked their way over my collarbone, though, and I groaned when shivers of desire chased through me.

"Not fair," I mumbled as he tucked a hand under my T-shirt and let his fingers span my ribs. There was something stupidly possessive about the way he held me like that; it was *such* a turn-on. "This is psychological warfare."

Kody's chuckle feathered over my skin and I found myself uncurling from my ball, eager for more.

"Whatever works, babe. Give me a good training session this

morning, and I'll reward you afterward." His tone was mischievous and full of promise.

I cracked an eye open.

"Elaborate."

He sat back, giving me a smirk. "You'll just have to trust me, babe." His eyes sparkled. "You *do* trust me, don't you?"

I groaned. "You know I do, you shithead."

His smile spread wide. "Yeah, but sometimes it's nice to *hear* it." The look he gave me was more pointed than his words, and I knew what he was getting at. But fuck him, I wasn't confessing my love when he was dragging me into the gym when I should be sleeping.

Still…

With a sigh, I pushed myself up to sitting and looped my arms around his neck. "Kodiak Jones…"

"Hmm?" His bright gaze danced between my eyes and my mouth, like he was fighting the urge to kiss me. What was with these boys lately?

I licked my lips, which only distracted him further. Then I grinned. "I need to tell you something," I whispered, catching his gaze and holding it intently. "You're my penguin too." A flash of amusement rippled across his face, and I wrinkled my nose. "Or *one* of my penguins. Is that okay? Can I have three penguins?"

Kody gave a short laugh. "Nah, fuck them. Archer is more of a sea lion anyway. But I *know* what you're saying, even if you're being too stubborn to fucking say it. I love you too, babe."

He sealed his lips to mine, kissing me slowly and letting all that emotion pour into me, warming me from the soul up. Fuck me, Kodiak Jones was too damn perfect sometimes.

"Mmm," I mumbled when our kiss ended, "I'd love you more if you let me go back to sleep right now."

He scoffed a laugh, then kissed me again, harder. "Nice try. Now, are you going to get up, or do I have to carry you into the gym wearing that?"

192

I glanced down at my oversized T-shirt and panties, then sighed. "I guess I'll change. Give me half an hour."

With a bark of amusement, Kody climbed off the bed and headed for the door. "Not a damn chance, babe. Five minutes or I'm dragging you down there no matter what you're wearing... or *not* wearing."

He left my bedroom laughing, and I flopped back onto my bed with a groan. But I couldn't be mad at him, despite how much I wanted to stay asleep. He was training me because he loved me. He wanted me to have the best possible chance of protecting *myself* rather than sitting in my ivory tower and waiting for my knights in shining armor to save the day.

I loved that. I loved that my guys wanted to empower me, not weaken me. They believed in my abilities...but in return I needed to play fair and show up when Kody had time to train me.

Dammit.

Groaning way too much, I rolled out of bed and changed into a crop top and yoga pants. That'd have to do.

I scraped my hair up into a high ponytail as I made my sleepy way down to the gym, yawning every three steps, then damn near swallowing my tongue as I entered the gym.

"Come on!" I exclaimed with my hands on my hips. "This isn't fair."

Archer just laughed from where he was doing pull-ups in nothing but a tiny pair of tight boxer shorts. Prick.

"Sorry, babe," Kody called out over the thumping music, "can't hear you over all that hypocrisy. Hey, nice workout outfit." He strolled over to me with a smug grin, his hands on his hips. He wore a pair of loose basketball shorts and *nothing* else. Seriously. I could see his dick swing when he walked. How the fuck was I meant to concentrate with him like that?

My frustrated gaze shifted back to Archer, but he just shot me a wink and an air kiss as he flexed harder.

Pop.

My ovaries just exploded.

"Kody…" I whined. "You're being mean."

He just grinned. "Payback's a bitch, babe. The number of times I've suffered through a session with you while dealing with a hard-on…" He shook his head and clicked his tongue. "Now, let's get started. I wanna work on your actual combat skills today."

I pouted, but he was making good points. I did tend to wear minimal, skintight clothes to work out in, knowing full damn well I was driving him nuts. Apparently, it was time for me to take a bit of my own medicine.

"Isn't that what we've been doing for weeks?" I asked, following him over to the cardio machines, where he always started me for a warm-up.

He nodded. "We have in theory. But I want to see you put some of those skills into action. Arch has kindly offered to be your sparring partner."

My jaw dropped. "You want me to fight Archer?" My voice was a shocked squeak, and I jerked my head to glare at the big asshole. "I can't fight you!"

His smile was pure evil. "Why not, Princess? I'll go easy on you."

"Why not?" I exclaimed. "Are you kidding? You'll annihilate me!"

"Only if you ask me really nicely," he replied with a hungry look, and my cheeks instantly heated. They seriously wanted to kill me this morning.

Kody chuckled to himself like he was enjoying his sick little idea. Bastard. "Come on, ten-minute warm-up while I sort through some shit with Arch, then you can have at it. I won't even call foul if you throw some dirty fists."

Now, I could have been wrong, but that sounded a whole lot like Kody suggesting I punch Archer in the junk, which left me with a conundrum to ponder the whole time I was warming up on the elliptical machine.

On the one hand, Kody was basically giving me permission to fight dirty and take Archer to his knees. On the other hand, at the moment I quite liked Archer's dick intact.

Ugh, talk about caught between a rock and a hard place!

When the timer beeped on my machine and Kody told me to get some gloves on, I was no closer to a decision. I guessed I would just wait and see how *easy* Archer wanted to go on me.

As it turned out, despite the boys teasing, they still intended to take my training seriously. For the next half hour or so, Archer was the perfect sparring partner. He was patient and calm, offering constructive criticisms and supporting Kody's training techniques. I actually felt like I was *learning*, which wasn't at all what I'd expected from a sparring session with Archer in those tiny shorts.

But then Kody asked us to work on grappling, and that's where my professionalism fast evaporated.

In my defense…I was only human.

"Kate," Archer warned as I arched my back and ground my ass against him, "stop it."

I let out a low chuckle, despite the way he held my arm trapped behind my back. He was *supposed* to be demonstrating a wrist lock, but all I could think about was how Kody'd bound my hands with his belt when he fucked me several weeks ago. *Then* I started thinking about Archer's mention of fun features in his new bed frame and…well…I was no longer interested in learning to fight.

"You guys started it." I rolled my hips again and felt his cock thicken against my backside. Yep, I wasn't the only one done with fight training.

Kody blew out a breath, scrubbing a hand over his hair. "Babe, you're killing me here. Maybe we should call it a day." He checked his watch, then nodded. "Yep, I think we're done."

"Thank fuck," Archer muttered as he released my arm. He gave me no time to recover, though. I let out a small scream of surprise as he twisted and lifted, throwing me over his shoulder in the same motion as he stood up.

"Arch—" I started to protest, then shut the hell up when he smacked my ass. *Hard*. He started striding out of the gym with me over his shoulder.

Kody's shout of protest made Archer pause. "Hey, what the hell, man?"

"Sorry, bro," Archer replied with a snicker, "my expertise doesn't come for free, you know." He was teasing, obviously, implying that he needed to be paid in sex for his sparring time.

Kody folded his arms, glaring. "Arch—"

My fingernails dug into Archer's sides and excitement fluttered through my upside-down belly. "Archer, play fair. Kody called dibs this morning."

In all honesty, I knew there was no freaking way Archer was going to back down and hand me over to Kody. For one thing, I wasn't a damn sack of flour. For another, his big-dick energy was already kicked into high gear and he might legitimately explode if forced to shove it all back in a box.

So yeah, I was messing with him. But also, Kody was giving me *that* look that gave me all kinds of naughty ideas. Sometimes Kodiak Jones and I were damn near sharing a brain.

"Fine," Archer snapped, a frustrated growl threading through his voice. He started walking again with me still slung over his shoulder. "Are you coming or what, Kody?"

Fuck yeah. That was easier than expected.

Kody's satisfied chuckle followed us as Archer all but ran up to his room, then dumped me onto his bed. I was still sweeping my sweaty hair back from my face when Kody entered the room and kicked the door shut behind him.

"Well, this is an interesting turn of events." I leaned back on my hands and eyed the two of them. They were both hard, their choice of clothing doing nothing to hide that fact, and I licked my lips.

"Fucking hell," Kody muttered. He crossed the distance between us and grabbed my face in his hands. His lips met mine in a flurry of desire, his tongue tangling in my mouth in a way that told me exactly how this was all going to play out. Archer might think he was the biggest alpha-hole in the house, but Kody was no beta.

Fuck me. I was in for a rough ride with these two, that was for damn sure.

"Get that bra off," Archer ordered, moving to his nightstand, then pulling the drawer open.

Kody released my lips, and we exchanged a grin as I lifted my arms up and he stripped my tight crop top off to leave my breasts bare. He tossed the garment aside, then cupped my breasts with a soft groan.

"Your tits are insane, babe," he murmured. "I think about them way too fucking often."

I grinned and arched my back to push into his hands a little more. I loved having his hands all over me.

Archer returned to us with a wicked look on his face and something in his hands. "Wrists, Princess," he ordered, and I dutifully extended my hands to him.

He bucked a thick leather band around each of my wrists, like mini-belts with a metal loop on the outside of each. Kody perched on the bed beside me, watching with curiosity while Archer fastened the straps.

"I'm so fucking intrigued right now," he murmured as he adjusted his erection. "I always knew you were a kinky fuck, Arch."

Archer scoffed a laugh. "Right. Last I checked, I wasn't the one getting metal shoved through my dick."

Kody cringed and I grinned. "Don't knock it till you try it," I purred, inspecting my new bracelets. "But what are we doing with these?"

Archer smirked. "Wait and see."

"Oh," Kody murmured with a short laugh. "Archer's playing that game."

I scowled. "What game?"

Kody shrugged. "Your curiosity is insane, babe. He's gonna drive you nuts wondering what those cuffs are for. Probably nothing." He shot Archer an amused look. "Or maybe something. Guess you'll have to be patient to find out."

I wanted to yowl. Those bastards! Total psychological warfare going on in this house today. Still, I couldn't deny how well they'd read me. I needed to turn the tables on them and regain some power. Apparently, we all had a healthy dose of alpha bullshit in us.

Sliding off the bed and onto my knees in front of Archer, I ignored the intriguing cuffs around my wrists. I peered up at him through my lashes as I hooked my fingers under his waistband. His cock was huge and hard, straining against the tight fabric, but I hesitated a moment.

"You sure you're okay with this, Sunshine?" I gave him one last chance to back out. "I think Kody and I both know you're not into the sharing aspect of this relationship. No hard feelings if you want to back out now."

But because I played dirty, I placed a lingering kiss on his dick through the fabric of his shorts, just to push his decision in my favor. It worked too. His hands moved to my head, encouraging me to keep going even as he let out a frustrated growl.

"It's fine," he muttered. "I'm fine with this."

Kody and I both snickered at the same time. "Liar," I accused.

Archer scowled down at me, but his eyes glittered with desire and his cock twitched as I let my warm breath tease him. "Fine, then I'm curious enough to let this play out...*once*. Keep questioning me and I'll change my damn mind and kick Kody out now." His brow twitched with the threat, and I bit back a smile.

"Works for me." I peeled his shorts down to free his erection. Kody muttered something under his breath and shifted on the bed behind me. His shorts hit the floor a second later, as my hand circled Archer's shaft, so I took that as his consent as well. Not that Kody's willingness to share had ever been in question.

"Princess." Archer grabbed my hair by the base of my ponytail. "If you don't open your fucking mouth soon…"

There was no need for him to finish that sentence. I eagerly parted my lips and swiped my tongue over the head of his dick.

Archer let out a small groan, his grip on my hair guiding me as I took him farther into my mouth, sucking and licking at him like his cock were made of candy. It may as well have been, as badly as I was addicted to the damn thing.

"Fuck yes," he murmured on an exhale when I swallowed him deeper, taking him into my throat.

Kody shifted to stand with his own erection in his hand, and I reached out to wrap my fingers around him. Whoever said I couldn't multitask?

One of them—or both of them—let out a moan as I went to town, sucking Archer off while my hand worked over Kody. A moment later, Archer gave my hair a tug, pulling out of my mouth and nudging me toward Kody.

If my mouth hadn't been quickly filled by Kody's huge cock, I would have smiled. Apparently, Archer could play nicely with others…given the right incentive.

Still, Archer kept control of my head with his strong fingers wrapped around my ponytail as he forced me to take Kody deeper. Then he grunted when my fingers tightened on his dick.

"Fuck me," Kody whispered on an exhale. "I need to taste you, babe. Get on the bed."

I did *not* need to be told twice. I scrambled up off the floor but barely made it halfway up the bed before one of them grabbed the waistband of my yoga pants. A second later the stretchy fabric was stripped—along with my panties—down my legs in one fluid movement. Then I found myself smoothly flipped onto my back.

My breath caught in my throat as I eyed the two of them. They both stood there at the foot of the bed, shoulder to shoulder, stark naked, with their impressive dicks hard and on display in front of them. If I didn't know any better, I'd question if I was in some sort of coma with my imagination running wild. Because, seriously, I was living every girl's wet dream.

By some unspoken agreement, they each placed a knee on the bed, and my heart pounded faster. The hungry way their eyes traveled over my naked body was driving me wild with anticipation, and then there was still the leather cuffs around my wrists...

"Babe," Kody murmured, trailing his fingers up my leg. He kissed the inside of my knee, then nudged my legs apart. "Have I told you lately how sexy you are?"

I let out a moan as he kissed his way up my inner thigh, but I couldn't respond. Archer claimed my mouth in a bruising kiss that stole my breath away and made my pulse race. When Kody's mouth found my core, I gasped into Archer's kiss.

Archer took that as an invitation to kiss me harder, his huge hand cupping my face possessively as he dominated my mouth, and I leaned into him eagerly.

Kody's tongue found my clit, circling it teasingly before flicking over the sensitive flesh and making me moan. He just chuckled, his fingers digging into my thighs as he spread me wider and feasted on my pussy.

As Kody's tongue moved down to my soaking core, Archer broke away from our kiss to watch what his friend was doing between my legs. For a moment, he seemed mesmerized, watching Kody tongue-fuck me as I tried my absolute best not to writhe around. It wasn't fucking easy, though. Especially with Archer watching.

Fucking hell. Kody was right. I needed all three of them in bed with me...sooner rather than later.

"You're so fucking responsive, Princess," Archer murmured, his face dipping to my breast even as his eyes remained glued to Kody's mouth between my legs. He sucked one of my hard nipples into my mouth, and I shuddered, proving his point. When I grasped his head between my hands, he took hold of my leather-clad wrists and moved them over my head. The way he pushed them into the mattress told me on no uncertain terms *don't move these*.

He was far from done, though. His hand smoothed over my stomach, his fingers tracing the ridge of my scar before moving lower. When his index finger found my clit, I died.

"Arch," I gasped, squirming in need while fighting to keep my hands where he'd put them. He was teasing me—he was fucking *teasing* me. His fingertip stroked over my clit ever so lightly; then he just skirted around it. Mother*fucker*, I couldn't handle much more of that torture.

"Yes?" He traced his tongue around my nipple.

Kody turned his face and bit the inside of my thigh playfully as he slipped two fingers into me. I bucked against him, and he snickered.

"MK wants to know what the cuffs are for," he translated for me, guessing my thoughts exactly. "Don't you, babe?" His fingers pumped in and out of me, and I writhed with a low moan.

"Is that right, Kate?" Archer murmured, the pad of his thumb pressing down on my clit and making me gasp. "You wanna know what they're for?"

I nodded, my breathing coming faster as he and Kody toyed with me.

"Maybe they're just decoration," Archer suggested with a smirk.

I narrowed my eyes at him. "Bullshit."

His grin spread wider. "Ask nicely, baby girl."

I groaned a protest, even though I secretly loved it. "Pretty please, Archer, tell me what the cuffs are for."

"That's more like it," he told me with pure, cursed condescension. I glowered and he smirked. But he *did* shift off the bed to open the nightstand drawer again.

201

Kody shot me a curious look, climbing up my body to lie beside me. His fingers slipped back into my pussy when he was comfortable, and I groaned under his touch.

"Weren't you supposed to have clients today, Kodiak Jones?" I mumbled as his thumb found my clit and my back arched off the bed. Fuck me, I wanted to come so damn hard, but I wanted to do it with one, or *both*, of them inside me.

Kody scoffed a laugh. "And miss this? Hell no. I think it's about fucking time I cut back on my client list anyway."

Archer moved in my peripheral vision, but before I could turn my head to see what he was up to, Kody grabbed my lips in a demanding kiss. His fingers worked faster between my legs, and I moaned against his mouth, almost missing the click and tug of my cuffs being clipped together.

Almost, but not quite. It was pretty much what I'd expected, that the metal loops would allow them to be joined. What I *didn't* expect was that when Kody let up on me with a mischievous grin, Archer took his place, dropping a rough kiss against my lips, then biting my earlobe.

"Get on your knees, baby girl." His order was husky in my ear, and I shivered with excitement. With my wrists bound, he needed to lift me up; then when I was balanced on my knees, he lifted my arms over my head...then clipped my cuffs to another chain hanging from the canopy of his bed.

My lips parted in shock as I looked up, then back at Archer. "What..."

He just grinned, kissed me, then reached across to a cord beside the bed. He yanked my arms higher, so I could only barely reach the bed with my knees.

"Ho-ly *shit*." Kody murmured his approval, reclining beside me on the bed. I was dead center on my knees, my arms extended so far I couldn't move even if I'd wanted to. I was also wetter than Niagara Falls. "I'm so down with this."

Archer flashed his friend a grin, then turned his attention back to me. "How about you, baby girl? You down with this?"

I let out a frustrated groan. "I will be once you show me what you have in mind here."

He huffed a laugh, then spun me around on the bed so I faced Kody with Archer's hands on my hips. "Spread your legs, Princess." His whisper in my ear sent pulsing waves of desire straight to my cunt, and I obediently slid my knees wider on the mattress.

Archer's hand moved around to the front of me, found my pussy, and spread me wide, giving Kody a prime view from his position. Something he clearly appreciated, if I were to judge by the way he groaned and stroked his cock.

"Yeah," Kody murmured, mostly to himself, "yeah, this is worth losing a few clients." He shifted against Archer's pillows and lazily fisted his erection. He watched with hungry eyes as Archer lined himself up with my pussy from behind and pushed his way inside *slowly*.

It was a damn good thing I was suspended from the chains above us because that was the only thing keeping me upright as Archer filled me up with his cock and played with my clit. By the time he'd fully seated himself in me, I was panting and cursing unintelligible words. I was already so damn close to coming from Kody playing with me that Archer was going to send me over the edge in no time at all.

"Kate," Archer rumbled in my ear, his lips tugging on my earlobe, "don't fucking come until I tell you to."

I shuddered out a laugh, letting the cuffs take my weight as he began to move, fucking me slowly as his fingers explored my clit. Kody still watched, jerking himself, and his eyes on me made every sensation a hundred times more intense.

"What's funny, Princess?" Archer growled, his teeth nipping my neck.

"You," I replied with a lust-filled snicker. "Telling me not to come. It's cute 'cause that's totally not how it works."

Archer stilled, his cock buried deep inside me. Kody's grin spread wide, and he shook his head like he could hardly believe I was back-talking while suspended by my wrists from the ceiling.

Fuck it, if they wanted a sub to play with, they'd better get used to handling a bratty one. But I thought it was painfully clear I'd make a shitty submissive.

"I'll come when I damn well want to, Husband dearest," I told Archer in a low, seductive voice while I locked eyes with Kody. "Then I'll come again and again...and if you're doing things right—"

My words broke off as Archer grabbed my face, tilting my head back to claim my mouth in a harsh kiss that made my pussy tighten around his cock. Yeah, he knew I was right.

My point was proven only a few moments later when he caved and started fucking me again, harder and faster than before. My cuffs rattled above us, and I moaned long and loud as I came, my internal muscles clenching and fluttering around him.

"Jesus fucking Christ," Kody breathed as my orgasm tailed off and Archer's hands swept up to clasp my breasts. "How secure did you make that?" He jerked his head up at the chain connected to my wrists.

Archer scoffed, his fingers kneading my breasts as I shuddered through a couple of little orgasm aftershocks. "What do you fucking take me for, bro?"

Laughing, Kody rose to his knees in front of me, then reached up to tug on the chain connected to my wrists. "Just checking. Now fuck off and give me a turn before my balls drop off from frustration."

I half expected Archer to refuse, but instead he just tugged my head back for another deep kiss before withdrawing out of my pussy. "Fine," he muttered, "but I put you in this position for a reason, baby girl." He winked, then Kody's fingers were threading into my hair, pulling my face back to his.

"Hey, babe?" he whispered against my lips as he positioned his dick against my cunt.

"Mmm?" I murmured back. I wanted to push my hips forward and sink down onto him but lacked enough range of motion.

His lips, still brushing against mine, curved in a smile as he slipped just the tip inside me. Fucking tease.

"I love you, MK," he whispered in a husky voice, then filled me up with one swift thrust. I groaned, long and low as he stretched me out. All my boys were blessed in the pants department, but Kody held the top spot. Had I not already been soaked from coming on Archer's dick, there was no way he'd have had such an easy passage.

"Fuck," I breathed as his hands gripped my hips and he started fucking me. Archer was up to something, though, and the fact that I couldn't *see* him was driving me crazy. I could hope, though…

Archer didn't keep me waiting long. The mattress dipped as he returned, and his hot breath feathered my spine as he took position behind me. Every damn nerve was lit up with anticipation, waiting for him to take that final step in our three-way. *Come on, Sunshine…*

I moaned as Kody's thrusts slowed and tipped my head to the side to let him kiss my neck while Archer's hand smoothed over the curve of my ass. Fuck yes. *Yes!*

"You want me to fuck your ass, don't you?" he rumbled with an edge of amusement. "You're mentally cursing me out and *begging* for it right now. I can see it written all over you, Princess."

I moaned but didn't disagree. He was spot-on.

"Say it out loud, baby girl," he urged me, even as his fingers parted my cheeks. A cold drip of lube ran down my crack, and I almost convulsed.

"Yes," I panted. "Yes, fuck, yes, Arch…" I whimpered as he teased the lube over my ass. Kody had all but paused, his cock fully seated in me and his hips only moving with minimal thrusts as if to keep himself sane while he waited. Meanwhile, it was driving me *in*sane.

"Archer," I groaned, "please, please, Arch, fuck my ass. Please, I need to feel you both inside me. I need you to stretch me out, fuck me raw, fill me with cum…" My words dissolved into a gasp as he pushed his finger into me and spread the lube around. He pumped that finger a couple of times, then added another and made me see goddamn fucking stars.

"Please, Arch," I moaned. "Please, I need your dick. Please…"

Kody grabbed my face, kissing my words away like he was jealous of me panting his friend's name, but I'd said enough. A moment later, Archer swapped his fingers for his cock, and I cried out against Kody's kiss.

It took a couple of seconds for Archer to push all the way in; then I had to send a mental thanks to how strong his chains were. My whole body had gone limp, and only the cuffs on my wrists held me upright.

When the two of them started moving, taking turns to thrust in and out of me, I turned into a quivering, boneless heap. A lightning- fast orgasm stole through me, making me scream and shake, but they didn't even pause. If anything, they fucked me harder all the way through my climax, then even harder still until I came again.

Kody grunted curses as my cunt tightened around him, over and over, and my muscles spasmed. His pace faltered, and he pulled out without coming, making me squeak a protest.

"Chill, babe," he laughed. "I'm like three seconds from coming, all right?"

I licked my lips, trying to regain enough moisture to form words, but his intention became clear a second later as he stood up on the mattress and shoved his hot cock into my mouth.

"Fucking hell," Archer muttered as I sucked Kody's dick greedily, moaning around his girth.

Archer's grip tightened on my hips, and he screwed my ass with punishing thrusts as Kody's hands yanked my hair, fucking my throat in synchronicity. A moment later, Kody's hips jerked and his hot seed hit the back of my throat. I swallowed, moaning, then licked his entire length as he withdrew.

"Shit," Archer grunted. "I'm gonna come in your ass, baby girl." It was a statement, not a request, and I panted my encouragement.

Kody sank back to his knees, holding my gaze as Archer's dick rammed me. He reached down, found my clit, and rubbed furiously as Archer cried out his climax. I shuddered, coming again as Kody's fingers worked me over, then let myself hang limp from the cuffs.

Holy. Shit.

CHAPTER 23

Kody decided to blow off his entire day of work, then made some calls to find replacement trainers for a few clients. He'd been thinking about doing it for a while. After Steele had been shot, he'd started taking extra precautions, but I was still glad. This meant even less opportunity for someone to shoot at him while we were split up.

We gave Anna the night off—after she insisted on hand-making our pizzas rather than letting us order in—and made sure the whole house was locked down before settling into the den. The boys played Xbox on either end of the sofa while I snuggled between them texting Bree.

"How'd she do with her ankle surgery?" Kody asked, peering over at my phone when Archer killed his character *again.*

"Sounds like it went well," I replied, showing him the smiling picture of Bree and Dallas with a big bunch of flowers. "She got the flowers we sent."

Kody made a thoughtful sound. "They look good together."

Archer tossed his controller onto the table and slouched back on the sofa. "Bree and her flowers?"

Kody rolled his eyes. "Bree and Dallas. I wouldn't have picked those two as a match, spoiled rich brat and gangster ex-con. But they work."

I smiled, agreeing, but Archer just scoffed as his fingers massaged my calves. "Please, they were destined for each other. Sheltered rich girls can never resist an inked-up bad boy. Right, Princess?" He shot me a smug look, and I jabbed him in the ribs with my toe.

"Arrogance is a bad look on you, Sunshine," I replied in a tart voice, leaning my shoulders into Kody as he looped an arm around me.

Archer grinned. "Don't lie; my arrogance is hot as hell."

I rolled my eyes but didn't deny it. "Well anyway, that reminds me, Bree's worried about Dallas and his obligations to the Wraiths. I told her I'd talk to you guys about it because I can't think of a solution."

Archer cocked a brow at me as his thumbs rubbed a particularly sore spot above my knee. "You think we can get Dallas out of his oath to Charon?"

I shrugged. "He *is* your uncle, and you've got him under your thumb, don't you?"

Archer shook his head. "He's my uncle by blood only, and he's nowhere near under my thumb. He just has enough self-preservation that he won't piss me off."

I sighed, understanding. "I get it. You don't mess around in his business, and he steers clear of yours. But there has to be some way to help Dallas out. He's likely to end up getting killed before his baby is even born."

The guys exchanged a look; then Archer grimaced. "I don't know that we need to be borrowing trouble right now, Kate."

My sound of protest was cut off when Kody added, "What about a tradeout? It's happened before."

Archer frowned, thinking, then shook his head. "We have no one to offer, and Moore wouldn't be any better off with the Reapers. Worse, even."

Kody sighed. "Good point. Zane would jump at the chance to make an example out of him. I'm guessing that's what Ferryman is doing too. Dallas has made it way too obvious he's loyal to MK over anyone else."

I cringed. "I can imagine that's a pretty big no-no in gangs."

"Yeah, you could say that," Archer murmured. "Leave it to me; I'll have to think about it, okay? I still don't fucking like Moore, and I trust him even less. But I can see Bree's happiness is important to you..." He ground the words out like it caused him physical pain to be a nice person. It was cute as hell.

Grinning, I slipped out of Kody's embrace and climbed on top of Archer to crush my mouth against his in a grateful kiss.

"Thank you, Sunshine," I whispered when our kiss ended, my arms still tight around his neck and his banded around my waist. "I promise, Dallas and Bree deserve our help. We need more allies anyway, right?"

Archer grumbled a noise but kissed me again in response.

"You guys keep that up and we're gonna have to test Archer's willingness to share again," Kody warned, giving me a sly grin when I looked over at him.

Archer huffed, then shocked the damn pants off me. "I'm not against the idea," he muttered as he dipped his face to kiss my neck.

I swallowed a gasp of surprise and shook my head. "You're in a rare mood, Archer D'Ath," I commented with a laugh. "But it'll have to wait. Our *lovely* wedding planner is calling in around twenty minutes, remember?"

Archer sucked lightly on my neck, making me groan. "So what you're saying, *Wifey*, is that we need to make you come in less than fifteen minutes? That's easily doable."

I laughed, then pushed back from him with my hands flat on his chest. "Did you get fucking body snatched or something?"

"Also, we don't even have fifteen," Kody added, checking his phone. "Zed's on his way over now to discuss floorplans and artillery."

Archer let out a long sigh, then ruffled his ink-black hair with his fingers. "Fine," he growled. "To be continued."

My brows flicked up, but I nodded anyway. I sure as hell wasn't saying no when he was in a sharing mood. My pussy was already damp in anticipation of *later*.

"If we're expecting company, I better get dressed," I said with a sigh, then reluctantly climbed out of Archer's lap. I was wearing just a baggy T-shirt—one of Kody's—and hot pants underneath—good enough when it was just the three of us but probably not acceptable for company.

I hurried up the stairs, and the doorbell rang before I reached my bedroom. By the time I'd changed into jeans and put a bra on, I'd already missed half of the discussion with Zed. Not that I fully understood what was going on anyway.

They all sat at the dining table with blueprints of our wedding venue—a nondenominational chapel on the north side of Shadow Grove—spread out between them. They were discussing choke points and lines of sight, and within around two minutes, they'd totally lost me. Which was fine because I wasn't going to make them sit there and explain it all to me. I didn't *need* a crash course in the tactics of an ambush. I just needed *them* to know what they were doing.

I had one role at this wedding.

Bait.

I tuned back in when Zed nodded his head at me. "What precautions have you put in place for your girl?" His question was aimed at Archer, even if his cold, assessing gaze was on me. "She can't exactly wear Kevlar. First fucking clue that the wedding is a sham, when the bride arrives in a bulletproof vest."

"I'm glad we agree on that point," I murmured, giving Archer an *I told you so* look.

He rolled his eyes and exhaled heavily. "We're still working on it," he admitted reluctantly. "For now, we just need to focus on ensuring all vantage points are covered by our men so there's no opportunity for Kate to be shot by a ranged weapon. Clear?"

Zed jerked a nod. "Clear. We want to bait the trap, not throw food to the rats." His phone vibrated on the table, and his brows twitched up. "Excuse me, I need to take this. Boss doesn't like voice-mail." He rolled his eyes; then brought his phone to his ear. "Hades."

That was all he said in greeting, and then he listened in silence as Hades spoke on the other end. Eventually, his eyes flicked up at Kody and a grin arched across his lips. "Yes, sir," he finally said into the phone. "I'll tell him."

He ended the call and cleared his throat.

"Tell me *what*?" Kody asked suspiciously.

Zed smirked. "Hades watched surveillance footage from the car crash. Wanted to tell you that your aim has improved vastly over the years 'cause you used to be a lousy shot."

Kody scowled. "I was not."

Zed glared. "You fucking were. Remember when you shot *me*?"

Archer snickered. "I forgot about that."

Kody was sulking now, though. His arms were folded tightly over his chest as he glared back at Zed. "It was only a graze, you big baby. Steele has since fine-tuned my skills."

"How is he doing anyway?" Zed dropped the teasing edge from his voice. "That was a close fucking call."

"Too close," I murmured, shuddering as I remembered the light fading from his eyes right after the bullet struck his chest.

Archer grunted his agreement. "He was lucky, that's for fuck-ing sure. I sent an extra guy to tail his ass while he's with his parents for Rachel's memorial."

Zed grimaced. "I forgot about that. I'll send a donation in Hades's name when I get back to the office." He gave me a tight smile, then pushed his chair back and gathered up all the papers from the table. "It's a good plan, boys. Just work out how you're protecting your girl on the day."

With a nod, Zed left the dining room just as my phone rang. I grimaced when I read the display.

Heaving a sigh, I answered the call and clicked the speaker-phone button. "Hi, Alyssa," I greeted my wedding planner.

"Madison Kate!" She all but sang my name, and I cringed. "My beautiful bride! Are you getting excited? There's only two weeks to go!"

Archer gave me a smug grin across the dining table, and I flipped him off. Kody had gone to see Zed out of the house and reset the perimeter alarms, so I decided to share the fun.

"I'm *so* excited," I fake gushed, giving Archer a wicked smile. "Actually, I have you on speaker and Archer is here too. Say hi to Alyssa, honey."

He extended his middle finger back at me. "Hi, Alyssa," he said, though, holding my gaze. "I can't tell you how much I'm looking forward to this day. It feels like I've been waiting to make this gorgeous girl mine for *years*."

There was a thread of total sincerity to his statement, despite the act we were putting on for our wedding planner, and my insides turned to mush.

Alyssa squealed in excitement on the phone, then launched into a whole spiel about various spreadsheets she'd created to help manage all the details of our *big day*.

I tuned her out for the most part because Archer was eye-fucking me across the table and making it damn near impossible to concentrate. I only tuned back in when I realized Alyssa had asked a question that required my response.

My cheeks heated with embarrassment. "Sorry, I missed what you said there," I admitted. "The line broke up a bit." *Lies.*

"Oh, I'm so sorry. I'm driving, so maybe I went through a patch of bad reception," she replied with a small laugh. "I asked about your bridesmaid? I know your best friend was in a horrible accident, but did you have the name of her replacement for me?"

I blinked down at the phone, my mind blanking. I hadn't even given it a second thought since our first meeting.

"I'll email it over to you," Archer smoothly offered. "Did you need anything else from us, Alyssa?"

"Oh yes, let me think." She hummed a tune for a second, then snapped her fingers. "Right. Rehearsal dinner—"

"We're not having one," Archer cut her off with a firm voice.

"Oh." Alyssa sounded totally gobsmacked. "But—"

"I'm sorry; I should have told you sooner. But we have an intimate family dinner planned. My girl hasn't seen her father for several months, you see? So we just want to make the night before our wedding a really special *family* moment. You understand, of course."

I couldn't fight the smile creeping over my lips as Archer reached over and ended the call on my phone.

"Family dinner, huh?" I asked him with narrowed eyes.

He shrugged. "What better wedding present for my bride than a pound of flesh?"

I groaned, letting my eyes roll back. "You say the sweetest things sometimes, Husband."

An evil smirk played over his lips. "Come over here and I'll show you just how sweet I can really be." His eyes flashed, and his hand moved under the table as he leaned back in his chair.

Fucking hell. With an offer like that...I didn't even bother pushing my chair back. I just climbed directly over the table and into his lap. We could spare a couple of minutes for a quickie.

Or a not so quickie, as it turned out.

214

CHAPTER 24

Later that night, Steele called me. I grabbed my slices of cold pizza that I'd just swiped from the fridge and told the guys I was going to my room. As much as I was loving having the whole day with Archer and Kody, I wanted to talk to Steele alone.

"Hey, you," I murmured, answering his call on my way up to my room. "I thought I might have heard from you sooner than this."

His heavy sigh gusted down the phone. "I'm sorry, Hellcat." His voice was thick and his words slightly slurred. "I wanted to call… You're all I can think about."

I closed my bedroom door behind me and made my way over to my bed. "Max…are you drunk?"

He yawned. "Yup. Super drunk. Told you I would be."

My heart hurt for him. This weekend with his parents was clearly painful, and I badly wanted to be there.

"Steele…" I trailed off with a sigh of frustration and flopped down onto my bed. "Can I ask you something?"

He hiccupped. "You can ask me anything, beautiful."

"How come your parents never came to the hospital? You almost died, Max, and they never even came to see you." I swallowed heavily, knowing I was picking at an open wound. I wanted to understand him better, though. I wanted to know what had happened between Steele and his parents that they cared so little for him, because I couldn't imagine how it was even possible when I loved him so hard it hurt.

Steele let out a small groan, and I could picture him running his hand over his face. "The short answer? They're bad people. It's why I don't want you meeting them, Hellcat. Maybe they're not bad enough to deserve a bullet to the head and a trip to Benny's... but I don't want them in our life."

Our life.

Sorrow rippled through me at the bitterness in his tone, but I understood. Apparently none of us had much luck in the parent department. Maybe that's why we all fit together so well.

"Can I play for you?" Steele asked, changing the subject. "My dad tried to force me to play at the memorial earlier, and I told him to get fucked. But Rachel used to love when I played for her... Can I play for you tonight instead?"

"Of course you can," I whispered, getting comfortable against my pillows to listen.

There was a short pause, I imagined while he was getting to a piano; then he hiccupped again and groaned. "Mixing wine and spirits was probably a bad idea," he mumbled, almost to himself. "Or maybe it was the half bottle of tequila. Something like that. Eh, anyway. I'm in the hotel lobby," he told me with a short laugh. "Apparently I don't care who else hears me play so long as I'm playing for you."

When he started playing, I sucked in a gasp and bit my lip. "Max..." I groaned. "I know this tune."

He gave a small laugh, his breath heavy like he was trying to balance the phone between his shoulder and ear while he played. Apparently being drunk hadn't impacted his coordination.

"I should hope so," he murmured back. "I finished writing it,

216

though. Even gave it a name…first time I've ever named one of my own songs. Usually Rachel named them."

My chest ached at the sorrow and pain in his voice as he spoke of his dead sister. It was no wonder why he'd had his back ink done to honor her memory.

"So, what's it called?" I asked gently, wrapping my arm around myself like the hug I wanted to give him.

He huffed a short laugh. "'Release.'"

I laughed. "Seriously?"

I could hear the grin in his voice as he replied. "Absolutely. I couldn't have thought of a better name to reflect the emotion behind this piece if I tried."

I grinned like an idiot up at my blank ceiling. I held fond memories of the *release* I'd found when he first played this tune for me over the phone.

This time, though, I just lay there and listened, absorbing every note, every keystroke, every raw emotion that Steele poured into his music in a way I'd never heard before.

Angry male voices interrupted the serenity of Steele's music a moment later, though, and the song cut off abruptly as the phone line clattered like he'd just dropped his device.

I sat up in a panic. My ears strained to hear what was being shouted but couldn't make out the words. All I could hear were raised voices from at least two men, then a woman's scream.

Fuck. *Fuck.* Max was in trouble.

"Max!" I shouted, despite how futile it was when he clearly wasn't holding his phone anymore. "Steele! Hey, what's going on? Max!"

A second later, the line clattered again, and a heavy sigh reached my ears, followed by a muttered curse from Steele. "Sorry, Hellcat," he murmured with a groan. "Apparently my father needed a lesson in manners."

Cold anxiety washed through me, mixed with relief. It wasn't an assassination attempt, only his dad. Fuck me.

"What happened?" I asked in a strangled whisper, my pulse still racing.

Steele made a hissing sound, like he'd hurt himself. "I knocked his ass out," he mumbled. "If that doesn't send the message that I'm *done* with this family, I don't know what will."

Oh, shit. Steele's voice practically dripped venom and despair, like he could hardly believe he'd finally been pushed that far. He was hurting so damn much, and I should have been there for him.

"Come home, Max," I whispered, my voice choked as tears for his pain streamed down my cheeks. "Come home to us, please?"

"Yeah," he said on another heavy sigh, like the weight of the damn world was on his shoulders. "Yeah, I'm leaving now. I'll be home by morning, Hellcat."

The relief that his words brought me was staggering. If I hadn't been sitting, I would have fallen. "I love you, Max," I told him, my voice firm and my words heartfelt. "I fucking love you. Come home safe."

"I will, Hellcat," he murmured, his breathing labored as I guessed he was making his way back up to his room. "I love you more."

With that declaration, the call dropped out. He'd likely just stepped into the elevator, but it didn't matter. He was coming home, and he loved me. That was *all* that mattered.

After my phone call with Steele, I couldn't sleep. After way too long tossing and turning in my big, *empty* bed, I gave up and climbed out again. I couldn't sleep alone anymore, and I was kidding myself to think otherwise.

Tucking my arms around myself, I padded down the hall and checked both Kody's and Archer's rooms, finding them empty. Curious—because it was well past midnight—I went to find them.

First place I checked was the gym. Sure enough, Archer was in there with his music blasting as he rained blows on his BOB training dummy. He had another big fight coming up the week after our "wedding," provided we all lived that long. It was no surprise to find him squeezing in a late-night training session.

"Kate," he grunted when he spotted me. "Are you okay? What's wrong?" He lifted the front of his shirt to wipe sweat from his face, and I tried *really* hard not to drool.

"I'm fine," I replied with a smile. "Just couldn't sleep. I won't interrupt you, though. Keep going."

He gave me a worried frown for a moment, then jerked a nod. "Kody's in the office if you're looking for him."

I flashed him a reassuring smile. "Cool. I'll find him." I nodded to his training dummy. "Keep working; you gotta win that fight if you wanna chain me up again."

Archer's jaw dropped. "What? Princess, that's three weeks away! You're not serious."

I laughed and exited the gym without answering him. I definitely *wasn't* serious, but he didn't need to know that. It was too fun messing with him.

The last time I'd stepped foot in the "office," I'd thought it was my father's. I'd thought that he owned this house and that the boys were simply freeloading off his wealth. Now I understood it was the other way around, and the guys had pretty much erased what minimal signs of Samuel Danvers remained on the property.

Thank fuck for that too.

The lights were on, and I found Kody slouched in the leather office chair with no shirt on as he talked into a headset.

Wait a second. Hold up.

Kody was speaking *Japanese* into his headset, with his computer open in front of him on the desk.

I paused in the doorway, staring at him with impressed shock as he spoke fluent Japanese to whoever was on the other line. When he spotted me there, his lips tugged up in a smile, but he didn't falter in what he was saying.

Instead, he crooked a finger at me, beckoning me closer as he listened to what the response was on his headset.

Intrigued, I made my way across the fancy Persian rug to the corner of his desk. He patted the top of the heavy oak desk beside his laptop like he wanted me to sit right there.

Excitement zapped through me, and I did as he indicated. I sucked a breath and tensed when the cold wood met my bare thighs.

Kody grinned, then clicked something on his computer before quickly rattling off more foreign words to whoever he was speaking to. A quick glance at his screen showed me three people in the conference call with him, one dressed sharply in a suit, the other two more casual in sportswear. Kody's box on the call was blank, and I realized he'd just switched his video feed off.

My eyes widened, and he sat forward in his chair, his hands coming to my thighs. I tensed, ready to swat him away, but he just shook his head and placed a finger over his lips, telling me to be quiet.

Ugh. Fuck. His camera was off, but his microphone wasn't. What had I been thinking, responding to that crook of his finger so easily? Of *course* he was up to no good. He was *always* up to no good.

Fucking Kody.

Still, I couldn't seem to tell *fucking Kody* no. Ever. So when he hooked his fingers under the sides of my panties, I obediently lifted my ass up for him to strip them off my legs.

He continued his conversation with the Japanese people on his screen. He chatted away like it was his native fucking tongue, all while spreading my knees open and taking a long, hungry look at my aching cunt.

His eyes flashed, and he bit his lip. His gaze snapped up to meet mine as his fingers parted me and found my clit. A small moan escaped me, and he quickly brought his finger to his lips to remind me that I needed to be silent.

I clamped my mouth shut, swallowing my whimper, then internally screamed as he licked his finger. He returned it to my throbbing core, pushing into me with a soft exhalation as he laughed about something on his phone call.

My brow creased and my body shook as he slipped a second finger into me. He played as he chatted, but his steady gaze locked on mine told me in no uncertain terms I was not to make noise. That in itself drove me just as wild as the way he fingered me.

When his thumb found my clit, my legs began to shake. He grinned, smug as fuck, and stood up from his chair to clamp a hand over my mouth. Then he really went to work. He fucked me hard and fast with his fingers while I writhed and shuddered silently on his desktop.

When I came, I just about blacked out. The only thing keeping me quiet was the tight grip Kody's hand held over my mouth.

A moment later he released me and sat back in his chair. He held my gaze and sucked his fingers in a way that made me almost come all over again. Fucking Kody. That wasn't fair *at all*.

When he started speaking again, I narrowed my eyes and slipped off the desk—literally *slipped* because the polished wood was all kinds of slick where I'd just been sitting.

My knees hit the carpet in front of his chair, and his brows hitched all the way up. Still, he didn't hesitate to tug his shorts down and free his rock-hard dick for me.

Good boy.

I wrapped my hand around his base, then closed my mouth over his tip. Eager and drenched in arousal, I sucked and licked at the generous smear of precum already lubricating his dick.

His breath hitched, and he stumbled over his next sentence in Japanese, needing to repeat it twice as I took him deeper into my mouth. Yep, payback really was a bitch, huh, Kodiak?

His hand went to my head, his fingers threading into my hair as I worked my mouth up and down his shaft, my fingers around

221

his base, echoing the motion of my lips. His abs tensed, and I glanced up to see his head tossed back and silent curses on his lips. Perfect.

I let my teeth scrape down his soft skin, loving the way his hand tightened in my hair as I did so. He pushed my head down, his cock hitting the back of my throat and choking me a second before he let up.

It was fucked up, but that was one of my favorite things about giving head, when my mouth and throat were so full of cock I could hardly breathe. It turned me on like nothing else, and I found myself bringing my free hand to my pussy.

"Oh fuck," Kody breathed, soft enough that his microphone might not have picked it up, but still… A second later, I got the impression he was ending the call; then he moaned long and loud.

"*Fucking hell*, babe!" he cried out as I swallowed him deeper and played with my own clit. "Holy shit, fuck, you're touching yourself. Goddamn that's hot."

His hips bucked, his hand on my head forcing more and more of his dick down my throat as I gagged and choked; then his laptop let out the distinctive sound of an incoming video call.

"Fuck!" he shouted. "Fuck, shit, *fuck*. Babe, I have to take this call." He tugged on my hair, and I released him from my mouth just long enough to smile wickedly.

"So?" I challenged him. "You started this game. Take the call, Kodiak."

His eyes widened, his brow creasing as I held his gaze and ran my tongue around the tip of his glistening cock.

"Babe, I have to answer with the camera on. It's—"

"Better hurry," I taunted, cutting him off. "They'll think you're not here." I shuffled back a bit until I was mostly under the desk, then pulled him closer on the wheeled chair. Before he could formulate any further protests, I took him back into my mouth, and he let out a curse.

A second later, the call connected, and Kody needed to put on his bravest face while I did everything possible to break him.

But I had thought it was his Japanese business contact calling back about something. So I just about choked in shock when I heard him speak quite clearly in English.

"Hi, Mom," he said loudly, and my fingers around his dick squeezed hard.

"Hi, Kody," a frail-sounding woman replied from the computer. "I'm sorry to keep you up so late. These time zones are such a bear to work out."

"Totally fine," he replied. He sounded a bit like he was gritting his teeth, and I didn't totally blame him, all things considered. I tried to back off, deciding it *wasn't* cool to suck his dick while his mom was on video chat, but his hand tightened on the back of my head. The implication was clear. He was calling my bluff. "I was up late for a conference call with Tokyo anyway."

Well, two could play at that game. After all...it wasn't *my* mom.

For a few minutes, Kody and his mom chatted about his business with Tokyo. Apparently that call that I'd walked in on had been discussing the sportswear line Kody had mentioned weeks ago. It would be launched in Japan in a couple of months, then expand to the rest of the world.

I listened with curiosity, delighting in the strain to his voice as he tried to converse normally while I was giving him the blow job of his damn life.

Then his mom said something that almost killed me.

"Are you okay, Kody? You look a bit funny. Are you sweating?"

I snorted a laugh, thankful for my gag to stifle the sound, but the way Kody bucked his hips told me he knew I'd laughed.

"Yeah, fine, Mom," he replied. "Just pulled a muscle earlier in the gym, that's all."

"Oh, that's no good, honey," she replied, sympathetic. "You'll need to get a massage. Maybe this new girlfriend of yours can help out?" There was an edge to her voice that suggested she was fishing for information, and I froze. "When do I get to meet her anyway? You always tell me so much about her; I'm dying to meet the magnificent Madison Kate."

Oh god. What? Kody tells his *mom* about me? He's never even *mentioned* his parents to me!

"Actually," Kody replied with a small laugh, "she's right here."

What?

"She is?" his mom replied. "Where? Can I say hello?"

"Um," Kody murmured, giving a small grunt as I threatened him with my teeth. "She can't talk right now," he finally said. "Her mouth is a bit full."

Oh my lord, I'm going to murder him.

"Really?" His mom sounded confused. "Bit late for a snack, isn't it?"

Kill me now.

There was a scraping sound on the desk, like a pen on paper; then Kody handed a scrap of notepaper down to me.

Make yourself come, babe.

"Yeah, we've been keeping weird hours lately," Kody lied to his mom as both of his hands threaded into my hair. "I've been training MK in the gym, so she stayed up late with me to do my Zoom calls."

His hands forced my face back down, filling my throat with his dick as I obediently slipped my fingers back between my legs. Damn him, I was soaked and needy, despite the fact that his mom was on the line.

"That's nice of her," his mom said. She sounded pleased that her son had such a thoughtful girlfriend. Whatever else she said was muffled as Kody controlled my head, fucking my face faster as he approached his orgasm. He'd given me an order, though, and I knew he intended for me to follow through before he would.

I found my clit with my fingers, rubbing furiously as he punished my throat. It only took seconds before I shattered. Fuck it, if his mom heard me, then it was his own damn fault. I moaned my release, shuddering and convulsing on my knees under the desk as Kody's hips started bucking.

His hot load hit the back of my throat only moments later, his shaft so deep in my mouth that my hand had slipped down to his balls. Still, he managed to keep quiet as he came. He just clenched his teeth—along with every other muscle in his body—until he finished with an exhale.

When he finally released my hair, I collapsed under the desk in a boneless heap, licking my lips as he finished his call with his mom some minutes later.

As I lay there, I made a mental note: *Don't play sexual chicken with Kody. He will win.*

CHAPTER 25

Steele woke me sometime around dawn with a soft kiss on my cheek and his finger pressed to my lips, telling me to stay quiet. I still smiled wide at the sight of him, despite how rough he looked.

Silently, I slipped out of Kody's sleeping embrace and followed Steele out into the hall, where he swept me up in a hug that took my feet off the floor.

"I missed you, Hellcat," he murmured into my ear, his voice husky.

I grinned into his neck and clung to him like a monkey. "I missed you too, Max. Don't go away that long again, okay?" Even though it had only been three nights…it was too damn long.

He chuckled, then started walking with me still wrapped around him and I let out a squeak in protest.

"Aren't you going to put me down?" I pulled back from his neck so I could glare at him properly.

He just smacked a kiss against my lips. "Nah. I like having your legs wrapped around me."

I rolled my eyes. "Steele, you shouldn't be—"

"I'm *fine*, gorgeous. I promise. Better than ever, okay?" His gaze was serious, and I let the subject drop. I was still worried he was overdoing it; it had barely been a month since he was shot in the chest and nearly died. But even I had to admit that he really did seem back to normal.

"So where are you taking me?" I asked when he bypassed his bedroom and started down the stairs.

His grin spread wider. "I made us breakfast. I'm guessing Arch had a late gym session if he's still asleep now, so I thought I could get you alone for a bit."

I snuggled back into his neck, stupid-level happy to have him home, and he carried me through to the kitchen. On the table, a huge spread was set up with fresh pancakes, fruit, orange juice, coffee…

"Holy shit," I exclaimed as Steele finally placed me on my feet and pulled out a chair for me. "You did all this?"

He gave me a sheepish look. "Anna helped a little bit—but only because she was worried I'd make a mess of her kitchen. Otherwise I would have been totally capable on my own."

"Well, I'm impressed. Who made the coffee?" I gave him a cheeky smile as I tentatively sipped it. It was good, not burnt, and I hummed my appreciation.

"Me," he replied with a smirk. "You know Anna can't work your fancy machine."

I licked my lips, impressed at how far his barista skills had come. "Well, Max Steele," I murmured as he took his seat beside me, rather than across the table, "you're a man of many skills. I'm suitably impressed."

He chuckled, dropping a kiss to my bare shoulder, where Kody's T-shirt had slipped down. "Good. Now eat before Kody and Arch wake up and smell the pancakes."

He had a good point. For about ten minutes, we ate together in a weird little domestic bliss, chatting about light subjects, like Archer's upcoming fight or Kody's clothing line…but eventually I couldn't ignore the elephant in the room much longer.

"Max…" I murmured with a sigh, pushing my plate away because I'd eaten so much I was about to burst. "Can I ask you about last night?"

Steele let out a sigh, his fingers tightening on my knee. He'd sat beside me so he could constantly touch me while we ate, which I was more than okay with.

"Yeah, I figured you might have questions," he admitted with a weak smile. "You want to know what happened with my parents?"

I nodded, my concerned frown pulling my brow as I searched his face. "If you don't want to talk about it—"

He shook his head, cutting me off. "No, it's fine. I want you to know all the parts of me, even the shitty ones." He pushed his own plate away and scrubbed a hand over his face. He looked exhausted, with dark circles under his eyes and longer than usual stubble on his cheeks. The knuckles of his right hand were red and slightly swollen, but it didn't look like he'd done any lasting damage.

"I'll…just keep it brief," he muttered with a bitter smile. "My parents adored Rachel. She was their angel and could do no wrong. Seriously, she could have murdered the family dog right in front of our parents and they'd have blamed me for it."

I wrinkled my nose. "That's not fair."

He shrugged. "I know, but that's how it always was. The *only* thing I could do that would earn even an ounce of my parents' good graces was succeed with piano. I swear, I can still remember the last time my mother actually smiled at me. It was when I won a classical composition contest when I was twelve." He blew out a long breath, shaking his head at the memory. "Anyway, suffice to say, they're just all around shitty humans. When Rachel died on her way to attend my concert, they blamed me…and they haven't stopped. This memorial was a crock of shit. Just an excuse for them to milk their rich friends for sympathy and money."

My jaw clenched as I read between the lines. "Were they ever violent toward you?" My question came out hoarse and full of worry.

He flashed me a sad smile. "Frequently. Until Phillip pulled me into his training camp and I met Arch. Then they were too scared to test me."

"Then I'm fucking glad for whatever led you to Phillip. I'm glad you and Arch met and that you can defend yourself. But your parents—"

"Can go burn in hell for all I care," he cut me off. "I'm done with them, and they no longer have any power over me. I have all the family I will ever need right here under this roof." He leaned in and pressed his lips to mine in a kiss that touched my damn soul.

Family. He included me in that, and it left me totally speechless. Since my mom died, I'd barely even known what that word meant.

"Yo, who made breakfast, then didn't wake me up?" Kody exclaimed, staggering into the kitchen looking all adorable and sleepy. His hair was sticking up all over the place, and his shirt was nowhere to be seen.

Oh wait, it was on me.

"I made breakfast for MK," Steele told him in a dry voice. "You can fucking fend for yourself."

"Lies," Kody scoffed. "You love me too much to make me—" He cut off as he yanked the oven open, then whooped with satisfaction. "Ta-da, see? I knew you cared." He pulled out a whole additional plate of pancakes that had been kept warm in the oven for him.

He brought them over to the table and sat heavily in the chair opposite me while Steele returned his hand to my thigh.

"So," Kody said, smothering his stack in syrup, "what have we been discussing?"

I quirked my brows at the huge pile of pancakes on his plate. "You saving any of those for Arch?"

"Hell no," Kody scoffed. "He needs to stay in shape for his fight anyway."

"Fuck you," the big guy himself rumbled as he slouched into the room, yawning heavily. He pulled out the chair beside Kody and snatched three pancakes off his plate without even bothering to use a fork.

"Hey!" Kody protested, swiping at Archer with his blunt knife, but the bigger guy just growled insults back and guarded his stolen food on a spare plate.

"Fucking children," Steele commented with a laugh.

Archer just rolled his eyes at Steele as he licked syrup from his fingers, then took a huge bite of a rolled-up pancake.

"Actually now that you're all here, we have mail," Steele told us with a grimace. He reached over to the end of the table and pulled an envelope out from under a stack of other, less sinister mail. The handwriting was chillingly familiar, once again, and I groaned.

"Not again," I whined.

"Sorry, Hellcat," Steele murmured, handing the envelope to Kody when he held his hand out for it. "But this time we caught him on camera. Either his inside guy really is gone, or he can't hack through Leon's security."

My brows shot up. "We did?" Steele nodded, and then my hopes soured. "But let me guess. He disguised his identity so we're still no closer to working out who he is?"

Steele shrugged. "Yep. But at least we know our camera feeds are secure now."

"True," I muttered, "silver linings. What is it?" I directed my question to Kody, who had ripped the envelope open and pulled out a single sheet of paper.

"It's…" He trailed off, his eyes scanning the paper before he frowned. "It's a paternity test."

My eyes widened in surprise. "For me?"

Kody shook his head, holding the document out for me to take. "No, for Deb…or more specifically, for Deb's baby just before she was killed. It wasn't Zane's."

The silence that fell over our breakfast table was thick with tension. If my mom's secret pregnancy wasn't Zane's…whose was it? Samuel's? And did that mean Zane was back on the table as a murder suspect?

"Well," I murmured, scanning the document and comprehending very little of the information there, "that's one way to kill the mood over breakfast."

Steele winced. "Sorry, Hellcat."

"Not your fault," I replied with a sigh. "Just a reminder that we're nowhere even close to done with this mess. Do we think Zane might have…" I trailed off with a wince and handed the document over to Archer to read.

"Do we think he could have killed Deb if he found out he wasn't the father?" Archer tilted his head to the side, considering. "Maybe. It depends if he even knew about this, though. This is addressed to Deb, not Zane. There's every chance she had the test done without his knowledge."

I groaned and rubbed at my eyes. "So it could have been Samuel's baby. Which caused Zane to flip his lid and kill my mom, along with the entire household staff, then, I don't even know, come *back* six hours later and let me out of the closet…" I wrinkled my nose. Even knowing Zane, that didn't make sense.

Steele nodded, thinking. "Or it was someone else's baby entirely."

"Fucking hell," Kody muttered, then took another forkful of food.

"Why do I get the feeling my stalker *wants* to help us find my mom's killer?" With a sigh, I dropped my head into my hands. "Which would then mean he doesn't know that we already know Kruger is behind it. This is getting really confusing."

231

Steele's hand moved to my back and rubbed soothing circles. "We'll work it out, Hellcat. You're not in this alone, remember? We'll take care of the assassins *and* Kruger in a little over a week. Then we can deal with the stalker. I give it a month and we'll be free to start over on a tropical island somewhere."

I gave a bitter laugh. "I hate beaches; sand gets everywhere. Can we get some sexy mountain cabin near a lake or waterfall or something?"

Archer shot me a grin across the table. "Somewhere with awesome lightning storms?"

I moaned and nodded enthusiastically. "And snow. I freaking love the snow."

"Sold," Kody announced as he slapped the table. "I'll get my real estate agent onto it. In the meantime, Archer, you're late for training. If you don't win your fight in two weeks, MK isn't gonna give us that four-way you've been dreaming about."

Archer choked on the mouthful of juice he'd just taken, sputtering as he scowled at Kody. "What the—"

"Don't act innocent," Kody teased. "It's all over your face. You got a taste of group sex, and now you're a goddamn addict. You know you talk in your sleep?"

A faint blush crept up Archer's neck, barely noticeable under his tattoos, but he glared at Kody anyway and shook his head. "You're a dick," he muttered as he finished his juice and pushed back his chair. "You coming, Princess? I can help work on your grappling game again."

I let out a low laugh. "Nice try," I replied. "I'm going back to bed. Kody was nice enough to move my session to this afternoon." I shot my trainer a sly grin, and he winked back at me. Yeah, we'd had a late night.

"I hate you all," Archer mumbled, stalking out of the kitchen.

"Hey!" Steele shouted. "What'd I do?"

Archer just flipped him off and disappeared in the general

direction of the gym. Kody helped Steele and me collect up all the breakfast plates, then dropped a quick kiss on my lips.

"Actually sleep, babe," he told me in a murmur, "and make Steele *sleep* too. He looks like shit warmed up."

"Harsh, bro," Steele muttered as he rinsed off the sticky plates so we wouldn't attract ants. Despite the fact that we had household staff, the boys were surprisingly thoughtful in small tasks like that. I'd even caught Archer emptying the dishwasher several days ago.

Kody snickered and clapped him on the shoulder. "I call it how I see it. Now I'm gonna go make Archer wish he'd never met me." His evil chuckle lingered behind as he left the kitchen, and I couldn't help smiling.

I fucking loved that idiot, and I was well past due to *tell* him that.

"So." Steele looped his arms around my waist from behind and kissed my neck. "I'm pretty sure Kody just told you to sleep with me, Hellcat."

I chuckled and leaned back into his embrace. "He did. *Sleep.* Come on; you need a shower first." Linking my hand with his, I gave him a suggestive brow waggle and tugged him out of the kitchen with me.

He took no coaxing whatsoever. Especially when I generously offered to scrub his back for him in the shower. After all, Kody's order had only been about sleeping, not showering, and it was a proven fact that sleep was better after sex.

CHAPTER 26

Later in the day I was in the gym with Kody, punching his pads with gloved hands as he barked commands at me. He was all business for our training session, and I wasn't arguing. Our stalker mail always seemed to refocus me on the stakes at hand.

The intercom near the door buzzed, and I paused my punches to raise a brow in question.

"I've got it," Archer muttered, getting up from his seat against the wall where he'd been watching and offering critiques. He moved over to the wall-mounted intercom and pressed the button to answer the call. "Yeah?"

"Sir," the man on the other end said, "there's someone here at the gate asking to speak with Miss Danvers. Says his name is Barker?"

I frowned and swiped sweat off my face with the towel Kody passed me. Why the fuck would Bark be here? Chasing more alien theories?

"Sorry," the guard amended, "Professor Barker."

Even stranger still. Archer met my gaze, silently asking what I wanted to do, and I shrugged. "I'm curious. Aren't you?"

Kody snorted a laugh. "When are you *not* curious, babe?"

"Shut up." I socked a gloved punch at his hard abs. He let out an *oof*, even though I doubted it'd hurt him even in the slightest. My ego liked it, though.

Archer just shrugged and pressed the intercom button again. "Let him up," he told the gate guard.

Steele groaned and sat up from the weight bench, where he seemed to have been napping for the past half hour. "I'll grab some guns," he announced with a yawn. "Never can be too careful."

Holding my hands out for Kody to unstrap my gloves, I agreed with a sigh. "True that."

He tugged them off my hands, then smacked a kiss on my cheek. "Go get changed, if you want. We can make the good professor wait."

I gave a short laugh but took him up on that offer. I still remembered the leering way Professor Barker had offered me *extra credit* when my grades had started slipping. So I really had no desire to chat with him while coated in sweat and wearing just a sports bra and shorts.

When I returned back downstairs some fifteen minutes later, freshly showered and dressed in jeans and a long-sleeve T-shirt, I found the boys sitting with Professor Barker in the formal dining room. Or as I was starting to think of it, the interrogation room.

They weren't even trying to be subtle either. Archer sat opposite Professor Barker with his gun on the table in front of him. Steele leaned on the wall behind Archer, and Kody slouched causally at the head of the table.

"Sorry to keep you waiting," I commented with a tight smile, not meaning a damn word of my apology. "I'm a bit surprised to see you here, Professor Barker."

"Please, call me Roy," he told me with a brittle smile. He'd told me that once before, and just like then, I pretended I hadn't heard him.

"So, what can we do for you, Professor? I withdrew from your class weeks ago." I sat down in the chair that Archer pushed out for me beside him.

Professor Barker cleared his throat, his eyes flickering uncomfortably to the gun in front of Archer, then back to me. "Well, I got the feeling our last meeting might have left you the wrong impression of me, Madison Kate."

"It's Miss Danvers," Archer corrected him. "You're not on a first-name basis."

Professor Barker flashed a tight smile. "Or is it Mrs. D'Ath?"

Archer stilled beside me, and I gently placed a hand on his knee under the table. I wanted to hear what the fuck the creepy professor was here for *before* his brains decorated the ugly wallpaper.

The professor puffed up a bit, like he had regained a bit of his confidence. "See, I noticed your engagement announcement in the *Gazette* and thought it was a bit odd. After all, I could have sworn I saw your filed marriage certificate at the courthouse more than a year ago."

I heaved a sigh. "That's a shame."

His smile faltered. "What is?"

"You," I replied with a shrug. "We're *probably* going to have to kill you now. But I guess if you came here with some important information for us…?" I left the question open, quietly hoping he had nothing. I didn't like him; he gave me the damn creeps. Apparently I'd already become jaded because I had zero qualms about leaving Bark without a dad.

Professor Barker gave a short, uncomfortable laugh, like I was making a joke. Then his eyes flickered around at the boys, then at the gun on the table, and his face paled.

"Look, I'm not here to make trouble," he quickly told us, holding his hands up. "I just wanted to explain. I'm writing a book, you see? It's fiction, but I've based the crimes all on real events here in Shadow Grove. The more I dug into old case files and newspaper articles, the more I discovered, and I just got a bit…uh…obsessed. I guess. I knew your mom back in the day, but we were never involved or anything. She was *way* out of my league, you know?" He gave another uneasy laugh, and sweat beaded on his brow.

I drew inspiration from Archer's interrogation techniques and said nothing in response. The silence thickened, and Professor Barker shifted in his chair. Fuck, I hoped that was the chair Jase had sat in naked.

"Why'd you come here, Professor Barker?" I asked after a *painfully* long silence.

"I'm asking myself the same damn question," he admitted with a wobbly smile. "I, uh, I guess I just wanted to ask if maybe I could interview you properly at some stage? I'd really love to pick your brain about how all this crime in Shadow Grove goes so unnoticed by city and state officials."

Wow. Professor Barker seriously had a death wish. It was almost laughable.

I exchanged a look with Kody, who just cocked a brow at me. The implication was clear. It was my choice whether Professor Barker walked away on his own two feet…or became pig food.

Decisions, decisions.

Taking a deep breath, I gave Archer's knee a quick squeeze in a silent warning to *not* argue with me.

"Get out of our house, Professor Barker," I said in a cold voice. "I suggest if you value your life, or your children's lives, you won't keep digging. Stick to fiction, or you'll be killed. Understood?"

The professor blinked at me a couple of times like he thought I might be joking. Then Archer reached out and placed his hand over the gun on the table.

"You heard her, Prof," he snarled. "Go now, before she changes her mind."

It was safe to say I don't think my criminology professor could have escaped our house faster if he'd tried. I was surprised not to see a trail of piss following him, as petrified as he looked. How in the *hell* he'd stayed alive this long was a mystery.

"Should have killed him," Steele murmured when the front door slammed. Kody had followed to ensure the professor *actually* left our property, but Archer, Steele, and I remained.

I sighed, dropping my head onto Archer's shoulder, and leaned into him when his arm wrapped around me. "I know," I mumbled, "but I get the feeling we're going to be doing a *lot* of killing in the next few weeks. Maybe sparing professor Barker will balance the karma a little."

Archer scoffed. "Doubtful. But he definitely struck me as more annoying than dangerous. We'll pay him a visit later when he's not expecting it. You know, really make sure he understands the importance of keeping his mouth *shut*."

I shivered at the violence in his voice. "Damn it, Sunshine, you're getting me all turned on with that kind of dirty talk."

Archer and Steele both laughed at that, but *fuck*...I wasn't joking.

"Come on," Steele said, pushing off the wall. "It smells like Anna has dinner almost ready."

My stomach rumbled at that comment, and I happily got out of my chair to follow him. Now that we'd gotten used to Anna cooking proper meals, it was a bit embarrassing how dependent on takeout we had been before. Not to mention how limited our diet had been.

Now, though? Anna was turning us all into actual foodies, and she was openly proud of that fact.

Steele had been right. Anna was just putting out the last of the plates of food when we entered the kitchen, and she happily talked us through what she'd made for us: spinach and ricotta cannelloni with a side of freshly made garlic bread. Yum. So much yum.

After we all ate, I packed up the plates, then went hunting in the freezer for ice cream. Just because Archer needed to eat well to make weight for his fight didn't mean the rest of us had to deprive ourselves.

Except we were all out.

"Who ate all the ice cream?" I demanded, turning around to scowl at the three boys. All of them gave me innocent *who me?* faces, but I narrowed my gaze on Archer. He thought he was *so* sneaky with his late-night fridge visits, but I was onto him.

"You. Go. Buy more ice cream." I pointed at him, then at the door. "Now."

He shook his head. "Can't; sorry, Princess. For one thing, Kody is the ice cream thief. For another, I need to get back to the gym. Big fight coming up, you know?" He hurried out of the room before I could argue with him, so I switched my glare to Kody instead.

"Way to throw me under the bus, asshole," Kody grumbled, his cheeks pink. "But…I should really go and oversee his training."

I rolled my eyes. "You both suck."

Steele snickered. "I'll go, Hellcat. But only if you let me pick the movie when I get back, okay?"

"Deal," I told him quickly.

His eyes narrowed thoughtfully. "And you watch it with no pants on."

I grinned. "Deal."

"Dammit," Kody grumbled, "well played, Max Steele. Well fucking played."

I laughed, then followed Steele as he headed for the garage. "Wait up, I'll come with you."

He paused, arching a brow at me in question, so I just shrugged and slipped my feet into a pair of ballet flats at the front door.

"Safety in numbers, Max," I told him quietly. "Even on a trip to the store for ice cream."

His lips tugged up in a smile, and when I came closer, he wrapped an arm around my waist and pulled me into a long kiss.

"You're adorable, Hellcat," he murmured, then handed me a gun. "Take this. I've got a spare in the car." I gave him a wide-eyed look, and he shrugged back. "Better safe than sorry, gorgeous. And I have confidence in your gun-handling skills these days."

"Aw, you guys are going to give me heart failure with all these sweet comments," I teased as we continued into the garage and climbed into one of Archer's black Porsches. Steele had probably chosen it for the bulletproof glass, and for that I was thankful.

We drove to the closest store, and Steele carefully checked our surroundings before we exited the car and headed into the shop. Getting shot from a distance had made him hypervigilant, and I didn't blame him. We all felt that way so close to the wedding—and our trap.

"Just ice cream?" Steele asked as we headed to the frozen section of the little store.

I nodded, then hummed. "Do we have any Bailey's at home? That's *definitely* what I'm in the mood for: mocha ice cream covered in Bailey's Irish Cream." I moaned, already tasting it.

Steele chuckled and tucked an arm around my waist. His forearm rested over where I'd stored his gun, and it was a solid reminder that we *always* needed to be on our guard.

A point that was proven just moments later as I hunted through the freezer for an elusive tub of mocha swirl. It happened so quick I barely even had a chance to gasp. One second my head was buried in the freezer, the next Steele grabbed the gun from my waistband and pointed it at the hooded man who'd just approached.

"What," Steele growled out, "the fuck?"

The man put his hands in the air in front of him, a gesture to show he was unarmed, but his dark hood shadowed his identity.

"I'm sorry," he said in a rough voice. "I'm sorry; I didn't mean to startle you. Your gate guard wouldn't let me pass, and I just…I just need to know where he is. Okay? I just wanna know where Scott is."

I frowned, taking a small step closer. "Officer Shane?"

The man jerked a nod of confirmation and tipped his hood back slightly. I gasped when I saw his face. Or rather, when I saw the bruised mess that *had been* his face. Fucking hell, someone had seriously laid into him.

"Holy shit," I murmured, "what the hell happened to you?"

Scott's older brother gave me a startled look, his gaze flicking to Steele, to the gun, then back to me. "I tripped," he lied through gritted teeth. "Look, I know I'm breaking the rules, but I just want to know where my brother is and I know you know. Please just tell me."

"Rules?" I repeated, dumbfounded. "What rules?"

Shane's nervous eyes flicked to Steele again, and understanding washed over me. *Oh, I see.*

"Look, Shane," I said with a sigh, "I can't help you."

His brow creased, and he shook his head. "No, you can. You just *won't.*"

I said nothing because he was right. I wouldn't help because what the fuck was I supposed to say? *Yes, I know where Scott is because I'm the one who killed him*? I was reckless and a bit naive at times, but I wasn't that stupid.

"If that's all, Officer Shane?" Steele prompted, still aiming his gun at Shane and not even trying to disguise it. Apparently he had no worries about being reported to the SGPD.

The older version of Scott just glared venom, then stormed off with a slight limp to his gait.

Wordlessly, Steele and I paid for our ice cream, then hurried back to the car. Once inside, he handed the gun back to me. I tucked it into the glove compartment next to the one already in there, then reached over and grabbed him by the back of his neck.

I kissed him hard, loving the hardness of his tongue stud as I claimed his mouth. When I released him some minutes later, we were both breathing heavily.

"You beat up Officer Shane?" I asked in a low voice, licking my wet lips and already desperate to kiss him again.

Steele cocked a brow. "He called you a slut, Hellcat. No one does that and walks away unscathed."

I groaned, squirming in my seat. "Fucking hell," I muttered, "that shouldn't turn me on so damn hard."

Steele just gave me a cocky grin and turned the car on, letting the purring rumble of the engine vibrate my seat. "But it does, and I love that about you."

I laughed, then shook my head. "Hurry up and get us home, or I'll be forced to fuck you here in Archer's car."

He groaned in pain. "Hellcat, don't tease me like that; you know how much I like to flirt with danger." Because Archer would probably kill him for fucking me in his Porsche. Still, Steele put his foot down and tore out of the parking lot at about twice the speed limit.

We were just two streets from home when he jerked the wheel to change our direction.

I startled, then took in his tense frame, the way his knuckles grasped the steering wheel, and the rapid way he checked his mirror every few seconds.

"We're being followed," I murmured in understanding.

"Yep," he replied in a grim voice. "Let's see how good they are."

His foot pressed down on the gas, and I nervously grabbed my seat belt as we rocketed around the corner and down the long stretch of residential street ahead. It was evening, so there weren't too many cars out, but even so, we had a couple of hair-raising misses as Steele hurtled across intersections.

Then our pursuer started shooting. The first shot hit the back window with a loud crack, but the glass remained intact. The same couldn't be said for my tenuous hold over my panic, and a small sound of fright escaped my throat before I could swallow it down.

Three more shots were fired, but this time I was prepared and didn't flinch *as* much.

"Are you okay?" Steele asked, cool as a damn cucumber while rocketing through the streets of Shadow Grove with some asshole shooting at us.

I jerked a nod. "I'm fine," I lied. "Do we think it's Shane?"

Steele shook his head. "Nah, no way. He wouldn't have the range of motion right now to either drive like that *or* shoot from a moving vehicle. My bet is that these guys took the opportunity while it was just the two of us out of the house. Well, joke's on them; we don't need Kody and Archer to cream their asses." He flashed me a confident smile. "You're cool with that, right? Otherwise we can just head back to the house and let security handle them."

I frowned at him, then popped the glove compartment open to grab his gun. "Fuck that; we *can* handle this."

Steele's grin spread wide. "That's my girl."

Pride rippled through me as I nervously grinned back. "What do you want me to do?"

Steele checked his mirror again as more bullets peppered the back of the car. Thank *fuck* we'd taken Archer's.

"Okay, it's a guy hanging out the passenger side that is shooting. We've got two options here." He paused, clearly running those two options through his head and testing them for risk. "One option," he amended after a moment. "Because I'm not risking you getting hit by a lucky shot. I'm going to get us out to the warehouse district, then you're going to take the wheel. When I say, you'll jerk the wheel *all* the way toward you. Clear?"

I nodded. "Clear."

"Good," he murmured. "This should be easy. They didn't plan this out; it's just an opportunistic attack." He gunned the engine faster, speeding in the direction of the warehouse district. As we approached, he held out his hand, and I passed over the gun.

"You've got this, Hellcat. Let's clear a few more players from the board." He flashed me a wide smile, then nodded to the steering wheel.

243

I reached out, wrapping my hands around it as he wound down his window. His eyes were glued to the mirror and his foot still firmly on the gas; then he calmly said, "Ready? And...*now*."

At his command, I wrenched the steering wheel, sending our sports car into a sickening spin. The wheels slipped in the loose gravel of the warehouse area, which allowed us to slide as we spun, rather than catching and flipping. Steele aimed his gun from his open window, then popped off a series of bullets as the car spun him in the direction of our pursuer.

As quick as he'd fired, he handed the gun back to me and grabbed the steering wheel once more. A moment later, he controlled our spin and slowed the car to a jerking stop outside a series of shipping containers.

"You okay, Hellcat?" he asked sharply, reaching out a hand to sweep my hair from my face.

I nodded to reassure him. "Yeah, yes, yeah, I'm totally fine. Holy shit. That was insane."

His gorgeous face lit up with a smile, and he pressed a quick kiss to my lips. "You're fucking amazing," he told me with a groan. "Let's finish these fuckers off." He popped the glove compartment open again, took out the second gun, then unbuckled himself and got out.

I hesitated only a moment before following, staying slightly behind him so I wouldn't distract or interfere with his shots, should anyone attack. I needn't have worried, though. When we approached the crumpled debris of the other car, crashed into the side of a shipping container, it was pretty damn clear they were no longer a threat.

Somehow, my quiet, gentle, piano-playing lover had managed to hit both attackers with headshots while our Porsche was midspin on gravel.

"Ho-ly shit," I breathed, wide-eyed as I stared. "You're a little bit badass, you know that?"

Steele barked a laugh and pulled his phone from his pocket. "So are you, gorgeous."

He called the guys to advise them that we had a little mess to clean up, then walked me back to our car to wait.

Incredibly, the only damage to Archer's car was that back window. It was almost entirely frosted with spiderweb shatters, but it *had* stopped seven bullets from penetrating. Each one of them was lodged within the thick glass like a trophy.

"Ah shit," Steele commented, noticing something on the side of the body. "Arch is gonna kill me. I scratched the paintwork here."

Laughter bubbled out of me and it didn't stop until Steele slipped into the passenger seat then pulled me into his lap. I relaxed into his embrace and soaked in the reality that he was still alive. It was going to take a hell of a lot more than bullets to take my men away.

CHAPTER 27

By the time everything was cleaned up, my ice cream had well and truly melted. If that weren't bad enough on its own, it'd somehow managed to melt out of its carton and get all through the carpet-lined floorboard of Archer's Porsche.

Whoops.

On the other hand, his car had also been shot full of bullets, so what was a little melted ice cream?

It was past midnight by the time we made it back to the house. Sampson and one of the other trusted security guards were taking care of the bodies, and we'd had the other car towed to a wrecker where it could be dismantled. Neither of the dead men had any ID on him, but it didn't make much difference. Dead was dead, no matter who you were.

"Benny is going to have the most well-fed pigs in the state," I mumbled as we made our way upstairs to bed.

"Nah," Kody commented. "Sampson doesn't use pigs, as far as I know."

Surprise made me blink a couple of times. "There are other equally effective methods to dispose of bodies?"

All three boys chuckled at that, so apparently I was missing the joke somewhere.

"Okay, cool. I'm going to sleep; who—"

"Dibs," Steele cut me off.

Kody scowled. "That's not how this works, bro."

Steele folded his arms, positioning himself closest to my bedroom door. "Oh no? How have you two been choosing who sleeps in Hellcat's bed these last few days, hmm?"

Archer scoffed. "Obviously, we've been handling it like real men." He held his fist out, and Kody copied. Then... "Rock, paper, scissors."

"Oh, for fuck's sake," I muttered, ignoring their antics and letting myself into my room with Steele following close behind. I was almost positive they *hadn't* been deciding by rock, paper, scissors, but then...not much would shock me.

I fell asleep wrapped up in Steele's embrace but woke the next morning to find Kody on the other side of me. I smiled as I admired my two sleeping men, pleased to find that they could compromise after all. And a compromise that ended up with more of them in my bed? That was one I could happily get on board with.

Carefully I slid out from between them, not wanting to wake either of them up, and smothered a laugh when Steele reached out an arm and snuggled Kody.

Downstairs, I found Archer in the kitchen. He was sitting on a stool at the island, drinking a protein shake as he chatted with Anna.

"Morning." I scuffed my way over to where Archer sat. He reached out, tucking his arm around my waist, and I leaned into him. "Why are you awake?"

He gave a small chuckle, and Anna clicked her tongue at me.

"Because it's nearly evening, my girl. You and those boys have been asleep all day. I was getting worried that this lamb shoulder I've been slow roasting would go to waste." Anna gave me a smile to show she was teasing, and my stomach rumbled.

"Yum," I whispered, leaning into Archer farther and loving

247

how he held me so tightly. Whatever the time was, I was still yawning. "Can I have cereal first, though?" I asked hopefully, and Anna threw her hands in the air with mock exasperation.

"You can, but only because the lamb is still a good two hours from done and I don't need you passing out from starvation."

"Sit down." Archer lifted me onto the stool beside his before I could do as I was told. "I'll get it for you."

I watched in loved-up fascination as he went to the pantry and selected my sugary cereal from the shelf, then got me out the biggest bowl and filled it two thirds of the way. Then he topped it up with milk and placed it in front of me with a spoon.

Grinning, I pulled it closer to me. "How'd you know how I liked my cereal?" I murmured as he slid back onto his stool.

He just gave me a *look* in return as if to say, *Don't underestimate me, Princess.*

Anna's eyes crinkled as she smiled at the two of us; then she tucked her oven mitts back over the rail.

"Right," she said with her hands on her hips. "Two hours until dinner. I'm going to get some laundry done; you make sure the other two are awake, yes?" Archer and I both bobbed our heads in understanding. "Good."

She bustled off and left the two of us alone in the kitchen.

Less than a second after she was gone, Archer lifted me off my stool and sat me in his lap, then wrapped his arms around my waist.

I only let out a small grumble of protest, then dragged my cereal closer so I could keep eating while he snuggled me. It was stupid cute.

"Hey," Steele said with a yawn. He wandered into the kitchen still half-asleep. "How long have you guys been up?"

"Um, ten minutes?" I guessed with a shrug before taking another mouthful of loops.

Archer kissed the side of my neck, behind my ear, then replied, "Six hours."

Steele wrinkled his nose at his friend in disgust. "Gross. You should sleep more, bro."

Archer huffed a laugh, his warm breath feathering my skin and making me shiver. "I *was* asleep, but then I got a call from my guy over at Rainybanks pathology. He's sending over the results from James's test today."

I startled, then turned in his lap to stare wide-eyed. "What?"

"I haven't gotten them yet," he assured me, "but I figured I may as well get up and be productive until they came through. Except apparently James doesn't work Mondays, so he's not even here today."

I bit my lip, trying really hard not to get my hopes up. It was weird, wanting a virtual stranger to be my biological father rather than the man who'd raised me. But there it was. I *wanted* James to be my dad because anyone had to be better than Samuel Danvers.

"Well, I mean, it's probably negative anyway," I said in a forced light tone of voice. "James said he ran a test himself, and it was negative. So I doubt that was tampered with. Right?"

Archer just shrugged. "You never know in Shadow Grove."

"I'll see if I can track him down," Steele offered. "We must have his home address on file somewhere. Or a phone number at least."

Archer nodded. "Steinwick said he'd find those details for us, but I figured we'd wait and see what the results say."

"Fair enough," Steele said with a yawn. "I was thinking maybe we'd head up to the shooting range tomorrow, if you guys are up for it." He made it sound like a group activity, but I knew he wanted to test my marksmanship again—something I was more than okay with. Like Steele had told me when he first started teaching me to shoot, the more I fired a gun, the more natural it would come. I wanted to get as good as he was…one day.

I nodded with enthusiasm, and Archer's arms tightened around me.

"Sounds good," he rumbled. "Anna wants us back here in two hours for a slow-roasted lamb shoulder."

Steele let out a drooling sound, throwing his head back in silent thanks to our cook, and I laughed.

"All right, I'm going to go wake Kody up," I told them. "We can…I dunno. Run through the plan for Saturday again."

Saturday being our *wedding day*. Fucking hell…it was so soon. Even though it wasn't a *real* wedding, I was still getting all the nervous jitters and shit. It was also solidifying some things in my mind.

Despite the fact that it was a ruse to take out—hopefully—all of the active hitmen currently hunting my hide, it had made me realize that I *was* completely in love with all three of the guys.

Archer squeezed me again and kissed my neck before letting me slide out of his lap. Steele caught me by the waist as I passed him, kissed me thoroughly, then let me go with a lingering look.

Upstairs, instead of waking Kody up like I'd intended, I found myself crawling back under the covers and snuggling into his sleepy embrace.

"Babe," he mumbled, "you're cold."

I let out a small laugh. "Warm me up, then, Kodiak."

He made a sleepy, growling noise. His teeth playfully nipped the bend of my neck, and I gasped. "Careful what you wish for, babe." He pulled me closer, grinding his hard length against my ass.

"Maybe that's exactly what I want," I taunted, arching into him. It *hadn't* been what was on my mind when I'd come upstairs, but the second his arms had wrapped around me, all nonsexual thoughts had flown completely out the window.

He hummed a sleepy, contented sound as his hand snaked under my T-shirt to palm one of my bare breasts and toy with my hard nipple.

"I think," he murmured, his lips against my neck, "that you use sex as a stress reliever."

I stilled. "Is that a bad thing?"

"Hell no," he replied with a short laugh, "but it does make me worry what you're stressed about right now."

His fingers rolled my nipple, sending pulses of arousal through my body and making me squirm. "Does that mean you're not going to fuck me, Kodiak Jones?"

His teeth scraped against my neck. "Babe, I'll *never* refuse you, especially when it's helping to keep you calm." His hand left my breast, skating down my belly, then pushing my sleep shorts down. "But I still want you to talk to me," he continued, as I kicked my shorts off. He cupped my pussy when it was bare. "Tell me what's stressing you out, babe. Maybe I can help in more than one way."

He probably could because he had the physical angle totally covered. His hand left my mound just long enough to push his own shorts down, and then he pushed into me slowly from his big-spoon position.

I groaned as he worked his way in. He lifted my top leg and hooked it over his hip to offer a better angle. But when he fully seated himself, he paused there. Waiting.

"Archer is waiting on James's paternity test results," I admitted with a gasp, my pussy throbbing around Kody's hard shaft.

"Ah, I see," he murmured as he started to move within me. His hand moved back up my shirt, and he found my breast once more. "Do you *want* James to be your dad?" he asked gently, his hips rolling and his thrusts deep.

I moaned, shivering as arousal built and chased across my skin, then focused on his question. "I don't *know* James," I replied, a little breathlessly. "He's a total stranger to me. But yeah, I guess I want confirmation that I'm *not* Samuel Danvers's daughter."

Kody murmured a sound of understanding, then gripped my breast tighter as his pace quickened a bit. His movements drew moans and whimpers out of me as my lazy orgasm built up.

"What else is on your mind, babe?" he asked in a low voice, his lips brushing my earlobe.

My breath was quick, my hips rocking in time with his thrusts, and my climax taunting me on the horizon, but Kody was right. More and more, I was turning to sex to handle my stress, and while I saw *nothing* wrong with that—given I had three extremely virile lovers on hand—I also needed to recognize the opportunity to purge my mental load.

I groaned. "I'm marrying Archer in six days," I finally told him.

Kody's rhythm faltered a second before he recovered at a slower pace.

"And?"

My back arched and I pushed my ass back against him as my body begged for him to fuck me harder. "And...I want you to know something first."

He did the complete fucking opposite of what I wanted and slowed to a stop. At least he'd stopped when he was buried balls deep and not teasing me with just the tip.

"I'm listening," he all but fucking purred. Damn him to hell, he knew *exactly* what was on my mind.

I groaned, craning my neck so that I could look him in the eye. "I love you, Kodiak Jones," I told him in a husky whisper.

A wide grin spread over his face, and he crushed his lips to mine in a hard kiss. "Good," he murmured after he'd kissed me breathless, "because I love you too, Madison Kate."

The rush of oxytocin hit my brain in a dizzying wave, and I hummed a happy noise. "Will you please make me come now?" I asked sweetly, peppering more kisses against his lips.

His lips were still curved in a grin. "Say it again," he ordered me.

I huffed a laugh but obliged. "I love you."

He groaned, then thoroughly delivered. Kody fucked me so hard the bed slammed against the wall and cracked the paint. We came simultaneously with whispered curses and confessions of love. It was magical as fuck.

When Kody went to rinse off in my shower, I just lay there in the middle of my bed like a well-fucked starfish. My thighs were wet and sticky with his cum and my face raw from stubble rash, but I needed to take a moment to store that feeling into my mental lockbox of awesome memories.

"That…" Steele's voice startled me out of my haze, "is way too fucking tempting."

I raised my head slightly and found him leaning his shoulder against my doorframe. From my spread-eagle position, he'd have a prime view of my *everything*. Feeling evil, I simply parted my legs even farther, offering a silent invitation.

His eyes raked all over me, lingering on my swollen core, and then he muttered a curse. "I'm saving this as an IOU for later, Hellcat," he told me, "because Arch just got the results from the pathology lab."

I gasped as I sat bolt upright, staring at him in anticipation. "And?"

"And it was a positive match. James is your biological parent."

All the air whooshed out of my lungs, and the room spun. Fuck me, was I about to pass out? No, I could handle this news. I'd dealt with more shocking stuff. It still took me a moment or two to force my lungs to work again, though, in which time Steele crossed the room and crouched beside the bed. His hand rubbed soothing circles on my back until I nodded and assured him I was fine.

"Okay," I breathed. "Okay. Good. That explains a few things, right?" I met Steele's concerned gaze, and he nodded. "Does James know? Did we get in touch with him already?"

Steele grimaced. "Yeah, we found him." He sighed. "He's at the hospital. Someone apparently mugged him last night outside his apartment. He fought them off and they ran, but he took a knife to the ribs for his efforts."

My jaw dropped. "What the fuck? Is he okay?"

Steele nodded. "Should be fine. The mugger only got that far thanks to the element of surprise. James sounds like he's in a foul mood but will be released soon. He's coming by after he gets done filing police reports."

I snorted a bitter laugh. "For all the good that will do. This can't be a coincidence."

"Agreed." Steele stood up from his crouch and tipped his head toward my bathroom. "Go shower before I change my mind and take that invitation now." He left my room before I could tell him that I was *all* for a little more stress relief, so I made my way into my bathroom.

Luckily, Kody was still under the hot spray, all soaped-up and gorgeous.

Who the fuck needed therapy when you could maintain good mental health through copious orgasms, right?

CHAPTER 28

The following morning, James tagged along to the gun range with us. The conversation we'd had when he finally arrived at the house—just in time for dinner—had been awkward at best. But then, what else was to be expected? I was barely nineteen, and he'd never known he had a child. More than that, my mom hadn't been some great love of his life. She'd been a two-week romance that ended poorly.

It was weird; I was more than willing to admit that much.

But when Steele suggested James come to the shooting range with us, I was cautiously optimistic. Maybe we just needed to spend some time together and find some common ground?

To my relief, it was an enjoyable day. James's almost twenty-year career in the marines had afforded him a wealth of knowledge in weapons, and it took no time at all for him to relax. Before long, he and Steele were engaged in friendly banter about guns, and I was left with Archer overseeing my lesson.

"Princess," Arch murmured in my ear as he adjusted my stance with his hands on my hips, "are you okay with this?"

I wriggled my hips under his fingers. "With *this*?"

Archer huffed a laugh. "No, with *this*, James being here."

I glanced over at our new addition, my biological dad. He and Steele laughed together, and the scene touched something inside me.

"I am," I admitted, "but I still can't shake the paranoia that we shouldn't let anyone into our circle right now."

Archer murmured a sound of agreement. "Good."

I turned my face to meet his gaze. "Good?"

He jerked a nod. "I want you to be happy, Kate. I want you to know what it's like to have a family, to know your real father. But right now…"

I nodded. "I agree. Right now isn't the time. If he really means us no harm, then I think he should understand that."

Archer's hands moved from my hips, his arms tightening around me in a hug as he kissed my hair. "I'll take care of it when we get home. Keep shooting, Princess; you're getting good."

With that pep talk, he sauntered away and left me alone with my thoughts and my target for a while. I threw myself into it, mentally talking myself through all the instructions I'd been given by Steele and peppering my paper target full of holes.

Despite the chat Archer and I had just had, all three boys seemed to genuinely enjoy his company. Like minds and all that. I watched them from the corner of my eye as they chatted comfortably, and I wondered if this was what it was like for other girls when their boyfriends met their dad for the first time.

Obviously not because, for one thing, it wasn't even close to the first time they'd met. For another, most girls didn't have three boyfriends.

But they should. It was the fucking best.

"Hey, babe," Kody called out when I tugged my earmuffs off and placed my gun down. "We're going to go to the rifle range. Wanna see who's the best shot long range?" His eyes sparkled with excitement, and his smile was wide.

James scoffed a laugh. "Kid, you don't stand a damn chance. I'll cream you."

Steele shrugged. "I'm game."

Archer and Kody both chuckled, knowing full damn well that Steele would win, regardless of how good James might be.

"Go set it up," Steele told them. "I just want to run through some feedback with Hellcat while it's fresh in my mind."

Kody, Archer, and James all headed outside to the rifle range, and Steele moved across the room toward me with a predatory expression on his face.

I narrowed my eyes at him. "You have *feedback* for me, huh?"

His lips tugged in a smirk. "You're damn right I do." He moved past me, flipped the lock on the door, then turned back. "Put your hands on the table, Hellcat."

I arched a brow but did as I was told. Steele moved to stand behind me, his hands lightly on my hips as I bent forward.

"My *feedback*, beautiful," he murmured as he reached around to unbutton my jeans, then pull them down over my ass, "is that watching you with a gun in your hands is one of the biggest turn-ons I've ever goddamn seen."

I gasped as he impaled me on his studded dick, not even taking a second to warm up. He didn't need to when he was already hard as granite.

"Shh," Steele murmured when I cried out, "we only have a couple of minutes before one of them comes looking. I want you back out there with my cum soaking your jeans before anyone notices."

I groaned, then bit my lip. Fucking hell, just picturing that was turning me the hell on. Not to mention the way his dick piercings were rubbing me in *all* the right ways from this angle.

"Christ," I muttered when he started fucking me hard and fast. "You're gonna need to gag me to keep me quiet, Max."

He snickered but obliged. When I came a few minutes later, the sounds of my screams were muffled by his hand clamped over my mouth.

Two minutes later, I found myself uncomfortably trying to focus on shooting a rifle while trying to ignore how soaked my panties and jeans were.

Still, oxytocin had to be hands down the best antidepressant known to man, because I was on cloud fucking nine the rest of our day at the shooting range.

As the next few days passed, my anxiety kept building to the point that not even multiple orgasms could shake it for long. Come mid-week, I was near my breaking point.

"All right, spill," Archer growled, tucking his dick back into his shorts after a mid-workout fuck that I'd lured him into. "You're more keyed up than usual," he told me accusingly. "What's on your mind that you're not talking about?"

I pulled my yoga pants back on and searched for my crop top. It was hanging off the chin-up bar...however the fuck that had happened.

"That's what I've been trying to work out," I admitted sheepishly. "But...I think I know what it is." I wrestled my tits back into my bra, then sat down on the padded mat to stretch out my hamstrings. Archer had done this thing where he put my ankle on his shoulder while he fucked me, and it'd made me realize I needed to work on my flexibility.

"The suspense is killing me," he commented, grabbing a sweat towel to dry his face and chest off. No one could say he wasn't working on his cardio during our somewhat unconventional training sessions.

I grimaced. "Samuel," I admitted. "I'm worried about what's going to happen when he gets back on Friday."

Archer sat on the mat and handed me a water bottle. "He won't hurt you, Kate. I won't let him."

I gave him a dry glare. "No shit. And I wasn't worried about that…more about whether I would be able to actually go through with it. You know?"

Archer gave me a considering look. "With killing him?" I jerked a nod, and he tilted his head to the side. "If you don't want to—"

"No," I snapped, cutting off the offer he was about to make. "No, this is personal. I need to deal with him myself. He *sold* me, Archer. He could have had my mom murdered, he tried to have me committed *several* times, and fuck only knows what he did to my memories to erase them all so thoroughly. But most importantly… he fucking *sold* me. He didn't care if I died some horribly painful death, so I owe him the same courtesy."

Archer just stared at me with an unreadable expression for a long moment; then the corners of his mouth tweaked with a grim smile. "Sounds like you're resolute on what needs to happen."

I nodded, finding that I *was*. I just needed to make my peace with my decision.

"Yeah," I said softly. "Yeah, Samuel Danvers dies on Friday. No matter what."

Archer's smile spread wider, and he scooped me up off the floor, then tossed me over his shoulder. "Fuck training," he muttered, carrying me out of the gym. "Let's go break my bed."

———————

Friday morning I woke up with my stomach in a million knots from anxiety. The next day would be my wedding with Archer, but tonight…tonight I'd put a bullet in Samuel Danvers's forehead.

Or that was the intention. We'd already learned the hard way that plans rarely went smoothly, so a handful of contingency plans were also in place.

Samuel and Cherry were due to land in the afternoon, then meet us at the fancy restaurant we'd rented out for our "intimate family dinner" that would end in bloodshed. But before any of that, I had something else to do.

I rushed through my shower, then hurried to get dressed before Steele woke up. Kody and Archer were already in the gym, and I knew I was going to have a hard time getting them to approve my request. But...too fucking bad. I wasn't a prisoner, so they ultimately couldn't tell me no.

I hoped.

They both gave me suspicious glances as I entered the gym and perched on the edge of a weight bench to watch them spar.

"We going somewhere today, babe?" Kody asked as he dodged a kick from Archer and circled out of the way. "You're wearing pants."

I arched a brow at him and folded my arms. "You say that like I don't normally wear pants."

Both boys gave me a look at that statement, and my cheeks heated. They had a point... The last few days I'd spent more naked than not. But I was *stressed*, okay?

"Well, whatever," I grumbled. But still, I felt rather called out. "I actually have an appointment this morning."

"I'll take you," Archer offered. He stepped away from his fight with Kody and started to unstrap his gloves. I shook my head, though.

"Sweet of you to offer, but this is an appointment you can't come to." I shifted my gaze to Kody before he could offer. "Or you. I arranged alternative security for the day, if that's cool with you guys?"

They both frowned at me in confusion.

"What appointment do you have that we can't come to?" Kody mused out loud.

Archer's eyes narrowed suspiciously. "Are you getting that IUD removed?"

My jaw dropped. "What?" My voice was a strangled squeak. "No! What the fuck, Arch? We discussed this. No, I'm not getting my fucking IUD removed, and no, I won't even remotely consider it."

Kody's brows shot up so hard they almost hit his hairline. "You *discussed* this? When? Where the fuck was I?"

My cheeks burned, and Archer gave me a smug smile. Motherfucker was going to find my foot buried up his ass if he kept that shit up.

"This is off the topic," I growled, giving Archer a hard glare. "Point is, I have something to do today and you're not invited. End of story. I came in here to do you the courtesy of keeping you informed when I could well have just crept out without you knowing. Don't make me regret that choice."

Archer folded his arms over his chest. "Who did you arrange as security?"

I let out a small breath, relieved he wasn't sparking the whole *kids* argument again. "Sampson is coming with me," I told him, "and Cass." I checked my watch. "Actually, Cass will be here any second now. He insisted on escorting me from here instead of meeting me there."

Both Archer and Kody scowled at me.

"Cass?" Archer repeated. "Why Cass?"

I cocked a brow at him. "Can you think of anyone else with skills close to yours who seems to care enough about my well-being to both keep me alive *and* not try to hit on me? I'd have thought you'd approve of Cass being my bodyguard."

Archer's brow furrowed in a scowl. "I do, except for the fact that he's still Zane's second."

I snorted a laugh. "Yeah, for how long? Even an idiot can see that Cass is the real leader of the Reapers. You said it yourself—Zane has outlived his usefulness."

Archer tipped his head, acknowledging my point.

"Wait, hold the fuck up," Kody interjected. Poor darling looked confused as all hell. "Why am I just now finding out that there's been a conversation about MK's birth control? Are kids an option here?"

"No."

"Yes."

Archer and I glared at each other, having answered the question at the same time.

"Well," Kody murmured, his gaze bouncing between the two of us, "this just got serious."

Archer rolled his eyes and moved away from us to grab his water bottle. "Like it wasn't already, bro."

"Okay, that's my cue to leave," I muttered. I hurried out of the gym and flipped Archer off when he yelled my name out after me.

The front doorbell rang as I was stuffing my feet into ballet flats, and I opened the door to greet the giant, tattoo-covered gangster as Archer and Kody emerged from the gym.

"Take a damn gun, Princess," Archer snapped. In no time at all, he had one out of a hiding place and lifted my shirt to tuck it in my waistband. "You better not be on your bike, Cass."

The big grump just scowled. "What do you fucking take me for, Arch?" He jerked his head over his shoulder, indicating the vintage Pontiac parked at the bottom of the steps. "I'll bring your girl back in one piece."

"Let's go," I told Cass as I hurried him down to the car before Archer or Kody changed his mind. "Sampson will follow in his own car."

Both boys stood on the front steps, staring after us with their arms folded as I slid into Cass's car. I closed my door and buckled my seat belt, so I didn't hear whatever the Reapers' second-in-command said to my guys before getting into the car. The way he huffed a raspy laugh, though, told me he'd been taunting them.

"Troublemaker," I scolded him as we drove down the long driveway to the front gates.

He just gave a one-shouldered shrug. "They make it too easy." He glanced over at me as we passed through the front gates and gave the guard a small wave. "You ready for this, kid?"

I grinned with excitement. "Shit, yes."

Even though my wedding was a sham, I still wanted to mark the occasion. I wanted to do something to show my guys just how serious I was about this thing between us. Because it *was* forever.

CHAPTER 29

My appointment ran late, so rather than go home and risk the boys finding out what I'd been up to all day, I went to a salon to get my hair and makeup done. Then I ducked into a boutique nearby to get a dress to wear.

After I was ready, Cass dropped me off at the restaurant around fifteen minutes late. He tried to walk me in, but I assured him we had it handled. After all, the whole restaurant had been booked out, and we sure as fuck weren't here for the steak.

At least...not *beef* steak and sure as fuck not to eat. I wasn't averse to cutting strips from Samuel Danvers, depending on how badly he pissed us off.

I thanked Cass for his help, then threw on my thickest skin before pushing open the door to Osso.

Sampson had been tailing me, and I paused a moment inside the restaurant to listen as he locked the door from the outside with his set of keys. We, of course, had our own set too. But we would be taking the staff exit when we left.

"Oh, here she is," a crawlingly familiar voice jeered. "My darling daughter, the blushing bride, fashionably late as *always*. Did you get lost in your own reflection, dear?"

Samuel Danvers was drunk already, apparently. Chances were, he'd been drinking on the flight. The glasses of champagne in everyone's hands as I joined them in the deserted bar area were just decoration.

I didn't even bother faking a smile. Why *fucking* should I? I had to admit to a small amount of perverse pleasure as Samuel's smile faltered when I just glared at him blankly.

Cherry cleared her throat, so incredibly out of the loop it hurt. "Madison Kate, you look lovely," she told me in a dazed voice. "You and Archer make such a beautiful couple; I'm so happy for you both."

I couldn't help noticing how glazed her eyes were as I moved closer to her son, letting him pull me close as his arm wrapped around my waist. Did she really have no clue that we were already married? Had Samuel kept her that heavily medicated, or did she do that to herself?

Archer let out a breath, his fingers flexing against my waist. "Mom, did Sam tell you that he's broke? Last I checked, he had less than a million dollars to his name. Not quite up to your usual standards, is he?"

Wow. We were really just…going for it. Cool.

Cherry blinked at her son like an owl, but there was a glimmer of clarity in her wide blue eyes. Yeah, I was willing to bet she drugged herself to suffer through these painful, loveless relationships.

"Is that true?" she asked Samuel, her startled gaze jerking to her so-called sugar daddy. "You're broke?"

I wanted to roll my eyes so fucking hard at a million dollars being considered *broke*, but I guess Cherry was fishing for a whale, not a snapper.

Samuel's smile turned brittle, and I could practically see him gearing up to lie.

"Cherry, I suggest you cut your losses and leave," I told her in a cold voice. "I see you've picked up a souvenir for your troubles." I

265

nodded to the sparkling engagement ring on her finger. "But that's probably all you're getting out of this."

Her lips parted, and she flashed me a terrified stare, like she was scared what I might do now that I'd outed her as a gold digger.

"Just go, Mom," Archer told her in a tired voice, like this wasn't even remotely the first time he'd saved her from her own greed. "Trust me when I say you're better off walking away from this one."

Samuel's brow furrowed, and his face pinkened. He was a man *not* used to being dismissed so easily, and sitting there quietly while Archer spoke like that? It wasn't sitting well with his inflated ego.

Too bad for him, his time was up.

"Save it, *Dad*," I sneered. "We'll deal with you in a minute." I looked at Cherry and jerked my head to the exit.

She didn't need any more encouragement than that, rising from her seat on thin heels and giving us all a tight smile. "Well," she said in a breathy voice, "I think I should be going. Congratulations again, you two. I do hope I'm still welcome at the wedding tomorrow?"

"I wouldn't advise attending," Archer replied, his voice glacial.

Cherry flinched like she'd been slapped but jerked a nod. "I understand." Her whisper was sad, but she didn't argue any further as Kody escorted her out of the restaurant, using his set of keys.

"What the devil do you think you're playing at, *boy*?" Samuel spluttered the moment Cherry was gone. "We had a *deal*." He rose out of his seat as though he was more imposing while standing. News flash, he wasn't. "A deal that you're clearly enjoying the benefits of." Samuel sneered at me, at Archer's hand around my waist, like I was some kind of paid escort.

Archer was far from rattled, though, and I didn't react. It was exactly what I'd expected from the man who'd sold me on a dark web transaction.

"We did have a deal," Archer agreed, sounding bored. "And now I find myself changing the terms."

Samuel blustered. "Y-you can't do that. Contracts were signed. The deal is *done*."

Archer's arm tightened around me, and his tone turned deadly. "Contracts are only worth the price of paper and ink when one of the parties is dead, Sam."

A shiver ran through me, but it wasn't fear.

"Shall we head on through to the private dining room?" Steele suggested, standing up from his seat with a deliberate flash of the gun holstered under his arm.

Samuel Danvers nervously eyed the three boys—I still wasn't a threat in his eyes—and licked his lips. "You know what?" he said with a weak smile. "I think I should be going."

He started to move in the direction of the exit but froze when Kody's gun pressed to his temple. "Steele wasn't making a request, Sam."

Finally, my so-called father turned his panicked eyes to me, seeking help. What a joke.

I just gave him a doe-eyed smile back. "What's the problem, Daddy? I thought you liked playing gangster."

His glare darkened as understanding dawned. I wasn't some dumb pawn in all of this, nor was I a victim.

"Move it," Kody prompted, giving Samuel a solid nudge. Reluctantly, the older man did as he was told, walking ahead of us through to the private dining room. Only when he crossed the threshold did he balk.

"No, I think we've had some sort of misunderstanding here." He tried to backpedal, but with Kody blocking the doorway, there was nowhere for him to go. "Archer, come on. You're a business-man; we can come to some arrangement that suits us both."

"It's Mr. D'Ath to you, Sam," Archer told him in a bored voice as he entered the private dining room and motioned to the solitary chair. "Please, take a seat. We would hate to be bad hosts and leave our guest of honor standing at his own execution."

Samuel's face turned ashen. "Wh-what? No. No, that's not… We had a *contract*!" He sputtered his defense like that would even remotely save him. But he'd sold my last fuck on the dark web eighteen months ago. What a shame.

"Sit down, Dad," I ordered, folding my arms over my chest. My dress was long sleeved and jet black—to hide the blood—and I felt like a pink-haired Morticia Adams. "I have a couple of questions for you."

Samuel's eyes darted from me to the guys and back again. "Why should I answer *anything* for you? You're going to kill me anyway, that much is painfully clear." He gestured to the fact that the whole room was covered in plastic sheeting.

He wasn't wrong.

"Of course we are," I murmured, cocking my head to the side. "Did you expect anything less after you sold your daughter on a human-trafficking site?" Snapping my fingers, I gave him a tight smile. "Oh wait, you didn't do that, did you?" I stepped closer to him and felt a spark of satisfaction when he took a step backward. "No, you never sold your daughter. You don't *have* a daughter, do you?"

His eyes widened and his face grayed even more. All it took was a firm push to his shoulder and he stumbled into the chair we had set up and waiting for him.

"What my beautiful wife is trying to say, Sam," Archer added in a smooth voice, "is that whether or not you answer her questions will determine how painful your death is. We could make it so quick: just a pop between the eyes and you're done."

"Or we could make it *hurt*," Kody added with a malicious grin. "After all, we were trained extensively in the art of torture. You wanna guess how many bones I can break while keeping someone alive?"

"Or how many micro cuts a person's skin can handle?" Steele offered, shrugging like he was discussing the weather. "Ever heard

268

the saying *like a death by a thousand cuts*?" His lips pulled up in a macabre smile. "I can assure you you'd pass out before we even reached three hundred. Sayings are always so exaggerated."

Oh man, my guys were some scary-ass motherfuckers. I loved them so damn hard for it too. We were like four pieces of the most fucked-up puzzle, clicking together in perfect harmony.

"What do you want?" Samuel asked Archer. Of course he asked *Archer* and not me. Heaven forbid a woman ever hold his fate in her hands. Even staring down his own mortality, Samuel Danvers wouldn't drop his misogynistic bullshit.

Archer knew it too. "Don't ask me," he murmured, placing his hands on my hips and pressing a tender kiss to my neck. "Ask your *daughter*. She's the one with a score to settle. I simply live to please *her*."

I leaned back into his touch without even thinking about it. Although I knew he was being dramatic, there was all too much sincerity in his words. Too much truth and devotion. It equally warmed my heart and scared the ever-loving shit out of me. More and more I was admitting that this relationship wasn't a question of *me* giving *them* my heart. It went both ways, and right now I held all three of their hearts in my hands.

It was a hell of a big responsibility. One I was determined not to fuck up.

"Okay, okay, you figured it out," Samuel said with a forced laugh. "You worked it out. I'm not your father. So what?"

Every word from his mouth stoked my temper and made what was coming all the easier to chew.

"When did you find out?" I asked, keeping my tone cool and calm. In reality, there had been no dire blow when I found out for sure. Was I shocked that James was my bio dad? Hell yes. Was I upset or shocked that Samuel wasn't? Not even close. Somewhere, deep down, I'd always suspected there was something amiss.

Samuel scoffed. "I've always known. I had a vasectomy when

I was nineteen to prevent any gold-digging whores from trapping me with an unexpected pregnancy. The *only* way I could ever father a child is through IVF, which Debbie and I never did. Imagine my surprise when she announces a month after our wedding that she's pregnant. Fucking miracle." He snorted a bitter laugh, slouching in his chair like it was a throne.

I pursed my lips, mulling over those details. "Then it wasn't your baby she was pregnant with when she died either."

Samuel's face darkened, but it wasn't with shock. More like annoyance or disgust. "Doubtful. Debbie tried to pull that one over on me too when she realized she wasn't carrying her gangbanger boyfriend's spawn. Well, that fucking backfired. Not only was it *not* mine, that meant there was only one other person's it could have been." His smirk was pure poison. Fuck, I hated him.

"Spit it out, Sam," Steele drawled with a bored yawn. "If I get too annoyed, I'll start breaking your fingers."

A small shudder ran through me at the memory of how he'd snapped Hank's fingers for interrupting us while we spoke. Archer must have noticed, because he dropped another gentle kiss to the bend of my neck.

Samuel wasn't watching us, though; his nervous gaze was on Steele.

"Debbie claimed she was attacked," he told us, licking his lips anxiously. "Came home one night all bloody and bruised up, her dress ripped and shit. Told me she'd been attacked and wanted to go to the police."

"And did you?" Archer rumbled, his voice threaded with violence.

Samuel shook his head. "Of course not. She'd probably just pissed off that fucking Reaper and he taught her a lesson. I wasn't about to drag our family through the newspapers and risk exposing Debbie's infidelity. Any DNA test would have just proven she was a whore. That gangster probably kept her bra as a trophy or something anyway."

I froze. "What did you just say?"

He looked at me in confusion and disgust. "That I wouldn't let her take it to the cops? Bunch of dirty fucks they are anyway."

I shook my head. "No. What did you just say about her bra? Why'd you mention that?"

Samuel wrinkled his nose. "I don't know. She just kept going on about how he'd ripped her bra before she was knocked out. But she wasn't wearing one when she came home." He shrugged, like it was inconsequential.

Except it wasn't. Because I'd been gifted a ripped and bloody bra by my stalker as my *something old* for the wedding.

Fucking hell. My mom had been raped by her stalker. By *my* stalker. Her unborn baby had belonged to *him*.

Horror and revulsion washed over me as I processed all that information. My mom had been attacked and *raped* and Samuel had refused to report it to the police. What kind of low-life piece of shit—

My murderous thoughts were interrupted when Archer pressed my butterfly knife into my hand. I'd had it tucked into the garter of my stockings and hadn't even noticed him pull it out; I was that deep in my fury toward Samuel *fucking* Danvers.

"Make him bleed, Kate," he murmured in a darkly seductive voice. "Make him pay."

I looked down at my beautiful holographic knife, then gritted my teeth and looked back to Samuel.

"Why pretend to be my father?" I asked him in a hollow voice. "If you knew from the moment my mom told you she was pregnant, why not leave her then?"

His expression morphed into a sneer. "Because Debbie wasn't as smart as she thought she was. I'd met Katerina; I knew full fucking well that family was hiding something good. They were too damn quick to accept my prenup. All I needed to do was wait it out. Fifteen years of marriage and one child, then I was entitled to half of everything in Debbie's name."

My brows flickered up. "But she was murdered before you'd even been married for twelve."

"Exactly why I kept you around, my little meal ticket. *You* inherited everything. I just needed to work out how to transfer that ownership to *me*. Trouble was, Debbie had suspected something was happening before her death and went to some serious lengths to muddy the water." He scowled at that, like he was still pissed off at his dead wife. "Eventually I worked out that no matter what I did, your estate wouldn't pass to me because I couldn't prove I was a blood relation, so I cut my losses."

Anger burned through my veins like acid. "You sold me."

He didn't even look apologetic. "For fifty-two million. A damn sight more than I ever thought you were worth, Madison Kate."

Ouch. Even knowing he wasn't my father—and never had been in the ways that mattered—that comment still stung because it totally summed up his whole attitude toward me my entire life. I was an asset with an assigned value. Nothing more.

It made sense, though. He'd sold me while I was still seventeen, likely when he'd exhausted all other avenues to get his hands on my money. If I'd turned eighteen, he'd have lost the power to marry me off and lost his chance at clearing his bad debts.

I looked down at the knife in my hand, then up at Samuel. It was hard to reconcile this revolting man with the one who'd forever been the head of the Danvers household. When I'd been a child or even a grief-stricken teen, he'd been someone to be respected and awed. Never loved. But now? Now he was simply better off dead.

"What are you going to do with that?" Samuel taunted with a laugh, eyeing the pretty purple blade in my hand.

My gaze rose, locking with his as I released the blade with a practiced flick of my wrist. I was rewarded with a flash of real fear across his face.

"Well," I said with a shrug, "someone told me recently that I deserve to take my pound of flesh from you. After all, I deserve vengeance for being sold in a slave market. Now that I've heard how you treated my mother, how she came to you after being *raped* and you refused to help her?" I took two steps closer, letting the silence thicken as Kody and Steele moved in on Samuel's chair from either side. They locked his wrists and ankles to the chair with handcuffs before he could struggle or try to run.

Samuel finally seemed to understand. The danger in this room wasn't from Kody or Steele; it wasn't even from Archer. No, this time it was all from me. This was *my* story to tell and *my* revenge to seek.

"Now, *Daddy dearest*, I think I might take that turn of phrase literally." I bent at the waist, bringing the tip of my blade to rest on the fabric of his suit pants, just above his knee. Only then did I hesitate.

Could I seriously do this? Could I deliberately cause so much pain simply for my own gratification?

Kody shifted in the corner of my eye, and I knew he was silently offering to do it for me. But I gave a small headshake, denying him. I needed to do this. I needed the closure this bloody act would bring, even at the cost of my uneasy mind.

Drawing a breath, I plunged the knife down into Samuel's leg.

He howled, thrashing against the handcuffs and dragging my blade all over the place as I held tight. Idiot. Blood spurted everywhere, but I closed my mind to it and focused on my task at hand.

Several moments later, I lifted a handful of severed flesh and inspected it with a critical eye. "What do you think, boys? Is that about a pound?"

Steele damn near looked like he was about to start laughing— sick fuck—but he nodded his agreement. "I'd say so."

Samuel was still screaming and crying, begging for his life, but it all fell on deaf ears. I tossed the chunk of his flesh onto the plastic-coated ground beside his chair and eyed him critically.

Blood gushed from the mess I'd made of his thigh, and I was willing to bet I'd cut something vital.

In my defense, I was no trained butcher. Just a pissed-off chick looking for vengeance.

Steele wordlessly handed me a gun, and I took it in my slick, blood-covered fingers.

"Any last words, Dad?" I asked Samuel in a chillingly cold voice as I aimed Steele's gun at his face.

He started to curse, but I squeezed the trigger. Fuck his last words—he didn't deserve them.

CHAPTER 30

I took my time in the fancy restroom at Osso, scrubbing the blood from my hands with their expensive hand soap. It washed off easier than it should have, but I carefully checked around my fingernails, then inspected my face in the mirror. Sure enough, spatters of blood peppered my cheeks and neck like macabre freckles.

I sighed, then wet one of the fabric hand towels to dab it off. Hazards of murder, I supposed.

The door opened, and Archer entered, letting it swing shut behind him.

"You okay?" he asked me in a quiet voice.

I nodded at him in the mirror. "Yeah. Sorry I'm taking ages."

He shook his head. "Take as long as you need, Kate. Kody and Steele are taking care of the cleanup."

"Cool." I dabbed another spot of blood from my neck, then inspected my reflection for any I might have missed.

Archer just stood there, watching me.

Eventually, I dropped the washcloth into the dirty laundry basket and turned to face him.

"What?" I asked, meeting his gaze.

His brows flicked up. "What?"

My eyes narrowed. "You're watching me like you're worried I'm going to fall to pieces any second. Well, I'm not. I'm fine. Okay?" And strangely, I was.

He took two steps closer, crowding me against the vanity. "I wasn't looking at you like you might break, Princess." His voice was rough as his thumb and forefinger caught my chin and jerked my face up to hold his gaze. "I was looking at you and thinking how you might be one of the strongest women I've ever laid eyes on. But I also worry that I've broken something in you." His eyes searched mine like he could see all the way down to my damaged soul.

I drew a deep breath, feeling it flood through me and calm my tense muscles. "If you have," I told him in a whisper, "then I don't want it mended."

He groaned, then kissed me like his very life depended on it.

When he released me some moments later, my cheeks were hot, my lips swollen, and my heart pounding so hard it hurt.

"Come on," Archer said, "let's get home. In case you forgot, we're getting married tomorrow." His smirk was all mischief as he linked our hands together to tug me out of the restroom.

I grinned back at him. "How could I forget?"

The private dining room had already been stripped of plastic sheeting—and dead bodies—and all the chairs and tables were back in the rightful places. Archer led me through the empty kitchen and out the staff exit into the alleyway behind the restaurant.

Kody and Steele leaned against another nondescript, midsize sedan, laughing about something while they waited for us.

Kody spotted us first. "All good?" His sharp gaze ran over me from head to toe, then back to my face. He searched my eyes a second before he jerked a nod.

"Yup," I replied with a tight smile. I wanted to wrap my arms around myself, but I was pretty certain my dress was coated in blood too. The fabric stuck to me in a wet sort of way, and I didn't want to get it all over my hands again.

Steele crossed over to us and gave me a tight squeeze, kissing my hair. Apparently, he didn't care about the blood. "You're incredible, you know that?" He whispered the words in my ear, then released me before I needed to respond.

Archer rapped his knuckles on the trunk of the sedan. "You boys got this handled?"

"Absolutely," Kody confirmed, then reached into the back of the car and pulled out a pair of Kevlar vests. He tossed one to Steele and strapped the other on himself. "Not taking any chances tonight." He shot me a wink, and my stomach rolled with anxiety.

After all, bulletproof vests only protect against a body shot. What if this time my stalker aimed for a headshot?

"We'll be hypervigilant, Hellcat," Steele assured me in a quiet voice. "I promise you, we'll come home safe."

"Damn right we will," Kody agreed with a broad grin. "See you at home, babe." He smacked a quick kiss on my lips; then he and Steele slid into the body-disposal vehicle.

Archer and I made our way farther down the alley to where Sampson waited beside the Range Rover.

"That was quick," our head of security commented as we slid into the SUV. For once, Archer didn't take the driver's seat. Instead, he left it for Sampson to drive us while he sat in the back with me.

"The late Samuel Danvers would probably disagree on that point," Archer murmured with an edge of black humor that made Sampson chuckle.

I said nothing, just stared out the window as we drove. Only a moment later, Archer reached over and unbuckled my seat belt.

Fear jolted through me and I started to protest, but he just lifted me into his lap and pulled his own belt over both of us. I pulled a couple of deep breaths to force my car-crash fear back in its box and relax into his embrace.

"Remember that first night we drove to Rainybanks?" he

whispered in my ear, his breath warm against my neck. "When you sat in my lap the whole way, just to piss me off?"

I smiled at the memory. "Of course. You were *so* angry the whole way there."

He let out a low chuckle. "I was angry because with every passing minute holding you in my arms, your ass grinding my dick, I was losing myself to you…all over again. Except this time, I knew I'd never be able to let you go."

His arms tightened around me, emphasizing his point, and I just snuggled against him.

When we got home, he carried me all the way up to my bedroom. Silently, he placed me down on the edge of my vanity and reached for my zipper, but I stopped him with a hand to his chest.

"I've got this," I told him with a gentle smile. "Thank you."

His brow dipped, but he didn't argue. He left me to shower alone, probably going to use their shared bathroom instead.

I washed up quickly, then dressed in one of the many T-shirts I'd swiped from the boys and climbed into my big bed. Archer joined me just a few minutes later, flipping the lights off on his way into my room. His big body curled around me in a way that screamed of comfort and protectiveness.

Neither one of us spoke for the longest time, just lay there in our tangle of limbs for ages until I started to drift into sleep. That's when I heard him whisper against my hair, ever so softly.

"I love you with my whole blackened soul, Kate. You're my everything."

Sometime later, I stirred as the mattress dipped and Steele climbed in on the other side of me. His hands were cold, and I groaned as he pulled me out of Archer's sleeping embrace to cuddle me to him instead.

"Shh," he breathed. "Go back to sleep, Hellcat."

A moment later I heard another set of footsteps, then Kody's muttered curse when he found my bed already full.

Steele shook with silent laughter against me. "Too slow, bro," he whispered.

Kody grumbled some more; then it all went quiet again and I let myself drift back into deep, dreamless sleep.

The next time I woke, I could sense it was almost morning. A quick glance at my clock over Archer's shoulder confirmed that guess, so I ever so carefully climbed out of bed without waking him or Steele. Except I almost stepped straight on Kody, who had made a little bed on the floor beside my bed.

So damn cute. I needed to invest in a bigger bed.

Smiling to myself, I padded into the bathroom to shower and get ready for my wedding day.

Holy crap. It was finally here.

I washed and dressed quickly, then crept back into my room to find Kody and Steele both gone. Archer was still fast asleep, snoring softly and hugging one of my pillows to his face.

Too. Freaking. *Cute.*

Grinning way too damn hard, I grabbed my dress bag from the closet, then tiptoed downstairs. I'd get ready at the venue, where my hair and makeup artists would be waiting. For now, I needed food.

In the kitchen, I found Kody and Steele laughing and joking with each other as they mixed batter for waffles.

"How the fuck did you two go from dead asleep to baking in three point six seconds flat? It's not natural to wake up that quick," I grumbled, sliding onto a stool and accepting a kiss from Steele.

He just grinned back at me and tucked a loose strand of pink hair behind my ear. "We wanted to make sure you had some food before you left," he told me. His gaze was locked on mine and more intense than his lighthearted tone.

"You're sweet." I leaned up to kiss him again. "But I'm pretty sure my car is due any minute now."

"We'll make waffles to go," Kody told me with a wide smile as he poured batter into the waffle iron. "They can wait five minutes."

Steele nodded his agreement, checking his watch. "I better get changed. I'm coming with you this morning, Hellcat."

My brows rose. That hadn't been part of the plan. I was supposed to go off with a security detail to get hair and makeup done—just like a real bride—and the boys were checking all our reinforcements and artillery.

"We decided it's safer," Kody told me as Steele rushed out. "None of us feel good about leaving you alone, even with our security guys. Better that either me or Steele stick close to you this morning."

I wasn't even going to argue that point; I totally agreed. "So how'd Steele get the job?"

Kody grimaced. "Rock, paper, scissors."

A heavy knock on the door pulled our attention, and I slid off my stool to answer it while Kody checked my waffle. I peered through the safety glass, then double-checked our video monitor to ensure Sampson was alone before opening the door.

"Morning," I greeted the older guy with a wide grin.

His brows twitched in confusion. "Are you ready to go?" His big, black SUV idled at the base of the steps, waiting for us, and I jerked a nod.

"Yes, just give me two minutes? Kody's making waffles. Come in." I stepped back and held the door for him.

He gave me a puzzled look but did as instructed. Sampson had no idea about our plan today; none of our security did. Only the four of us and Zed's backup knew that this wasn't my *real* wedding day, so maybe I wasn't acting like a bride should? Fuck it. Whatever. Sampson would work it out soon enough, and if he really was on our side, he'd understand the subterfuge.

When we got back to the kitchen, Kody was putting the finishing touches on what he informed me was a "banana waffle sandwich," which he then wrapped with a napkin and handed to me.

"See, now you can eat it in the car," he told me, proud as punch, "but maybe take extra napkins for the syrup."

Sampson groaned and shook his head but said nothing as I took a bite of my breakfast. Steele came jogging back downstairs a few moments later and announced we were ready to go.

Kody followed us through to the foyer, then snagged my wrist before I could leave.

"Hey, babe?" He tugged me around to face him, and I awkwardly licked syrup from my lips. "Whatever happens today—"

"Kodiak Jones," I cut him off with a warning growl, "you better not be saying goodbye right now. *Whatever* happens today, we'll all make it out alive. Got it?"

He gave me a pained smile, but I grabbed the front of his T-shirt in my fist, yanking him down to kiss me. When I released him again, we were both breathing hard, but I wasn't done making my point.

"No one, Kodiak Jones, *no one* is separating the four of us again. Certainly not some piece-of-shit, limp-dick businessman throwing his fucking cash around. You're my damn penguin, Kody." I crushed another hard kiss against his lips, then smacked him on the ass. "See you at the altar, babe."

I hurried out of the house before he could stop me again because the last thing I needed was to start leaking from the eyes so early in the day. And that was exactly what would happen if I let him tell me he loved me like there was a chance one of us might die today. Nope. Not happening. Not on my watch.

"All okay?" Steele asked as I slid into the backseat beside him with my waffle sandwich still clenched in my hand.

I jerked a nod, then leaned over and kissed him too. He groaned against my mouth, his tongue flicking over my lips and his fingers threading into my hair to pull me closer.

"Are you gonna share that with me?" he murmured when our kiss ended some moments later. It took me a hot second to follow what he was even talking about, but that was all the time he needed to lean forward and take a huge bite out of my waffle sandwich.

With a shout of protest, I yanked my food away but he just grinned as he chewed his mouthful of stolen food. Bastard. But I couldn't even be all that mad at him—I loved the food-stealing prick too damn much.

Now I just needed to get fake married to my real husband and clean the slate of assassins. Then, maybe, we could entertain a happily ever after.

Maybe.

CHAPTER 31

My bridal suite was set up in a hotel room directly across the street from the chapel where the wedding would play out. The second we got inside, I was bombarded with women all talking at a million miles an hour. Steele just laughed at what must have been a deer-in-the-headlights look on my face, then murmured in my ear that he'd find us some coffee.

Fuck, I loved him.

Hours later, my hair was a perfect cascade of pink curls pulled back from my face in an intricate braid and threaded with small white flowers. My makeup was flawless, and I almost seemed to glow from the inside. Like I'd just swallowed Tinker Bell or some shit.

I'd just stepped into my wedding gown when I heard voices outside the bathroom door.

Frowning, I tugged my zipper up, then pulled the door open to find out what the fuck the problem was.

"Arch?" I asked, my voice sharp with alarm. "What's going on? What's happened?"

He and Steele both turned to look at me in unison, and for a second it seemed like they were both frozen in time, like someone just pressed pause on them. It was only broken by my wedding planner's shriek of panic.

"No!" Alyssa howled. "No, it's bad luck! Don't look!" She tried to somehow block Archer's line of sight by leaping between us, despite the fact that she was all of five feet tall and not blocking *shit*.

Archer's lips twitched in a grin, but his eyes didn't leave me for even a second. "I think we'll be fine, Alyssa," he told her with a hint of laughter. "Kate and I don't buy into superstitions much, do we, sweetheart?"

His teasing tone of voice made me think he wasn't here because our plans had suddenly gone awry, so I let the tension slip out of my shoulders somewhat. "He's right," I assured our panicked wedding planner, touching her shoulder gently. "Could you give us a minute, please?"

She looked confused but nodded anyway and started to hurry out of the suite with the hairstylist close behind her. Then she paused at the doorway and swung back around with a frown on her face. "Actually, Madison Kate, I was coming up to ask if you've heard from your father? I haven't seen him at the chapel, and we're getting awfully close to time." Her brows hitched high, like she was trying to remain optimistic but could quietly sense it all falling to pieces.

I gave her a tight smile in return, thinking of how my father had howled when I drove that blade into his thigh. "Oh, I'm sorry; he won't be able to make it," I told her "He and Cherry ate some bad shellfish on their flight home yesterday. They're both terribly laid up with diarrhea today."

Alyssa's smile slipped to a grimace. "I see. Okay, well, no matter. It's a modern wedding; there's no reason you can't walk by yourself." Except her tone suggested it was the *worst* thing in the world. How right she was. I'd be one hell of a target like that…but that was sort of the point. Become bait.

"Actually," Archer spoke up, "Sampson is going to step in,

right?" He gave our security guy a pointed look, and the older guy peered up at us from his phone.

"Um," he started, his sharp gaze flicking from Archer to me, then back again. "Yes, of course. I'm practically Madison Kate's surrogate uncle, so it's only right."

I bit my lip to keep from laughing at his fumbled lie, but as Alyssa was already gushing her enthusiasm for that plan, I doubt she'd noticed. Part of me felt a little guilty that I wasn't asking James to take that role, but the guys and I had decided to keep things cautious with him for now. A surprise biological father at this late stage of the game was just a bit too clichéd to trust him implicitly.

"Okay, cool, now that's sorted, so if you could…" Archer gave Alyssa a tight smile, the rest of his sentence pretty damn clear.

"Oh, yes, of course," she exclaimed, pressing her hand to her chest as her cheeks pinked. "Sorry, you wanted a moment with your beautiful bride. Please be quick, though. We're ready to start in just ten minutes."

With that, she bustled out of the room, and my hair and makeup girls followed. Archer gave Sampson a pointed look, and the security guard reluctantly got to his feet.

Before he also left, he gave us all a critical look and shook his head. "Look, I don't know what's all going on here today," he said quietly, "but I don't need to know. I'll guard you with my life, miss. Same as every day." He gave me a short nod, then exited the room, closing the door firmly behind himself.

I arched a brow at the boys, my hands on my hips. "Okay, what's going on?"

"I'm pretty confident Sampson is loyal," Archer replied as he moved over to the sofa and opened the silver briefcase he'd brought with him. Inside was a slim silver pistol, much smaller than the Glocks the boys favored, and a white leather holster.

"What's this?" I asked as I moved closer to get a better look.

Archer turned his face to shoot me a sly grin. "Princess, you didn't think we were sending you out there totally unarmed, did you?"

I rolled my eyes. "I'm not." Hitching my long, lilac skirts up, I showed him where I'd attached my butterfly blade to my garter belt. Except apparently showing them my sexy lingerie interwoven with a deadly weapon had hit their stun buttons again, and both boys froze with their eyes glued to my, uh, knife.

"Actually, Steele," Archer said, clearing his throat as he recovered first, "I wanted to talk to Kate for a moment in private. Do you mind?"

Steele rolled his eyes and folded his arms over his chest. He was already dressed in a sharp suit but hadn't put his jacket on just yet. "Bullshit, Arch," he snapped back. "Unless by *talk* you mean *fuck*, which I'd believe."

Archer glowered at his friend. "I'm serious, bro. Just give me five minutes."

I could tell Steele wanted to refuse. He wanted to argue and stay with me a little longer, but something in Archer's expression made his shoulders sag.

"Fine," he ground out. "Five minutes. Not even you can fuck that fast." He gave me a wink, then glared at Archer again before leaving the room.

When he was gone, I gave Archer a quizzical look. "Okay, you're acting kind of weird this morning, Arch." I sank down to sit on the sofa beside the gun case. He was on his knees, so it put us at eye level. "What's going on?"

His lips quirked in a half smile. "I can't just want to give my bride a gun on our wedding day?"

My glare flattened, even though I did appreciate the gun. "Steele could have given me the gun, Arch. Fess up; you've got something else on your mind."

He didn't disagree, but his gaze did drop away from my eyes and rake over my body, pausing over the dangerously low neckline and the generous curves of my breasts on display. "You look sensational, Kate," he told me, his voice rough. "Better than anything I could have imagined. You're a fucking goddess right now, you know that?"

I couldn't fight my smile but still shook my head. "Don't change the subject, Sunshine. What's going on with you?"

His smile turned almost apprehensive, and he let out a sigh. "I wanted to give you something." He reached into his pocket and pulled out a small velvet box. A fucking ring box. *What the fuck?*

"Arch—" I started to say in a panic, but he just shot me a lopsided smile and handed me the envelope that he'd pulled out with the ring box.

"Just read the letter," he told me in a gruff voice, running a hand through his hair anxiously.

I wrinkled my nose in confusion, one eye still on the ring box in his other hand, but I did as he asked and opened the envelope. With one more suspicious look at him, I tugged the letter out and unfolded the linen-textured paper.

My gaze lowered from Archer's stupidly handsome face and started taking in the elegant, flowing handwriting of the letter. The first thing that became totally apparent: it wasn't written by Archer. I'd seen his handwriting, and it was a far cry from the neat, looping cursive on the page.

It was addressed to me, and it only took a couple of words to realize it was from Archer's grandmother. I read another sentence, then glanced up at Archer with a frown.

"Have you read this?"

He shook his head. "No. She was pretty clear with me that letter is for your eyes only."

Relieved, I bit my lip and turned my attention back to the letter. Line by line, word by word, Constance D'Ath reached through the page and wrapped me in her arms, in her love, and in her *approval*. It was hands down the most heartfelt thing I'd ever read, and by the time I reached the end, my cheeks were wet and my vision blurry.

"Baby girl," Archer breathed, "don't cry." He gently dabbed my cheeks with a fabric handkerchief, and I let out a short laugh.

"Sorry," I groaned, taking the handkerchief from him. "Fuck, I've messed up my makeup, haven't I?"

The corner of his mouth hitched in a half smile. "Nah, you still look like a fucking angel."

I rolled my eyes and dabbed underneath them to try to clean up what was likely a mascara mess. Yep, sure enough, black smudges came away on the handkerchief. "Fallen angel, more like."

Archer's smile spread wider. "My favorite type."

The ring box still in his hand caught my attention once more, and I nodded to it. "So are you going to show me what's in the box?"

His gaze dropped down to it as he turned it over in his fingers thoughtfully. Then he cleared his throat. A faint blush crept up his neck, which was starting to freak me right the fuck out, but then he opened the box.

My breath caught. "Holy shit."

"Kate," Archer said in a soft voice, his gaze capturing mine despite the gorgeous, sparkling diamond ring in his hand. "I know everything that's happened has been just all kinds of fucked up. I messed things up from day one, and I'll probably spend forever trying to make up for it. Hell, I *want* to spend forever making up for it because that'll mean we're together…" He trailed off, but my throat was so tight I couldn't have said anything even if I had words to say.

Archer drew another deep breath. "I'm not asking you to marry me."

A smile tugged at my lips. "Because we're already married. Yeah, you skipped that step."

His eyes flashed with some deep, painful emotion. "I did. But this might be as close to a real wedding as you'll ever let me have, and…" He trailed off, his gaze dipping to the ring. "I dunno. I guess I wanted to make it more real. I don't want to put some cheap costume jewelry on your finger, Kate. Not today, not ever." He pinched the delicate ring between his way-too-big fingers, making it look comical as he offered it to me.

I bit my lip, my pulse racing, but I didn't flinch as he slid it onto my finger. It was a perfect fit. Of course it was.

"This came from my great-grandmother." Archer's thumb stroked over the glittering diamonds as he gripped my fingers tight.

I drew a long breath, feeling the weight of his gift. This had nothing to do with today's fake wedding and everything to do with us. Just us. Archer and me…and our unconventional marriage.

"What are we calling this, then?" I wet my lips as his gaze met mine once more.

He gave a one-shouldered shrug. "Fuck if I know. I just want my family ring on your finger, Princess. Don't ask me to analyze it any more than that."

I swallowed a laugh but couldn't wipe the grin from my face. "Well, it's stunning. But—"

"I know," he cut me off with a shake of his head. "I know. When this is all over, I swear I'll personally file our divorce papers if that's what you still want. But in the meantime…" He gave another small shrug. "In the meantime, just let a man hold out hope that you might not want that."

My brows shot up, and a rush of *something* surged through me. But it wasn't panic like I'd have expected. More like…I didn't even know. Excitement? Was that weird? Ugh, everything about us was weird, so be it.

"I…don't even know what to say," I finally admitted after sitting there with my eyes locked on his for way too damn long.

His lips slanted in a half smile. "You don't need to say anything, Princess. I just want you to know I'm in this one hundred percent. I love you more than I even knew I was capable of, and I—"

"I love you too," I whispered, cutting him off.

His eyes widened. "What?"

"You heard me."

"I don't know that I did. Say it again."

I rolled my eyes, and his fingers tightened around mine. "I said I love you too."

The smile that lit his face was an image I immediately banked into my memory. It was a smile I never *ever* wanted to forget. He looked at me like I'd just changed his whole damn life, and it gave me all the fuzzy feelings.

"What, that's it?" he teased, tugging me by my hand and bringing me closer to where he knelt. "No extended declarations of how I'm the light of your life?"

I squinted at him. "Don't push it, Sunshine." He smirked, and I couldn't help but add, "You already fucking know you are."

"Yeah, but it's something different to hear it from your lips, Princess." His other hand wrapped around my waist, and he pulled me closer still, until my ass was just barely on the edge of the sofa and my knees—covered in lilac silk and tulle—bracketed his body. "It's officially my second favorite sound from your lips."

My brows quirked up in curiosity. "Only your *second* favorite? What's better than me telling you that I love you?" He shivered slightly as I said those three words again, and it made my heart race. Fucking hell…these boys were the best addiction that I never wanted to quit.

"You wanna know?" He released my fingers and brought his hand up to cup my face. His own lips hovered just an inch away, so close I was dying to kiss him. Still, I also wanted to play his game because Archer's games *always* ended well for me.

So I nodded as much as his grip would allow. "I wanna know."

"Well then, I better show you," he replied with a wicked grin. He closed the gap between us, his lips meeting mine in a kiss so tender it made my heart ache, and I let out a small moan. Then froze.

"Wait, was that it?" I asked, jerking away from him.

Archer grinned and shook his head. "Not…*quite*." He found the hem of my skirt and started bunching it up. His hands trailed up my legs. "But it was close."

I groaned, licking my lips in anticipation. "Steele is gonna be back *any* second." But I didn't exactly protest when his fingers found the satin thong I was wearing under my gown.

Archer just threw me a wicked smirk. "So? He can watch. I bet he gets off on that shit too." His fingers hooked my panties aside, then stroked along the length of my aching pussy. Fucking hell, if he left me all keyed up and twitchy before this wedding, I'd kick him straight in the balls.

"He'd be more likely to wanna join in," I murmured, then gasped as Archer's fingers pushed into me. Thank fuck, he wasn't messing around. "Oh shit," I breathed, grabbing his wrist tight.

"Close," he chuckled, his fingers pumping into me as his thumb found my clit and teased circles. I moaned long and low as I dropped my head back and rode his hand. I was already riding the endorphin high of the whole "I love you" situation, so making me come wasn't exactly going to be difficult. I was already halfway there even before his lips dropped to kiss my chest.

"Arch," I gasped as he pushed the fabric of my dress aside to expose my breast. His lips seized my hard nipple, and his fingers pumped between my lips, building my orgasm with alarming speed. It only took a few moments more, and then I was done for. My climax hit hard, and I moaned out his name while my pussy tightened around his fingers.

He snickered, his breath teasing my damp flesh as he tugged my dress back over my tits. "*That* is my favorite sound off your lips, baby girl. When you moan my name mid-orgasm. Nothing fucking sweeter."

I groaned, watching him with heavy-lidded eyes as he brought his fingers to his mouth and sucked them. Why was that so fucking sexy? Whatever the reason, it sent a shudder straight through me, and my breath caught.

"Holy shit," I whispered. "I need you, Arch."

One of his brows flicked up in silent question, but we didn't have time to discuss it. Instead, I just grabbed up an armful of my long skirt so I could turn around to kneel on the sofa with my hands on the back of it.

Arching my neck to look back at him, I let a teasing smile play over my lips. "Quickly, Sunshine. If your dick isn't inside me in three seconds, I'm taking this ring off."

It was safe to say I'd never seen him undo his pants faster. Two seconds later, my panties were ripped clean off and I screamed as he filled me up in one hard thrust. My fingers tightened on the velvet back of the sofa, and I arched my spine to push against him. We were on borrowed time already, and I wanted to feel him come. I *needed* it.

"Fuck yes," I moaned as he fucked me, his hands gripping my hips where my wedding dress was all bunched up. He let out little grunting pants with every thrust, and I grinned at how much I craved that sound from him too. "Harder," I begged him, "faster, Arch. Fuck me like you own me."

Magic. Fucking. Words. His control snapped. He gripped a handful of my perfectly curled hair and tugged it tight as he rode me hard. Every stroke, every slap of skin made me cry out, and I could already see stars.

My moans of encouragement were coming more and more breathy, my hands gripping the back of the sofa tight to prevent us both tumbling over. Archer released my hair as my climax started to build, brushing it over my shoulder to expose my back, and I smiled.

He slowed, then stilled within me.

"Princess," he growled in a husky voice, trailing a finger down the top of my spine. "What is *this*?"

I grinned wider, wiggling my hips to remind him what we were still in the middle of doing. He took the hint and started moving again, but this time it was slow. Gentle. Fucking *loving* as his finger traced the new ink on my spine.

"What does it look like, *Archer*?" I teased as I rocked on his cock, chasing my orgasm.

He let out a deeply masculine rumble and leaned forward to trace that small tattoo with his lips as his hands closed over mine. "It looks like you tattooed an arrow on your skin, Kate." His hips rolled, his thick shaft pumping all too leisurely in my desperate cunt. "Why would you do that?"

I let out a small laugh, loving how heavily he leaned on my hands. "Because, idiot," I panted, "I fucking love you. That's why."

He let out a soft moan, and his hips bucked a bit faster, making me shudder as my orgasm built up again. "I fucking love you too, Princess," he confessed, then bit me.

I cried out, and he took that as his cue. I came so hard my ears rang and my vision went spotty, and I knew he joined me right there. His fingers laced together with mine on the sofa, and I couldn't stop staring at the way his huge, inked hand gripped mine as we came. The glittering, diamond D'Ath ring bit into his skin, and a smear of blood marked my pale flesh, but that in itself couldn't have been more perfect if it'd been scripted.

Someone cleared their throat, interrupting us before Archer even pulled out of me. I turned my face to smile at Steele.

"Hey, Max," I greeted him, licking my lips.

He glared at the two of us. "You have no idea how thin my self-control is right now, Hellcat. *Don't* look at me like that."

Archer snickered as he tucked himself back into his suit pants, then smoothed my dress back down.

"I better get cleaned up," I murmured with a faint blush as I climbed off the sofa and felt the slickness between my legs.

Steele rolled his eyes but tossed me a packet of wet wipes left behind by my makeup artist. "I should have come back in five minutes like I said." He crossed over to me when I was done with my speedy cleanup and ran his fingers through my curls to tidy them somewhat. He swiped a thumb under my left eye and his brow furrowed. "Have you been crying?" His accusing gaze shot to Archer, who raised his hands defensively.

"Don't look at me like that, shithead. It wasn't me."

"It was Connie," I assured Steele. "She wrote me a very sweet letter."

He still frowned but jerked a nod and gently pushed me to sit so he could help me strap my gun in the thigh holster included with the weapon onto my leg. "All right, everyone is in place. Arch, you better go." Steele nodded to the door. "I'll stay with MK until the last possible second; then we're at go time."

Archer nodded his understanding, then stooped to kiss me possessively. "Stay safe, baby girl," he murmured. "I love you."

I bit my lip, but he was gone before I could reciprocate the sentiment.

Steele just arched a brow at me. "You ready for this, Hellcat?"

I nodded, firm. I was *more* than ready for this.

CHAPTER 32

The second Alyssa gave Sampson and me the nod to say it was go time, I almost keeled over. The processional music had just started playing, and a thick knot of emotions choked me. It wasn't some cheesy wedding march by Bach. It was Steele's song for me, played by a string quartet.

What the fuck?

These boys were piling on the sweet gestures as though this were a real wedding. It was tripping my nerves out, and my arm was trembling in Sampson's.

"Don't worry, miss," he murmured under his breath. "Your boys got me all strapped up in Kevlar. If anyone shoots, you go down and I'll cover you, got it?"

I jerked a nod. I couldn't tell him that I wasn't even remotely worried about getting shot; I was shaking because my heart was too fucking full of love.

The faces of the guests were totally anonymous, almost all planted there. Of course we'd made excuses for Constance and Ana not to come; there was no way in hell we would have risked them being caught in the crossfire. Samuel was dead, Cherry had been told she wasn't welcome, and Bree was still in the hospital. Aside from our security team, I recognized *no one*, and that was exactly how I wanted it.

I held my breath almost the entire way down the chapel aisle. It wasn't a huge venue, which played into our "intimate guest list" bullshit, but I was torn between wanting to soak up the sound of Steele's music being played by the string quartet and remaining alert for any assassination attempts. The plan should safeguard me from long-range attacks, though. I had to trust in the plan.

Still, my palms were sweating as Sampson delivered me to the end of the aisle where my groom waited, looking sexier than I'd ever fucking seen him. Maybe that was helped by the fact that I was equally in love with his two best men, both sharply dressed in tailored suits that made my inner submissive pant with desire.

The three of them stared at me like they were seeing me for the first time, and it was a feeling I never wanted to get used to. It made my chest tight and gooseflesh break out all over my skin, but I couldn't stop fucking smiling.

Fucking hell, MK, this is an ambush, not a real wedding. Pull it together!

Our celebrant started droning on with his canned-wedding-speech crap, and I totally tuned him out. My attention was all for my boys. My gaze ate the three of them up, and everything else faded into the background. Not the smartest move when we were actively *expecting* someone—or several someones—to try to kill me today, but...too fucking bad. Like Archer had said, this may be the closest we ever came to a real wedding, so why not make the most of it?

I had faith in our plan. It was airtight.

Yet as the ceremony progressed, I started getting uneasy. Archer's brow was furrowed too, as he held my gaze, and I could sense he was just as concerned. They should have tried something by now. All our intel on the four hitmen who'd taken my contract while the listing had still been active suggested each of their standard MOs was to take an easy target. That's exactly what we were giving them. Yet…nothing had happened.

Not a single person had tried to attack throughout the ceremony. Not one. No one had even *attempted* to interrupt the whole bullshit wedding, and I soon found myself tripping over vows that I hadn't remotely prepared to say.

I made the best of it, though, meeting each of my guys' eyes with each line of those trite, well-worn wedding vows. Because regardless of who I was already legally married to, I was in it for the long haul with *all three* of them. I hoped they all knew that.

"…may now kiss your bride." The celebrant's declaration shocked me. I gasped as Archer threaded his fingers into my hair and claimed my mouth in a searing kiss that I felt *all* the way to my toes.

"What the fuck is going on?" I whispered against his lips, letting the fall of my pink curls hide our faces from the clapping fake guests. "What went wrong?"

"I have no idea," he murmured back, his thumb stroking my cheek. "But I'm kind of glad it did."

And just like that, the chapel exploded.

Not metaphorically. A goddamn fucking bomb detonated and took the entire back of the chapel off. Archer threw himself over me, guarding me with his body even as he pulled his gun from his underarm holster. Gunfire rang out from every damn angle, and my gut churned with anxiety. Something had gone seriously wrong with our plan.

"Stay down," Archer barked as he lifted his weight off me somewhat.

I didn't argue, just scrambled to shelter behind our dead celebrant as Archer stood and started shooting at one of our attackers. One of our *many* attackers.

"Babe, you good?" Kody demanded, appearing beside me as he ejected the magazine of his gun and slammed a fresh one in.

How had he already used an entire fucking magazine? Boy was a machine.

"Yep," I replied. "Go. I'm fine."

He jerked a nod, then rose to his knees and squeezed off at least five shots before reaching his feet. I had no doubt they'd all hit their intended targets too. Steele really had trained him well.

Gripping the long silk skirt of my gown, I quickly hitched it up and retrieved my own gun. No way in hell was I going down without a fight. No. Fucking. Way.

Still using the celebrant as a shield, I rose up enough to get a look at what was going on. Not that it helped, much. There was almost a wall of suited guys shielding me, so I couldn't see much of anything. That didn't stop a sneaky fuck from creeping up on me from the opposite direction, though. Only the flash of his movement in the corner of my eye tipped me off, and I reacted quickly, doing exactly as Steele had trained me.

Shoot first. Ask questions never.

The man dropped to the floor, my shot finding its mark as my heart raced.

Fuck. *Fuck.* We hadn't expected an attack like this, but luckily we'd planned for all circumstances.

"Hellcat!" Steele roared from somewhere past the line of suits protecting me. "Plan C, gorgeous!"

"Got it!" I shouted back, already having guessed that's what we'd do.

"Count of three, babe!" Kody shouted from somewhere else. Then, "Three!"

I surged out of my protected spot and dove through the gap between two of the suited soldiers, tucking and rolling in a snowball of lilac wedding gown. As I found my feet—totally blinded by dress and pink hair—I leaped straight into Kody's arms. Together we bolted down the short aisle and barreled straight into the waiting SUV at the front door.

298

"Go!" Kody shouted at Sampson behind the wheel, but he didn't need to be told twice. He was already thumping back down the short stairs, with the heavy-duty, off-road tires of our SUV handling it like a walk in the park. Kody yanked the door closed as we peeled into the street and left the shootout in our dust.

"Are you okay?" he asked, turning to me in concern as he tucked his gun away and grabbed the back of my neck. "Are you hurt? Fucking hell, I never would have expected them to blow the fucking church up; that was nuts!"

"I'm fine," I assured him, "not even a scratch. That was a hell of a lot more than four assassins, though, Kody. And they were working together?"

He grimaced but nodded. "They must have recruited help. We'll know more when we get to Club 22." His thumb stroked across my cheek. "Are you sure you're okay?"

"Positive," I promised him. "Even though that wasn't what we'd expected, Plan C worked flawlessly. Right?"

"How many backup plans were there?" Sampson asked from the driver's seat, looking at us in the mirror.

Kody just shot him a smirk. "Enough."

Sampson inclined his head. "Fair enough. Club 22, yeah?"

"Yep," Kody replied, snaking his arm around my waist and pulling me closer to him. "Hades thought it'd be entertaining to throw a reception, banking on us all coming out of the wedding alive, I guess."

Sampson grunted. "Safe bet. I spotted plenty of armed Timberwolves fighting on our side there."

Kody gave a short laugh. "Yeah, we over-gunned this one. Better safe than sorry." His arm was tight around my waist, but I was still nervously sweating that I didn't have a seat belt on.

Before I could free myself from his grip to reach for it, Kody snagged my belt with his other hand and clicked it securely over me. My held breath rushed out in instant relief, and he kissed my forehead.

"I've got you, babe," he murmured. "You're safe with me. Always."

I didn't doubt that statement for even a second. But what about Archer and Steele?

CHAPTER 33

The club was quiet when we arrived, most of the "guests" still back at the ruined chapel with my attackers. Not to mention the fact that it was only midday, and I doubted Club 22 was much of a day-drinking venue.

I hated running away from that fight, *hated* it, but it was a topic that had been thoroughly debated over the past few weeks. Even I couldn't deny the logic in getting me out of there as fast as possible. Not only was I the number one target, I was also exposed without Kevlar and the least experienced soldier. Yeah, I hated running from that fight, but I got it.

One of the gorgeous dancers greeted us as we entered the club and told me she had a change of clothes ready for me in the backstage area. I hesitated, wanting to keep my lilac wedding gown on, but a quick glance down my front made me grimace. At some point, maybe while I was using a dead celebrant as a shield, I'd soaked up a decent amount of someone else's blood. Not the best look.

Kody tailed me through to the backstage area where a couple of dancers were getting done up for their sets onstage, but the pretty brunette—Venus—led me to a private dressing room where a dress bag was hung up on the rail and a brand-new shoebox sat below it.

"The boss sorted out a backup outfit, in case your wedding dress didn't survive the day," Venus told me with a warm smile. "It should fit, but if it doesn't, just give me a yell. I can work wonders with a handful of safety pins."

I thanked her, and she ducked out of the room, closing the door softly behind herself. Kody stayed, his eyes intense on me as I reached for my zipper.

"You just gonna stare at me while I get changed?" I teased with a grin.

His eyes darkened, and he prowled closer to me. "Changed? Nah. I was hoping more for just undressing." He shot me a wink and smoothed his palms down my neck, then pushed my gown from my shoulders. It pooled around my ankles in a flutter of blood-soaked fabric, leaving me in nothing but a garter belt, empty gun holder, garters, and stockings. My panties were long gone, and the dress hadn't been suitable for a bra.

Kody sucked in a sharp breath, his gaze pleading as he cupped my breasts in his hands. "Babe, you blow my fucking mind," he whispered. His lips found mine when I tilted my head back. He kissed me tenderly, tracing the lines of my mouth like he was committing my kiss to memory.

I gasped as he gripped my waist and boosted me onto the low vanity behind me.

"Kody," I protested in a low chuckle as he pushed my legs apart and stepped closer to kiss me again. "I get the feeling we probably shouldn't fuck in one of Hades's dressing rooms. It feels a little too close to disrespectful after all the help we just got."

He groaned, kissing my neck, then sighed. "I guess you make a good point. Fuck, I want you, though. Seeing you walk down that aisle in your dress was like I was trapped in the most incredible dream." He grabbed my earlobe in his teeth and sucked on it, making me squirm.

"Kodiak Jones," I scolded with a laugh, "just help me get

302

dressed. I need to get out there and make sure the boys made it back in one piece."

He sighed heavily but backed off a step, catching my eyes. Then he gave me a knowing smirk and threaded his fingers into the tangle of my hair, tipping my head to the side so he could kiss the fresh tattoo below my ear. I shuddered at the slight ache of my fresh ink, but it was a good kind of shudder.

"I saw this when you were halfway through those fucking cardboard wedding vows to Arch," Kody murmured next to my ear, his lips brushing soft kisses over the little penguin design I'd had inked into my skin. "I almost shoved that fuck out of the way so I could kiss you right then. I fucking love you, MK."

I grinned, deliriously happy with his reaction to my tattoo for him. "I love you too, my penguin," I whispered back, then let him kiss me until I was light-headed and aching for him.

"I better let you get dressed." He brushed his thumb over my lower lip like he badly wanted to do that with his dick. "I'll call Arch and make sure he and Steele are alive."

I winced at that flippant comment. It was still too fresh after Steele had nearly died from a shot to the chest. "Please do," I muttered. "I'll be quick."

Kody left the dressing room, only opening the door far enough to slip out, then closing it firmly. I knew he would be right on the other side of the door while he made his calls. He wouldn't leave me alone right now; we were all too keyed up and paranoid to do dumb shit like that.

I hurried to unzip the dress bag left for me and found a gorgeous, floor-length ivory gown. It was almost entirely made up of intricate glass beads and soft fringing, with a silk slip underneath it all. Very on-theme for the *Gatsby*-era club and utterly stunning.

Grinning, I quickly stepped into it and pulled the zipper up at the back. It fit like a glove, and the shoes provided—champagne-glitter Jimmy Choos—were exactly my size. There wasn't much I could do about my hair and makeup, so I just finger-combed the tangled pink curls and re-pinned a couple of the pins holding my braid secure.

With a shrug at my reflection, I decided I was done. Anxious nerves were already knotting my stomach anyway. I needed to get out there and find out if my boys were okay. I needed to know everyone had made it out of that chapel safely.

I pulled the door open and found Kody leaning against the wall directly opposite, his phone to his ear and his eyes meeting mine. My brows shot up in question, and his lips curved in a half smile.

"All right, no worries, bro," he said into the phone. "Get cleaned up, but take your time. I'm more than happy to entertain our bride alone for a while." He snickered at whatever the response was to that, then ended the call.

I let out a long breath in relief at the relaxed expression on his face. "Everything's okay?"

He nodded. "Everyone's alive that should be alive."

"Thank fuck." I closed the gap between us and threw my arms around his neck. "Fucking hell, I don't think I could handle it if one of you got shot again. We should make Kevlar part of your everyday wardrobe or something."

Kody laughed, but his arms stiffened slightly.

A cold wash of dread rolled through me. "Kodiak?" I prompted, pulling away far enough to glare at him. "No one was shot, were they?"

He winced. "Everyone's alive," he evaded, and my panic ratcheted up even higher.

"Kody!" I snapped. "Who got shot? Was it Steele? Did Steele get shot again? Oh my god, I'm gonna—"

"Steele's fine," Kody cut me off with a grin. "It was Arch." He actually started laughing. How the hell this situation was *funny*, I had no clue.

"Kodiak Jones, explain that in more detail, or I'm castrating you with my knife."

He cringed and cupped his junk. "I don't believe you. You enjoy my dick too much to mutilate it. But seriously, he's fine. That was him on the phone being all surly and shit about it."

I bit my lip, waves on waves of concern crashing over me. But if he was well enough to be talking to Kody on the phone...

"I promise, babe." Kody brought his hands to my face and kissed my lips gently. "Arch is fine. It was just a flesh wound on his arm. He's just pissed because it messed up one of his favorite tats."

I rolled my eyes. "Really?" My tone was drier than a nun's nasty. "He said that?"

Kody snickered. "Not in words, but I know that's what he meant. So precious. Anyway, he and Steele are swinging past home to get patched up by James before they come here. Hades isn't super appreciative of people showing up with bleeding bullet wounds. That sort of thing attracts all the wrong attention for a *legitimate* business."

The way he stressed *legitimate* made me pretty confident the clubs were just the tip of Hades's empire. Not that it was any of my business. Regardless of the deals and connections between my boys and the criminals of Shadow Grove, none of us were interested in running our own crime syndicate.

"You're *sure* he's okay?" I pressed, still worried as hell about the fact that Archer had gotten *shot*. These guys were going to kill me with sheer stress before my assassins could get me.

Kody nodded. "Do you want to call him back and check?" He held his phone out to me, but I shook my head.

"No, it's fine. If you say he's okay, then he's okay." I still bit at my lip, though. "Okay, maybe I'll just text him?" I grabbed the phone from Kody's hand as he gave a chuckle.

I jabbed him playfully with my elbow and spun around to lean my back against his chest as I typed out my message to Archer.

Kodiak Jones: Sunshine! You got SHOT? WTF?!

I didn't think I needed to elaborate on the fact that it was me messaging him. The idea of Kody ever calling Archer *Sunshine* was enough to make me laugh.

There was a pause before the message was marked as read. Kody hugged me against his body, his arms around my waist and his lips finding the penguin tattoo behind my ear again.

Archer D'Ath: Blame Steele. Dickhead.

I frowned in confusion at the message, but before I could reply, another came through.

Archer D'Ath: I'm fine, Princess. Just a graze, I promise.

He ended the message with a heart emoji, and the tension seeped out of my bones. He was okay. He wasn't dying. I couldn't handle another life-or-death race to an emergency room.

Kodiak Jones: Good. Just…get here. I need to see you both alive with my own eyes.
Archer D'Ath: Yes, ma'am.

He followed that one with a winking face, and I grinned. Yeah, he was fine.

Before I handed the phone back to Kody, it buzzed again.

Archer D'Ath: I love you, Kate.

Oh fuck. That was a whole different thing to see in writing.

I only hesitated a second, glancing up at Kody, before I wrote my reply knowing full well he could see the screen.

Kodiak Jones: I love you too.

I added a heart emoji, then quickly spun around to hand Kody his phone back with my cheeks warm. For whatever reason, I was a hundred times more awkward about saying the L-word in front of the other guys than having sex in front of them. Truly a testament to how broken I was.

Kody wasn't judging me, though. He just took his phone and tucked it back in his pocket, then cupped my cheek in his palm.

"I *also* love you, babe," he whispered before kissing me softly. "Let's go get some champagne. It's a party, after all."

"Is it weird to be partying at midday when a whole freaking chapel just got blown up and countless people killed this morning?" I pondered aloud as we linked our fingers together and made our way back out to the main bar area. It had filled up more since we'd arrived, and I spotted a whole bunch of barely concealed weapons on the patrons who were drinking and laughing already.

Kody shot me a grin. "Nah. This is mostly a reward for Hades's guys who helped us out this morning. Plus, they've opened to VIP guests as well, so it'll be a proper party and not just a sausage fest. Any excuse for a good party when your business relies on liquor sales, babe."

That seemed like good enough reasoning, and certainly everyone seemed to be having a good time already. A pretty waitress in a sequined flapper dress approached and invited us to follow her to a reserved table, where she had set up several champagne flutes and an ice bucket holding a still-sealed bottle of Perrier-Jouët Belle Epoque Rosé.

Kody thanked her but waved her off when she offered to open and pour the champagne for us. Apparently, I wasn't the only one still feeling all kinds of paranoid because he carefully checked each of the flutes to ensure they were, in fact, empty. When he was satisfied, he popped the cork from the champagne and poured for both of us.

"You think someone would try to drug us *here*?" I asked quietly as I accepted my drink from him.

He just shrugged. "I think there's no harm in being cautious. It wouldn't be the first time, babe."

I wrinkled my nose, remembering all too clearly how I'd almost died of a fentanyl overdose not that long ago. "Fair call."

Taking a sip of my drink, I caught sight of a familiar face across the room. He spotted us a moment later and headed over to our booth with a look of determination.

"Zed." Kody greeted the sharply suited guy with a nod. "Everything pan out as planned?"

Zed sat down with a sigh and accepted the glass of champagne Kody poured for him. "As much as it ever can, yes. Twenty-three assailants was definitely on the upper end of all the scenarios we'd run, but nothing we couldn't handle."

"Thank you for your help on this," I told him seriously. "I can't even begin to tell you how much I appreciate it."

Zed stared back at me a moment, then jerked a nod. "I can imagine. It was a solid plan; I'd do the same if I were in Archer's shoes. If anyone put a hit out on the woman I love..." He trailed off with a shake of his head, but Kody snorted a laugh. Zed shot him a sharp glare before anything else was said, but I filed that away to ask Kody later.

"You invited the Reapers?" Kody asked, changing the subject and nodding toward the bar. I couldn't see who he was talking about but sincerely hoped it wasn't Zane. Our last interaction had left me feeling all kinds of slimy, and I was starting to question just how much he'd truly cared for my mom.

Zed took a gulp of his drink and shrugged. "Reapers are good for business. But only Cass was extended an invitation to *this* party. No one wants a D'Ath family reunion here today, thanks."

I perked up at the information that Cass was here. I liked that grumpy bastard.

"Ah shit, trouble's here," Zed groaned. A moment later, a beautiful girl with silky copper hair came bouncing over to us with a

308

wide, somewhat innocent smile plastered across her face. She was dressed casually in jeans and a tank top, so she looked out of place with all the suits and glittering dresses of the club patrons.

"Kody!" she squealed, basically leaping into my man's arms as he stood up to greet her. "Oh my god, it's been ages! I've missed you! What happened this morning? No one will tell me anything, *again*." She shot a pointed glare at Zed, who just sipped his drink. "But I heard you and Arch and Steele were going to be here with—" She broke off with a gasp, releasing Kody and locking eyes with me. "You! Oh wow, you're Madison Kate Danvers! Holy shit. Oh my god, didn't you and Arch just get *married*? I can't believe he didn't invite me, but whatever, I'm so excited to meet you!" She all but shoved Kody aside so she could sit in his place and hug me.

I stiffened up in her embrace, and she quickly released me with a blush rising in her cheeks.

"Sorry. Shit, sorry. I shouldn't have hugged you. Sorry." She was tripping all over her words and looking all kinds of embarrassed, and it was throwing me for a loop.

I shook my head. "It's fine, seriously. You just took me off guard. I'm not really a hugger." Which was true, with the exceptions of my three loves. With them, I could hardly get enough of the feeling of being wrapped up in their arms.

The girl smiled at me again, her whole face lighting up. She was *really* pretty and seemed around my age. Maybe a bit younger. "I'm Seph," she said, introducing herself. "I bet these fuckers have never even mentioned me too." She rolled her eyes dramatically, and I bit back a laugh. Archer had, in fact, mentioned her to me.

"Seph," Zed growled from across the table. "You're not even supposed to be here. You want me to call Hades?"

Seph's eyes narrowed. "Don't you dare. Just let me have, like, five minutes of harmless fun, Zed. God, you're such a fucking buzzkill."

"You're underage, Seph. Get the fuck out of here before you

land in more trouble than you already are." Zed pulled his phone out of his pocket, and Seph let out a small scream of protest.

"Zed, don't be a fuck-nugget. Madison Kate is underage too!"

Zed shrugged, a teasing grin playing across his lips. "And yet it's you who will get my ass chewed out by Hades later." He nodded his head to Cass, who'd just arrived at our table. "Cass, do you mind escorting Seph home?"

Cass gave me a nod of greeting, then turned his dark eyes to the vibrant girl beside me. Maybe it was a trick of the light, but I could have sworn his gaze softened with affection. "My pleasure, Zed," he rumbled, holding out his hand to the girl.

"Screw you, Cassiel," she snapped back, folding her arms under her breasts. "You all need to stop treating me like a little kid. I'm seventeen, not seven. I want to hang out with Madison Kate and Kody."

Cass and Zed exchanged a look, and Kody seemed to be trying not to laugh. Man, I wanted to understand how all these pieces connected.

"You don't wanna be treated like a kid, then stop acting like one, Seph," Zed replied, sounding tired. I got the feeling this wasn't the first time they'd had this argument. "Go with Cass, or I'm calling." He held up his phone, showing the call screen cued up with *Hades*.

"Sorry, girl," I whispered to her sympathetically. "It was nice to meet you, though."

"You too," she mumbled back to me. "Maybe one day I'll be let off my damn leash and we can hang out properly. I already know we could be good friends." Her smile was wide, and I couldn't help returning it. Weirdly, I thought she could be right. I remembered all too clearly what Archer had told me about this girl, Persephone. He'd saved her from being sold as a sex slave at age *thirteen*. No wonder Hades was overprotective of her, considering she was only seventeen now.

"Come on, Seph," Cass growled, "I've got better shit to do than babysit your bratty ass." Except I knew that grumpy fuck, and he didn't seem annoyed by the job at all. Curiouser and curiouser.

Seph's jaw tightened, and her eyes narrowed at the big, tattoo-covered Reaper. "I'm not going with you, Cass. I'll find my own way home." She turned to me and smacked a quick kiss on my cheek, then did the same to Kody. "Say hey to Arch and Steele for me."

"Will do," Kody promised her.

She flipped Zed and Cass off, then started to make her way across the bar. Zed just gave Cass a silent look, and Seph only made it another couple of steps before she found herself thrown over the Reaper second-in-command's shoulder. She kicked and screamed as he carried her out of the club, but I wasn't worried for her. Cass wouldn't hurt a girl like that. He was a good egg, and he clearly held some level of affection for Seph.

Oh. What if *she* was the girl he'd been pining for? His "place-holder" had been a redhead too.

"Sorry about that," Zed said, addressing me. "Seph knows she shouldn't come into the clubs, but she's going through a rebellious phase." He grimaced, and Kody laughed.

"Yeah, good luck with that," Kody scoffed, sitting back down beside me and wrapping his arm around my waist.

Zed just rolled his eyes and took another sip of his champagne, then hit call on his phone screen. Raising it to his ear, he grimaced. "Boss, Seph was here. Cass is escorting her home now." He paused a moment, and he winced at whatever was being said on the other end. "I needed to stay so I can debrief when Archer gets here. Cass has it handled; he won't let anything happen to her." Another pause, and Zed scrubbed a hand over his clean-shaven face. "Yes, sir. Understood."

He ended the call, then downed the rest of his drink in one gulp.

311

Kody just grinned and offered him a refill. "You're playing with fire, Zed," he commented lightly, and the older guy just shrugged.

"Nothing new there, Kody." He flashed a grin, then shifted his attention to include me once more. "Now, you guys wanna tell me who has enough money and motive to put out a hit that hardcore? Someone really wants you dead, Madison Kate."

I wrinkled my nose. "No shit."

CHAPTER 34

Archer and Steele arrived about an hour later, and I almost tripped over the table trying to launch myself at the two of them. I hugged Steele first, my arms banding around him and my face buried in his neck. He hugged me back just as hard, then loosened his grip slightly.

"Hellcat, I'm fine," he whispered in my ear, then kissed my cheek. "We all are. Promise."

I huffed. "That's not true." I let him go and turned to face Archer with my hands on my hips. "How the fuck did you get *shot*, Archer D'Ath? You're supposed to be invincible!"

His full lips curved in a grin. "Am I? Huh, I didn't know that. Sure would make these gunfights easier if I were." He rubbed his chin thoughtfully but used his left hand.

My eyes narrowed, and I patted him firmly on the right arm, taking a guess. He flinched and hissed in pain, so I glared harder. "That doesn't seem like you are, D'Ath. Start talking."

He grimaced, then shot Steele a dark look. "Steele shot me. Get mad at him instead."

My jaw dropped, and I spun around to give Steele an accusing glare. But he was just shaking his head at Archer in disappointment.

"Smooth, bro. Real smooth. Just push me right in front of the bus, why don't you?"

Archer snorted a laugh. "Well, you did." Leaning into my body, he pressed a kiss on my cheek. "But I'm fine, Princess. Stop stressing." With a quick kiss to my lips, he moved over to our table and let Kody pour him a scotch from the bottle he and Zed had been sharing.

"Max Steele," I snarled, spearing him with my glare. "What the fuck?"

He just smiled at me and reached out to grab my hand. "Hellcat, it's not as bad as it sounds," he said with a laugh, tugging me closer, then lifting me into his lap as he sat.

"Uh-huh, so you didn't shoot Archer?"

His gray eyes met mine, full of amusement. "I didn't. I shot the guy who was about to stab Archer in the kidney, and his fat arm just happened to be in the way of my headshot. It's really his own fault."

I blinked at him in disbelief. "You...hang on. Wait. You're telling me you *deliberately* shot Archer?"

"Grazed at best," Steele corrected with a small eye roll. "He's just being a baby about it. Better a grazed bicep than a knife in the kidney, I'm just saying."

"Max Steele!" I shrieked in outrage. "You could have killed him!"

"My point exactly," Archer agreed with a smirk at Steele. Clearly, I was the only one freaking out about Steele *literally* shooting Archer.

Steele just grinned and kissed the tip of my nose. "That wasn't even a possibility, Hellcat. Have you seen me shoot? I don't miss."

Zed and Kody were chuckling quietly, and I just threw my hands up in frustration.

"Hey," Steele whispered, tightening his arms around my waist. "You did well with the plan, Hellcat. I saw you cap that guy in the head."

A stupid amount of pride rolled through me, and my lips quirked in a smile, despite how mad I was at him. "Yeah?"

"Yep," he replied, kissing my neck, "hottest thing I've seen all week. Don't even get me started on that perfectly executed tuck and roll you did." He let out a sexy sort of moan that went straight to my cunt. Damn him, using my libido against me like that.

"Max..." I groaned in protest, then gave up on my anger. I turned my face, cupped his cheek in my hand, and kissed him hard. His lips curved into a smile against mine, and he deepened our kiss to the point that I was squirming in his lap and desperate for more, despite our audience.

Hell, I'd totally forgotten Zed was even there until Steele released me and I spotted him eyeing us with curiosity.

"Poly relationship, huh?" he murmured to Kody with a raised brow.

Kody shrugged. "Don't knock it until you try it, friend."

Zed snorted a laugh, shaking his head. "You're braver men than me, that's for sure."

Archer refilled his scotch, then clapped Zed on the shoulder with a grin. "For the right girl, Zed, you'd be surprised what you'd agree to."

I caught Archer's eye across the table, and the look he gave me was pure adoration. It made my pulse race and my insides warm, and I smiled back at him with total infatuation. The fact that he'd accepted our unconventional relationship constantly blew my mind.

He and Zed slipped into a casual debriefing about the mission, and I snuggled back into Steele's embrace as we took some time to just enjoy the party.

The boys had all moved on to scotch, leaving the champagne for me, so it wasn't long before the warm buzz of drunkenness started rolling through my limbs. The music was catchy, and without even meaning to, I found myself swaying in Steele's lap.

His fingers tightened on my hips, and he let out a small groan some moments later. "Hellcat, you keep grinding on me, and I'm gonna have to fuck you in the bathroom."

I laughed but rolled my hips against him harder. "Maybe we should go dance," I suggested. "I need to work off this energy somehow."

"Take Kody," Archer told me before Steele could accept.

I cocked a brow at him. "Why?"

"Because," he replied with a smirk, "for one thing, Steele can't fucking dance. For another, he shot me and doesn't deserve rewards."

Kody snickered and stood up, holding out his hand to me. "Come on, babe, you know I love dancing with you." The wink he shot me said it all. Every time the two of us had danced together, we'd ended up making out or more. Perfect.

We made our way over to the busy dance floor, giggling together as I tripped on the edge of my dress. Kody caught me before I could fall, of course, and dipped me like it had been an intentional dance move. Smooth as *fuck*.

"Hey, babe?" Kody said as he pulled me into his arms and started moving with the music. We were pressed close together, and I was already cursing the amount of clothing between us. He'd ditched the bulletproof vest, but even so…naked would have been better.

"Hmm?" I looped my arms around his neck and gazed up at him with adoration. I was so fucking smitten with my guys it was insane.

He grinned back at me, like he knew exactly what I was thinking. "I noticed Arch gave you a gift this morning. Does that mean you're not filing for divorce?"

My eyes widened, and I brought my hand between us to look at the ring in question. It fit me so perfectly, it felt like it had been made for me. It was unquestionably stunning too, and clearly a priceless antique. Yeah, that ring was more than just a casual trinket.

"I…" I had no words. Is that what it meant? What did it say for our whole relationship if we started out with a divorce? Ugh, then again, it shouldn't have started with a forced marriage. But still...what harm was there in leaving things as they were for the time being?

Kody took my hand in his, brought it to his mouth, and kissed my ring finger. "It's okay," he murmured. "I was just curious to see where your head was."

I gave him a lopsided smile, my heart pounding at the tender way he'd just kissed my ring—like it was a ring from all of them, not just Archer. "Right now?" I said with a laugh, changing the subject, "right now, my head is a bit fuzzy from champagne but also laser focused on how I can drag you into the bathroom for a quickie before anyone notices."

Oh yeah, I was drunk. Kody's brows rose at my confession, and a sly smile crept over his face. "Is that right?"

"Yup." I licked my lips. "But also, I'm so in love with you three, it actually scares me. Can we just make it through this whole, you know, assassin and stalker shit before we start thinking long-term? Let's just stay alive for now."

Kody's eyes searched mine for a long moment, our bodies still swaying together in time with the music. "We can stay alive," he agreed, "but you deserve so much more than just *surviving*. You deserve to *thrive*, babe."

"We all do," I replied in a soft voice.

He gave a short nod, like we were both on the same page. "Good. Then let's start now."

He didn't give me a chance to question him, linking our fingers together and pulling me through the crowd on the dance floor. I let out a laugh as I spotted the direction we were heading.

"Kody, we can't." It was a weak protest at best, and I was still laughing as I said it. He just shot me a smirk and pushed the door to the ladies' restroom open.

"We definitely can." He spun me around and kissed me like a starving man. I moaned into his kiss, parting my lips to let him claim my mouth in a possessive, desperate way that made my knees weak.

Then someone flushed a toilet, and we broke off our kiss in shock. A woman exited one of the stalls, then did a double take when she saw Kody standing there with his hands on my waist. Yeah, it was pretty damn obvious what we were up to, and Kody seemed to give zero fucks. Aside from that initial surprise of realizing we weren't alone, he was relaxed as ever, his hands still holding me tight against him.

The woman cast her eyes over my man as she washed her hands; then she met my gaze and smirked in an approving way. "The last stall has the most space," she told me with a wink, then quickly dried her hands and left the restroom.

My jaw was hanging open with shock, but Kody didn't need to be told twice. None of the other stall doors were closed, and he wasted no time pulling me into the one on the far end. Sure enough, it was larger than a normal stall, with a little bench seat tucked behind the door and a mirrored shelf on the wall as though the club were condoning drug use. Oh wait, it was a Timberwolf club, they probably were.

"Kody," I said on a laugh as he pushed me against the wall and started kissing my neck, "we *really* shouldn't fuck in Hades's nightclub. It seems super disrespectful or something. Even if it was my idea."

He just laughed and kissed my penguin tattoo again— apparently his new favorite thing—sending shudders of toe-curling desire shooting through me.

"Trust me, babe, Hades won't care. At least we've taken it to the bathroom; Zed is known for fucking girls right out in the main club." He was so unconcerned it was easy to let my own apprehension drop.

Screw it. We were already in here.

"Gross," I commented in mild disgust at Zed, but at the same time I reached for my dress zipper and shucked the heavily beaded gown from my shoulders.

Kody groaned his appreciation as the garment slithered to the floor and cupped my bare breasts with his hands. "Fuck yes," he murmured, bending to suck one of my nipples into his mouth.

"We better be quick," I told him in a breathy sigh. "Or someone will come searching."

"Let them," he growled back, his voice pure sex.

I grinned, biting my lip at the hungry, lust-soaked look in his gaze. My fingers made quick work of the buttons on his shirt as we stared into each other's eyes; then I pushed both his shirt and jacket off in one movement.

His body was *insane*. Before meeting the guys, I'd thought all bodies like his were a trick of photoshop. But nope, he was just straight up cut, and I could safely say I wasn't ever going to get enough of all those hard muscles and chiseled lines.

"Fucking hell, you're perfect." I trailed my fingers all over his inked chest and washboard abs. I was too damn turned on to drag out the foreplay much longer, so the second I reached his waist, I tugged his belt and pants open to free his straining erection.

Kody groaned as I palmed his dick, my fingers closing around his sizable girth. "Fucking hell, babe," he whispered into my neck, his lips moving against my skin. "I need to be inside you so bad it hurts."

"Well, what are you waiting for?" I hitched a leg up around his waist in invitation. He took the hint, moving his hands under my ass to lift me up and pin me to the wall, and I crossed my ankles behind him.

He let out a small groan as he held me with one hand, using the other to line his huge cock up to my soaking core. Once he'd pushed his tip just inside, he moved his hand to my face. He gripped my jaw in a way that forced our eyes to lock and held eye contact as he surged forward, filling me and stretching me in the most delicious way.

"I love you so fucking hard, MK," he told me in a gruff voice when his cock was fully seated. "So. Fucking. Hard." He punctuated that statement with several rough thrusts that almost saw me coming already.

Tightening my grip around him, I tilted my head back to seal my lips against his. We probably needed to be quiet, and Kody's tongue seemed like as good a gag as any. Well…in the absence of Steele's or Archer's dick, that was.

Kody kissed me the same way as he fucked me: hard, fast, and deep. His thick cock lit up every damn nerve in my pussy, striking me at the best possible angle that saw me clenching and writhing all over him in a matter of seconds. I was so lost in ecstasy that I didn't even hear the main door open as someone came into the restroom.

He heard them, though. His pace slowed and his kiss gentled as he whispered a warning.

"Stay quiet, babe," he urged me. "Not a sound, okay? We don't wanna get thrown out by security or something."

Worry zapped through me, making me gasp and tighten up around his dick. He just groaned softly and kissed me again.

"Shh," he breathed with a laugh. "Be silent, and I promise I'll make you come again before we leave this club tonight."

My eyes rolled back with a silent groan. How the hell could I refuse an offer like that? Kody knew it too. He let me have his lips once more, keeping me quiet, then went to *town* fucking me into a quivering mess. His fingers snaked between us, finding my clit and shattering my whole damn world as I came all over his dick.

Small whimpers and moans slipped out of me, but he swallowed the noises with his kiss, his hips bucking as he chased his own release.

My head was spinning, my breathing heavy as Kody released my lips just as the restroom door closed again.

"Are we alone again?" I asked in a breathy whisper.

He licked his lips, his cock still twitching inside me. "Why? You wanna go again already?"

I snickered. "Always. But I meant more about sneaking out of here unseen."

Kody pouted teasingly but gently placed me back on my feet, then grabbed me a handful of toilet paper to clean up. Still, he watched me with predatory eyes as I wiped away the evidence of our quickie, and I knew he'd make good on his promise to make me come again soon.

Refusing to give in to temptation *too* soon, I ignored the way he eye-fucked me and wiggled back into my dress. "Zip me up, babe," I told him, lifting my hair out of the way.

He did as I asked, then tugged his shirt back on, only buttoning it halfway. He tucked the front back into his pants but let the back hang out. Like he *wanted* everyone to know we'd been fucking in the bathrooms.

Then again, this was Kody. He *did* want people to know. I couldn't even tell him off because I quietly loved how much he wanted people to know that I was his.

He cracked our stall door open and peered out before giving me the all clear. Before we re-entered the main club, though, he pinned me to the wall and kissed me breathless. Then he swiped his thumb over my lower lip and grinned.

Goddamn. I had it *bad* for Kodiak Jones.

CHAPTER 35

The rest of the night turned into a bit of a blur. I remembered Kody following through on his promise by snaking a hand up my skirt while we were at our table. Archer and Steele knew full well what was happening, and that had only turned me on even more. Their eyes stayed locked on me the whole time, and I'd never felt like more of a queen.

Archer had arranged us a hotel suite for the night, but sometime between the club and the lobby, I fell asleep. I had vague flashes of being carried out of the car and soft, low murmurs of conversation between the guys in the elevator, but then it was all blank.

When I woke again, sunlight streamed through the gauze-covered windows, and my head was aching.

"Ow," I mumbled, bringing a hand to my eyes to cover them.

Someone laughed at me, and a set of strong, warm arms tightened around me. That made my hangover infinitely more bearable, and I snuggled into the hard body behind me.

"Good morning, gorgeous," Steele murmured in my ear, then kissed my neck.

"My head hurts," I admitted on a sleepy groan, my ass pushing against his morning wood. Fuck, I loved sleepy sex. Hopefully, we were on the same page because...

"Hellcat," Steele replied as his fingertips trailed down my body, his hand then cupping my mound, "I have it on good authority that the best cure for a headache is an orgasm."

I moaned, writhing in encouragement when he pushed his fingers into me. "Hell yes," I gasped, "I'll take that cure."

He gave a soft chuckle. His lips kissed along the curve of my neck as he pumped his fingers into me and his thumb found my clit. God*damn*, he was talented with his fingers.

"Max," I said on a breathy sigh, "I want your dick."

He gave an amused grunt and nipped my neck playfully. "How can I refuse a request like that? Are you okay to sit up?"

I nodded eagerly and let him guide me into straddling his waist, reverse-cowgirl style. Oh, *hell* yes. With all those piercings? My hangover had already evaporated.

"Oh shit," I gasped as I sank down onto his hard, studded length. I felt every damn one of those piercings as he raised his hips to push into me deeper, and a strangled scream escaped my throat.

"Is that okay?" Steele asked, his own voice tight with arousal.

"Okay?" I snorted a laugh. "That's fucking *incredible*."

I braced my hands on his thighs, spread my knees wider on the bed, and leaned forward to take him to a deeper, different angle. I'd barely even started moving, riding his laddered cock slowly, when the bedroom door opened.

Archer said nothing when he saw us, just closed the door behind himself and leaned his shoulders against it. His gaze was dark and sultry, though, his gray sweatpants already swelling as he watched me ride his friend.

"You just gonna stand there and watch, big guy?" I asked in a teasing voice. Or it would have been teasing if it wasn't threaded with a sex-drenched moan.

His brows flickered up. His bicep was wrapped in a thick bandage, but the rest of him was muscular, tattooed perfection. "What's the alternative, Princess?"

Steele's hands gripped my hips, urging me to keep riding him, and I grinned wickedly.

"Come over here and fuck my face, Sunshine. I wanna make you come." I punctuated my offer by licking my lips, and Archer's sweats hit the floor faster than I could blink.

A moment later, my mouth was full and my hair swept up in a knot around Archer's fist while Steele took over the pace below me. Shit, *yes*. Goddamn, *yes*.

Steele fucked me from below, his piercings doing dirty, amazing things to my cunt, while Archer gave me exactly what I had asked for. He was forceful, demanding, damn near choking me as he fucked my throat harder with every damn thrust. My eyes watered, and I just gripped onto his ass, begging for more.

I came first, my pussy clenching and fluttering around Steele's dick as he slammed into me harder and harder. My screams were muffled as Archer jerked my head forward again. He cried out a curse as he came a moment later, his hot seed shooting straight down my throat as I swallowed eagerly.

Steele only needed a couple of moments more, his fingers tight on my hips as he fucked me faster and I licked down the length of Archer's shaft.

"You're a fucking goddess," Archer growled. He cupped my face and kissed me as Steele grunted his release inside me. "I came to ask what you wanted for breakfast, Wifey."

I moaned into his next kiss, still writhing around on Steele's dick. "This was a pretty good breakfast so far," I admitted with a cheeky grin. "But I'll take waffles, if you're ordering room service."

Archer smacked another kiss on my lips. "Done." He pulled his sweats back on and exited the bedroom once more.

Exhausted, I climbed off Steele's cock and collapsed beside him with a lazy grin. "You were right," I told him, snuggling up until we shared a pillow. "Headache is completely gone."

He smirked back at me. "Always trust Doctor Max, Hellcat. He knows what's good for you."

His loved-up, gray-eyed gaze held mine steady as his fingers traced light patterns over my skin, starting at my shoulder, then pausing when he reached the side of my left breast. There, he ever so slowly, ever so gently followed the lines of my third tattoo.

"Is this what you ran off with Cass to do the other day?" His tone was sleepy and relaxed, and my whole damn body was just one giant warm and fuzzy for how in love I was.

I nodded. "Do you like it?"

Pushing himself up on his elbow, he leaned over and kissed my tender skin where I'd inked a design just for him: a treble clef that turned into a pulse line. I couldn't even begin to tell him how long I'd stared at the beeping pulse line of his heart monitor after he'd been shot, so when I'd seen the design Cass had drawn, I'd known it was perfect.

"I love it more than words can even describe, Hellcat," Steele told me in a husky whisper. "I love *you* more than words can describe."

He kissed me again, letting his lips speak all the emotions that were too big for the spoken language. Who even needed breakfast anyway? Sure as hell not me.

The bedroom door opened again before I could coax Steele into round two, and Kody raised a brow at us.

"Not cool, guys," he told us with a scowl. "Where was my party invitation?"

I grinned and shrugged. "Pretty sure I left it in the shower. Wanna help me and Max find it in there?"

Kody's lips parted as his gaze heated to scorching, but he let out a long breath and shook his head. "So fucking tempting, you have *no* idea. But we just got a tip on some intel about Kruger."

I sat up in shock. "What? We did? What was it?"

Kody grinned. "I have no idea, so get dressed and we can find out. Food should be here in fifteen too, so hurry the hell up."

I did as I was told, racing through my shower and grabbing fresh clothes out of the overnight bag Archer had stashed in the car for me yesterday.

When I emerged to the living room of our suite, the room service was just arriving. Apparently, the events of our wedding day hadn't eased anyone's paranoia because I spotted no fewer than seven unconcealed weapons out while the tense server pushed her cart in.

Kody signed the bill, and she hurried out of the room like her tail was on fire. Only after the door closed firmly did everyone relax somewhat.

"Okay, if we're all this on edge, how do we know our food hasn't been poisoned?" I planted my hands on my hips and frowned at the food cart.

Kody lifted all the lids from our plates and shrugged. "We don't, but I'm fucking starving." He grabbed one of my waffles and took a bite before I could yell a protest.

"Kody!" I darted over and slapped my breakfast out of his fingers.

He just swallowed his mouthful and grinned. "Tasty waffles. The rat poison seasoning gives them a real kick."

I rolled my eyes, grabbed my plate, and carried it over to the dining table. "Ha-ha, asshole. That'd be *hilarious* if we'd actually been poisoned. So what's the news about Kruger?" I posed my question to Archer, guessing that he'd been the one to receive it.

With a one-shouldered shrug, he took the seat beside me and hooked one of my legs over his knee. "Don't know yet. Cass left me a rather cryptic message and said he'd call back again shortly."

I frowned and took a small nibble of my waffles. They tasted okay...I guessed. But now that the idea of poison was in my head, I was going to be imagining it in everything.

"That's annoying." I frowned thoughtfully. Why would Cass leave a vague-as-fuck message like that, then say *he'd* call back. Like it wasn't safe for us to call him.

"Right?" Kody agreed. "More annoying that Arch missed the call in the first place because he was busy *waking* you guys up." He wiggled his brows suggestively, knowing full well we'd had a quick fuck before breakfast.

"I've got Sampson and James looking around," Archer told us. His hand rested comfortably on my knee that he'd hooked over his. "One of them will get back to us soon, I'm sure."

Steele nodded his agreement as he ate his bacon and eggs. "It's a fucking shame Danny and Leon had another job to get to; they were useful as hell."

"Tell me about it," Kody agreed, then smirked. "You reckon those two are hitting it?"

Archer rolled his eyes and sighed. "Who cares? They're mercenaries, basically one step away from being actual demons, given how black their souls must be right now."

My brows shot up. "Uh, sorry, is that a judgment I hear? Hypocrisy, thy name is—"

"I wasn't judging, Kate," he growled, cutting me off, "just questioning whether *any* mercs have enough humanity left for relationships. Also pointing out that it doesn't matter if Danny and Leon fuck like bunnies—it'd never interfere with their job. Mercs aren't hired onto their company easily, and getting fired for underperforming is a hell of a lot more permanent than any other job."

I took that information on with curiosity, but before we could gossip any more, Archer's phone rang.

"James," he snapped on answering the call, "what did you find?" He switched the call to speakerphone and placed his device down on the table for all of us to hear.

"Boss," James replied, "you were right. Kruger is in Shadow

Grove, arrived two days ago via private jet under a fake name and ID. Brought a small army of guys with him, but by my guess he's missing around a dozen of them after yesterday."

My lips parted in shock. That explained where some of the additional attackers had come from during the wedding. But what the hell did he hope to achieve by being here personally?

"Do you have a location on him?" Archer asked in tight, clipped tones.

His phone pinged with an incoming message as James replied, "Just sent you the address. He's staying in a private home up the coast a way. Based on satellite imaging, he's got about twenty-odd guards around the house. He's one paranoid motherfucker, that's for sure. I'd need to get a better look from the ground to get a clearer picture, though."

Archer seemed annoyed by that, scrubbing a hand over his long stubble.

"Sampson and his guys all there at the house with you?" Steele asked in the silence.

"Sure are," James replied, all business. "Except for Ryan and Adamson on your detail right now. Want us to meet you at Kruger's location?"

The three guys exchanged a series of meaningful looks, too fast for me to follow.

"Yes," Kody answered. "We'll give you an ETA when we're on the road."

"Got it," James replied. "And Madison Kate?" There was an edge of hesitancy in his voice as he asked about me. Because he was worried? Or...something else?

"Safe," Archer replied. "We'll be in touch shortly." He ended the call without waiting for a reply, then dropped his hand back to my knee. His fingers bit into my skin, but I didn't protest. I knew he was working through his base instinct to be a dick about this change of events.

Just for something new, I thought I could make it easier on everyone. "I don't need to tag along," I told them. "You can leave me here with Ryan and Adamson."

All three of them looked at me like I'd just grown two heads.

"Babe," Kody said on a laugh, "are you feeling okay? That sounded way too reasonable for this time of the morning."

I flipped him off. "Funny, prick. I'm serious; this job sounds like it's *way* over my pay grade. If I stamp my feet and insist on coming with you, then, for one thing, you'll all be so preoccupied with *my* safety, you'll likely get shot...again."

Archer scowled at Steele, who just grinned.

"And for another thing," I continued, "this could well be a trap to get to me. Kruger doesn't strike me as the careless sort, considering how many other deaths he has arranged to get his hands on my family estate. He's not likely to bungle it now when I'm the only person who could take it away from him."

"So what if the trap is to lure us away from you?" Kody countered, looking thoughtful. "Lay a false trail that he knows we will follow, then snatch you away from us here. I don't trust Ryan and Adamson enough to keep you safe, if that's the plan."

I shrugged. "Okay, so what other options do we have? Ignore the tip and live in fear of Kruger forever?"

"Or we can split up," Steele suggested. "Two of us follow up on the tip, and one of us stays here to protect you along with the detail."

I nodded. "That works. I'm sure we could call Cass for extra backup too."

Archer wrinkled his nose. "I'd rather steer clear of the Reapers as much as we can. I could call Zed and see if any of his guys would help out, though."

"Who's staying with MK, then?" Kody asked, sitting back in his chair and folding his arms over his chest.

Steele shrugged. "I will."

Kody snorted a laugh and rolled his eyes. "I fucking bet you will. No way. You're the best sharpshooter, so you're the logical choice to take a shot at Kruger." He looked up at the ceiling, then released a long sigh. "Arch, you're staying."

Archer jolted like he'd been stabbed with a fork. "What? No. This is my mission to run. I'm going to choke the life out of Kruger with my bare hands." His voice was dark and laced with menace that made me shiver.

"You're not doing shit with a fresh bullet wound in your dominant arm, dickhead," Kody snapped back at him. "Bad enough that you're going to fuck up your fight next week; we're not risking you getting killed today for being a damn cowboy."

Archer started to protest, and I cleared my throat. "You got a problem staying here with me, Sunshine?"

His jaw moved, but no sounds came out as he quickly recognized the lose-lose situation he was in. Yeah, smart boy.

"All right, good chat," Steele said with a laugh, pushing back from the table. "Come on, Kody, before Hellcat changes her mind."

I rolled my eyes and finished off my waffles as they hurried to get dressed and armed up. Archer muttered under his breath but placed a call to Zed to see if he could spare any backup to keep an eye on the hotel.

"We'll wait until the wolves get here," Kody told us as he checked his own phone.

"Don't," Archer replied. "Every second we hesitate, we risk Kruger slipping away. We're not leaving this room, and nothing is getting past me in the next fifteen minutes. Just go."

"Seconded," I agreed. "Besides, I'm not exactly a helpless damsel anymore either. Arch and I can handle ourselves; you guys go deal with that motherfucker who killed my mom."

Both Kody and Steele looked torn but quickly kissed me and headed out to meet up with James. As the door closed behind them, I turned to face Archer with my hands on my hips.

"What's that look for?" he asked, his eyes narrowed in suspicion and his brow furrowed.

"Sunshine," I replied with a stern voice, "you're not seriously still planning to fight next week?"

One of his brows raised. "Why wouldn't I?"

I gaped at him. "Oh, gee, I dunno, maybe because you have a gunshot wound in your arm?"

He just let a slow smile creep over his lips as he tugged me into his lap. He was sitting on the sofa, so I straddled his waist but carefully avoided touching his bandaged bicep.

"Princess," he replied with a low chuckle, "it's adorable that you're worried for my well-being. But this little scratch isn't going to stop me from fighting...or *anything* else."

I dragged my teeth over my lower lip, locking eyes with him. "Oh yeah? Prove it."

A wicked grin flashed over his face, and the next thing I knew, I was flat on my back against the couch with his heavy frame on top of me. I let out a shriek of laughter as he pinned my wrists over my head, but whatever he had planned next was cut short by the ringing of his phone.

"Answer it," I urged him, sobering up. "It might be the guys."

He let me go and grabbed for his phone, wincing slightly at the movement on his injured arm. The scowl he gave his screen told me it wasn't Kody or Steele, though.

"Cass," he said, answering the call on speakerphone. "What's going on?"

"Wish I knew," the older gangster rumbled back. "Is the kid there with you?"

"I'm here," I spoke up, frowning at the tense way he snapped out his words. "What's wrong?"

He blew out a sigh. "No idea. But Zane's up to something. I reckon it's got something to do with you."

Archer and I exchanged a worried glance. "Why do you think that?" Arch asked cautiously.

Cass grunted. "Little fuck had a meeting this morning with his inner circle."

"Nothing suspicious with that," Archer murmured, confused.

"*Without* me," Cass elaborated. "He's been acting shady for a few weeks, but shit just got weird these last few days."

Archer snorted and rolled his eyes. "Since when is Zane *not* shady?"

"Worse," Cass grunted. "Anyway, I don't have much more. Just keep all eyes on the kid. Whatever is going on, it's about her."

I bit my lip, meeting Archer's concerned gaze with my heart in my throat. We *really* didn't need to add another player to the board this late in the game.

"Gotta go," Cass growled. "Stay alert."

He ended the call, and Archer ran his hand over his hair, then cursed.

"What do we do?" I asked in a quiet voice. Worry was knotting my stomach, but I had confidence in all Archer had already done to safeguard us.

He shook his head, thinking. "Nothing," he finally said. "The worst thing we can do right now is leave here. Ryan and Adamson are still guarding the door, and the Timberwolves will be here as backup soon. We just stay put and hope my brother isn't really stupid enough to try anything."

I groaned. "He is, though, isn't he?"

Archer sighed. "If he is, I'll kill him. Simple as that."

Yet somehow, that didn't make me feel better. Did I want Archer to have his own brother's blood on his hands? It was bad enough that I'd carry Samuel Danvers's death with me forever— not that I regretted killing him for even a second—but I'd rather spare Archer that.

"Let's hope it doesn't come to that," I murmured, then sighed. "Wanna watch a movie with me? Sounds like it could be a while before Kody and Steele get back."

He let out a long sigh and tossed his phone onto the coffee table, then sank back into the sofa. "Sure, why not?"

We settled in together to watch some lighthearted comedy, but neither one of us was paying attention to the screen. We were both tense and alert, knowing it would just be a matter of time before something happened.

About ten minutes into the movie, Archer's phone pinged, and he groaned.

"Bad news?" I guessed.

"Maybe," he murmured, thoughtful. "Zed's guys are held up in traffic. Some accident on the bridge that blocked two lanes."

"Could be a coincidence," I offered.

Archer shook his head. "I don't believe in coincidences."

As if with choreographed timing, the fire alarm screamed to life. It damn near deafened us with its piercing volume, and I clapped my hands over my ears on instinct.

Archer gave me a silent command to stay where I was, then grabbed a gun and rushed over to the door. He took a second to peer through the peephole, then tugged the door open to speak with our security guards.

"Decoy?" he asked one of them, but the guard shook his head.

"Uncertain," he replied.

Archer jerked a nod. "Stay alert; I have a bad feeling." He closed the door again, then hurried back over to me. "Here, take this." He handed me his gun, then strode through to the bedroom.

I got to my feet, following him with the gun in hand. I needed shoes on at the very least, just in case we did need to evacuate.

Archer was quickly dressing, pulling a black T-shirt over his muscular chest. So I sat on the end of the bed to put my socks and shoes on, then swept my hair up in a high ponytail. The alarm was still screaming, making my head ring, but I ignored it.

"Wear this," Archer told me, ripping open a carefully wrapped gift box. He lifted a delicate necklace out. "It's a gift from Steele, but I doubt he'll mind me giving it to you."

I frowned in confusion at the odd timing for a present but lifted my hair out of the way so he could clasp it behind my neck for me. The pendant was a small, gold music note that sat just an inch below the hollow of my throat.

"Arch—" I started to say, but was interrupted by heavy pounding on the front door.

Both Archer and I grabbed our guns before hurrying back through the suite to open it.

"Not a decoy," the guard informed us. "Smoke is coming up through the south fire escape. Hotel is on fire; we gotta get out of here ASAP."

Archer spat a string of curses, then grabbed a second gun to tuck into the back of his jeans. He handed me two extra clips for mine, and I stuffed them into the pockets of my hoodie.

"All right, stay close. I'll put money on the fact that this is a trap." Archer looked grim, but I knew where his head was. What were our other options? Stay put and risk burning alive? That certainly didn't sit high on my list of preferred ways to die.

We moved out quickly, heading for the north stairwell to get out. Adamson took the lead, followed by Archer, then me, and Ryan took our rear. At each and every bend of the staircase, they followed military-style procedures. Despite the pressing need to get out of the burning hotel, no one was taking chances at being ambushed. We'd waited so long after the alarm had initially gone off that the stairwell was empty, all the other hotel guests probably having already made it outside.

Around the time we reached the seventh floor, the heavy sounds of boots on stairs traveled up to us from below, along with voices.

Archer and Adamson exchanged a flurry of hand signals; then Adamson took off ahead, hurrying down the next few flights well ahead of us. Meanwhile, Ryan peered over the railing and gave a small shrug.

"Looks like firefighters, boss," he told Archer in a low voice.

Archer gave a nod, peering over the railing himself. "Probably," he murmured. Stay close anyway, Kate."

We continued down and soon ran into a half-dozen fully geared-up firefighters. But…no sign of Adamson.

"Hey," Archer barked when the firefighters were on the landing below us. "Where—"

That was all he got out before one of the "firefighters" pulled a gun from under his heavy jacket and shot Archer straight in the chest.

"No!" I screamed, reaching out to grab Archer. My fingers snagged his T-shirt, but he was already falling. His weight tipped forward, and I could do nothing but watch in horror as he toppled down the short flight of stairs toward the firefighters.

Ryan grabbed me faster than I could fully react, shoving me behind his body and around the low corner of the stairs as he popped off a series of bullets toward our attackers. He dropped three of them, but then he, too, collapsed.

My pulse thundering, I clutched at my own gun. I kept low, hiding behind the low railing but knowing it'd only be a matter of seconds before the remaining attackers were on me. Tears burned in my eyes, but there was no time for falling apart. If I was going down—and I probably was—then the least I could do was take some of them with me.

With that thought, a calm resolve flooded through me. I slipped into a cold, emotionless trance and let my fresh training take the reins.

Quicker than a whip, I rolled out of my hiding place and fired on my attackers. There were more of them now, but I wasn't shooting to stay alive. I was shooting to inflict damage, and as much of it as possible.

When my body jerked and searing hot pain flooded my veins, I hit the ground with the sweet satisfaction of knowing I'd dented their numbers. That, apparently, was the best I could do.

My limbs lost feeling and my vision blackened, but I still held on to enough consciousness to watch one of the firefighters crouch down beside me, then sweep his helmet off.

Fuck.

"You *cunt*," I spat with damn near my last breath.

"Such language, Madison Kate," Zane scolded me. "Your mother would be horrified."

I wanted to curse him out, to tell him my mother would have personally cut his balls from his body for this. But...I had nothing left.

The fire alarm continued to scream in my ears, but my whole world went black and my body gave up the fight.

CHAPTER 36

Ever so slowly, consciousness crept back into my brain. For several moments, it was just a daze of confusion and pain, but after a series of deep, calming breaths, I found my wits once more.

Enough that I connected some important dots. The first of those was I hadn't been *shot* like I'd thought. I wasn't bleeding, and I wasn't dying. I'd been tranquilized. That gave me a surge of hope that Archer had only been tranqed too… It certainly would explain the way he'd instantly crumpled and the lack of blood spray.

The second thing I assessed was that I was bound. A thick gag covered my mouth, and my wrists were tightly tied behind me. Worse yet, I was in the trunk of a car. Again.

Fuck.

A weak, pathetic sound of fear whined out of my throat before I could get a handle on it, and my body trembled with anxiety.

Pull it together, MK. You survived every other small space; you'll survive this one.

Still, it was one thing to give myself a stern pep talk. It was another to calm my panicking body down. As it was, I was tugging frantically at my wrist restraints and trying to free myself. The effort was totally futile, and I already knew this, but I couldn't stop trying anyway.

The car was moving, the rumble of the engine vibrating through the trunk, and I couldn't stop the flood of worst-case scenarios washing through my brain. What the hell was Zane up to? Why had he suddenly flipped on us? I'd never totally trusted him, but I'd really believed he was looking out for my safety. Why else would he tell me about Archer's marriage arrangement? Why help me out with a place to stay and...?

But the answer was clear. Because it all hurt Archer. And he *hated* his little brother. Hated the fact that he was beholden to him and that he could do nothing to wriggle free. Until now, it seemed. Zane had made his move, and I could only hope it was all about to spectacularly blow up in his sneaky, lying face.

Fuck.

I had a weirdly confident gut feeling I knew where Zane was taking me. Like Archer had said, we no longer believed in coincidence, and it was all too coincidental that Kruger was in Shadow Grove at the same time that Zane pulled a reckless move like this.

None of my thrashing was loosening my hands at all. It was just exhausting me. So instead, I bit down hard on my gag and turned my effort inward. I needed to survive however long I was going to be left trapped in the trunk of this car. I needed to overcome my claustrophobia, or I'd be no use to anyone when I was eventually let out.

It was hard. It was *so* freaking hard, and by the time the car had stopped, it felt like I'd been locked in that trunk for *days*. But despite the cold sheen of terrified sweat all over my body, I was still okay. I was still holding on to my sense of self and hadn't dissolved into a mindless puddle of panicked goo or worse.

The engine shut off, and car doors slammed. Muffled voices reached my ears through the trunk, and more cars arrived. More voices, and the distinctive clicks of guns being loaded with fresh ammunition. There was no doubt in my mind this was going to end in bloodshed.

I just hoped it would be Zane's and the Reapers', not mine.

When the trunk finally opened, I needed to blink a thousand times to make my eyes refocus. It didn't help that it was dark outside and several cars parked nearby had their high beams on to illuminate the parking lot.

"Oh, good, you're awake," Zane commented with a cruel snicker. "I hate shooting people when they're unconscious. Half the fun is seeing that look of blind terror in their eyes a second before they die." He wasn't looking for a reply from me. He just reached into the trunk and grabbed a tight handful of my ponytail, using it to all but drag me out of the trunk.

Without the use of my hands, I tumbled onto the gravel as soon as he let go of my hair. My cheek stung with a graze, but it was nothing compared to the heavy kick Zane delivered to my ribs.

I couldn't even curse him out because my mouth was gagged so securely. It didn't seem to deter him, though, and he kicked me again just for fun. Pain lanced through me, and I moaned in desperation.

Fucker was gonna pay for this when I got free. Because I *would* get free. Somehow.

Zane hauled me up to my knees by my hair and crouched down to sneer at me. "I warned you I was a businessman, Madison Kate. And I smelled money to be gained in keeping you alive. Turns out I was right, huh?"

His smile was wide, and his pupils were unevenly dilated. He was high as *fuck*.

"You wanna know how much the hit on you was increased to after yesterday's wedding bullshit?" He let out a peal of hysterical laughter. "Your family *really* wants you dead, little girl. Far be it from me to stand in the way of that, huh?" He backhanded me then, making me lose my balance and eat gravel once more.

One of the other Reapers yelled something out at Zane, but my ears were ringing too hard to make out the words. All I knew was that Zane's drug-jittering intensified, and he slammed a fist into my face so hard I felt my teeth rattle.

My boys were going to *murder* him for this, even if I didn't make it out myself. *Especially* if I didn't.

"You know," Zane confessed, yanking me back up to sitting. His face was so close to mine that I could feel his breath on my aching cheek. "Kruger paid extra to have you delivered alive, but he didn't say unharmed. Guess that means he doesn't plan on keeping you breathing for long, huh?" He patted my face, sending spikes of pain through my skull, but I could do nothing but glare.

The sound of more cars arriving pulled Zane's attention, and I decided to throw caution to the wind. How much worse could my situation really get, right?

I dropped to the ground, letting my body crush my bound hands into the gravel as I kicked out my legs.

Boom. Nailed it.

Zane howled, clutching at his junk and spitting curses at me. I tried to roll to my feet but was stopped by a scruffy, bearded Reaper. He swung a fist at me as I staggered up from the gravel, knocking me straight back down again. This time I wasn't getting up so easily. A high-pitched whine had started ringing in my ears, and my vision was getting spotty.

How hard had that motherfucker just hit me?

Zane gave me no time to pull myself together either. His hand went around my throat, and he climbed on top of me for better leverage. The sheer hatred twisting his face was what scared me the most. His eyes were so similar to Archer's, but the fury and disgust spoke to years of instability.

"...fucking whore," he was snarling at me, but my ringing ears were only picking up fragments. "...like Deb...baby..."

If I wasn't being choked to death, I'd have had something to say about that. He clearly thought my mom had been cheating on him when she got pregnant, when in reality she'd been *raped*. Then again, Zane wasn't proving himself any more of a man than Samuel, so maybe it wouldn't have made a difference to him either.

A loud bang sounded somewhere close by, and Zane startled enough that his grip loosened. I greedily sucked gulps of air, refilling my aching lungs as I blinked the tears out of my eyes, but Zane just seemed more pissed off by whoever had interrupted.

"...something of mine?" Someone was asking him, and the Reaper leader scowled deeply.

"I'm just doing you a favor," Zane snarled at the newcomer. "You wanted her dead, right? Consider this a freebie."

Apparently my distant relative didn't like Zane's offer because a moment later a gun was pressed to the older D'Ath's forehead.

"If you want to be paid, Zane, I suggest you hand over my property immediately," the man said in a cool, accented voice.

Zane scowled down at me again but slowly raised his hands and climbed off me to back away.

I wasn't about to be shot lying down, though, so I rolled over and wriggled up to my knees to face my would-be killer head on. I wanted to look into the eyes of the man who'd murdered my mother and grandmother. The man who'd probably pushed his own wife down the stairs to paralyze her and take control of her estate.

"That's quite far enough, Madison Kate," the man told me in a bland tone before I could stand up fully. "You're one tough girl to catch, you know that?"

All the punches and choking on the ground had loosened my gag enough that I could spit it from my mouth and wet my lips.

"Maybe you just weren't trying hard enough," I retorted, my voice husky and edged with pain. My whole damn body hurt, and a sharp agony when I breathed hinted at a broken rib.

Karl Kruger just tossed his head back and laughed. His gun didn't waver, though. A quick glance around the parking lot told me just how outmatched I was too. Zane had six guys with him, all decked out in the full gangster costume with bandanas and tattoos on display. Kruger had brought twice that with him.

Where were Kody and Steele? Had they found him, or was the whole thing just one big setup? Or worse yet…had they walked into a trap and been killed?

No. No way. I refused to even consider that possibility. They were alive, they were *all* alive. There was no other option.

"I have to confess," Kruger told me with a smile, "I haven't had this much fun since I tracked your mother down."

My stomach rolled with disgust, and he just clicked his tongue.

"Silly me, I was so worked up from the excitement of it all, I never dug too deep. Maybe if I'd stuck around, I would have worked out what she did to cover you up. You…the one and *only* blood heir to Wittenberg."

"What about Selena?" I asked, glaring up at him and trying my very best to ignore the gun pointed at my head. "Your wife is a blood heir. Isn't that what this is *all* about?"

Kruger parted his lips to reply, then grinned and shook his head. "Nice try, girl. You won't trap me into confessing all my deep dark secrets here for one of these criminals to use later." He jerked his head toward the Reapers. They'd backed off a small way, but they hadn't left. Probably hanging around to get paid once I was dead.

"Anyway, that's enough banter," Kruger continued, giving me a banal smile. Fuck me, he looked like a mild-mannered accountant, not the man who'd murdered our family's entire household staff, then beaten my mother to death. Then again, what better way to disguise a monster than make them look *normal*. Boring. Unremarkable and totally forgettable.

The villain of my story shifted his grip, and I coiled my leg muscles. No fucking way was I going to kneel there like a good little girl while I get shot in the head. He wanted to kill me? He was gonna work for it.

Before he could pull the trigger, I launched straight at him. My body stayed low as my shoulder slammed into his gut with my full weight, knocking him off his feet. A gunshot ripped through the air, deafening me momentarily, but his shot had gone wide.

He got no time to recover either. One second I was tackling him into the ground, and the next we were smack in the middle of a full-blown gun fight.

Kruger sat up slightly, his eyes wide as several of his men dropped from perfect headshots. "No!" he shrieked.

I wasn't hanging around to chat, though. I rolled like a damn alligator to get away from him, aiming for one of the freshly dead guys and praying he'd have a knife on his body somewhere. Anything sharp to cut my hands loose so I could fight back properly.

Kruger recovered faster than I'd expected, though. He grabbed my arm in a biting grip and hauled me against his body like a human shield. Mother*fucker*, that's exactly what he was using me as.

"Stop!" he shrieked, pressing his gun to my head. *Ah fuck.* "Stop, or the bitch gets it!"

The gunfire died down, and my heart raced. Surely the guys weren't falling for that bullshit; he was about to kill me *regardless*. He was only keeping me alive now to try to guarantee his own exit.

"Let her go!" Archer shouted from across the parking lot. The high beams from the cars made it hard to see exactly where he was, but I had no doubt my guys had the important players in their sights: Zane and Kruger.

Forcing myself to take calming breaths, I let my gaze track around us, hunting for someone in particular. Someone who would need a good line of sight, and—*there*.

About a hundred feet away, I made out the vague shadow of Steele on top of a shipping container. Only the reflection from his scope and my knowledge of his habits clued me in to him being there, but once I found him, my relief was tangible.

"Not a chance," Kruger yelled back at Archer. "If you're

invested in keeping her brains *inside* her pretty head, then you'll let me leave here unharmed."

I locked my eyes on that shadow that I was *sure* was Steele. I couldn't make out his features, but I knew he was watching us through his scope. I knew he could read my lips as I mouthed *Do it* at him.

"Let her go, and we'll make it a quick death," Archer countered, not even bothering to pretend Kruger could leave this scene alive.

Kruger barked a bitter laugh, but I blocked him out. My focus was all on Steele, and I glared harder, silently yelling at him to quit fucking around.

Shoot him. I mouthed the words as clearly as I could. *I trust you.*

My heart thudded hard. Once. Twice.

Crack.

The sound of a rifle shot echoed through the parking lot, and Kruger jerked like he'd been electrocuted. A sharp flash of pain burned across my temple, and I collapsed to the gravel as Kruger's grip on me loosened.

He hit the ground a fraction of a second after me, his dead eyes staring into mine and the perfect hole in his forehead seeping blood down his face.

Commotion and gunfire exploded around me again, but this time I was too shocked to move. It was only a few seconds, though, until a blade sliced through my wrist restraints, and Kody dragged me behind one of the parked cars for protection.

"Babe, are you okay?" he asked in a panicked gasp. His hand pushed my hair back from my face but froze when I hissed in pain. "Shit. Motherfucker."

"I'm okay," I replied through gritted teeth, fresh blood pouring down my face from my newest injury. "Just a graze. Give me a gun."

Kody's eyes widened, and then a grin curved his lips. "Yes, ma'am." He pulled a spare from his ankle holster and helped me wrap my stiff fingers around the grip. "Let's finish this, babe."

He rolled out of our protection, popping off three shots before he found his feet once more, and I followed somewhat slower. My ribs hurt more with every passing second, and the blood running down my face was starting to get in my eye. The last thing I wanted was to accidentally kill the wrong person.

Luckily, though, the fight was already over.

I spotted Cass across the parking lot, standing over the bearded Reaper who'd punched me. He seemed to say something to the man, then shot him straight in the face.

That left just one enemy alive, and he was on his knees with his brother's gun to his head.

"You're a fucking traitor," Zane spat at Cass, who sauntered over to stand beside Archer with his gun held ever so casually in his hand. "You think you can just take my place? My family *created* the Reapers. They'll never follow a snake like you."

Cass just arched a scarred brow and shrugged. "Well, that's not really your problem, is it? You signed away your life the second you made a move against Archer, and you knew it."

Zane snarled. "Fuck you, Cass. *Fuck you.*"

"You're boring me," Archer commented, his voice dry and devoid of any human emotions. "And you broke the rules."

Bang.

Just like that, the Shadow Grove Reapers saw a change of leadership.

CHAPTER 37

There was no question about it: I was in *rough* shape. James had arrived with the guys and firmly insisted on patching me up before I was allowed to do anything else.

The tally of my injuries was enough to make me cringe from just listening to James mutter under his breath. So far, he'd decided two of my ribs were most probably broken for which he gave me a dose of a decent analgesia to dull the pain. I also had a sprained wrist and an absolute shitload of bruising. My entire torso from bra to jeans was already darkening with blackish purple, and every movement ached.

Then there was the bullet graze. Steele's shot had been flawless, and the cut it'd opened from the edge of my hairline really wasn't *that* bad. James cursed about needing to stitch it, but a second opinion from Cass confirmed what I was saying, that it wasn't *that* bad. So a bit of surgical glue was as good as it was going to get.

"Archer!" I shouted out as I spotted him swing a punch at Steele.

Snatching the wet cloth from James—he'd been trying to wipe some of the blood off my face—I rushed over to break up their fight.

"What the fuck do you think you're doing?" I demanded, putting myself physically between them. Kody just stood back, watching with his arms folded across his chest. Unhelpful shithead.

"He *shot* you!" Archer roared back, his face a mask of fury.

"He *saved* me," I corrected him in a hard voice. "It's a fucking graze, Arch. You know better than anyone how minor a bullet graze is, and I for one was happy there was no fucking around with Kruger in that situation."

Archer's jaw clenched, his temple throbbing as he glared down at me. "If he'd missed—"

"He didn't. So quit throwing your big-dick energy around and focus on this cleanup. I don't know about you, but I want to go the fuck home and not worry that cops will be arresting us all for multiple murders." I held his gaze steady, even though one of my eyes was throbbing painfully. "*Now*, Archer."

He scowled back at me another moment, then shot Steele a narrow-eyed glare before storming away to help Sampson's guys clean up the bodies.

"You too, Kodiak," I snapped, pinning him with my gaze. "Quit stirring shit up."

His jaw dropped in protest. "I wasn't—"

"Bullshit." I cut him off before he could deny it. "Go help Arch; I need a moment with Max."

Kody grumbled but closed the space between us and gently kissed my cheek. "You scared us, babe," he whispered in my ear. "Don't do that again, okay?"

I gave a small nod but a grim smile. "No promises."

Kody winced, then sighed. "Fair enough." He dropped a soft kiss to my lips, then headed over to help the cleanup.

Steele wouldn't look at me. He was quite deliberately looking at his shoes, even as he rubbed his face where Archer's punch had landed. He hadn't even tried to dodge it either, which told me everything I needed to know.

"Max Steele," I scolded, moving close enough to tip his chin up with my finger. "Don't you dare."

His eyes, when they met mine, were flooded with guilt and regret, and I shook my head before he could even try to apologize.

"You did exactly what needed to be done, Max; don't start beating yourself up over it now." I held his gaze, not letting him sink into self-flagellation over what had been a necessary and damn brave move to eliminate the threat.

His brow creased in a pained grimace. "Hellcat," he breathed, "I shot you. If my aim had been even a fraction off—"

"It wasn't." I cut him off just like I'd done to Archer a moment ago. "It never is. I trusted you, and you did exactly what needed to be done. No regrets here, Max."

He studied my eyes for a long moment like he was seeking the truth behind my words—or maybe searching for some level of accusation or anger. If so, he wouldn't find it. A moment later, he let out a long breath and let his shoulders sag.

"I don't deserve you, Hellcat." He looped his arms ever so carefully around my waist and pulled me into his body.

I snorted a laugh that hurt my bruised face but hugged him back. Gently. "Pretty sure that feeling is mutual, Max Steele. Come on, you can come keep me warm while the boys clean up." I linked my fingers with his and pulled him back over to the SUV, where James had set up his medical supplies. I slid into the backseat, wincing at the movement, but urged Steele to slide in beside me.

"I should probably help out." He glanced guiltily in the direction of the guys, who were using battery-operated angle grinders to slice up the dead Reapers. A handful of Zed's guys had arrived with them, and they'd gone to pick up some plastic tubs to transport the, uh, meat.

I yawned. "Nah, they're fine," I told him. "I wanna hear what happened. I missed a whole crapload while I was knocked out. How'd Arch get away from Zane? What happened when you and

Kody went to find Kruger? And how the fuck did you guys find me right in time?" I squinted at the sloppy, bloody mess that was being made across the parking lot. "Also, why are they cutting the bodies up so small? We've never done that before."

Steele looked in the direction I was staring, then gave me a lopsided smile. "Ah, Benny's stressing out that there's been too much activity lately, so he asked us to give his place a break for a couple of weeks."

I gave him a curious look. "So…how are we disposing of this mess?"

He gave me a lopsided smile. "I don't know if you'll believe me if I tell you."

"Try me."

Running his hand over his buzzed hair, he gave a wry grin. "Snapping turtles."

I blinked at him several times. "Say again?"

"Snapping turtles," he repeated. "The Japanese garden in Rainybanks has a turtle pond with about two hundred of the vicious bastards. They're just a bit slower than pigs, so we have to, uh, dice up their food a bit first. It's closed for pathway repairs for a few weeks too, so no one will see the chunks before the little snappers are done eating."

Bile rose in my stomach, and I gagged a bit. Snapping turtles ate dead humans? Now I'd really heard it all. "Gross," I whispered, and Steele gave a short laugh.

"But effective. The guys will load up all the chunks into some tubs, drive them over, and dump them in. Then we can get this ground pressure-washed with some peroxide, and the job is done." Steele looked so damn casual about it, but his eyes tightened with tension as they flickered over my glued-together head wound again.

"What about the cars?" I changed the subject before he could start feeling guilty all over again.

"Tow trucks should be here in a couple of hours. They'll be

taken to a somewhat less-than-legal chop shop and dismantled for parts. Don't worry, Hellcat; we've got this all under control." Steele took my hand in his, weaving our fingers together. My wrist was tightly bandaged, thanks to James, but it was only a dull ache compared to my various other pains.

"Okay, so catch me up on everything else," I urged, leaning my head back against the leather headrest.

Steele nodded, his thumb tracing gentle patterns over my scraped hand. "There's not too much else. When we arrived at Kruger's property, it was already empty; we'd missed him by a matter of minutes. Arch called not long after that. Zane got arrogant and wanted him captured, not killed, so he could make Arch watch while you were shot." Steele's fingers tightened around mine, and his jaw clenched with anger.

"But he got away?" I guessed, pushing forward and not dwelling on what could have been.

Steele jerked a nod. "The Reapers Zane had left to transport Arch thought better of it. Apparently, they were fine with helping kidnap and kill you, but they lost their nerve when it came to Arch."

"So they told you where I was?"

He gave me a crooked smile. "Uh, no. Arch killed them both before thinking about questioning them. Luckily, he'd remembered to give you my gift before you left the hotel." Steele reached over and touched the musical note pendant. "It's something I worked on with Leon while he was staying with us. There's a tiny tracking device embedded in the metal that would be totally undetectable to anyone searching. Not that Zane has the technology to scan you for trackers anyway. But I'm fucking glad Arch was thinking on his feet in the moment."

My jaw dropped slightly, and I touched a hand to the delicate necklace. Zane wouldn't have even given it a second glance, and it had led my guys straight to us. "I'm impressed," I murmured. "I did think it was a really weird time for Archer to give me jewelry, not gonna lie on that one."

Steele gave a short laugh, raised our linked fingers to his lips, and kissed my hand. "Well, it saved all of us, so feel free to keep wearing it always, Hellcat."

"Noted," I replied. "So what do we do now?"

He gave me a long look. "Can you be persuaded to go to a hospital and get checked out properly?"

I arched a brow at him. "You and I both know they will do nothing for me. Ice and painkillers, nothing I can't get at home. And I really, *really* just wanna go home with you guys. Can we please do that?"

I knew he wanted to argue and insist I go to the hospital, but after a long moment, he just sighed. "Yeah, I get it. Wait here; I'll make sure we're all okay to head back. I just need to know no one else has taken the hit on you after Zane accepted it. We badly don't need more half-baked hitmen coming at us tonight."

He kissed my fingers again, then slid out of the car and left me alone. I stared down at my hand for a long time, my eyes locked on my new diamond ring, and felt a strange sense of relief that Zane hadn't taken the heirloom. I was crazy attached to the thing.

James popped the door open sometime later and handed me a bottle of water with a couple of painkillers. I only hesitated a second before taking them, which probably spoke to how much pain I was really in. They made me sleepy, and I just let myself doze for a while. My lids were cracked halfway open, my gaze locked on the guys, but otherwise I was mostly asleep.

Eventually, they returned to the SUV I was in, and Archer slipped behind the wheel. Kody peeled off his sticky, blood-covered T-shirt and jeans outside the car, then crawled into the backseat with me in nothing but his boxers.

Steele was the last to rejoin us, having stayed to speak with

James and Sampson a few moments longer, and he climbed into the passenger seat.

"We all good?" Archer asked him in a clipped tone. Apparently, he was still pissed off.

Steele jerked a nod. "Sampson is staying here to supervise the rest of the cleanup. Gill, Dave, and James are all heading home in front of us to run a safety check. The hit has been officially canceled, though, thanks to Kruger's thumbprint on his laptop."

Kody blew out a long breath. "Thank fuck for that."

"Yup," I agreed, my voice thick with sleep and pain meds. "Let's go home."

Archer started the car, and Kody gently lifted me into his lap before buckling the seat belt around us both. Not technically the safest thing in the event of a crash, but I doubted I could ever feel anything *but* safe in his arms.

———————

The drive home took several hours. Zane had arranged a meeting point with Kruger *well* out of Shadow Grove, which in itself showed how he really had feared his little brother's wrath if he was caught.

I slept most of the way, my head on Kody's shoulder as he gently stroked my hair and whispered all kinds of heart-stopping promises.

When we reached the front gate, we needed to wait several minutes until the security guys gave us an all-clear. Not that any of us expected *more* bad guys waiting in our highly secured mansion, but it didn't hurt to remain cautious.

Archer didn't bother parking in the garage, instead just stopping directly in front of the entrance, then climbing out. He popped my door open as Kody unbuckled us, and then Archer carefully lifted me out into his arms.

"I can walk," I told him in a groggy voice, but he just ignored me, carrying me into the house.

Gill was waiting for us in the foyer and exchanged a few words with the boys about the house being secured, then left us alone. Archer carried me straight upstairs to my bedroom and kicked open the door to my bathroom.

He only put me down briefly, perching me on the edge of the vanity so he could turn my shower on. I was sleepy enough not to protest, just yawn and watch him strip his own bloody clothes off.

"Are you okay to stand in the shower?" he asked me with overwhelming concern as he helped me out of my T-shirt. I winced as the movement pulled on my damaged ribs but gritted my teeth.

"I'll be fine." I unclipped my bra as he worked on my jeans, and within seconds I was groaning under the hot spray of my shower.

"Just be careful not to get your head wet, Princess," Archer murmured as he adjusted the angle of the spray. "I don't know if you can get that glue wet so soon."

I just mumbled some sound of agreement and leaned against his hard body to stay upright. It was safe to say that was the worst beating I'd taken in a long time. Or…ever. Not even my car accidents had bruised me up so badly.

Then again, I hadn't been stabbed this time, so there was a small victory.

"I can't believe he fucking shot you," Archer whispered in outrage, his lips feathering over my forehead near the bullet graze.

I let out a small laugh. "I told him to do it, Sunshine, so stop being a bear about it. You know how good Steele is; there was no way he'd take that shot if he thought for even a second he might miss."

Archer just made a sound in his throat that was neither agreement nor disagreement. Regardless, he was the definition of caring as he gently washed dried blood, dirt, and grime from my battered skin. When I was clean, he hurried to rinse off himself, then bundled me up in a towel to carry me out.

"I really can walk," I told him with a laugh as he carefully deposited me into bed.

He just shrugged. "So?"

That was an argument I couldn't win, so I just let him fuss around to get me comfortable. When I was all tucked in, he fetched me more painkillers and a sleeping pill, which I happily accepted.

Before he could leave, I grabbed his hand. "Stay with me. Just until I'm asleep or something? I don't...I just need to feel you close."

Archer gave me a small frown of concern, then nodded and climbed into my bed beside me. I clenched my teeth against a grimace of pain as he got comfy, then carefully snuggled into his embrace.

"I thought you got shot for real," I confessed, my words mumbled into his chest. "I thought..." I couldn't even get the rest of those words out. It was bad enough watching Steele almost die of a shot to the chest, so when I'd seen that gun, heard a shot fired, then seen Archer collapse, my heart had stopped.

Archer knew what I meant, though. He just rubbed soothing circles on my back and kissed my hair.

"Baby girl, I'm like a cockroach. I can't be taken out so easily."

I smiled at that image, then let my eyes close as the sleeping pill worked its magic over me. Terrifying, shadowed creatures lurked in the edges of my mind, though, filling me with anxiety and holding true sleep at arm's length.

"It's not over yet, is it?" I whispered into the darkness.

Archer's chest rose and fell under my face as he heaved a sigh. "No, Princess. It's not. But it will be really soon. I promise."

CHAPTER 38

The next two days passed in a flash, mostly due to the fact that—aside from a trip to the hospital that next morning, for X-rays on my broken ribs and to check for facial fractures—I slept almost around the clock. I woke up for occasional meals that the guys brought to me in bed and to pee. That was about it. By the time I dragged my ass into the shower on day three, I was feeling a hell of a lot better, even if I didn't look it.

Actually, I *really* didn't look it. My face was a mess of purple and yellow bruising, and my ribs made me cringe just to look at. No amount of concealer was going to hide the state I was in, though, so I just tied my hair up—careful not to tug on my healing head wound—then headed downstairs to find the guys.

"Hellcat!" Steele was the first to notice me enter the kitchen. "What are you doing out of bed?"

I gave a small shrug. "I slept for the better part of three days; I got bored. And hungry. Is that pizza I smell?"

"It sure is," Anna replied, pulling a fresh one from the oven and sliding it onto her chopping board. "But, girl, you look a mess. Have you put any bruise balm on that face?"

I blinked at her in confusion. "That's a thing?"

The look of utter exasperation that she gave the boys over that comment was priceless.

"Unbelievable," the cook muttered. "Just because you three think bruises make you look *cool* doesn't mean you should let Madison Kate suffer. Goodness me. Wait here, sweetheart." She patted me on the shoulder and hurried out of the kitchen, leaving the fresh pizza uncut on her board.

I wrinkled my nose at the guys in confusion, then winced as it moved my bruises. Yeah, if she had something to help, then I was all for it.

"Come here, babe." Kody reached out his hand to me. When I took it, he pulled me—carefully—into his lap rather than onto the empty barstool beside him. He kissed my slightly less-bruised cheek and gave me a light squeeze. "How are you feeling?"

"Like I got beaten the hell up," I replied with a snort of laughter, "but actually a shitload better than I did. What time is it anyway?" I had no idea where my phone was and hadn't even tried looking for it.

"Dinnertime," Steele told me, grinning wide as he cut the pizza up in Anna's absence. He had flour streaked over his face and an apron tied around his neck, so I had to assume he'd been assisting.

Anna came back in carrying a little purple tub of cream and instructed Kody to spread it all over my bruises. He did as he was told, smoothing the peppermint-scented cream over my face with gentle fingers.

"We might need to move to the couch to do the rest," I told him when he finished rubbing the bruise balm onto my puffy cheekbone. He followed me over to the sofa in the open-plan living area off the kitchen, and I pulled my T-shirt up for him to access my ribs.

Kody's brow furrowed as he worked—carefully avoiding the area where my ribs were broken—and I knew it was out of concern for my injuries. When he was done, I cupped his face in my hands and kissed him hard.

"I'm fine, Kodiak," I whispered against his lips. "It's just bruising."

He kissed me back, but his brow was still tense and furrowed as he smoothed my T-shirt back down over my peppermint-scented skin.

"You shouldn't be getting hurt like this, babe," he murmured in a low voice. "What fucking use are we if we can't keep you safe?"

I got it. I did. I'd felt the same fucking way when Steele was shot. But self-pity never changed the past, and there was nothing to be gained by entertaining what-ifs. So I bopped him on the nose with my finger.

"Stop it."

His brows shot up in surprise. "Uh…"

"No, seriously, Kody. Stop it. What's done is done, and you know what? It actually worked out for the best. We killed Kruger. The hit on me was canceled. We got rid of Zane and his slimy little lieutenants. I feel a hell of a lot better with Cass in charge of the Reapers, don't you?"

A loud crash of breaking glass cut off whatever he might have replied, and Kody all but threw me down into the couch. He covered me almost completely with his body, blocking my view of whatever the fuck was going on.

Not that I needed to see.

"Gas!" Archer shouted, the alarm in his voice clear as day.

"Stay behind me," Kody ordered. He rolled off me and deftly caught a gun that Steele tossed him from the cutlery drawer. "Cover your mouth and nose," he added, coughing.

It wasn't hard to see what he meant. Several canisters of gas had been tossed through the smashed windows and were spurting thick plumes of chemical smoke into the room.

A moment later, four men clad entirely in black with full-face gas masks climbed through those broken windows with guns drawn. More fool, them. They should have waited longer for the gas to do its trick because all four of them were dead before they'd even taken two steps into the kitchen.

"MK, get to the panic room!" Kody barked, covering his face with his T-shirt and holding his gun steady as he waited for more attackers to enter.

The gas was getting thicker, making my head swim and my vision blur, but I staggered in the direction of the foyer. I needed to get across the garage to the hidden panel.

"Here!" Anna shouted, tossing me a wet washcloth. She had one clasped to her own face and a heavy skillet in her other hand.

I followed suit, breathing through the wet fabric to filter the gas somewhat, then watched in shock as a gas-masked man appeared from the corridor and grabbed for Anna. She was ready for him, though, and smacked him so hard in the face with her skillet that blood spattered the wall as he collapsed.

"Fuck," I exclaimed as she smacked the man one more time before collapsing herself.

"Run, girl," she croaked at me, then dissolved into coughing as her eyes rolled back.

Tight fingers circled my upper arm, and I almost lashed out before recognizing Steele behind me. "Hurry," he told me in a strained voice. His face was deathly pale, his lips turning a weird shade of blue, but his eyes were determined.

I dragged a lungful of air through my washcloth and raced out into the foyer, leaving Kody and Archer shooting at people behind us. Fucking hell, how many attackers were coming for us? But more to the point, *why*? The hit had been *canceled*. Kruger was *dead*. What the fuck was even happening right now?

Steele ran with me through the marble foyer to the garage, but jerked me out of the way a fraction of a second before I passed through the doorway. Not a moment too soon, either. Two gas mask–wearing men came through the doorway, and Steele dropped the first one with a shot. Then his gun clicked empty. Thinking quick, he charged at the second man, shoving him back through the doorway, and slammed the door shut and locked it.

"Shit," he wheezed. With a panicked look, he pushed me in the direction of the stairs. "Other entrance," he ordered me. "Run, don't stop. They must have gassed the AC."

That was all he managed to tell me before several gunshots fired through the flimsy door and narrowly missed hitting him.

"Go!" he roared, ducking out of the way as the door burst open in a shower of splintering wood.

I stumbled, coughing, but the adrenaline coursing through my veins pushed me forward. Taking the stairs three at a time, I barely even breathed, not wanting to inhale the gas and succumb to unconsciousness. Shouts and gunfire echoed through the house below me, but I didn't look. Anyone who'd watched a slasher flick knew the second you looked, you'd trip, fall, and ultimately die a painful, gruesome death. No thanks.

The guys had said there was a panic room access point from the second linen closet; I just needed to get there without being caught. Or, *fuck*, was it the third linen closet? On the left or the right? Who the *fuck* had so many closets anyway?

Taking a gamble, I went with my first instinct and yanked the door open as my vision swirled dangerously. I needed to hurry the hell up, or I'd pass out.

Someone had to be smiling down on me, though, because it only took a few seconds to pop open the hidden panel and slip into the darkness of the narrow staircase. I descended so fast I practically tumbled the last few steps, then slammed my palm onto the biometric scanner.

The door slid open immediately, and I threw myself forward. My vision was almost entirely black and my limbs felt like they were moving through custard as I reached up and pressed the button to close the door.

It slid closed silently, but not before I saw a gas mask–wearing man storming down the tight corridor toward me.

"Too late, fucker," I croaked as the door sealed, cutting him off from me as securely as Fort fucking Knox.

There was a moment of dead silence, then a soft whirring started up and a cool breeze washed over my face from the vents near the floor. A spike of panic shot through me, but I quickly remembered the panic room operated on an independent AC unit from the main house. Thank fuck too. I inhaled deeply, groaning as the clean air filled my lungs and cleared my head.

A buzz sounded through the panic room, and a chill crept over my skin. Whoever was outside was using the intercom.

Drawing a couple more deep breaths, I climbed up off the floor and opened the panel beside the door, which would show me whoever was outside. Unsurprisingly, it was the gas-masked attacker who'd just missed me as the door closed.

Biting my lip, I stared at the screen. Did I know this person? Or were all the gas-masked fucks just hired muscle? I sure as fuck wasn't letting him in, regardless of whether I knew him or not. So I didn't know what the point of buzzing me was.

And yet he buzzed again.

My temper got the best of me, and I stabbed the *talk* button on my panel. "What the *fuck* do you want?" I snapped.

"Open the door, Madison Kate," the man responded. His voice was muffled by his mask, his identity still a total secret. He was head to toe in black, even wearing gloves, so there were no distinguishing tattoos or marks.

I scoffed a bitter laugh. "Yeah sure, let me just open the door and let you murder me. Shall I make it easier and just shoot myself in the head so you can save some bullets?"

There was a long pause where I imagined my attacker might be pondering how useful that would be. If my offer hadn't been dripping in sarcasm, that was.

"Open the door, Madison Kate," he repeated after a moment. "I won't hurt you. I'm trying to keep you *safe*."

My jaw dropped. Then realization washed over me. This was my stalker. My *actual* stalker. In the fucking flesh. Holy shit. *Holy shit!*

"Madison Kate, they can't keep you safe," my stalker continued, his tone totally flat and even. Not a shred of emotion carried through, and that just scared me all the more. "Look at what happened the other night. You almost died because those boys don't *care* about you. Not really. Not like I do."

What. The. Fuck.

All the messed-up, sick, and twisted things my stalker had done over the last year crossed my mind in a flash. The dead animals. The Barbie dolls. Drew getting her throat cut, me getting drugged and locked in a trunk, the human heart, the mutilated blogger... the list went on. And then there were the crimes against my mom. Her attack and rape. Her *pregnancy*.

Fuck. Holy *fuck*.

Terror flowed freely through my veins, making my whole body tremble, but I didn't take the bait and reply. Instead, I turned my back on the door and made my way over to the surveillance desk. There were eight flat-screen monitors mounted on the wall, and a tap to the keyboard brought them all to life. In an instant, I had eyes on the entire estate, but I couldn't see my guys anywhere.

I spotted plenty of unconscious or dead assailants, all in black and none of them looking remotely like my guys...so that was something.

"Madison Kate," my stalker at the door called out again. I must have left the intercom turned on. "Just open the door and come with me. I won't hurt you. I've never wanted to hurt you. Just look at all I've done to keep you safe."

My gaze scanned the screens again as I desperately searched for my guys and still came up blank. Fuck. Where were they? Had they gotten out of the house? That was the logical thing to do when the vents were pumping gas through the house. They'd have gone outside to stay conscious.

Unless they hadn't made it that far.

Shit. Now what the hell did I do? Were there guns in the panic room? Of course there would be. There was a gun in the cutlery drawer; there would *definitely* be at least one in the panic room.

"Do *not* keep me waiting, Madison Kate," my stalker snapped, finally showing some emotion. It was anger, but still. It was something. "You do not want to piss me off."

Sneering, I returned to the door panel. "Or *fucking* what? You're gonna stand there and stamp your feet like a brat? You can't get in here, and you fucking well know it. You lost this round."

I was confident his primary objective was me. He wasn't here to kill the guys; he was here to abduct *me*. So as long as I was out of reach, we were at a stalemate. Right?

"Very well, you want to play hard to get." My stalker sounded almost amused. How was it that being amused was scarier than angry? "I'll fetch some more incentive, then. Don't go anywhere, my sweet. I'll be right back."

He didn't wait for me to reply—if I even had anything to say—just spun on his heel and stalked away from the panic room with determined strides. His gait was strong and confident with not even a hint of a limp. That crossed Officer Shane off my list of suspects.

After he disappeared from my door camera, I raced back to the surveillance panel and followed him from screen to screen.

"What the hell are you doing?" I muttered aloud, chewing at my lip as he passed through the den and exited out to the back patio. A burst of movement on another screen grabbed my attention, though, and I spotted Archer locked in a hand-to-hand fight with one of the black-clad attackers.

My heart in my throat, I watched enthralled as they traded punches, but instantly I knew something was wrong. Archer's movements were too slow. Sluggish. And he was massively favoring his right side, like he'd taken an injury there recently.

Even so, he was getting the upper hand on his opponent. Until my stalker entered the frame. How I knew it was him, I had no idea. Call it a hunch.

I gasped, internally screaming because there was nothing I could do to warn Archer. Every fiber in my being wanted to *scream* at him to turn around, to *look behind you!* But it was futile. They were in the gym, way too far for me to get up there. I could do nothing but watch as my stalker picked up one of the dumbbells from the weights rack, then struck Archer in the back of the head with it.

Archer crumpled, a smear of blood showing vividly against the light blue floor as my heart tore in half.

My stalker turned his masked face directly toward the surveillance camera, and I knew perfectly well he was sending me a message. Not only was this *my fault* for taunting him, he was also telling me he knew *exactly* where the hidden cameras were. But of course he did. He'd been hacking the footage and tampering with angles right up until Leon and Danny secured our network, after all.

"Holy shit," I whispered, my voice fading into a bit of a whimper.

In the gym, my stalker used the assistance of the guy Archer had been fighting and, between them, dragged my man out of the room. Once again, I followed them from screen to screen, even though I knew full well where they were going.

By the time they'd dragged Archer's unconscious body along the narrow corridor outside the panic room, my face was wet with tears and my stomach churning with bile. Where were Kody and Steele? Were they even still alive?

The intercom buzzed, and I staggered over to it with dread in my veins. He had me. He totally had me, and he knew it. There wasn't *anything* I wouldn't do for my guys…including give myself up.

"Let him go," I ordered my stalker as I turned the intercom back on. I wanted it to come out as an order, but my voice was croaky and thick with despair. Archer was still out cold, face down on the floor at his captor's feet.

"Open the door, Madison Kate," my stalker replied. "Or I'm shooting your not-so-new husband in the head." He drew a pistol from the back of his waistband and aimed it at the back of Archer's head.

"You shoot him, and you'll *never* get me out of here," I bluffed, choking over the words. Every instinct in me wanted to open that door, but I *knew* Archer would curse me out six ways to Sunday if he were conscious.

My stalker gave a small shrug. "See, here's the thing, Madison Kate. I planned to kill these three regardless of how tonight worked out. They failed to protect you, and they need to be eliminated. So you can stay there and watch as I kill them in front of you, one by one." There was an implied second option, and I was too weak to resist the bait.

"Or?"

"Or you can open the door, Madison Kate."

I wet my lips and swallowed past the hard lump in my throat. He didn't have Steele and Kody…not yet anyway. But if I didn't act fast, Archer would die.

"You'll kill them," I replied, feeling my heart shatter into a million pieces with those words. I wanted nothing more than to trade myself for Archer, but like my stalker had *just* said…he was going to kill them regardless. What good would it do to hand myself over only to have them shot anyway?

"Maybe I won't," my stalker replied. "Maybe I will. The only certainty here, Madison Kate, is that if you *don't* open the door in the next five seconds, Archer *will* die." He paused, tilting his mask-covered face to the side as he faced the camera. "Is that shred of uncertainty enough, my love?" I shuddered at the endearment.

"Let's find out. One…two…three…" He wasn't even pausing a full second between. I had no doubt he would follow through on his threat when he reached five. "Four…"

I slammed my hand down on the door release.

The sharp chemical smell of gas hit my nose the second the door slid open, and I swallowed heavily.

"Good girl," my stalker purred. He offered his hand for me to take, and I looked down at it with horror, like he'd just presented me with a live snake. "Don't keep me waiting, Madison Kate." His other hand still held a gun aimed at Archer's head, and the threat was clear. Crystal fucking clear.

I swallowed heavily and placed my hand in his.

"Such obedience," my stalker murmured, "so unlike your mother. She made things so difficult for herself toward the end there."

Revulsion burned in my throat, and I gagged. But then maybe that was the gas getting to me. In the time I'd spent in the panic room, the gas had thickened through the house, and I was already lightheaded and dizzy. It was no wonder Archer had been losing his fight. In fact, I was amazed he'd even still been conscious at all.

"You have me now," I announced in a strangled voice. "Leave everyone else alone."

My stalker's gloved fingers tightened around my hand as he dragged me along the corridor away from Archer. Away from his buddy, who remained standing over my fallen love.

I stupidly let myself hope. I let myself have a spark of relief that he must have decided on mercy now that he had me. But as he dragged me up the narrow staircase to the garage entrance, the deafening crack of a gunshot echoed through the small space.

An agonized scream tore from my throat, and I tried desperately to wrench my hand free. But the gas was doing its work. I was weaker than wet tissue paper and just sagged to the ground instead.

My stalker barely even skipped a beat, stooping, then throwing me over his shoulder as he made his way through the garage. Several cars were peppered with bullet holes, but I was too broken to care.

Consciousness swam, my vision blacking in and out, and my stomach lurched. The gas was nauseating me as well as knocking me out, but the way my captor strode through the house—confident, like he knew the layout intimately—told me we weren't hanging around. He had his prize; now he was getting the fuck out.

He carried me through the pool area to a door beside the steam room. It led out to some of the meticulously maintained gardens, and a few gulps of fresh air helped to clear my head enough that I recognized the whirling sound of helicopter blades.

Fuck. I'd halfway counted on Steele or Kody catching up to us on the road, but how the hell would they follow a helicopter? Wait. My necklace. I still had my tracker necklace on… Maybe they would find me eventually after all.

A gunshot rang out through the night, and my captor jerked to a stop, then dropped me behind some low hedges. He aimed his gun at someone, squeezing out a couple of shots.

He must have missed whoever he was aiming at, though, because he ducked behind the hedge with me and muttered a string of curses.

I couldn't stop the bitter, mocking laugh bubbling out of me as the gas faded away. "I thought you *never missed*. Looks like that was just wishful thinking, huh?"

He didn't dignify that jab with a response, but I didn't fucking care. I just wanted to take a swipe at him and distract him so that whoever was shooting could change their position. I was also working my jellylike arm into the pocket of my sweatpants and praying to all things holy that my butterfly knife hadn't fallen out.

My fingers touched metal, and I grinned.

That caught his attention, though. "What are you smiling at?" he demanded, and I knew it'd be a matter of seconds before he found my weapon.

Now or never.

"This," I replied, whipping the blade out of my pocket and slamming it into his side.

He cried out, falling backward, and I didn't waste my opportunity. I left my knife in his flesh and fucking *ran*.

My bare feet pounded the damp grass as I raced toward Steinwick and Anna's cottage, but I only made it halfway there before my attacker tackled me to the grass.

I went down hard but rolled immediately and kicked out furiously, fighting him off as he tried to get his hands around my throat. All my bruises and injuries from just three nights ago were screaming, my entire body a mass of pain, but it was incredible what could be achieved when there was nothing to lose.

My stalker cursed at me, something about not fighting him, but I was lost to an almost total panic state. Fight-or-flight had well and truly set in, and seeing as I *couldn't* flee, I was damn well going to fight with everything I had.

My legs bunched under me, and I kicked out, trying to push him away, but he was heavier than I expected. Not to mention my legs were still so weak with the lingering gas in my system. Seeing it wasn't working, I swung a fist, trying to break his mask or knock it loose, but he caught my wrist in a crushing grip. It was my sprained one, and I let out a scream of pain.

"Stop fighting me!" he roared, his grip tightening even more. Tears stream from my eyes at the crushing pain. His face was so close to mine that I could see his eyes through the mask, and there was something eerily familiar about them. They were an unusual violet blue…just like mine. Just like my mom's.

Panicked and desperate to free myself, I just struggled harder. This time I swung my other fist, aiming for the spot where I'd stabbed him. He cried out, and something snapped. White-hot pain lanced through my arm, and my vision blacked for a second. He'd broken my wrist.

He reared back, releasing my wrist to reach for my knife, where it was still buried in his side. That was my opportunity. I pulled my knees up to my chest and kicked like a donkey. My heel caught him in the chin, snapping his head back. His gas mask skittered away across the grass, and I gasped in shock.

"Dave?" I exclaimed in disbelief. But…that didn't make sense. The eyes didn't match. I would have noticed something like that, as many times as I'd spoken to the man in the past months. He had brown eyes, I was *sure* of it.

Unless, of course, he wore color contacts.

Fuck.

My shock held me frozen, but it no longer mattered. A split second later a bullet ripped through our two-faced security guard's chest, splattering hot blood all over me.

"Babe!" Kody shouted from somewhere nearby, racing out from the shelter of some trees to scoop me up in his arms.

Dave seemed almost frozen in place, still upright on his knees with a look of abject horror on his face. A second shot tore through his shoulder, jerking his body, and a moment later, Steinwick appeared from freaking *nowhere* and slammed his fist across Dave's face.

"Steinwick?" I exclaimed, even as Kody tried to carry me away to safety. "No, Kody, put me down. It was Dave. It was him all along. Stop!" My order echoed through the suddenly quiet night air, and Kody froze in his tracks.

"Babe, you need—"

"No!" I cut him off. "I *need* answers. Put me the fuck down!"

He only needed to look into my determined gaze for a second before doing what I asked. He trusted me not to be an idiot, and I really didn't want to disappoint him. Besides, it was my wrist that was broken, not my ankle. I could walk just fine.

Okay, so it was more of a stagger as I made my way back to Dave and found Steinwick standing over him with a gun. Fucking *Steinwick*.

"Nice punch," I murmured to him as I dropped to my knees in the grass. Dave wasn't going anywhere. Not with two bullet holes in his chest.

Several more shots rang out, and I barely flinched. Now that I knew Kody was here, I was sure Steele was on the other end of that rifle. He must be cleaning up any remaining attackers.

James jogged across the lawn toward us, a rifle of his own tucked under his arm and blood dripping down his face. I ignored him, though, turning my attention back to the dying man before me.

"Why?" I demanded. "What connection did you even have to my mom? To me?" All his background checks had been clear. There had been no reason to suspect him. Not one…or not anything that we'd found.

Blood bubbling from his chest wounds, Dave gave a gasping laugh. One bullet had struck him near his shoulder, not an immediately fatal wound. The other looked a whole lot more serious, though.

"We need to get him to the hospital," I announced to anyone who was listening.

Kody scoffed. "Fuck that, I'm not saving this sick fuck."

I shook my head. "I don't want to *save* him, but this is too fast. Too merciful. He needs to pay…painfully. For *days*. He can't die this quickly; he doesn't fucking deserve it."

James crouched down beside us and shook his head. "Sorry, kiddo. That hole in his aorta will see him dead before we could even get him into a car."

Frustration burned through me, but I just gritted my teeth and glared down at the security guard who we'd thought to be so trustworthy.

"Who are you really?" I demanded. "You're dead in minutes, might as well rip the mask off, *Dave*."

Blood ran from his lips, but his familiar gaze was steady on mine as he tried to form words. Fuck. *Fuck*. He'd better not die before giving me at least *one* answer. Because right now all I had were *more* questions.

His lips moved again, and I crouched lower to try to hear him. There was a sickening wheezing sound mixed with the gurgle of blood, but right on the end of his last exhale, I got my answer.

"*Declan.*"

It took a second for that name to click in my brain, but when it did, I felt like I'd been hit by lightning. Horrified, I jerked back from his lifeless gaze and lost my balance, putting my hand out to brace myself. But I forgot about my broken wrist.

An agonized scream ripped out of my throat, but it wasn't just from the pain in my hand. It was for my mom—because the man who'd stalked her, *raped* her, was her own twin brother.

CHAPTER 39

There was no stopping the vomit after all those pieces clicked together in my brain. I crouched on my knees, emptying my stomach into a garden bed while Kody rubbed my back. Steele arrived just a minute later, his rifle tucked under his arm and a fresh bruise blooming on his cheek.

"Hellcat," he exhaled when he spotted me shivering under Kody's arm. "You're okay?"

Kody snorted as I wiped my mouth off on my forearm. "What the fuck does it look like, bro? She's far from okay."

I gave him a small jab in the ribs. "I'm okay," I told Steele. "Nothing that won't heal."

Movement from the house drew everyone's attention, and both James and Steele swung their guns up to aim before the person staggered out of the shadows and into the light from the security spotlights.

"Thank *fuck*," I exclaimed, staggering to my feet to run at top speed across the lawn. My broken wrist and multiple bruises were totally forgotten as I threw myself at Archer, clinging on to him as I sobbed into his chest.

He let out a small grunt of pain, but one arm wrapped around me tight, holding me against him with just as much desperation as I was feeling. I'd thought for sure he was dead. That hit he'd taken from the weight, then the gunshot…but of course he wasn't dead. This was Archer D'Ath; he was basically indestructible.

"I'm okay, baby girl," he murmured in my ear, his lips moving against my skin. "I'm alive. It's okay, shh, don't cry."

His words made sense, but I couldn't stop. I was shaking all over, tears pouring from my eyes and my chest aching with an overload of emotions.

"Hellcat." Steele stroked a gentle hand down my back. "Gorgeous, can you let go for a second? Arch needs his shoulder popped back into place, and your wrist needs attention."

I jerked back with a gasp, my gaze taking in the way Archer's arm hung limp at his side and the steady drip of blood coloring the grass at our feet.

"Shit, I'm so sorry." I sniffed to try to control my tears but had exactly zero luck. "S-sorry. Arch, you're bleeding really hard. Steele, he's—"

"We've got it, babe," Kody cut me off in a smooth, gentle tone. "Come, sit with me over here. Will you be okay a couple of minutes while James stops Archer's bleeding?"

Nodding quickly, I let him lead me over to the outdoor table and took a seat when he pulled it out for me. James and Steele— the only ones who actually knew what they were doing—went to work on Archer where he stood.

Steinwick came rushing back over the lawn carrying a large medical kit, which he must have just fetched from James's shed. Anna appeared out of the house, looking pale and shocked, but rushed straight over to where I sat with Kody.

"Oh, my girl, what a mess," she murmured as she took in my newest injuries. "Wait here."

Not like I was going anywhere, but I nodded. My eyes were glued to Archer, though, watching with choking concern as James peeled Archer's T-shirt up to inspect the bullet hole on his side. Steele handed him wipes, and they quickly patched it up with gauze, then wrapped a bandage tightly around his waist to hold pressure against the wound.

They then worked in tandem to pop Archer's shoulder back into place. It took them several tries, and when it eventually slid into place, Archer's face was gray and sweat beaded on his brow.

"Just keep that there," Anna said to me, and I blinked rapidly, not having noticed she'd returned. An ice pack was wrapped around my broken wrist where it rested on the table, and I had no recollection of her having done it. Shock must have been setting in.

"Ambulance is just two minutes away," Steinwick informed Kody, touching him on the shoulder to get his attention. "Archer will need to be taken in with Madison Kate. That gunshot wound needs stitching properly." He nodded over to where James was asking Archer a series of questions.

"His head too," I added, my voice hoarse and thick with emotions. "He got hit in the back of the head with a dumbbell."

Kody's brows shot up, and Steinwick nodded his understanding, then crossed over the lawn to tell James this additional information. Archer shot me an accusatory look, like I'd just tattled on him, but I didn't fucking care. He could have had a concussion or something, and he needed that checked out properly.

"Babe," Kody said, carefully cupping my face and stroking his thumb over my less bruised cheek. "Hey, stay with me. It's all over now. It's done. No one else is going to hurt you, I swear."

It wasn't until he started speaking that I realized I was shivering. More than shivering, I was damn near convulsing. My wrist was numb from the ice, but my whole arm ached with a dull pain. Frowning, I forced myself to draw a couple of deep, slow breaths. I needed to calm down, or I'd do more damage than I already had.

Two ambulances with lights and sirens came speeding across the grass from the direction of the front gates, and I breathed a sigh of relief. Archer needed their help, and Steele needed to be checked out too. Who knew how hard he'd been hit to make that bruise on his face—not to mention whatever the fuck we'd all been gassed with. Shit, *everyone* needed to be checked out.

"What do we do about the bodies?" I asked Kody with chattering teeth. "Where did he even get so much backup?"

Kody grimaced. "Wraiths. I spotted a gang tattoo on one of the first attackers. Trust me, babe, Charon has a lot to answer for after this mess."

Surprisingly, no cop cars followed the ambulances onto the property. But then, that wasn't actually so surprising, was it? Archer D'Ath was above the law, at least in Shadow Grove. They'd attended the scene when Bree's car had crashed because it had been so public. But here? On our private property? They were firmly turning their heads the other way. And thank fuck for that.

It took some time for the EMTs to check everyone over, but at the end of It, only Archer and I needed to go to the hospital for further treatment. Steele had taken a solid hit to the face but was given the all clear with only a mild concussion.

Kody, though? *Fucking Kody*. Not a damn scratch on him.

"Seriously?" Archer grumbled at his friend while the EMTs strapped him into a stretcher and stabilized his arm. "How the fuck are you so slippery you didn't even catch a black eye or something? This is such bullshit."

Kody just grinned like a shithead. "Hey, man, don't hate the player, hate the game. I can't help that I'm just a bigger badass than you."

Archer glared daggers but couldn't do anything as he was loaded into the back of the ambulance.

"Don't worry about all of this," Steele told me as I frowned in the direction of Dave's—or *Declan's*—body. "After you get that wrist sorted, we can debrief. Your injuries take priority, Hellcat."

I jerked a nod of understanding and let the nice, older female

EMT coax me into the other ambulance. Even though I was the only one who'd heard my stalker's dying confession, I was a long way from being able to pass the information on. It was so much worse than I'd ever anticipated, and just the idea of voicing the reality made my stomach churn again.

Nope. No, Steele was right. It could wait a couple of hours.

———————

That couple of hours turned into the rest of the night, as Archer was admitted for observation, despite his protests. After my wrist was X-rayed and set in a cast and I'd been given a couple of pain-killers for all my other bruises, I'd given him a stern talking to.

James had accompanied us to the hospital, offering to keep an eye on me while Kody and Steele dealt with the cleanup, and I weirdly appreciated his company. I liked him, despite really know-ing very little about him. A small part of me hoped that maybe we could get to know each other when my life was less blood soaked.

After all, he was the only genetic family I had left. Chosen family, though? I had plenty of that. Archer, Kody, and Steele owned equal parts of my soul; they were my fucking *everything*. But the events of the night had brought me clarity regarding the other members of my new family. Anna and Steinwick had gained my undying respect. I doubted I'd ever forget the image of Anna beating a man to death with a skillet.

"He'll be out for a while," James told me softly as I sat beside Archer's bedside. "They've given him some sleeping aid to help his body heal."

I nodded, tired as fuck. "Probably smart," I mumbled. "He wouldn't rest otherwise."

James gave a soft laugh. "Ain't that true. Never met a man so hardheaded in my life." He paused, but I could sense he had more to say.

I didn't push him, though. I was too damn exhausted.

Eventually he sighed, sitting down beside me. "You know...I never even thought about kids. It just never seemed to be in the cards for me, and I was content with the life I had."

I said nothing, but I was curious to see where he was going with this.

"I *definitely* never thought about what it'd be like to have a daughter, that's for fucking sure. And I sure as fuck never thought I'd be the father to a grown-ass woman who is perfectly capable of standing on her own two feet." He ruffled his hair with his fingers and blew out a long exhale. "Listen, you don't know me from a bar of soap, but for what it's worth..." He trailed off like he had no idea what the right phrasing was for what he wanted to say. Eventually he just shrugged. "You've got three guys who would quite literally die for you, Madison Kate. They love you with a force I never even knew possible. I guess...that's all any parent could want for their kid, right?"

It didn't sound like a rhetorical question; he was genuinely asking if that was the right reaction to his newly discovered adult daughter dating three violent killers.

Glancing over at him, I gave a small smile. "Don't overthink it, James," I advised with a hint of amusement. "It just is what it is."

He gave a small grimace somewhere in the realm of awkward embarrassment. "Well, anyway." Another pause. "Are you happy, Madison Kate? I mean, if you could ignore all the shootings and bombings and stalkers...if you were just a normal girl, dating three guys who loved her equally, would you be happy?"

I raised my brows, not totally sure what point he was making. "Um...well, I don't think I can ignore all those things. Without all of that, I might never have met Archer, Kody, and Steele, so then the answer would be no. I can't possibly picture my life now without the three of them in it. They're *it* for me, and I love everything that comes with them—blood, violence, and all. So if your real question is would I change anything if I could? Hell no. This is me now. The real me. And they're just the other parts to my whole piece."

James held my gaze for a moment, his eyes curious but not judgmental. He just wanted to understand, and I appreciated that about him.

After a second, he jerked a nod. "Well, good. I'm pretty glad I took the job with Archer, that's for sure. I never could have seen this coming, but I'm surprisingly okay with how it's worked out."

I returned his smile. "Me too."

James cleared his throat a bit awkwardly, then gave another short nod. "I'll leave you be. Whenever you want to head home, I'll be in the waiting room, okay?"

"Actually, I'm probably going to stay awhile," I told him with a yawn. "Bree is still upstairs, so I want to go and see her when she wakes up. You can head home and get some sleep; one of the guys can come get me later."

James just gave me a tight smile as he paused in the doorway. "Nah, I'll wait. Take as long as you need; my gardens can wait a day." He gave me a joking wink, then left the room.

A warm feeling had settled over me as we'd spoken, and in his absence, I found myself smiling. He might never be my *dad*, but he was a damn sight better than the one I'd known growing up.

I yawned again and rested my head on the side of Archer's bed. It was only four in the morning; Bree wouldn't likely be awake for a while yet. Maybe I'd just…close my eyes a moment.

CHAPTER 40

"Babe, wake up." Kody's gentle voice jerked me out of my deep sleep, and I sat up with a gasp, then groaned in pain. "Hey, whoa, take it easy, MK."

"Ow," I complained, trying to rub my eyes and accidentally bashing myself in the face with my plaster cast. "What's going on?"

Kody smoothed his hand over my face, rubbing his thumb over my nose, which I'd just whacked. "You were asleep on the side of the bed," he told me in a low whisper. "I was worried your neck would be hurting. Let me take you home, babe. Arch will be fine here."

I shook my head. "No, I wanted to…" I trailed off, blinking at the clock on the wall. "Oh damn, I was asleep for more than five minutes." It was past eight in the morning. Bree should be awake by now. "I wanna go and see Bree." I stood up from my chair and *every* stiff muscle screamed at me. Holy crap, I was feeling rough.

Kody didn't argue with me, just nodded and took my good hand in his. I hesitated before we left the room, glancing back at Archer's sleeping form with indecision. It felt wrong to leave him so vulnerable.

"I've got Arch, Hellcat," Steele told me, coming from down the corridor with a tray of coffees in hand. "Here, take one of these, kiss me, tell me you're fine, then go do what you were doing."

I couldn't help smiling as he handed me a coffee. Rising up on my toes, I pressed my lips to his in a tender kiss, which he leaned into.

"I'm fine, Max," I whispered against his lips. "And I love you."

His mouth curved in a blissful smile. "I love you too, Hellcat."

"One of those for me, bro?" Kody asked, plucking a coffee from Steele's tray without waiting for a response. It was a damn good thing all four of us drank our coffee the same way; it made ordering easy as hell. "Come on, babe. Let's go see Bree, then head home for sleep."

I grumbled about not wanting to leave the hospital without Archer but sipped my coffee and followed him along past the nurses' station to the elevators. We passed through the waiting room on the way, and I was genuinely surprised to see James still sitting there, waiting. Just like he'd said he would.

He was in one of the uncomfortable plastic chairs, reading what looked like a well-worn paperback romance novel that he must have found in the stack of magazines and coloring books. He was a decent way through it too.

"All okay?" he asked us, his gaze flicking up from his book when he noticed us there.

I nodded and gave a small smile. "You're fine to go home," I told him. "You look wrecked."

His gaze flipped between Kody and me before he replied. "Nah, I'm good. I'll hang out in case you guys need something. I've heard how much coffee you go through, Madison Kate. You might need a refill soon."

I snorted a laugh, shaking my head. "Suit yourself. And it's MK. Only people I don't like call me Madison Kate."

James bobbed a nod, a hint of red creeping up his neck. "MK. Got it." Then he shifted his gaze to Kody, and his eyes turned hard. "Don't take your eyes off her."

Kody just nodded and nudged me over to the elevators. He kept his face neutral until the doors slid closed; then his lips curved in a wide grin as he glanced over at me.

"What?" I asked, suspicious as fuck.

He snickered. "Babe, I reckon your dad might actually kill us if you get hurt again. He's got that whole protective papa-bear look *nailed*."

I rolled my eyes, shaking off his teasing. "Stop it. James probably finds this whole dynamic just as weird as I do."

Kody shrugged, sipping his coffee. "Maybe, but I think he's adapting pretty well. But for the record, he wouldn't need to kill us if you got hurt again." His joking demeanor evaporated, and his tone darkened. "I'd do it for him."

The elevator doors slid open on Bree's floor, and he took three steps out before noticing I was frozen to the spot. He turned back to me, a small frown creasing his brow.

"You coming, beautiful?"

"Yeah." I forced my feet to move, swallowing past the seriousness of that moment we'd just had. I knew *exactly* what he was feeling, though. It was the same thing I'd felt watching Steele and Archer both nearly die in front of me.

Joining Kody, I leaned into him as he wrapped his free arm around my waist. My hands were occupied holding coffee and wearing a plaster cast, but I still appreciated the half hug as we headed down the corridor to Bree's room.

Her door was closed, so I tapped lightly before cracking it open to check if she was asleep. To my relief, she was awake already and eating breakfast with her TV on.

"Hey, girl," I greeted her, pushing the door open fully to enter.

She looked up with a wide smile, which quickly fell when she saw the state of me. Crap. I hadn't even told her about the showdown with Zane and Kruger. Hell, I hadn't even turned my phone on since before the wedding.

"MK!" she shrieked, her face a picture of panic. "What the hell happened? Oh my god, you look like you've been run over by a truck!"

I smiled and quirked a brow at her pointedly, and she scowled.

"Not funny," she snapped back. "I wasn't run over. Just run *into*."

"Okay, semantics," I said on a snort of laughter. "I'm fine, though. Just bruised."

Bree glared at Kody, who'd followed me into her room. "Why the hell does Kodiak Jones look like he just woke up from a lovely, refreshing sleep? Where was he when you got beaten the hell up, girl? What fucking use are three boyfriends if they can't keep you safe?"

Guilt and regret flashed over Kody's face, and a flicker of anger passed through me. "Bree, stop it. Kody saved my ass multiple times. He just always looks good; you can't hold it against him."

The smile Kody shot me was doing little to hide his guilt over me getting hurt, but that was something for us to work through ourselves. Hopefully naked.

"Anyway, I wanted to come see how you were getting on with everything," I told Bree, changing the subject. "How's baby doing?"

She shot Kody another warning look, not dissimilar to the way James had just eyed him. But then she refocused and smiled as she rubbed her growing belly.

"Baby is happy and healthy. This bed rest bullshit is suiting him nicely, that's for sure. I'm *dying* to get out of here, though." She groaned a bit like being trapped in the hospital was physical torture.

I smiled, knowing all too well there were a million worse places to be. "What did your doctors say about your bones setting? Are they happy with everything?"

She nodded enthusiastically. Her wrist was still bandaged heavily from a recent surgery to correct the way it was all healing. "Going as well as anyone could have hoped. The only concern now is my stupid placenta. They have to keep giving me transfusions for the baby, but they seem confident it will sort itself out soon. I'm quietly hoping they'll let me go home for the rest of the pregnancy. I *really* don't want to be stuck here for another five months."

"Yeah, fair enough." I sat down in one of her guest chairs with a groan. Whatever show she was watching had super-catchy music, and I watched it for a minute. "What's this? You finished *Gilmore Girls*?"

"Yup," she replied. "This show is my new obsession; it's about this chick and her ghost band, who—" She broke off and narrowed her eyes at me, tilting her head to the side. "Fucking never mind what I'm watching. What the hell happened to you?"

I exchanged a look with Kody, but he just shrugged. The message was clear. It was entirely my call what I wanted to tell Bree about all that we'd done in the past few days. How many people we'd killed. Fucking hell.

Biting my lip, I agonized over what I'd actually come to ask her. Then I gave myself a quick mental slap to get it over with.

"Hey, Bree, I want to ask something a bit out of left field," I told her, ignoring her question about how I'd ended up so battered.

She frowned in confusion but nodded. "Anything at all," she said. "What's up?"

I shifted in my seat and tightened my grip around my coffee. "Uh, I wanted to know…did you ever meet any of our new security guards?"

Now she looked even more confused. "Yeah, I did. I mean, not at the house; the last time I was there was…I don't even remember. Your boys sort of made it clear I wasn't welcome at the house, remember? They tried that BS with your dad threatening you to stay away from me." She snorted a laugh because we'd just taken to hanging out in the library at SGU instead. "But I met the bearded guy, Sampson?" I nodded. "Right. I met him when you were visiting Steele. And a couple of the other guys. Wade and Bill?"

"Gill," I corrected but nodded again. "Right, yeah, that's what I thought. I just...fucking hell." I chewed on the edge of my lip, really not wanting to keep going down this line of questioning. Kody was frowning at me too, like he had no idea what sort of thread I was picking at.

Bree gave a nervous laugh. "Okay, you're kinda freaking me out, girl. What's going on?"

"Bree, do you happen to have a photo of that guy you were seeing last year?" I let the question out in a rush, and she blinked back at me, more confused than ever.

"David?" she repeated with a squeak of alarm. "Why?"

I cringed at the name, cursing myself. Kody clued in there too and cursed profusely under his breath.

"Just...do you have a picture? It's kind of important." I didn't want to go jumping to conclusions if I was wrong. It was a pretty common name, after all. "You mentioned he was older and pretty firm on keeping your relationship quiet."

Bree's cheeks heated, and her eyes shot to Kody. She was clearly embarrassed, but...fucking hell. This was bigger than her bad taste in men.

"Kody's not judging you, girl," I told her in a gentle voice. "Please just tell me?"

She rolled her eyes skyward, blowing out a long breath. "Yes, he was older. Like...dad-age old. And he was a cop. So like, yeah. That would have been a bit of a fucking scandal if his wife had found out, right?"

My chest ached. He had a wife? This got worse and worse. I really, *really* hoped it was a coincidence and he *wasn't* the same Dave. Or maybe that his wife was a total fabrication.

Bree reached for her phone, looking depressed as fuck as she unlocked it and opened her photo gallery. "He never wanted me to take pictures of us," she mumbled. "I figured he was just super paranoid about his job or something. But I took one when he wasn't looking one day…I don't know why. I was just really in love, you know? Or I thought I was."

Tension sang through me so hard it was everything I could do not to snatch the phone out of her hands. The photo had to have been from almost a year ago, though, so it was going to take her a bit of scrolling to find it.

Kody cleared his throat. "He was a cop?" Bree nodded, still scrolling. "He's not anymore?" he asked, to clarify.

"Uh, I don't think so," she replied. "I saw him a couple of months ago in the grocery store downtown. He was in some kind of private security uniform, and last I knew SGPD didn't allow moonlighting. I just assumed he'd done something to fuck up and got fired. Maybe he was screwing other teenage girls and got caught." She shrugged. "I didn't exactly approach him to chat. Dallas was with me, and I didn't want to point him out, you know?"

I nodded my understanding. Dallas would have *slaughtered* him. Hell, that might have done me a huge favor if he had. But Bree couldn't have known. *No one* had known.

"Here." She expanded an image and passed it to me. "Not the best picture, but it's all I've got."

I took the phone and held my breath as I looked down at the screen. The man in the picture had his back to the camera, his face in part profile, but there was no doubt in my mind. That was Dave. Declan. Whoever the fuck he was. He'd targeted Bree, made her fall for him, *gotten her pregnant*, and all for what? To leverage her for information? For access?

I swallowed heavily and offered the phone to Kody.

He took one glance at it, then tightened his fist around the phone like he wanted to hurl it at the wall. A venomous curse fell from his lips, and Bree's brows shot up in shock.

"Guys, what the fuck is going on right now? Why are you asking all this shit about David? Did something happen?" She gasped, her eyes taking in all my bruises again. "Did *he* do that to you?"

I grimaced and gave a slight headshake. "No, most of this was from Zane." It was just my broken wrist that her ex-boyfriend had given me, but she didn't need to know that. "He was...David, I mean—he was one of our security guards at the house that was killed last night."

Bree gasped, covering her mouth with her fingers as her eyes swam with sadness. "Oh my god, that's... Holy shit." She shook her head in disbelief. "What *happened*?"

I met Kody's eyes, then sighed. "My stalker," I replied, keeping the details vague to spare her the inevitable guilt. She didn't need that burden added to her shoulders on top of everything else. She was innocent in Dave's scheme; she shouldn't have to suffer the guilt of knowing he'd used her. "He, uh, he tried to abduct me. It didn't end well."

She blinked rapidly, like she was fighting tears. "I can imagine."

"Bree, you mentioned he had a wife. Can you tell us anything about her? We'd like to inform her first, but his employment records never listed a spouse." Kody was a smooth liar, I'd give him that. I was in a weirdly quiet state of shock now that my suspicion had been confirmed, and any bullshit I tried to spin would have fallen all kinds of flat.

Bree shook her head. "I, um, no, he wouldn't tell me anything about her. But I know his home address, if that helps?"

Kody arched a brow at her. "He wouldn't tell you his wife's name or let you take his photo, but you have his home address?"

Bree flushed pink. "It was after I told him I was pregnant. He started acting *so* weird, like a totally different person. It freaked me out. So...I sort of followed him home. I wanted to confront his wife and tell her I was carrying his baby."

"But you couldn't do it," I guessed, my voice gentle and understanding.

She shook her head. "I couldn't be responsible for ruining her life. She'd find out he was a cheating fuck sooner or later, but I didn't need to be *that* girl. I just...I couldn't do it."

Kody passed her phone back to her. "Can you text me the address? I'll go over there today and, uh, break the news to his widow."

She nodded, her thumb flying over the screen as she typed the address into a message and sent it to him.

"Did everything...I mean, I'm guessing you guys caught the stalker last night?" She gave me a hopeful look, and I nodded.

"Yeah." I sighed. "Yeah, we got him. He's gone."

Her smile was relieved and genuine. "I'm really glad to hear it, MK. You didn't deserve that stress in your life."

My answering smile was weak at best. "Thanks, girl. We should probably go and meet David's wife." I awkwardly stood up from my chair and dropped a quick kiss on my friend's cheek. "I'll come back and see you later, okay?"

She bid us farewell, and I made a quick exit out of her room before I could totally lose my shit about the whole damn situation.

I managed to hold it together all the way to the elevators, tossing my half-drunk coffee in the trash on the way. But the moment we stepped inside, my knees buckled, and I slid to the floor.

"Holy fuck," I whispered aloud. "Holy *fuck*."

"You can say that again." Kody crouched down and wrapped his arm around me. "Come on, babe, let's get back to Archer's room before we talk." He half carried me when I stood up once more, and I wrapped my good arm tight around him as we walked back through the halls.

James was still in the waiting room reading his romance novel, and his brows hitched as we passed.

I made a snap decision to trust him and jerked my head for him to join us. He tossed his book down on the table.

The three of us entered Archer's private room silently and found him awake but groggy, laughing at something Steele was saying. That laughter cut short when his eyes met mine, though. No doubt my shock showed clearly all over my face.

"What's happened?" he demanded, wincing with pain as he sat up.

"Settle the fuck down," Kody growled. "You're going to split your stitches being all dramatic like that."

Archer just glowered at his friend in fury. "What *the fuck* has happened to make Kate look like she's seen a damn ghost?"

James closed the door firmly, pulled the blind down over its little window, then leaned his body against it to literally prevent anyone from entering while we spoke. I was liking him more by the minute.

"I went to see Bree," I explained, licking my lips. "Last night when I recognized Dave...I don't even know. I just had this uneasy feeling that I was missing something. Then when we arrived at the hospital, I remembered Bree."

Steele's brows shot up; he seemed to follow my line of reasoning faster than Archer. "Her secret boyfriend from last year?"

I jerked a nod. "I remembered his name was *David*. That, plus the fact that he insisted on her keeping their affair secret, and, well, you know we don't believe in coincidences, right?" I said that to Archer, and his smile of acknowledgment was grim.

"I take it Bree just confirmed David and Dave were, in fact, one and the same?" Steele correctly guessed. "Does she know?"

I shook my head firmly. "No. And I'd rather it stay that way because it's so much worse than you guys already know." I swallowed the lump of revulsion in my throat. "Remember when Demi gave us all that info on my mom's family? About Wittenberg and about how Katerina left Pretoria when my mom was a kid?"

They both nodded. Archer still looked like he wanted to leap from his hospital bed and Hulk-smash everything around him, but Steele was dissecting what I was telling him carefully. Kody was slightly behind me. I couldn't see his reaction, but I could guess he was just as curious and confused.

"Right," I continued, breathing a sigh. "Katerina had two children when she arrived here and changed their names."

"Deb and her twin brother, Declan," Steele said, nodding his understanding. "But Declan was killed in a home invasion when they were seventeen, leaving Deb as Katerina's sole heir."

I gave him a weak smile. "But was he? I don't remember what the file said about his death. Was there a body? Or did they just assume he was dead?"

Kody sucked in a sharp breath, and Archer's brows shot up.

"I never looked into it any further," Steele admitted, looking shell-shocked. "You think Dave was actually Declan? He faked his own death or something?"

I shrugged. "I have no idea. I don't have any good explanation for him faking his death, but I *know* Dave was Declan. That's what he told me before he died. And…he had my eyes. My mom's eyes." I shook my head, still partly in disbelief, despite seeing it with my own eyes. "He had to have been wearing contacts the rest of the time. I bet his hair was dyed too."

James murmured a curse, and Kody breathed a muttered comment of disbelief himself.

"How?" Steele exploded out of his chair, throwing his hands up. "How could this happen? How did he evade *all* our background checks? Hell, he even passed Leon's check, and he's the best fucking hacker in the mercenary guild. How the *fuck* did this bastard lurk under our noses *so long* without raising suspicion?"

I fucking wish I knew the answers to that. "It gets better," I muttered, my throat aching with tension from all the stress. "Bree mentioned he used to be a cop."

Archer scowled. "That we knew. Loads of private security come from the police."

"Right." I nodded. "But here's the thing. How many crime scenes did SGPD attend back in those early days? Every time a doll was delivered, when Steele's car was blown up…" I rubbed my forehead, feeling the thumping ache of a headache building. But the guys were following my line of thought.

"The police were involved in the first security system setup," Archer murmured. "He had access then. Kate, on Riot Night, do you remember if he was one of the cops that arrested you?"

My jaw dropped; I hadn't even thought that far back. "I have no idea," I admitted in a whisper. "I don't remember. I wasn't really paying that much attention."

Kody snorted a soft laugh. "Genuinely shocked, babe."

I swiveled around to glare at him in outrage, but he just shrugged and smiled. Fucker. He was right too. I had been particularly oblivious to everyone around me back then. Hell, I'd thought Anna's name was Karen for at least three years, and *no one* had corrected me. I'd only realized my mistake when I heard Steele call her Anna.

"How does this connect with Scott?" Steele asked. "Why frame *him*?"

I heaved a sigh and shrugged. "I guess we might find out more when we meet Dave's wife. Bree gave us his home address, and I'd put money on it that it's not the address listed in his employment file."

Archer looked genuinely sickened at this development. "He had a *wife*? You're not fucking going there without me."

Kody scoffed. "Pretty sure we are, big man. You don't have medical clearance to leave the hospital, and we're not waiting on this."

"Fuck clearance," Archer barked, reaching for his IV drip as though he wanted to yank it straight out of his arm.

Alarmed, I shot forward and slapped his hand away before he could complete the motion. "Don't you fucking dare, Archer D'Ath," I snarled. "You're not leaving this bed until a *medical professional* clears you."

His cool blue eyes met mine with a challenge, shining clearly. "Or what?"

"Or I promise you'll regret it, Sunshine." I wasn't backing down on this subject. Not in a million years. Not when his well-being was at stake. "Don't fucking test me."

He held my gaze for a long moment. But I didn't flinch or soften, and he was the first to retreat.

"Fine," he growled, like a grouchy bear woken from hibernation too soon. "But you're staying here with me."

I scoffed. "Fat chance. You're not sidelining me on this just because you're sulking. James will stay here and look after you, right?" I turned to arch a brow at my newly discovered father, and he jerked a quick nod back.

"Okay, sorted," Kody announced, clapping his hands. "We'll call you later, Arch." He nudged James out of the way so he could open the door, and I dodged as Archer tried to grab my arm. He had his bad arm strapped up in a sling, though, so he wasn't quick enough.

"Kate!" he shouted as I headed for the door and Kody exited.

I just shot him a grin and blew a kiss. "Love you, Arch."

His face froze; then his scowl softened. "I love you too, Kate."

Steele gave me a nudge, and I hurried out of the room before Archer could reel me back in again. James pulled the door closed after us, and the three of us made our way out of the hospital in silence.

One question kept gnawing at my mind the whole way out to Steele's car, and it was knotting me up with anxiety.

Had she helped him? We could well be walking into the viper's nest with a live snake lying in wait. God, I hoped not.

Please, please, please, let my uncle's wife just be a normal, clueless housewife. Please.

CHAPTER 41

The universe, it seemed, wasn't playing fair. Or it had a seriously fucked up way of cutting me some breaks. But one thing we quickly realized on breaking into Dave's house was that he *had* no wife.

What we found instead was a thousand times worse.

The house itself seemed so innocent, just a normal suburban home in a nice neighborhood. But none of the pictures on the walls had Dave in them. They were all of a pretty blond woman with her husband, who was very definitely *not* Dave.

At first, we thought Bree had been wrong. She'd given us the wrong address or he'd moved since then. But then we found the heavily bolted door to the basement, and chills raced down my spine.

"I don't even want to know what we're going to find down there," I confessed to the boys in a whisper. They both had their guns at the ready, but I was unarmed. My plastered wrist made it too difficult to hold a gun in my right hand, and I wasn't competent enough with my left.

"Same," Kody agreed, grimacing.

Steele holstered his gun and went to work picking the locks on the door. There were seven of them total, and nothing good could come from a basement with seven locks on it. Everyone knew that.

"Just stay back, Hellcat," he murmured as the last lock clicked open. "Stay behind us, okay?"

I agreed quickly, not in any mood to throw myself at whatever monster lurked in the basement. In fact, I was surprised they hadn't made me wait in the car or something. Then again, maybe they were just smart enough to know I'd never actually *do* that and decided not to even try.

The boys exchanged a look, both adjusting their grips on their weapons, and then Steele pulled the door open.

The first thing to hit us was the smell. *Holy shit*. The *smell* was enough to make us all gag and my eyes water. Something was seriously dead down there.

"Fuck me," Kody muttered in a strangled voice. "We should have left this for Archer to do."

I snorted a laugh, despite the situation, and Steele rolled his eyes.

"It's not *that* bad. Just block your nose." He still grimaced, though, and tried to flick the light on. Nothing happened, so he sighed and started down the stairs slowly with his phone light on. He kept his gun up and ready for anything jumping out of the darkness.

Kody followed him after a beat, and I took up the rear. As we descended into the darkness. I glanced down at the stairs and shuddered. They were the open kind, and I couldn't stop imagining a clawed hand reaching through and grabbing my ankles.

Steele reached the bottom step, using his mobile phone light to find another set of light switches. He flipped them all down, and this time the fluorescent tube lights lining the ceiling all flickered to life.

I'd never in my life wished for darkness *more*.

"Oh *fuck*," I breathed, bile rising in my throat and making me swallow heavily.

"This…is going to give me nightmares," Kody groaned, his face taking on an ashen pallor.

Steele made a gagging noise and covered his mouth with his hand, then turned to look at us in horror. "I think I might throw up," he admitted.

"Try not to," Kody replied with a grimace. "We really don't need to add to the smell."

The basement was huge. Several cages lined the wall under the stairs, like the type that would hold big dogs or feral animals. Lumpy shapes inside each cage suggested whatever Dave had kept in there hadn't been cared for in a while, though.

The worst part, the part that was going to be imprinted in my mind, was the serial-killer setup in front of us. A medical gurney sat in the middle, crusted with old blood and hanging with leather straps that he must have used to hold his victims in place. The work bench was scattered with dirty tools, a variety of both medical instruments and construction tools that he'd used to torture people. None of it was clean, but I guessed he hadn't been overly concerned about infection.

The *entire* wall above his workbench was plastered with images of me. Every available inch of wall space was covered in photographs, newspaper clippings, and information like my class schedules or my medical records... Literally my entire life was stuck to this sick fuck's wall.

To the side, there was a craft station set up, scattered with piles and piles of fabrics and a commercial-grade sewing machine. Somehow, I had a hard time imagining Dave sitting there and creating miniature doll clothes, though.

"Do we even want to open that freezer?" Kody asked, reluctantly pointing to the huge chest freezer against the wall.

Steele shuddered. "Fifty bucks says we find the guy who actually owns this house."

Kody snorted. "I'm not taking that bet; it's a sure fucking thing. Question is, will he be whole or cut up?"

"You two are fucked up," I whispered, brushing past them. I gripped the freezer lid. Then I paused, glancing around at the sheer volume of dried and still-sticky blood coating the floor around the makeshift operating table. "In pieces, I'll bet."

Before I could talk myself out of it, I lifted the lid and swallowed back the scream of fright that tried to escape. Sure enough, the man from the photos upstairs stared up at me with dead eyes from a decapitated head.

"I think I'm going to need therapy after this," I admitted in a soft voice. After the boys had taken a look, I dropped the lid back down, then wiped my hands off on my jeans. Like I could somehow wipe away the crawling sensation all over my skin.

"Steele, go check the cages," Kody prompted his friend, nudging him toward the area in question. The one closest to us seemed to be the source of the smell, and a small horde of flies were circling the lumpy contents of it. Yeah, that was on the boys. I'd opened the freezer; my part was done.

"No fucking way," Steele replied. "You check the damn cages."

I rolled my eyes. "*Both* of you do it," I told them with a thread of impatience. "I wanna get the fuck out of here. Fast. Let's just get this over with and then...I don't even know what we do with this mess. Call the cops? Or clean it up ourselves?"

Steele wrinkled his nose, his mouth twisting in disgust. "Cops are a waste of fucking time. We need to just set fire to this whole fucking house and scrub it of evidence."

Kody nodded his agreement. "We can do that. Easily done."

"Just make sure the neighbors are out of their houses," I warned them. "I don't want any collateral damage."

"Any *more* collateral damage, you mean." Kody nodded to the freezer, and I cringed. I was going to guess the decaying corpse in the cage would turn out to be that man's pretty, blond wife.

I heaved a sigh. "Stop stalling. Check the damn cages."

The two of them smirked at my authoritative tone but reluctantly did as they were told. Steele checked the first cage, the one with the flies, and gagged again.

"Yep. Dead body," he confirmed. "No idea who; her face is all messed up. But…she's got pink hair."

What the fuck?

Just when I thought it couldn't possibly get more fucked up, Dave proved me wrong from the damn grave.

"Guys!" Kody exclaimed, a sharp note of panic in his voice. "Guys, this one's alive!"

"What?" I squeaked, rushing over to where he crouched in front of an open cage.

The woman inside was *barely* alive, but he was right. Her eyelids fluttered, and her chest moved as she breathed shallow, gasping breaths.

Steele was already on the phone calling for an ambulance, and Kody ever so carefully lifted the emaciated woman from the cage. Her hair was stringy and dirty but clearly dyed pink.

Fucking hell.

I could do nothing but watch in abject horror as Kody carried the woman up the stairs in long strides, and Steele nudged me to follow. He was speaking to the EMTs on the phone in low tones, detailing the woman's condition from what we could see. I heard him mention starvation and lack of water for countless days, and I wanted to break down and cry.

What kind of sick bastard could do this to another human being? And how many people had he tortured, abused, or killed before her? Before the dead woman still in the cages or the decapitated man in the freezer?

Kody carried the woman all the way out to the front lawn, holding on to her for a few minutes until an ambulance came tearing down the street and into the driveway.

Seeing her handed over to the EMTs was surreal and such a relief that my knees buckled and I sank to my ass on the lawn. Steele said nothing, just sat down beside me and tucked his arm around me in comfort.

Kody stayed with the EMTs—one of whom I recognized from the night before—and talked to them as they set the woman up in a bed and inserted an IV line. No doubt she was badly in need of fluids. Who knew when Dave had last fed or watered his captives? No fucking wonder the other woman was dead.

"Do you want to wait in the car while we finish this?" Steele's tone was soft. His lips pressed a kiss to the side of my head, just below my bullet graze.

Normally, I'd have sucked it up and stuck it out because we were a team. All for one and one for all. But something about finding a *live* victim had rattled me so much harder than all the death I'd witnessed in the last few months. So I nodded silently and let him escort me over to the car where we'd left it in the street.

"Here," he said as I slid into the passenger seat. He handed me his phone. "Hold on to this; call Kody's phone if you need us for anything, okay? We'll try to make this quick."

I nodded, promising I'd be fine, then locked the doors as he jogged back to Dave's house. Or his victim's house anyway.

Anxiety and impatience started setting in only a few minutes later, and I found myself shifting around in my seat like I had ants in my pants. In an attempt to calm my nerves, I turned on Steele's phone and pulled up an internet browser.

My stomach knotted painfully as I typed in the address of the house and added the surname I'd seen on an envelope in the kitchen. It only took a minute of browsing results to find what I was looking for.

The pretty blond from the pictures was Samantha Clarke, a twenty-nine-year-old seamstress. Her husband, forty-one-year-old David Clarke, was a former FBI agent who'd retired several years ago after a knee injury that'd left him with walking difficulties.

I chewed at my lip, wondering if Samantha was the woman who'd lived or the one who'd died.

It took another hour before the boys were done. They returned to the car looking grim and exhausted. None of us spoke on the drive home, but as we passed through our front gates, I cracked.

"What will happen now?" I asked in a hollow voice.

Steele glanced over at me from the driver's seat. "We documented everything we found. The neighbors have been informed that there's been a gas leak on their street and not to come home tonight. Sampson will take care of the rest. By morning, there won't be a shred of DNA or evidence left."

"Sampson's still alive?" I asked, genuinely relieved. I had been so worried about Archer the night before that I hadn't given a second thought to what had happened to the rest of our security team.

Kody snorted a laugh. "He's basically indestructible, babe. If it weren't for him and Gill, as well as James and Steinwick, I doubt we'd have all made it out of that ambush alive last night."

"Gotcha," I murmured. "What about the woman? Is she going to be okay?"

Steele gave a shrug. "Only time will tell. She was in pretty rough shape; it'll be a while before we can speak with her, I'd think."

I nodded my understanding. What more could I really expect? Besides…what would I even say to her, given the chance? *Sorry my psychopathic serial-killer, stalker uncle held you captive and…*

Yeah. Maybe not.

But at least she was alive. That was something, wasn't it? We'd saved *one* of his victims. Yet all I could think about was how many more we'd failed for taking so long to stop him—how many other women he might have killed in the *years* he'd stalked me and my mom.

How the hell was I ever going to get past this?

The woman we'd saved was, in fact, Samantha Clarke. A week later she'd recovered enough to speak with Kody—posing as a police officer—and she filled in the remaining blanks.

The dead woman was her sister, Janette, who'd come over to check on her and been taken by Dave. He'd done horrific, nightmare-inducing things to both of them over the course of the last year, but he'd stopped feeding them a few weeks ago. Samantha told how they'd been thrown occasional scraps and given water, but then all of that had dried up about five days before we found them. Dave hadn't returned, and her sister had died two days before we found the house.

I hadn't gone to speak with her myself, aware that she'd seen my face on that wall facing her cage for every waking moment of her captivity. Seeing me now wasn't going to do her any good. The information Kody relayed was vague at best, and it was abundantly clear he was sparing me the details.

For that, I was thankful.

Less than twenty-four hours after Samantha was discharged into the care of her cousin, we found out she'd killed herself.

CHAPTER 42

The process of healing took some time and a healthy amount of therapy for me. Unlike the boys, I wasn't used to all the violence, death, and destruction. It plagued my dreams to the point I would wake up screaming and thrashing, even with one of them sleeping beside me. After a few weeks, I'd admitted to myself—and to them—how scared for my own sanity I was becoming. After that, they'd sourced me the very best therapist in the state, and with her help, I was slowly healing.

Archer had needed more time in the hospital than he'd been happy with, but we'd given him no option to decline. The bullet wound in his side had chipped a fragment of bone from his rib, which had started causing complications, and I wasn't risking his health over his stubborn pride.

There'd been no way in hell he could make his fight and had to forfeit. That, I guessed, was the thing pissing him off the most.

To my surprise—in a good way—after a few weeks, the guys started taking turns accompanying me to therapy. Not to babysit me but to participate. It was weird, but every damn time it made my heart happy. They were invested in this relationship and in my well-being. But more than that, they recognized the need for themselves to grow and heal along with me… They put their big-dick energy aside and welcomed positive mental health changes.

Not to say they suddenly became choir boys, hell no. But every damn day our bonds grew stronger and tighter until I could barely remember what it felt like to be without them, criminal activities and all.

The first weekend of summer, Archer woke me up early and announced we were going for a vacation.

It was out of the blue enough that I sat up with a confused frown. "Vacation? Where to?"

His answering grin was all mischief. "Wait and see, Princess."

I scowled back at him. Surprises were not high on my list of favorite things these days. "Sunshine…"

He silenced my sleepy protests with a long, lingering kiss that made my heart race. "Pack a swimsuit, baby girl. Or don't." His wink was pure sex, and a wave of desire rippled through me. "Come on, it's a long drive, and I promised we'd be there for lunch."

I frowned again. "Promised who?"

He just kissed me again, then reached over and flicked Steele in the forehead to wake him up. "Come on, metal dick. We're leaving in half an hour."

Steele flipped him off without opening his eyes, but Archer just smirked and headed out of my bedroom.

I thought for sure Steele had gone back to sleep again, but the second the door closed, his arm snaked around my waist and he dragged me back under the covers with him.

"Mmm, good morning, Hellcat," he mumbled into my neck as he kissed my warm skin. His hands roamed over me, slipping under my sleep shirt and gripping my waist.

I grinned as he ground his hard dick against my ass. "Max… you heard the boss. We gotta go in half an hour."

"I heard him," he replied in a sleepy voice. His fingers hooked into my panties and tugged them down my legs. "Half an hour.

So let's be quick, or I'll end up sharing you when he comes back to yell at us."

A low chuckle bubbled from me as he coaxed my legs open. "Don't need to tell me twice."

As it turned out, it was closer to an hour before we left the house. Steele and I used every second of that half hour, then still needed to shower and pack our bags for this mystery vacation.

Or rather, it was a mystery to me. Steele clearly knew where we were going because he helped me pack and discarded anything remotely dressy or formal. So that was my clue. Wherever we were going, it was going to be casual and comfortable the whole time.

It already sounded perfect.

We took one of Archer's black, bulletproof Range Rovers, and the boys gave me the front passenger seat. My phone rang before we'd even been on the road for five minutes, and a flash of anticipation raced through me as I looked at the caller ID.

"Leon," I answered, knowing he was the only one who'd call from a secured network. "How'd it go?"

"All sorted," the computer-genius mercenary told me. "I've emailed you with the three candidates I'd pick and earmarked my top choice. Up to you, though; it's your company to run."

I let out a long sigh of relief, feeling one less worry weighing me down. The past weeks had been a whirlwind of legal bullshit, red tape, and borderline nasty discussions with the board of directors at Wittenberg. Just eight days earlier, though, a court in Pretoria had officially signed off on my claim of ownership over one of the world's largest companies—and diamond mines.

I was no idiot; I knew damn well that the sheer volume of money Archer had been able to throw at the case had fast-tracked it through the legal system a hundred times quicker than it could have been done otherwise. But even so, my nerves had been on edge every time I had to speak with the suspicious, judgmental old men on *my* company board. Not to mention their flesh-eating lawyers.

Leon's help had been the relief I so badly needed. He'd felt so guilty about not catching Dave in his security sweep that he'd offered me a freebie—something I'd happily taken him up on when I took an instant dislike to the man who'd taken over from Kruger as interim CEO.

I was in no position to run a company I knew nothing about. But I'd be *damned* if I kept a misogynistic old fuck in charge. Especially one who talked to my tits for our entire Zoom call and insulted me with every second word. Nope. No way in hell.

Ideally, I wanted someone in charge who I could *trust*, at least for a few years, until I learned enough to become involved myself. In lieu of that, though, I wanted someone I could potentially grow to trust. Someone who would look after the interests of my family's company, not just line their own pockets. That's where Leon had come in. He'd run an extensive audit of the entire company's management team and then looked further abroad to competitors.

"Thank you, Leon," I said with a sigh. "I really appreciate your help."

He just scoffed. "It wasn't a favor, MK. I owed you, big-time. Anyway, get your legal team onto whichever of those candidates you like best. They'd all be poaching jobs from direct competition, though, so maybe a personal touch might work in your favor."

I grinned and thanked him again before ending the call.

Archer gave me a curious look before returning his eyes to the road. "Good news from Leon?"

I nodded and opened my email to see who he'd picked out. I had been keeping up with his whole investigation, which had started weeks before the company had been officially handed over to me, so I was already familiar with who I thought he might have chosen.

"Knew it," I said, reading the names of the attachment files out loud.

Steele whooped. "You suckers owe me fifty bucks each."

I looked up from my phone, turning to peer at him in the backseat. "You three taking bets on my future CEO now?"

Archer rolled his eyes, but Kody was the one who replied. "Steele guessed Leon would give you three female options; Arch and I thought he would throw one dude in just for variety."

I laughed, already pleased with the options Leon had chosen. "Well, he got a good read on what I wanted, that's for sure." I hit forward on the email and sent the files over to my new legal team, asking them to start drafting an offer of employment to the woman Leon had marked as his favorite.

That done, I tucked my phone away to enjoy the drive to our mystery vacation spot with my guys.

"So, when do you guys wanna tell me where we're going?"

The three of them all grinned, Kody catching my eyes in the mirror.

"Wait and see, babe," he told me. "Otherwise it's not a *surprise*."

I huffed and reached out to turn the stereo on. With music filling the car, I settled into my seat, and Archer's hand rested on my knee while he drove. It was all kinds of blissful, and I decided that maybe I didn't mind surprises so much after all.

Half a day of driving later, we pulled into a driveway lined by gorgeous old oak trees. I shot Archer a curious look, sitting up a bit straighter in my seat. He wasn't giving away shit, though. Neither were the guys in the back, but they were carefully watching me for my reactions.

The driveway wound down the side of a hill, then opened up at the bottom to reveal a stunning wooden house. Or more of a lodge than a house. It was enormous but breathtakingly beautiful, with multiple peaked roofs and an abundance of windows.

"This is gorgeous," I murmured, trying to take it all in as Archer parked next to several other cars. "Is it a hotel?"

Kody snickered, and Archer shook his head.

"No." Archer unbuckled his belt and climbed out of the car.

He came around and opened my door before I got to it, then offered me his hand to step out. "It's a house." He paused then, and the other guys joined us there as we looked up at the majestic mountain lodge.

"*Our* house," Steele added, and my jaw dropped.

"What?" The question was more of a shriek than a word, but they got the idea.

Kody's arm wrapped around my waist, and I leaned into his side without taking my eyes off the house. "Remember, you told us about your perfect house? The one you wanted to move to when our lives were less dangerous, somewhere to get away from the violence and prying eyes of Shadow Grove?"

"Y-yeah?" I was totally dumbstruck. They'd bought us a house? Like…for all of us?

Steele took a few strides forward, opened one of the huge wooden doors, and turned to grin at me. "We've been searching for the perfect one ever since that conversation," he told me, proud as fuck. "The owners of this one took a little convincing, but about two weeks after Dave, they agreed to sell. Welcome home, Hellcat."

"If you hate it, we can keep looking," Archer added in a low voice. "We just wanted to surprise you."

I shook my head in stunned disbelief. "You definitely managed that." I finally tore my eyes from the house to look at each of my guys in wonder. "It's perfect," I told them with heartfelt honestly. I didn't even need to look inside to see if it ticked my boxes. It was perfect because *they'd* chosen it.

"Well, that's not all," Kody announced with a wide smile. "Come on; we have another surprise for you."

They urged me into the foyer, then hurried me through the expansive, open-plan kitchen without giving me a chance to look around properly. It didn't take long to figure out what they were so excited about, though.

The gorgeous, sunny family room opened out on the other side of the house to reveal an enormous, sparkling mountain lake.

"Holy shit," I gasped, my jaw dropping as I took in the scenery. The lake was surrounded by rolling hills and tall peaks, and not a single other house was in view. It was like our own private slice of paradise.

They'd really nailed it. Every single detail.

"And it snows here in winter," Archer whispered in my ear as I stood there, totally dumbfounded. "That lake will ice over, and the road in will become totally snowed over. We could be trapped up here for months with no contact to the outside world if we wanted."

A shiver of excitement rippled through me, and I let out a small moan.

"It's fucking *perfect*," I whispered. "You guys are blowing my damn mind right now."

Movement down near the water grabbed my attention, and I squinted against the sun glare on the water. "Is that—"

"Surprise." Kody laughed. "Come on." He linked his fingers through mine and pulled me out of the house. A short staircase from the balcony took us down to a sloped lawn dotted with lovely shade trees, and at the water's edge, a gazebo held a barbecue and some comfortable outdoor lounges.

Along with our friends. Everyone I cared about seemed to have been invited, *including* Bree with her huge belly and Dallas with his fresh Timberwolf ink.

Happy tears stung my eyes as I hugged her tight, and she just laughed back.

"You look so freaking good," I said, letting her go again.

She just beamed and shrugged, her hand rubbing her belly. "Yeah, well, I have you guys to thank for that. Dallas has had a whole lot more time to spend with me now that he's out of the Wraiths."

My old friend met my eyes over his fiancée's head, and we exchanged a private smile. When we'd approached Zed about getting Dallas out of the Wraiths, he'd needed proof of loyalty. Dallas had delivered that and more, spending weeks hacking the Wraiths' accounts and uncovering paper trails to show they'd been stealing from the Reapers.

Then, after so many Wraiths had been complicit in the attack on me, Dallas had taken matters into his own hands and killed Charon in his sleep. After that, he'd needed the Timberwolves' protection more than ever, and Hades had provided it.

None of us had even known he'd done it until Cass had called for a meeting with Archer to discuss the change of leadership in the Wraiths. Skate—stupid name—had stepped up into Charon's role and been given stern warnings not to step out of line or he'd meet the same fate as his predecessor.

With a knowing wink to Dallas, I moved on to greet everyone else that had turned up. Constance hugged me like I was her own granddaughter and gave her nod of approval that I was still wearing the D'Ath family ring. Ana was with her, and they looked happier than ever.

Steinwick, Anna, and James were working the barbecue together, and the sight of our stuffy butler in pineapple-printed board shorts and an apron that had cartoon tits on it was enough to kill me laughing.

"Whatever you're cooking, it smells incredible," I told the three of them with a wide grin.

James wrinkled his nose at me in response. "It's a barbecue, MK. Don't tell me you've never had a barbecue before."

My cheeks flushed as I searched my memory. But...nope. It hadn't really been Samuel Danvers style.

"Sorry I'm late!" a familiar voice called out from the side of the house, and a bubbly redhead came bounding toward us. "MK, your house is to *die* for! I'm totally spending weekends here."

I grinned hard as my new friend crashed into me with a tight, way-too-friendly hug. I'd gotten used to it, though.

"Seph! Please tell me you have permission to be here." I freaking loved the girl, but I also didn't want to take the fall for her teenage-rebellion bullshit.

She scoffed a laugh. "Of course, I do. This time. Anyway, not even big, bad Hades could argue my safety when I said I was spending the weekend with you and your harem." She shot me a wink, then sighed. "I mean, I did have to accept a ride from Daddy Cass to get here, though."

I almost choked on my tongue. "You did *not* just call him that," I said in a strangled voice as the tattoo-covered, scowling biker came stalking across the grass carrying Seph's overnight bag.

She just shrugged like she didn't see the big deal. "Maybe he should stop acting like my dad then. Oh, Bree's here! Hey, girl!" She bounded over to my bestie like an overly energetic puppy. Seph was fast becoming one of my favorite people in the whole world.

"Kid," Cass greeted me with a grunt, nodding his head to my guys as well. "Sorry to crash the party. Little shit crashed her car into a ditch last weekend, and Hades wouldn't let her drive up alone."

My brows rose, and my lips curved in a mocking smile. "So you offered? That's awfully *nice* of you, Grumpy. You're not even a Timberwolf; surely someone else could have done the job."

He just glared at me. "Shut up." He shifted his scowl to Archer. "Where's the booze? I'm not suffering this sober."

Archer looked like he was biting back a laugh but clapped Cass on the shoulder and walked with him back into the house.

Kody and Steele walked with me over to the long wooden jetty that protruded out into the lake, and the three of us sat on the end of it with our feet dangling in the water.

"This is amazing, you guys know that?"

Steele's arm was around my waist, and Kody's hand rested on my knee, both radiating pride for their surprise well done.

407

"Well, we kinda figured this was a birthday gift to all of us," Kody told me, "seeing as none of us celebrated properly this year."

"Best birthday *ever*," I said with a groan of emotion. "What's that out there?" I pointed farther out into the lake, where there seemed to be a platform of some sort.

Steele kissed my shoulder and his lips curved in a smile. "Just a diving platform," he said with an edge of mischief. "We'll show you later."

Excitement buzzed through me at his tone, and I nodded. "All right, I'll play along. So far you guys are pretty much killing it with this surprise thing."

"Score." Kody reached out a hand to Steele, who slapped it with a high five. Fucking boys.

Leaning my head on Kody's shoulder, with Steele's strong arm around me, I could barely even handle how stupidly happy they'd made me. Everything we'd gone through almost seemed worth it to have such overwhelming happiness.

Archer joined us a few minutes later, lifting me into his lap as he squeezed his ass between his friends; then he kissed me until I was panting.

"Come on, Princess. Food's ready."

"I'm not hungry," I replied, licking my lips and darting my eyes between the three of them. "Not for food."

Kody let out a groan and scrubbed a hand over his face. Steele just threw his head back and laughed. Archer met my eyes with burning heat in his gaze.

"We've got guests, Kate. Play along, and we promise it'll be worth it."

I wanted to protest, but he was right. All our family was here, for *us*. It'd probably be bad form to sneak off to fuck while they were waiting to eat. And I *badly* didn't want Constance calling us out for bad manners.

"Fine," I grumbled, letting Steele help me out of Archer's

lap and up to my feet. "But I'm holding you to that promise, D'Ath."

He smirked. "I'm counting on it, Wittenberg."

I snorted and rolled my eyes. Part of my legal proceedings had been to drop the Danvers name, and it'd felt too weird to take D'Ath without Jones or Steele. So I'd taken my mother's maiden name.

I was now Madison Kate Wittenberg, and it felt *right*.

CHAPTER 43

The afternoon passed in a blur of laughter, conversation, food, and cocktails. Our little crew stayed outdoors, partying until well into the evening, but Bree was the first to call it a night, yawning heavily.

She and Dallas left to drive back to Shadow Grove, where they'd recently moved into their own place together. Anna and Steinwick left not long after them, citing old age.

I gave them a suspicious look as they left together, and Kody snickered.

"They're totally fucking," he whispered in my ear.

"You think?" I hissed back at him. "Steinwick must be, like, twenty years older than her."

He just shrugged. "So what? Age is just a number, and they clearly click."

I nodded, agreeing on that statement.

"I think we might turn in as well," Connie told us with a smile. "We'll see you kids at breakfast." She and Ana made their way up to the house, hand in hand, and I watched them lovingly. The fact that they were no longer hiding their relationship from Archer made my whole heart happy.

The guys and I stayed out on the gazebo drinking and chatting with Seph, Cass, and James for a while longer, then when it got late, Steele offered to show everyone their rooms. I was itching to see the rest of the house, so I jumped at the chance to come along for the tour.

Steele took his time with it too. And there was a *lot* of house to cover. After he delivered our guests to their rooms, he laced our fingers together and showed me the rest of the house. Namely, my bedroom.

"Wait, how's this going to work?" I asked, standing in the middle of my gorgeous master suite. "We have our own rooms?" He'd pointed out their bedrooms along the hallway before we reached mine.

He just shrugged. "It can work however you want it to, Hellcat. There are no rules. I sort of figure we'll all pretty much live in here anyway."

I nodded, agreeing. "Yeah, I mean, it's plenty big enough to share."

He laughed. "Even if it weren't, it's where *you* are. But we figured it's good to have spare rooms to store all our crap and also for nights when you need your own space."

"Oh, yeah." I blinked several times, looking around the room again.

"Is that...okay?" Steele sounded hesitant. "If you don't—"

"No!" I cut him off before he could misinterpret my silence. "No, fuck, this is all...Max, this is beyond perfect. It's just fucking *hitting* me, you know? This is *our* house. All of ours. Not Archer's house that we all happen to live in. It just feels really *real*."

His arms looped around my waist, and his lips pressed against my hair, kissing the faint scar from where his bullet had grazed me. "Are you okay with real, Hellcat?"

My breath rushed out in a long exhale. "God yes," I whispered. "I've never been so okay with anything in my life."

I physically felt the tension slide from his limbs, and he hugged me tighter. "Thank fuck for that. 'Cause we're never letting you go, Hellcat. You're it for all of us, forever."

Words couldn't encompass how much I agreed with that sentiment, so I let my actions speak for themselves. I kissed him with my *whole* heart, my hands clasping his face and my body curving into his as he kissed me back.

Before I could take it any further, though, he took a reluctant step away and gave me a predatory stare. "Too damn tempting, Hellcat," he murmured. "But we've already been gone for long enough. Kody and Arch will be getting impatient waiting for me to bring you back."

I got the feeling he didn't just mean that they would be bored on their own, so I let him pull me back out of the bedroom—*my* bedroom—and through the house.

From the deck, I could see lights out on the lake somewhere, and I squinted into the darkness, instantly worried.

"Max, what—" I grabbed his hand in alarm, but the smile he shot me said this was all part of their plan.

"You feeling up for a swim, Hellcat?" he suggested, giving me a wicked grin.

My brows shot up. "I'm not wearing a swimsuit."

His smile spread wider, and he tugged his T-shirt off in one smooth motion, dropping it in the grass as we continued down toward the pier. "So?"

My jaw dropped, but then he gave me *that* look. The one that so clearly challenged me. Fucking hell, he knew I couldn't back down when dignity was on the line.

We got to the end of the pier, and he pushed his pants off, then executed a perfect dive into the inky waters. Totally naked.

"Are you coming in?" he called back to me when his head broke the surface once more. "I promise it's not *that* cold."

I groaned, knowing full well how chilly it'd been on my feet earlier. Yet…I couldn't let him have all the fun.

Hesitant, I started to tug my tank top off, then looked back up at the house, which was lit up like a Christmas tree. "What about—"

"They won't see," he assured me before I could even fully form the protest. "It's so dark out here; I promise, we're totally alone."

That was all the reassurance I needed. I tossed my tank top aside, then my bra, then shimmied out of my shorts and panties. Gasping a deep breath, I plunged into the dark water and instantly felt the biting cold seize my body.

Not that cold, my ass.

"Wh-what th-the f-fuck, M-max?" I exclaimed when I popped up near him. "It's fr-freezing!"

He just laughed, the shithead, and dragged me into his arms. "You'll warm up in no time," he told me with a chuckle, then kissed me long and hard. "Come on, we have one last surprise."

He started gliding in the direction I'd seen the lights, toward where they'd pointed out a diving platform earlier, and I grumbled about being tricked as I swam with him. Goddamn sexy shark that he was, I couldn't resist.

As we drew closer, my breath caught all over again. A small boat was tied up beside the wide dive platform, right beside the pretty awesome waterslide. That boat explained how Kody and Archer had pulled off what had to be the most romantic date setting I'd ever seen.

The whole platform was set up with pillows and soft blankets and illuminated by a dozen hurricane lamps with flickering candles inside. Exquisite arrangements of flowers complimented the candles, and near the pillows, a dessert tray was all set up for the four of us. There was even a bottle of champagne chilling in an ice bucket. They'd thought of *everything*.

"Are you guys for real right now?" I gaped, holding on to the edge of the platform with my fingers.

Archer reached down to pull me from the water; then his

413

brows shot right up. "You're naked," he observed, shooting Steele a puzzled look. "What happened to getting swimsuits on upstairs?"

Steele just pulled himself out of the water and shrugged. "I got distracted. And I like seeing Hellcat naked, so win-win."

Archer rolled his eyes, and Kody tossed us towels to wrap up in. Steele had been right, though; once I'd gotten used to the water, it hadn't been as cold as I'd thought.

"You guys are seriously setting the bar high here," I teased as I wrapped myself up in the towel and made my way over to the pillows.

"Good," Kody replied, nudging me to sit down; then he knelt on one of the blankets as he opened the champagne. "Forces these unromantic fucks to keep stepping up their game, right?" He winked at me like we were in on a joke together, and Archer smacked him in the back of the head playfully.

"So you guys set up this ultra-romantic picnic in the middle of a lake with flowers, candles, champagne…" I accepted a glass from Kody and took a sip. I was already decently buzzed, but I really liked this champagne. "Just for fun?"

"Some might say we did it because we love you, Princess," Archer commented in a dry tone, and I laughed.

"Uh-huh, some might say that," I agreed, teasing. "But then Steele got me naked, so some might also wonder if you had ulterior motives."

Kody gave a fake gasp of outrage as he handed out drinks to the other guys before reclining into the pillows beside me. "Babe, I can't possibly imagine what you mean by that," he lied, holding my gaze unblinkingly as he took a huge sip of his champagne.

I smirked back at him, shaking my head but playing along. "I'm sure you can't."

"So, what do you think of the house?" Archer asked, changing the subject as he turned on a little portable stereo, filling the night air with soft piano music.

Steele's music.

My lips parted in surprise as I heard the original compositions that he'd been working on over the last few weeks pouring from the speaker. He gave me a knowing smile back but didn't comment.

"The house?" I repeated, refocusing on Archer's question. I screwed up my nose, gazing back at the lit-up lodge on the shore of the lake. "It's okay, I guess."

Kody choked on his champagne, and Steele clapped him on the back to help out.

Archer just gave me a flat stare. "Just okay, huh?"

I shrugged. "Yeah, I mean…is there even a gym? Where will you guys work out? And I didn't see a piano anywhere. We obviously need to add all of that."

His unimpressed stare melted into an adoring smile as he realized what I was saying. "Yeah, well, we didn't have a lot of time to get everything perfect. But *aside* from that…"

"Aside from that?" I turned my face to look at the house again, a soft smile on my lips. "You guys fucking nailed it."

"Thank fuck," Kody groaned, collapsing into the pillows and making me laugh.

I took another big mouthful of my drink, then placed the glass aside. "I've got one *really* important question, though."

Archer's brow shot up. "Oh yeah? What's that?"

"Are you *sure* no one can see us out here?"

Steele answered me. "Not unless they have binoculars, and I thoughtfully didn't provide those to any of our guests. Total privacy, Hellcat."

"Well then," I replied, loosening my towel and tossing it aside. "I believe someone has a promise to deliver on."

Archer met my stare unflinchingly and carefully placed his glass aside.

"Are you sure about this, Kate?" His tone was carefully even, like he was trying not to influence my decision. Silly boy.

415

I smirked. "I'm more than sure. Are *you*?" It was no secret that Archer was the least comfortable with sharing, but he'd come a hell of a long way in recent months.

He glanced over at Kody and Steele, but neither one of them said anything as they waited for his response.

After a second, he jerked a nod and prowled toward me on hands and knees. "Fuck yes, I am." His mouth crashed into mine with a force that pushed me back into the pillows, but I wasn't complaining. Instead, I kissed him back with equal fervor, my lips parting to give him access to my mouth.

Archer groaned as our tongues danced together and my legs wrapped around his waist to pull him tighter to me. He and Kody were only in swim shorts, and the thin fabric was doing little to disguise how *very* okay with this situation he was feeling.

He uttered a soft curse, pulling back from my lips and grasping my thighs with his huge hands. I barely had a moment to gasp before Steele tipped my face toward him, claiming my lips as his own.

I gave a delighted sigh as his tongue stud flicked over my tongue, and Archer kissed his way down my body, circling my belly button with kisses as he spread my legs wider apart.

Hell yeah, that's what I was here for.

Kody leaned in on the opposite side from Steele, kissing my neck and cupping one of my bare breasts with his warm, calloused hand.

"How do you wanna do this, babe?" he whispered in my ear, his voice low and seductive. "You're calling the shots here. Wanna make Steele sit back and watch as punishment for shooting you?"

"Hey!" Steele protested, breaking away from my lips to glare at Kody. "I heard that, prick. It was *weeks* ago, okay?"

Still, his eyes flashed with lingering guilt, so I cupped his cheek and brought his face back to mine to kiss. "You know I don't blame you, Max," I murmured against his lips.

"I do," Archer offered, then flicked his tongue over my clit and made me jolt with desire.

"Assholes," Steele grumbled, but he returned to kissing me, harder this time like he was still apologizing for grazing me with that bullet.

Archer's lips sealed over my clit as he sucked at the throbbing flesh, and I squirmed under his touch, needing more. I'd been turned on all damn day, ever since they'd announced having bought my dream house for all four of us to live in together. I didn't have the *patience* for drawn-out foreplay.

"Fuck," I moaned against Steele's lips. "Max...do me a favor?"

He pulled back an inch, his brow hitching in curiosity. "Anything, Hellcat."

I grinned at my small victory. "Fuck my mouth."

They were all used to my demands enough by now that he wasn't shocked. He just chuckled and shrugged, then unhooked his towel from around his waist and let it drop to reveal his hard, pierced cock.

"Yes, ma'am," he teased, rising up on his knees to offer me exactly what I wanted without Archer stopping in his task.

I licked my lips in excitement, then opened my mouth wide as Steele gripped the back of my head and guided his dick between my lips. When I swirled my tongue around his tip, he moaned, and Archer sank two fingers into my aching pussy.

Fuck yes.

My mouth too full to speak, I just groaned and took Steele deeper. His breathing hitched in the most delicious way as I gazed up at him, and his fingers tightened in my hair. He knew how I liked it and was more than happy to deliver. His hips moved, pushing farther and farther into my throat and forcing me to relax into taking all of him.

"Pretty sure I'm gonna need in on that," Kody told me, his teeth tugging on my earlobe. He shed his swim shorts, kicking them aside, then rose up to kneel on my other side with his own erect cock at the ready, waiting.

Steele groaned a small protest but released my hair and let his pierced cock withdraw from my lips. I barely had enough time to swipe my tongue over my lips once, and then Kody was filling my mouth with his huge, smooth shaft.

Archer played with me, his fingers teasing with shallow thrusts and his tongue circling my clit, and it was driving me nuts. I needed *more*. I needed him to fill me up and make me scream.

My hand reached out, wrapping around Steele's cock and stroking him as I sucked Kody off, but my hips were bucking against Archer's face. If he didn't put something more than his fingers into me soon…

I met his eyes over Kody's dick, and he read my mind clear as day. A second later he was shoving his shorts down and sinking his thick cock between my folds.

A low moan escaped me, despite how full my mouth was, and Archer grunted as he made his way farther inside my pussy.

Goddamn, there were so many things to split my attention when all four of us were involved. Steele smacked Kody in the shoulder, and they switched again. This time Steele slammed into my mouth so fast his piercings clicked against my teeth, and I gagged slightly as he hit the back of my throat.

Kody grabbed my hand to wrap around his shaft, slick with my saliva, and encouraged me to pump my fist up and down him.

Archer started moving between my legs, his hips bucking forcefully. My legs were already quivering, and I knew there was no way they were letting me off with any fewer than three orgasms before this was over. One for each of them…if not more.

He met my eyes as Steele fucked my mouth, then quite deliberately sucked on his fingers before reaching between us and finding my clit.

Yep, I had no hope. They were driving the ship; I was just along for the ride. But holy hell, *what* a ride!

I came, gasping and moaning around Steele's dick, and he showed mercy in withdrawing while I shuddered through that intense first climax. Probably worried I was going to bite him, come to think of it.

"God, I'll never get used to that sound," Archer commented, his voice strained as he withdrew from my pussy and fisted his own cock.

The only response I was capable of was a groaning whimper as my limbs trembled with orgasm aftershocks. Steele's fingers were still tangled in my hair, and he looked down at me with raw hunger, licking his lips.

"I want to fuck your ass so bad right now, Hellcat," he admitted in a rough, lust-filled voice.

Kody snickered, slipping from my grip as he reached for something tucked into the side of the champagne bucket. "Got you covered, pin cushion." He tossed a miniature bottle of lube to Steele with a wink. "Can't have you doing any damage just because we weren't prepared."

Steele's dick literally twitched with excitement as he sat back into the pillows. His eyes locked on mine, he patted his lap. "Come here, gorgeous."

Grinning like a maniac, I scrambled over to him and let him position me reverse cowgirl again, facing both Kody and Archer on my knees. The first drip of lube on my ass made me flinch because it was *cold*, but as soon as Steele started working it in, pushing his finger into me and stretching my ass, the cold was forgotten.

"Arch," I said in a breathless pant. "Archer, come here."

He shuffled closer on his knees, knowing exactly what I was asking for. His eyes were locked on Steele's fingers in my ass, though, even as he gathered my wet hair up in his fist and pushed his cock into my mouth.

419

I could taste myself on him, and it just turned me on harder. Knowing he'd just been in my pussy and that Steele was about to fuck my ass...yeah, it was turning me right the fuck on. A low moan pulled from me as Archer fucked my face and Steele stretched me with another finger. More cold lube. God, the anticipation was killing me.

The boys seemed to be working on intuition or ESP or something because just when I was about to lose it, Archer released my face and Steele's hands gripped my hips. He guided me back, coaxing me to sit up as he positioned his tip against my slick asshole.

"Just take it slow," he said to me, but the way his hands held my hips, pulling me down onto him as he pushed up, told another story.

I gasped and panted as he filled my ass, feeling every damn piercing—all eight of them—as he pushed deeper and deeper into me. By the time he was fully seated in me, I was shaking and breathless, my hands braced behind me on Steele's hard abs.

"Oh my god," I exclaimed on an exhale as he paused, giving me a second to adjust.

"You okay, babe?" Kody asked, licking his lips as he stared. I was fully spread open, Steele's dick in my ass and my pussy on display, so I didn't blame him.

I jerked a quick nod, not fully trusting my voice.

Archer just made a sound of amusement and moved around beside me with his dick in hand. "Remember how you said you wanted to take us all at once?" he asked in a heated voice, his fist stroking his own cock lazily as Steele started to move under me.

I just nodded again, too damn worked up to reply. But shit yes, I remembered. I'd said it the first time we fucked, on the side of the road in the pouring rain.

"Ready to make good on that, babe?" Kody teased, his fingers stroking my pussy, teasing my clit, then sinking inside.

"Fuck yes," I breathed, my voice holding a heady moan. "Kody..."

He just smirked, two fingers in my cunt as Steele slowly fucked my ass. "I got you, babe. Just let me play a minute." His head dipped low, his mouth closing over my clit, and his fingers filled me up, making me cry out.

"Fuck, you're gorgeous," Archer muttered, stroking his hand down my face and dragging his thumb over my lower lip. I bit his thumb, then sucked on it as I held his eye contact. Then Kody did something with his tongue that made me scream.

That was enough to snap Archer's patience, and his grip tightened on my hair once more, his dick tapping my lips. I eagerly opened for him, sucking him hard as Kody and Steele worked together to push me into another orgasm.

When I came again, no sounds escaped me as Archer damn near suffocated me with his cock. That only intensified my climax, and Kody's face was thoroughly damp when he sat up wearing a wide, self-satisfied grin.

His fingers were still in my pussy, though, and Steele's hands gripped my hips tight enough to bruise as he tried to pace himself.

"Kody," Archer grunted, "quit messing around. We've got the rest of the night to take turns, but right now—"

"Yeah, yeah," Kody snickered, licking his lips slowly like he was savoring the taste of my climax. "Hold your load, big guy." He shot me a wink, then gripped his cock as he shifted positions.

"You good, babe?" Kody double-checked as he rubbed the tip of his dick over my soaking pussy. He was teasing because I was clearly in no position to chat, a fact Archer reinforced by thrusting back down my throat again and making me moan.

My eyes said it all for Kody, though. He held eye contact with me as he pushed inside my cunt, breaking my gaze only as his hips met my pelvis and his eyes rolled back slightly.

"Holy crap," he muttered. "That's a different experience with Steele's pierced dick, that's for fucking sure."

Steele snorted a laugh from under me. "You can feel that,

huh?" He pulled out of my ass almost entirely, then slammed back in quickly. "How about that?"

Kody looked like his brain was short circuiting. I understood the feeling.

"Holy fuck," Kody muttered with a laugh. "I mean, I'm not into dudes. But I could get used to this." He gripped my knee, adjusting his angle.

I looked up, meeting Archer's eyes and encouraging him. I wanted them all. I wanted to feel them fuck me every damn way imaginable, and I wanted them all to come inside me.

Archer's eyes darkened, flashing with heat, and he gripped my hair tight. He used his hold on my head to fuck my face, punishing my throat as Kody and Steele alternated thrusts into my other holes.

Steele was the first to lose it. His pace stuttered and his fingers gripped my hips harder; then he cried out as he came. Kody just fucked me faster, like Steele's climax had forced him to prove something.

I came again a moment later, feeling the slide of Steele's cum against his piercings in my ass like an overload of lube.

Archer grunted, withdrew from my mouth, and pushed Steele to move him out from under me. Kody must have guessed what he wanted, because he pulled me into his arms, moving us until he was flat on his back with me riding his dick.

"Oh fuck," Steele commented with a laugh. "I'm gonna be hard again before you two even finish."

I just shot him a grin and a wink, challenging him to make that happen.

Archer moved behind me and pushed me flat into Kody's chest with a hand on my back. Except, instead of taking my ass like I'd expected, I felt a startling, unfamiliar stretch as he pushed into my pussy *with* Kody.

A low, sex-drenched moan escaped me as my cunt adjusted to

accommodate two cocks together, and my breath came in short, sharp pants. It was *incredible*.

"You okay, baby girl?" Archer asked in a rough voice, his body shadowing me and his lips at my ear.

I nodded, frantic, and Kody just chuckled. He wasn't objecting, though. Far fucking from it. He and Archer just went to town, fucking me in tandem and making me come twice more before they each chased their own climaxes.

When they withdrew, I was aching, throbbing, soaked in cum, and more satisfied than I could ever remember being in my entire life. Yet as Kody and Archer collapsed into boneless heaps on the pillows, Steele caught my eye with a smirk. His dick was in his hand, hard as a damn rock again.

His brow cocked in question, and I nodded, licking my lips. My limbs were too jellylike to do much, though, so I just lay back on the blanket as he climbed between my legs. A few minutes later, he came again, filling my cunt with his seed and kissing me like I was his very reason for existence.

Yeah, it was safe to say they'd officially changed my opinion on surprises. One hundred and twenty percent, I *loved* their surprises.

EPILOGUE

Halloween night

Steele's fingers ruffled my freshly blow-dried hair, and he kissed me softly. "You're so fucking hot as a blond, Hellcat," he confessed with a groan. "This is gonna be way too hard to keep my hands off you all night."

I grinned wide, loving his reaction to my new hair color. After everything with Dave—or Declan—I'd tried to pretend I was okay. I'd tried to act tough, like nothing had left a lingering mark thanks to my therapy. But the sheer relief I'd felt when my hairdresser stripped the pink dye from my hair and returned me to my natural blond? It was staggering. Maybe because all those creepy Barbie dolls had had pink hair. Or maybe because his captive slaves had been forced to dye their hair to match mine. Or maybe I just needed to feel like a truer version of *me*.

Whatever the reason, it felt like a thousand tons had lifted from my shoulders. Steele's jaw dropping when he saw me only made it so much sweeter too. Bree had lost her ever-loving shit when I video-called her from the hairdresser but then fell asleep halfway through our call. I totally didn't blame her either;

her baby boy was giving her karmic justice for her own diva personality.

Kody and Archer were already at The Laughing Clown prepping for the fight, but Steele and I had told them we'd meet them there. For one thing, they needed to focus before Archer's fight. For another, Steele wanted to sit me on his grand piano and eat me out as he played his latest composition. It sounded complicated, but he was a talented man—he made it work.

"Well"—I flipped my platinum hair over my shoulder and pulled a pair of panties on—"I never said you had to keep your hands off me. Just don't distract me from Archer's fight this time. I wanna see the whole thing."

Steele dragged his thumb over his lower lip, his face already full of ideas. "Well, in that case why are you putting panties on? If we're not allowed to take you away from the fight, you gotta make it a bit easier."

I snorted a laugh and shook my head. "I'm sure you'll make it work."

He shrugged, knowing full well my panties would prove exactly zero deterrent when he set his mind to it. Then again, if they knew I was going commando under my oversized hoodie, it'd drive them crazy.

With that evil thought, I stripped my underwear off again and left it on Steele's music stand.

"Come on, Max, we're gonna be late." He grabbed for me, and I laughed, dancing out of his reach on my dangerously high heels. I'd dressed to kill for tonight's fight, wearing my favorite, personalized *The Archer* hoodie—which fit me like a dress—paired with thigh-high, lace-up, black stiletto boots.

Steele sure as fuck seemed to appreciate the image it cut as I sat on his piano with my legs spread.

We climbed into one of his cars, a cherry-red Corvette that had recently been modified with bulletproof glass, and he took his time kissing me before pulling out of our old mansion. Because the fight was being held at The Laughing Clown, we'd gotten ready at our former residence. Technically it was still ours, but we hadn't spent more than a handful of nights there since that weekend the guys had surprised me with the mountain lodge. *That* was our home.

The Laughing Clown had recently undergone an extensive refurbishment. Hades had decided to take over a lot of my father's Shadow Grove revitalization projects. Except instead of doing it as a front for embezzlement for sleazy motherfuckers like Bree's dad, the Timberwolves were doing it to run them as actual businesses.

So, the creepy, old, abandoned amusement park that had haunted my nightmares way too damn often was getting a face-lift and a new name.

Anarchy.

It seemed oddly appropriate, considering the crowd it'd attracted for Archer's fight. Steele and I made our way through the costumed spectators, and I couldn't wipe the smile from my face. I knew Halloween was just a good excuse for a party—and therefore, alcohol sales as well as sales in the less legal side of gang business—but the Timberwolves were really doing me a favor with this fight night.

Closure was a beautiful thing. Being able to attend Archer's fight, knowing everything we'd been through in the two years since Riot Night, was cathartic. The fact that Steele was at my side, his fingers tightly linked with mine, made it all the better.

"We should have reserved seats," Steele told me, his lips against my ear so he could be heard over the crowd and thumping music. Everyone was crazy hyped up for this fight, and the excitement was infectious.

Archer hadn't taken any fights since canceling the one after he was shot. He'd been offered plenty, sure, but he'd turned them all down. His official line was that he was still recovering, but I suspected he was just enjoying himself without the pressure of a

426

looming fight to train for. Certainly, he'd healed quickly from his injuries, and Kody had been kicking his ass around our new home gym enough.

The boys had taken it on themselves to train me in just about every possible martial-arts and self-defense technique they knew, but I had no desire to try my luck in the octagon. That was all Archer's domain.

Steele and I found our front-row seats, emblazoned with The Archer's two corporate sponsors—Brilliance Diamonds and KJ-Fit.

Music started pounding through the speakers louder than before, and a heavy death-metal tune announced the first of the fighters into the cage. He was a big guy, strongly muscled and sporting a full-back Timberwolf tattoo.

When Archer had been approached about the fight by Zed, he'd laughed and mocked the Timberwolf second that it was going to be embarrassing when he kept wiping the floor with their guys. Yet he couldn't turn it down. Not here, not on such a meaningful anniversary.

Still, I suspected this guy was going to give him a good run for his money.

The overly dramatic commentator did his bit to intro the Timberwolf fighter, and a huge section of the crowd went nuts for the big guy. Apparently, he also had a promising career in the professional MMA circuit. Hades had been aiming for star power to launch Anarchy, that was for sure.

Then Archer's intro music started, and my grin spread so wide I could barely contain it.

"I fucking love this song!" I needed to yell to be heard over the deafening roar of Archer's supporters, and Steele just gave me a self-conscious smile back. He knew how much I loved it, though, and just watched me with adoration in his eyes as I danced around to *his* tune, which he'd licensed to an up-and-coming rock band out of Hollywood.

It'd taken a bit of convincing for Steele to go *mainstream*, but the lead singer was the older brother of one of Seph's school friends. When I'd heard them play, I'd known they'd do justice to Steele's compositions.

Kody entered the fight cage with Archer to give him the usual pep talk; then he took Arch's hat and hoodie from him. Archer's eyes were locked on me from the moment he entered my line of sight, though, and my heart swelled to bursting with sheer pride for my guys.

I blew him a kiss as the commentator rattled off the intro stats and whipped the crowd up into a screaming frenzy. He just winked back at me. A promise for later, after he'd won the fight.

Kody climbed out of the octagon and came over to where Steele and I waited, then greeted me with a long, passionate kiss. His hand firmly gripped my ass through the hoodie, and he groaned against my lips.

"Fuck me, you look so damn hot I'm tempted to drag you into the bathrooms before this fight even starts, babe." He was only halfway joking, and I knew it all too well. "This hair… Holy crap, I didn't know it was possible for you to be more breathtaking."

My eyes narrowed at him. "Not tonight, Casanova. I'm here for the fight. You can all fuck me senseless later."

Kody huffed a laugh and released his grip on me, but he kept his arm around my waist loosely. "I'll hold you to that, gorgeous."

I licked my lips, grinning as I met Archer's intense stare once more. He bounced on his toes, throwing warm-up punches, but his attention was all on me. We could have been in an empty warehouse for all he noticed the crowd of spectators.

"Go," I urged Kody, pushing him back toward Archer. "Help him win this so we can celebrate."

He kissed me again but did as he was told. He turned his KJ-Fit cap backward as he strode around the cage to Archer, laser-focused on the job at hand.

"Wanna take bets?" Steele murmured as I sat back down beside him when the referee started the fight. We both knew the first part would just be Archer testing out his opponent, checking his speed and weaknesses, so we saved our energy for when it heated up.

I snorted a laugh. "We're not betting on Archer to lose, you asshole."

He just smirked. "You never know; Jimbo is a tough cookie and Arch is out of practice. The big bad wolf might mop the floor with your Sunshine."

I just rolled my eyes. "Jimbo. What a stupid name for a gang-affiliated UFC fighter. And Archer's hardly out of practice with how hard he's been training." He'd also had several mock fights at our mountain lodge with a few of UFC's greatest, so yeah, I was pretty confident he had this fight against Jimbo in the bag.

Sure enough, halfway through round two, Archer unleashed his inner beast. Blood flew, spattering the blue floor of the octagon, and the next thirty seconds were a heart-racing flurry of hard fists, sharp elbows, and stealthy knees. Then it was all over. Jimbo hit the deck with a crash as a final right hook snapped his head back and turned out the lights.

"Told ya." I turned to Steele with a victorious grin.

He just laughed, then jerked his head to the cage. Archer was at the mesh, beckoning for me to come closer. Kody grabbed my hand, hauling me up into the octagon with him as he jumped around and whooped his excitement over Archer's win.

Once Jimbo was back on his feet, the referee did his bit to officially announce Archer as the victor. Then, the second his gloved hand was released, Archer grabbed my face and kissed me long and hard, right there in the middle of the former big top.

The after-party was held in the old fun house. Hades converted it into a seriously funky nightclub, but I still needed to swallow past a lump of lingering fear as the four of us made our way through the front door.

Inside, though, not a trace of that horrible old fun house remained. The only nod to what had been there the last time I'd been inside was the abundance of mirrors everywhere, except now they just reflected flashing strobe lights and scantily clad dancers. I tried not to ask too many questions about the Timberwolves—their gang was none of my damn business—but I was getting the distinct impression the less legal side of their income came from the sex trade. Prostitution, I meant, not human trafficking. Given how Archer had saved Seph, I'd think Hades might be firmly *against* the skin market.

A handsome guy in nothing but a pair of black latex hotpants greeted us as we approached the bar and advised us that we had a table reserved in the VIP section. He escorted us over to it, shaking his ass in time to the music as he walked, then left with our drink orders.

As soon as we were seated, I looped my arms around Archer's neck and kissed him again. "Congrats on your win, Sunshine," I told him in a husky whisper.

He just gave a lopsided grin and tucked a loose, blond curl behind my ear. "I don't think you've ever looked hotter than when I saw you dancing beside the cage tonight."

I scoffed. "Uh-huh, 'cause I'm wearing your hoodie."

Kody cleared his throat and tipped his head at Archer like he was trying to remind him about something. Or maybe just hurry him up.

"Right," Archer muttered. He swept his hand over his wet hair—fresh from the shower—and reached inside his jacket. "Kate, seeing as tonight sort of marks an anniversary for all of us, especially *here*, I wanted to give you something."

He placed a folded stack of papers down on the table in front of me, then a single sheet of folded paper beside it. Steele pulled a pen from his own jacket pocket and placed it beside the papers.

"For all the bad memories October 31 holds for you, Hellcat, we hope this might be the start of repairing them." His gray eyes held mine for a moment, sincerity shining through.

Kody shifted in his seat, leaning forward with his elbows on his knees. "This might *seem* like a gift just from Archer, but it's really from all of us."

Archer rolled his eyes. "Right. But mostly from me. Open this one first." He tapped his finger on the thicker stack of paperwork.

Frowning in confusion, I picked it up and unfolded it carefully. My eyes scanned the top page, and my heart stopped. Dread pooled in my stomach, and I flipped through the pages until I found Archer's signature already on the appropriate lines.

Hurt squeezed my chest, and my gaze flicked up to meet Archer's eyes. "You're divorcing me?"

His expression stayed carefully neutral, not giving away any emotions as he stared back at me. Was… Were they breaking up with me? If so, this was a monumentally *shitty* way to repair my lingering fear of Halloween.

"I married you without your knowledge or consent, Kate," he told me in a carefully even tone of voice, despite the booming music all around us. "I'm giving you the opportunity to start over…if that's what you want."

My brows flicked up, and a sharp streak of stubborn anger shot through me. "And what if it's not?" I slapped the divorce papers back down on the table, and my diamond ring glittered under the lights as if mocking me. "What if I don't want this?"

Archer drew a deep breath, his jaw tight as he picked up the single sheet of folded paper. "Well, then you could take this one instead."

Seething, I snatched it from his fingers and flipped it open. I wasn't sure what I expected to find there, but it sure as hell wasn't the simple legal document with his signature at the bottom.

My brows shot up even higher. "A dissolution of our prenuptial agreement?"

Steele cleared his throat, pulling my attention from Archer's blank face. "We thought...if you're happy with things the way they are—"

"I am," I snapped, cutting him off. "I thought you all were too."

"What?" Kody exclaimed, panic flashing across his face. "Of course we are. Why would you—?" He broke off, understanding dawning. "Oh shit. You thought—"

"You guys gave me fucking *divorce* papers; what am I supposed to think?" I demanded, feeling my cheeks heat. I was so fucking confused. What the hell were they trying to achieve here?

"Princess," Archer murmured, placing a finger under my chin to bring my gaze back to his, "we're not ending things. We're offering you a fresh start on equal footing with all of us. That's all. Trust me, Kate, nothing on this entire damn earth could make us leave you now. We all love you too damn much."

Relief washed over me in waves, and I could finally breathe again. I'd jumped way into the wrong conclusion there, and my panic had momentarily blinded me to logic. But I got it. He was trying to right his first wrong against me.

"Oh," I murmured, all other words failing me.

Archer's lips curled in a smile. "Exactly." He knew I was on the right page with him now.

"So, you don't *want* to divorce me?" I bit my lip, still tense. Of course, it was always going to be a messy situation with the four of us. I couldn't legally marry them all, but...Archer and I were already done. We'd even had a wedding, complete with multiple fatalities. And cake. We'd had wedding cake...albeit licked from each other's bodies in the kitchen of a bakery.

His pale blue eyes softened, and his thumb tugged my lip from between my teeth. "I *never* want to divorce you, baby girl. You're my reason for living."

My heart thudded faster as my breath caught.

"For the record," Kody added, his tone dry, "Steele and I

432

already have IDs made for you in alias names, you know, in case you ever wanted to make things *semi*official with us one day."

Shock held me frozen for a second; then a bubble of way-too-excited laughter worked its way out of my throat. Shaking my head in disbelief, I picked up the divorce papers again, then ripped them into confetti.

"Does that answer the question?" I asked, meeting each of their gazes one at a time.

Archer's grin was wide as he smoothed the other document out on the table and handed me the pen. "Sign this, Kate. I don't need or want any legal claim over your estate. I just want *you*."

Groaning inwardly at the delicious things his declarations of love were doing to my lady bits, I took the pen and scribbled my signature on the line marked with my name.

Satisfied, Archer folded the document back up and tucked it into his jacket once more.

Steele grinned, nodding his head across the club. "How's Seph's impeccable timing?" he joked as my bubbly friend bounced her way through the crowd. She had a bright, fruity cocktail in one hand and body glitter smeared down her arms. Seph clearly intended to have a good time tonight.

"Hey!" she shouted, coming over to join our table with a broad smile pasted to her face. "Oh my god, Archer, that fight was *insane*. Totally insane. I've never even liked fighting before, but that was…" She trailed off with her jaw slightly unhinged as she gave my husband heart eyes.

"Down girl," Kody teased. "Don't make MK shank you for drooling on her boys."

Seph's mouth snapped shut, and her eyes widened as she gave me a guilty look. "Sorry, MK," she squeaked. "You totally can't blame a girl, though." She burst out laughing, and I just shook my head as I chuckled.

"Actually, there was one other thing we needed to clear from the air," Archer admitted, his arm tucked around my waist as a waiter delivered our drinks to the table.

I cocked a brow. "Oh yeah? What else?"

He just shrugged. "We all promised you there were no more secrets between us, but something you said the other day made us realize we had let something slip through the cracks—entirely unintentionally, I'll add."

"Definitely unintentional," Steele agreed with a grimace. "More just from force of habit."

"And old loyalty," Kody added.

Seph wrinkled her nose, looking as confused as I felt. "What the fuck are you guys talking about?"

Archer ignored her question, addressing me. "We realized, Princess, that you still haven't met Hades in person."

Seph choked on her drink, laughing. "Yes, she has!"

Archer rolled his eyes at my younger friend. "Not *officially*. Anyway, now seems as good a time as any." He nodded at a familiar face approaching our table. "Kate, meet Hades, leader of the infamous Tri-State Timberwolves."

My jaw dropped; then I burst out laughing. "You've got to be kidding me."

Want to stay in Shadow Grove?
Read on for a sneak peek of
the first book in the Hades series

7TH CIRCLE

CHAPTER 1

Ice clinked in my glass as I swirled the amber liquid. It was my fourth straight whiskey, and it'd barely dented my shitty mood.

It was my own fucking fault. I knew better. I knew he didn't feel the same way about me, but…ugh. I was such an idiot!

I'd all but thrown myself at him—at a man I still needed to deal with in a professional capacity on a far-too-frequent basis. Well, as professional as anyone was in our line of work.

Keeping the upper hand with him was going to be all too uncomfortable now that I'd gone and made a pass at him. And been rejected.

His harsh words still echoed in my mind. "I don't fuck children." Like I was a fucking teenager or something. I wasn't. I was a twenty-three-year-old successful businesswoman—among other things—and I was far from the immature, blushing virgin he must think I was. Maybe he was getting me confused with my eighteen-year-old, naive-as-fuck sister, Persephone. That's how he'd just treated me, anyway. Like a little kid with a crush.

"Rough night?" A smooth voice asked, and I glanced over as a gorgeous man slid onto the barstool beside me. The bar was busy, no question, but not so busy that there weren't other seats available.

I cocked a brow at the ballsy stranger and sipped my drink. "Nope," I lied, baring my teeth in a mockery of a smile. "Best night of my life." My sarcasm was thick enough to wade through. Maybe those whiskeys had started hitting me after all. "You?"

"Me?" He flashed me a blinding smile, and my pulse raced in reaction. He was fucking stunning, model-level beautiful with a strong jaw dusted with scruff and dark lashes any woman would kill for. "Nah, I'm celebrating. Can I buy you a drink?"

A grin curved my lips despite my shitty mood. "Sure." I gave a small signal to the bartender, silently ordering another of the same, then nodded to the handsome man beside me to indicate he was paying. He asked for the same as I was drinking and didn't speak again until our drinks were delivered in front of us in beautiful cut-crystal glasses.

"Cheers," he murmured to me, clinking his glass gently against mine, then downing his whole drink in one mouthful. He ordered another, then slid his gaze back to meet mine.

His eyes were a pretty mix of green and blue, and I found myself smiling at him.

"So, what are we celebrating?" I asked, letting my words drawl in a clear indication I didn't actually believe him. Based on the way he'd thrown that drink back, his night was going about as well as mine was.

The model-handsome man let his own lips curve in an answering smile. "My new job," he announced. His gaze flicked away from mine for a second, sweeping over the busy club and pausing briefly on the podium dancers. Both of them were down to their underwear, and the girl was climbing the pole with admirable ease. Totally mesmerizing.

"Oh yeah?" I prompted, suddenly curious about my new drinking buddy. He was ballsy enough to approach me; maybe he could cure my shitty mood tonight. Best way to get over a guy was to get under a new one, right? "Congratulations. What's your new job?"

His perfect face flashed with tension for just a second, then cleared into an easy smile again as he nodded to the male dancer on the podium. "That."

I choked on my drink. Just a little bit. Just enough to shock me and flood my cheeks with heat as I dabbed my lips on a napkin.

"That?" I repeated in a strangled voice, indicating to the gorgeous black man gyrating his hips in nothing but an electric-blue G-string. "You're a stripper?"

My new friend grinned wider, turning back to me and sipping his new drink. "Male entertainer," he corrected with a small nod. "Yep, sure am." There was pride in his voice, but also an edge of something darker. Disappointment?

Curiosity shoved aside my shock, and I ran my gaze over him as subtly as I could. He was pretty enough, no doubt, and the way he filled out his shirt spoke to a well-built frame. Yeah, he could definitely make good money taking his clothes off. Great money, when combined with that mischievous look in his eyes and the pure-sex way he brushed a droplet of whiskey from his lip and then licked his thumb.

"That's cool," I commented. "So, which lucky club snapped you up? I bet you're going to be in high demand."

His smile turned suggestive. "Did you just call me sexy?"

I snickered a laugh. "Was that too subtle? You're scorching. I'm not surprised you got the job. So…?" I really, really wanted to know which club had picked up this diamond.

The easy smile on his face faltered a split second as he answered. "This one, of course. 7th Circle is the hottest club in Shadow Grove; everyone knows that. And they pay their dancers better than all the other shitty clubs in town. I wouldn't even consider anywhere else, given the choice."

AUTHOR'S NOTE

Hey, you… Yeah, you! The reader currently glaring at this page like maybe the next line will be all "ha-ha April Fool's, here are the answers you seek!"

Spoiler alert: it's not gonna happen.

Let's clear the air real quick before this gets out of hand. That, the minor detail that made you just curse me out and yell "WTF Tate?!" That was not a cliff-hanger. You know this. Steele getting shot? Yeah, that one counts, but this was just sparking interest in the next Shadow Grove series! Besides, it just wouldn't be the same without those death glares you're shooting me right now. It's all part of the fun! All those muttered curses about what a monster I am? They keep me so nice and toasty warm at night.

Besides, I'm already neck deep in Timberwolves and it's so, so much fun! I hope you'll enjoy them as much as I do! But if you don't…well…fuck it. At least I tried! I've said it before, I'll say it again, I don't make this shit up. My characters have a story to tell, and I just write up the incident reports for it all.

But back to the matter at hand. Madison Kate's story is OVER! That was a pretty wild ride, am I right? I'm still finding it a little bit nuts that she's done. This series took almost half a million words to write and has totally consumed my writing brain for the last five months. (Yep, this was all released over just five months!)

2020 was a fucking rough one, and I know lots of you agree. For me, I've dealt with the Australian Bushfires looming on my doorstep for months, then cohosted a book signing event, got flooded in by the worst flood my area has seen in a hundred years, dealt with coronavirus isolations, and…my mum died.

For anyone who read my author's note in *Hate,* you already know, my mum was my first and biggest fan, so this whole series for me has been bittersweet. I feel like it's my best work to date, but it's the only series my mum never read. I hate that. I hate that she won't read my next series too. Or the ones after that… All I can do is hope like hell that she would have loved them, or that she'd have been proud of how far I've come in this career.

My mum started me on my love of books as a kid; she would read *Watership Down* to my brother and me every night, before we could read chapter books for ourselves, and she did the worst voices for all the rabbits. But from there, my love of books only exploded. She never censored my reading or told me I wasn't old enough for certain content, which was how I ended up reading *The Horse Whisperer* at about age ten and getting totally hooked on romance from there on out.

When I told her I was writing a book, it was never even a question whether she would read and give feedback. She didn't even know what reverse harem was but went off and did some thorough Googling so she could fully appreciate the genre. She never blinked when I started writing graphic sex scenes and grisly death, only gave me notes on characterization and realism.

If it weren't for my mum, I wouldn't be here, writing this. This was my thirtieth book, and I never would have made it past number one if she hadn't been standing there in my corner, supporting me and cheering me along every step of the way.

So…what I'm saying here is Fuck 2020. Seriously. Fuck it right up the ass with a cactus, and then fuck it some more. It's been rough as shit, but I'm so lucky to have the support of some incredible friends and crown-fixers who have been keeping my head above water, even when I wanted to hibernate and quit.

My awesome content editor, Heather, has been with me through this whole series, pumping me up and cackling at new ideas and scenes as we've gone. She was also the first person to guess that MK was living in D'Ath Mansion—not Danvers Mansion— and the first to figure out that it was Dave doing the stalking. Although I did cackle with glee that she never saw the Declan twist coming!

All in all, I like to think of her as that little devil on my shoulder, whispering, "Yeah, good, but make it worse. Make them cry!"

See that? Just backed a bus over Heather. Beep beep!!

Anyway, I should wrap this up. It's time to shift gears into Hades! *drool* I can't wait for you to see what the Timberwolves have been up to behind the scenes in Shadow Grove.

Thanks for sticking with MK through her series! It means the world to me, and I hope these books have offered you some kind of break from the clusterfuck of 2020.

#FuckCovid #FuckCancer #FuckDaveWithAChainsaw

ABOUT THE AUTHOR

Tate James is a *USA Today* bestselling author of contemporary romance and romantic suspense, with occasional forays into fantasy, paranormal romance, and urban fantasy. She was born and raised in Aotearoa (New Zealand) but now lives in Australia with her husband and their adorable crotchfruit.

She is a lover of books, booze, cats, and coffee and is most definitely not a morning person. Tate is a bit too sarcastic, swears far too much for polite society, and definitely tells too many dirty jokes.